If the Invader Comes

Derek Beaven lives in Maidenhead, Berkshire. His first novel, *Newton's Niece* (1994), was shortlisted for the Writers' Guild Best Novel Prize and won a Commonwealth Prize. His second, *Acts of Mutiny* (1998), was shortlisted for the *Guardian* Fiction Prize.

For more information on Derek Beaven's *If the Invader Comes* and to download a reading guide, visit www.4thestate.com/derekbeaven

If the Invader Comes

DEREK BEAVEN

FOURTH ESTATE • *London*

This paperback edition first published in 2002
First published in Great Britain in 2001 by
Fourth Estate
A Division of HarperCollins*Publishers*
77–85 Fulham Palace Road,
London w6 8jb
www.4thestate.com

10 9 8 7 6 5 4 3 2 1

The right of Derek Beaven to be identified as the author of
this work has been asserted by him in accordance with the
Copyright, Designs and Patents Act 1988

A catalogue record for this book is available from the
British Library

ISBN 1–84115–592–6

Typeset by Palimpsest Book Production Limited,
Polmont, Stirlingshire
Printed in Great Britain by
Clays Ltd, St Ives plc

For Peter

If the Invader Comes is a work of fiction. Except for historical figures, all its characters are imaginary, and their names were chosen for no other reason than euphony.

Contents

I
A Contract

IT OPENS IN paradise, with my great-uncle. He was woken by a thud from the ceiling directly over his head, followed by a flurry of squeals, as the little cobra that seemed to have got into the roof caught another rat. In the darkness of the bedroom, Dr Wulfstan Pike lay under his mosquito net and listened to the drench hitting the bungalow thatch and the cascade of rivulets from the eaves on to the garden outside his window. He could distinguish, too, the pelt of huge globes of water into the puddles in the compound. The steamy rot smell from the old carpet mingled with the flavour of his own sweat.

He felt under the sheet for the woman lying at his side. Selama stirred in her sleep and turned over towards him; his palm traced the child-stretched skin of her belly to rest on the prominence of her hip. He smoothed the curve to her waist, and, as he bent his head near her hair on the pillow, he caught both the savour of the food she prepared, and the deeper note of her body's secretions. The spicy confluence in his nostrils was so tender that he woke her with his kisses.

Later, they slept until dawn. When he got up, he felt confident, as if the world these last two weeks really had not been shifting under his feet. Outside, on the veranda, the view towards the coast showed each leaf for miles rinsed and urgently viridescent. The huge sky was mottled with pearl.

He stood, taking it in, still hardly believing after so

many years the sublimity that lay around him – until a waft of fresh coffee announced that Musa, the *kuki*, was up and doing. A queue of patients had already begun to form on the other side of the front steps.

The coffee pot, on its Chinese tray, had been served neatly to the sideboard in the dining-room. Dr Pike took his cup and clomped in his boots and dressing-gown to the teak table. Its top was completely covered with cut-out newspaper stories; but as if they were no more than a scrapbook in process he was at pains not to notice them.

Most mornings Selama sent the cook, Musa, off to do housework or buy groceries, and made breakfast herself in an old shirt she'd taken a fancy to, a frayed blue one with cooking splashes down the front. Most mornings during the last fortnight she had begun the meal by objecting to Dr Pike's mess of papers all over the breakfast table.

Today, however, she wore the red kimono he'd bought her once in Kuala Lumpur. And, seeing her like that, he wished he could hold time still with Selama sitting opposite him just as she was, her brown eyes looking up for a second, her quick smile showing the missing front tooth, and her fine, slightly greying hair spilling down on to red silk.

Isolated words from the expanse of print caught his attention: *Blitzkrieg, cathedral, armour-piercing, Bydgoszcz*. They flicked up at him with venom. He felt Selama watching him. She guessed exactly what was in his heart – of that he was certain. She knew he thought of quitting Malaya, of simply failing to return from his next leave. Part of him wished they could discuss his dilemma, another was relieved they never did. She knew he could never take her with him.

Neither spoke over a breakfast of last night's rice pancakes, heated up again and buttered. When they'd finished, he rose and went to kiss her cheek. 'Dear, you know how I need you.'

'I know and I don't know.'

'You know.' In the haven of her neck, breathing her, he was overcome.

'No, Stan.' She stood up, crossly, and rearranged her lapel. 'Haven't you got patients to see?'

My great-uncle sighed. Taking his quinine from the sideboard, he went to get dressed.

As always, he stood in front of the long mirror in his wardrobe door. It showed nothing youthful, nor romantic; merely an ample, red-and-white Englishman with grizzled body hair. He was no more than his reflection, and age had caught up with him.

How strange not to notice. Sag had occurred in several regions quite recently taut. And how thoroughly bald he'd grown. Only the eyebrows and moustache appeared to flourish, sprouting ever whiter and more luxuriant. Wrinkles he'd rather thought of as charm were bunched under the pale blue eyes. Surely his nose had enlarged while he slept. The jowls, simian; the ears, elephantine – it all added up to little more than roguishness.

The *amah*, the Chinese woman who'd first looked after his daughter and still remained with the household, had left a jug of tepid water on the bedroom floor. A large enamelled tin bowl was the apparatus he generally used for washing his privates. Planting his feet either side of it, he would lower himself on to its rims and then work up a good lather by the action of his hands, diving all about, leaving no crevice of his life unexamined. But for some reason this morning found him too picturesque for his own good and he left the mirror. He went instead to the little bathroom which adjoined, in order to sluice himself from the monumental earthenware jar kept permanently there. The cool water slipped deliciously from his back and belly and disappeared through the slats in the floor.

As he returned, dripping, to rummage in a drawer for

underwear, Selama knocked at the door. 'Stan! What're you doing? It's getting late. Are you lazy?'

'Just thinking.'

'You think too much.'

Dr Pike's old thatched bungalow was on stilts. Standing next to the bedroom window as he hauled on his khaki shorts and snapped his braces over his shoulders, he looked down on smiling faces. A child waved. He recognised her. Under his care, she'd recovered from a paralysis, which the mother had insisted was caused by an ill-wisher. On such matters he kept an open mind, for he'd proved the abracadabra of medicine himself, countless times. The body might be decently addressed with an instruction to heal – and quite often it really would, throwing off even the most tenacious bug. Therefore, he allowed, in wickedness it could be told to become sick, and might comply.

Shaving, he reminded himself that his daughter, Clarice, was arriving at teatime.

'They're waiting for you. Hurry up, dear!'

'All right, woman! D'you want to make a chap cut his bloody throat.'

HE LEFT THE bedroom as soon as he'd finished, and carried the little desk and cane chair out from the study to the veranda. There he called up the first patient to stand before him, and without more ado began examining the sore in a plantation worker's leg. With its ring of ooze, it was a bad wound to come across first thing. It lay beside the shin-bone, an obscene, pointless crater in the structures just below the knee.

In fact, his head swam at the sight of it. He actually felt as though he were going to pass out – something that hadn't happened since the day Clarice broke her arm.

That had been on her seventh birthday, in England. His pale daughter had stood before him holding the shocking misalignment with her good hand and he'd fainted against the bookcase corner, the one by the door in the Suffolk house, and almost knocked himself out. Little use it would have been then to her, having a doctor for a father. All at once the plantation worker's lesion meant nothing to him. His brain refused to focus, and he lacked any notion of the routine treatment called for. The only thing he could sense was that the sufferer seemed unusually sullen and unco-operative.

Dr Pike was an intuitive. As a healer, he relied on the inner 'click' – that moment when body responded to body – by which he'd know how to begin. Just now, its absence was unnerving, and, while the sweat broke out on his brow, his skin grew incomprehensibly cold. The sore mocked him. It threatened to widen and erupt before his eyes. He felt his other patients waiting, watching from the garden. A fly settled on the raw flesh; a couple more. His relationship with Selama was racially illicit. It was September 1939. The paradise was altering around him.

There had once gone out in that world an imperial edict, the Concubine Circular. After its issue, 'native women' had become less and less permissible in a government or company bungalow, no matter how unpretentious. While new men sat at the famous long bar at the club in Seremban, older Malaya hands would describe the passing of the Romance of the Orient. Before the Great War, most white officials had Malayan mistresses; the practice had been so ordinary as to be beyond comment.

Nowadays, men brought out their wives from England. There were roads, cars, telephones. Among the English there was a polite society of sorts, an urban sentiment, and with it a heightened racial feeling, for white women looked on the natives as unfair competition. Dr Pike brushed

7

the flies away. The accumulation of fester was already dangerous. Tentatively, he began cleaning the mess with a spirit swab, trying to gather his wits.

He hadn't set out to take up with a Malayan woman – nor was he the typical imperial servant I might already have led you to suspect. He'd left England in desperation because his young wife Mattie's family couldn't be trusted, and would never suffer her to be free of them. From London the couple's first escape had been to East Anglia with the child, Clarice. When Suffolk failed to lighten the marriage, my great-uncle had prescribed this more drastic relocation and trained for the tropics. But Mattie had taken sick: of climate, of separation from home, of jungle fever or falling fever, or perhaps wilfully of some yet-to-be-identified complaint.

He and Selama had met at the cottage hospital. A ward sister, she had been recently widowed. In the way of doctors and nurses, they'd worked together over a period, brought close by several problem cases and their shared determination not to give up on them. Gradually, they'd become attracted enough to risk love. Both had been gratified. He'd immediately found a happiness, which had lasted.

But their liaison broke rules and crossed boundaries. Even after Mattie died, they thought of themselves as an embarrassing throwback, a white man and his 'keep'. They were inadmissible among either his or her people, tolerated only so long as they kept on the very edge of society.

Now his daughter was a grown woman, and only last month a Mrs Christopher, a Perak District Officer's wife *en route* northward through Seremban, had sent in a complaint about him: that Dr Pike's liaison made his daughter's social position impossible. Everybody knew about it except the girl herself. The plantation worker flinched at the swab's touch. There was a dull hatred in his eyes, as if this *tuan doktor* were cause rather than cure. Dr Pike pressed into the weeping tissue, trying to do the right thing. Or was even this called in question, he asked himself? Had one person ever the right to intervene in the condition of another? It was his duty, surely, at least to clean up the damage. The man groaned and muttered through clenched teeth.

A whole region of clotted blood and pus finally came away. In the exposed corner of the sore, just under a film of partially healed skin, Dr Pike spotted a blue-grey shape, like a gaping comma, sharply defined. He stared at it in surprise. It was the head of something. 'There's a good chap,' he told his patient. 'You've been very brave.'

He finished off with the swab and rinsed his hands. Then, as if the treatment were complete, he prepared a fold of powder at his desk. 'I'd like you to take this, three times a day after meals.' He repeated the formula in his best Tamil, and handed over the paper.

The patient relaxed, visibly.

'Oh. One thing. Sit down here.' He stood up, and gestured to his own chair.

The man complied, and, apparently half-amused, settled himself in.

Dr Pike picked up one of the sharp slivers of bamboo he kept ready and split it to make a springy clip. He returned almost casually, before pain could be anticipated, knelt down, and inflicted one deft but absolute stroke.

A sharp scream echoed round the compound. It was still dying away as the doctor stood, triumphant. From the bamboo in which its head was trapped, a strange marbled worm hung curling like three inches of theatrical macaroni. 'Found you, rogue. My God, but you're an altogether different kettle of fish.' And it was true: he had not seen the like before.

Laughter and applause broke out in the queue below the veranda. He could have sworn he felt the thing twitch at the sound; and he called over his shoulder, 'Selama! Come and look! Tell me if you've seen one of these!'

The plantation worker darted a strained glance behind him towards the bungalow's interior, from which Selama's voice came back, high and still irritated, 'Whatever it is, I don't want to see!'

'Don't be silly. Come here, woman. Just take a look at this.'

There were calls for Selama from the lawn. At last she came out, an apron round her fine red kimono and a feather duster in her hand. 'You're dreadful, Dr Pike. Get away with you. My, my, a very bad animal.'

Everybody laughed, except the worm's host, who looked offended. As for doctor and nurse, it was imperial farce, and the incident restored them. Dr Pike made up a dressing, sent both his patient and his lover away, and found himself able to proceed.

BY TWELVE THIRTY he'd finished. He'd treated three vitamin deficiencies, a lethargy, a broken toe, the child with the paralysis, two toothaches, two animal bites and a knife wound; advised one man to smoke less, another to smoke more; and monitored, through their husbands, the progress of several pregnant women. His last patient left a chicken in a bamboo cage which would answer for tomorrow's dinner, and which also reminded him of East Anglia, where a parish doctor might find a brace of dead pheasants on his doorstep in lieu of payment.

The worm lay in a dish, faintly convulsing. He spoke to it. 'What have you been up to, eh? Don't imagine I don't know.' He took his trophy to the larger, mahogany desk in the den, poured himself a Scotch, and turned to his books to attempt identification.

He had small hope. There was such great variety in the forest, so much speciation. Manson's *Tropical Diseases*, he knew, was both limited and soggy: the pages clung one to another at this time of year. Usually, he didn't mind – the rubber company got him new volumes whenever the print started actually coming away. Today, however, it put him out. He unpeeled the relevant chapter and read. For large worms there was always the Hippocratic method, whereby nematodes such as *Dracunculus* were teased slowly out of the human lymphatic system, poulticed, rolled week by week around a piece of stick. Manson also listed a biblical technique for them: Moses had once nailed a brazen snake to a pole. Though Dr Pike lamented the lack of such kit from his issue, he dismissed these findings as irrelevant. In this part of the world *Dracunculus* was not a problem.

His own specimen began in a sightless head, was bloody, much shorter, and fringed with liverish stalks. It had visible segments. He imagined sharing his own body with such a thing, while it strove and grew. The sweat broke out again, this time soaking his collar and the armpits of his shirt. He prescribed himself another whisky.

With the usual filariases and helminth infestations, the difficult ulcerations, the mysterious wastings and crippling diarrhoeas, Dr Pike was generally more successful than science alone could have made him. Obvious incurables were packed off to the government hospital in Seremban, but where there was a chance, flair could tip the scales. He did see strange cases, and story-book monsters of the kind that lay in the dish seemed to long to be understood. Sometimes he had literally to wrestle with them; at others they required a long and teasing dance. Dr Pike was prepared to entertain the notion of a medical borderland, and was unconventional enough to meet the jungle half-way.

It was a far cry from an English surgery. The little lurking ticks, the mischievous snails, the local threadlike *Wuchererias* and *Brugias* concealed themselves within the abundant Malayan woodland, glued under leaves, afloat in pools, suspended from threads, or cunningly ciphered in the bodies of insects, waiting only to hide yet again in the tissue of a passer-by. They reproduced by threading species and air, being and space in the most ingenious stitchwork. Parasitical colonisation was the defining disease of Malaya, and Dr Pike felt both the worm's malice, and its repulsive yearning to find a place for itself. Nature, so secretive, so abundant, so enterprising, actually craved attention. The worm *desired* a name. Dr Pike spluttered into his glass.

The creature was beginning to dull into a mass. There was already a putrid stink to it. It made his gorge rise again, as if today he lacked all stomach for research. To stretch it out and examine it thoroughly, to take the omens, how revolting. Thankfully the Scotch was always in good supply. In the heat it went straight in at the mouth and out at the pores, hardly touching the bloodstream. He splashed in another couple of fingers.

Now Selama knocked on the study door. 'Stan! I've made lunch.'

She served him neat vicarage sandwiches filled with spiced egg. Afterwards they went to the bedroom. He undressed her, and the kimono cascaded round her feet in a silken rush; but when she responded to his embrace and huddled herself close, the room suddenly emptied for him, as though a plug had been pulled, and he was left afloat on nothing. He recalled his lapse of mind on the veranda, that feeling of being lost, disconnected.

'Sorry. Sorry, dear.' Horrified, he turned away from her. 'The bloody Scotch, I expect.'

'It doesn't matter.'

'No. Sorry.'

'Stan. It doesn't matter.'

'No. I expect not. Sorry. I'm so sorry.' He couldn't think. Her body, always so desirable, like a home, a flame, a frontier, had become strange. Because of his failure, she was almost unbearable to him. 'Must be getting old,' he said. The forced chuckle sounded like a rattle. His mind offered him only the image of the worm.

She held out a hand. 'Come. Lie down.' He obeyed, and allowed himself to be led to the bed and settled. Naked, she lay beside him.

He tried again, pouncing on her, almost; capturing her breasts and kissing them, pressing her belly, prising her legs apart.

'Stop it! Stan, you pack that up!'

'Yes, of course. Sorry.'

'What are you playing at?'

'Well . . . Hasn't done any good anyway.' The bedroom seemed far away, tinged with a juiceless aerial light, her anger terrible, but so remote. 'Hasn't done any bloody good.'

THEY LAY ON the bed, in the heat of the afternoon. He wished he could be sure she was asleep, but fancied she was merely pretending, lying there hating him. After an hour she got up and stretched in front of the window. Her silhouette, the back he knew he loved, the waist, the fullness of her hips, all struck him with fear.

'Clarice will be here soon, won't she?' she said. 'I'm going to Ibrahim, then. Straight away.' Her son's family lived closer to Seremban itself. 'I'll be back tomorrow after dark, when your daughter has gone. Don't worry yourself, though. He'll bring me.' She faced away from the doctor as she tied on a batik skirt, slipped into a brown cotton jacket and left the room.

He followed, useless. He found her by the print-strewn dining table, and struggled for words. 'He's good to his mother, Ibrahim.'

'Yes, Stan. He is.' She picked up one of the plates left from their lunch and placed it waitress-like on her arm. Then she waved her free hand crossly at the strewn cuttings. Outside, it was about to rain again.

'So what's happening? Eh, Stan? You tell me what's happening.'

He had no answer, but only peered down at the evidence he'd assembled. There were reports out of the *Straits Times*, the *Malay Mail*, the *Tribune*, *Planter*, and clippings, too, from the English *Times*, the *Manchester Guardian* and the *Daily Telegraph* – in fact whatever of the Fleet Street press had managed to find its way up to Seremban, hot off some RAF plane into Singapore and already quite overtaken by events. Shamed, he shifted his weight from foot to foot like a schoolboy up before the beak. Selama stacked the other plate on top of the first, and disappeared towards the kitchen.

'Shall I drive you?' he called after her.

'No, thank you.'

'Till later then. Goodbye, dear.' He handed the umbrella out of the bamboo hall-stand. 'You'll need this.'

From the veranda he watched her go down the length of the garden path, the umbrella under her arm, still rolled even though the first warm drops had begun to fall. Musa, the *kuki*, hovered with a broom in his hand on his way to the back bungalow, pretending not to look. At the mud road Selama turned in the direction of the town, refusing to glance back and wave. Failing her, betraying her, he watched until she was hidden in the tunnel of large, overarching trees at the bend.

Almost immediately out of the same gap a Malayan lad appeared on a bicycle, coming towards him, bringing the latest paper. The boy hurried to where the doctor stood on the veranda. '*Selamat petang.*' He presented the broadsheet. '*Tuan.*'

There was also a letter, from England.

'*Terima kasih.*' Stan Pike fished a small coin from his pocket, and then remembered himself. 'May your deeds also be blessed.'

The newspaper contained flashed accounts of the Russians going into Poland from the east, together with more evidence of German barbarities as they'd made their way through from the west. The letter was from Phyllis, Mattie's niece, whom he hadn't seen since she was a scrap of a kid.

Then Clarice arrived in the town's ancient taxi.

'DON'T BE RIDICULOUS, Daddy.' Ensconced in a cane chair, Clarice held her cup and saucer balanced in one hand and brushed with the other at the rain splashes on her shoulder and sleeve. Dr Pike was proud of his daughter's looks: Clarice had Mattie's features, fine and regular. Her hair, though, had always tended towards his own sandy colour. It was now further bleached and streaked from her trip up-country. Today, she wore it pinned, visibly ridged with the traces of a perm.

He was proud, too, of her dress sense. She'd put on a cool, belted day dress in pale grey crêpe de Chine. Leaning back somewhat languidly, with her legs elegantly crossed, and conducting a minute rhythm with the toe of one slim black shoe, she appeared more assured and sophisticated than he'd ever seen her; more mature, certainly, than her twenty-three years. As for himself, he stood facing her from the doorway to the dining-room, holding the teapot, with sweat already sopping the armpits of his shapeless tropical kit. 'I'm not ridiculous,' he said.

'Who in their right mind would choose just now to up sticks? And England of all places. Even if they're not bombed to bits, I certainly don't want to go back to England. What was it you said once? Malignant middle class, beaten working class, and Mummy's relations. I thought you *never* wanted to.' She squinted at him, with a puzzled expression.

'There comes a point when one thinks of retiring,' he muttered.

She chided him. 'And don't be lame, either. There's years in you yet. You're not the retiring kind. Anyway, Malaya's your life. Weren't you planning to go up to the hills? Gunung Angsi, buy a little place?'

He changed the subject. 'What about this young man of yours? You might have brought him with you.'

'Oh, Robin,' she said, airily. 'I would have done. But he said he had some business at the club. You can meet him when he comes to pick me up in the morning.'

'A nice trip?'

'Fine, thanks. Absolutely fine.'

Clarice got up, still holding her tea. 'Daddy, you're looking terrible. I didn't like to say it as soon as I came in, but honestly . . . What is it?'

'It's nothing.'

She placed the back of her hand on his brow. 'Hadn't you better sit down? I'll get your medicine, shall I?' Taking charge, she moved past him into the dining-room. 'And what on earth have you been doing here?'

He saw her put down her cup on the strewn table. 'Don't do that,' he said.

'Why not? I'll just see if I can find a sponge for you – and some water, too.'

'No!'

But she went off despite him towards the bedrooms. He sat down to mop his own brow.

He sometimes wondered how much Clarice had suffered, lacking a mother, trailing about the world alone like a lost soul, sometimes at school in England, at other times mured in this old-fashioned colonial bungalow, back and forth. Her mother's death had come when she was fourteen and she'd taken ship directly back to Malaya for a period of mourning with him. Selama had moved discreetly out.

Then Clarice had gone home to finish her schooling and Selama was reinstated. Clarice had returned once more, and, once more, he'd kept up appearances. Now Clarice moved in higher social circles than his own. Singapore was a fortress.

But even if he could maintain her there indefinitely, he wasn't sure what her place was in the scheme of things. Daughters were supposed to be married off. Or she should have some career? Whatever, there was some strong element in it of a father's duty; though Clarice had shown little sign of knowing for herself what she wanted.

At times she'd thrown herself into helping him on his rounds, like a devoted nursing auxiliary. Dr Pike had distrusted her motives; they smacked of spinsterism, possibly of religion. In any case, if he'd wanted a nurse he had Selama, and Clarice muddled his drug cabinet. But now she seemed the composed one, while he sat baffled, ghostly, and afraid of his decision.

He dabbed at himself with his handkerchief. The core of his fear was the subject no one at the club would discuss: that the Japanese would come as they had to China, and there'd be nothing anyone could do. People at the club said he was being alarmist. They seemed to lack the imagination to grasp the meaning of what had gone on in Nanking. Dr Pike had been left alone with the vision culled from his newspaper cuttings: of the Japanese Army occupying a Malaya left defenceless because Britain was suddenly locked into a struggle on the other side of the world – of the merciless rape of the two women in his life over his dead body. Nobody believed it could happen, yet for the two weeks since Britain had declared war on Germany he hadn't been able to shut the thought off.

He wondered whether he really was in for a bout of his fever. His preoccupation might be delirium. He tried thinking of Selama, of all his familiar textures, the closeness of his house, the rattan chairs, the boxed discs of chamber music for the wind-up gramophone, the pictures on his walls, his specimen cabinets, his rack of Dutch cigars.

Clarice returned with the sponge. 'Call yourself a doctor, Daddy? I can't leave you, can I? Thought you'd have known better. And why have you left those wretched pieces all over the dining table?'

Eyes screwed shut, he tilted up his face for her. How he wished he could put aside the buzz in his ear which said, Take Clarice away from Malaya, go now while you can. Or was it in his bones, his blood, this gathering intuition of crisis?

'I'm not being ridiculous, Clarice,' he repeated. 'I really think we have to leave.'

'I've no intention of going anywhere except Singapore,' she said. 'Now take some of this.' She held out the quinine bottle.

Later, he staggered out of his bedroom just as Musa was serving Clarice's dinner over the arrangement on the table. He did try to explain. He picked up a cutting from the *Times*. Dated 18 December 1937, it was by C. M. Macdonald, the only British correspondent to have remained in Nanking during the Japanese army's entry into that city. He scanned past the descriptions of murder to the part of the report which glared by its tale of omission, *But it is a fact that the bodies of no women were seen.*

Clarice was firm with him. 'Daddy, I'm terribly tired, actually. Would you mind awfully if we did the political lecture another time. I know you've probably got something gruesome to demonstrate, but to be honest I'd rather not hear it just at the moment. I'll have to make an early start tomorrow. You won't be offended if I call it a day, will you? Just go back to bed. Come on. This way.'

'We have to get out.'

'You have to get some sleep.' Stifling a yawn, she kissed him good-night. 'And so do I. Now you'll take care of yourself, won't you?' She turned to go.

'Of course,' he said, submissive now. 'Sorry. Sleep well, darling.' He still held the cutting in his hand but was glad, after all, that he didn't have to explain to her how the missing women hadn't been chivalrously spared.

IN THE NIGHT he got up. He was very frightened. His desire to put things right, to do his duty at last as a father – that was what had turned him into this parody of a supreme commander, pacing agitated, solo, around his dining-room table as if it contained the relief map of the theatre of operations. If he could assess the situation accurately, the enemy's strength and disposition, then and only then would he know how to act. The evidence was laid out before him. Thousands of miles away, Poland, a fully functioning European state with a considerable army and a fine cultural history, had been reduced to rubble in a week or two. Some terrible permission had been given. Reports confirmed both the astonishing German tactical brilliance and the brutality of the assault. He tapped his foot on the floorboards. Rain outside drowned out the sound. What if Britain and France got drawn in and bogged down? If America stayed on the fence? What of the imperial supply lines if the thing really got going? Any ship between Singapore and the English Channel would increasingly become fair game for a U-boat.

He rummaged for Selama's sharp sewing scissors in the sideboard drawer and cut out a piece from the newspaper that had just arrived. It counted the total sinkings as two dozen British ships, so far. No such announcement had come through on the short-wave radio. The liner *Athenia* had been torpedoed by a submarine.

If his vision was right, Clarice must not stay. But he couldn't just send her away – to nowhere, to Mattie's family – cast her adrift as she'd been set to drift already, this time on dangerous seas. He'd been a wretched parent, if the truth were told. Booting her out once more would be to fail her utterly. The whole thing was repeating itself. Supposing England were more fire than frying-pan, and he were deliberately hurrying his daughter under a cloudburst of bombs. Then, as her father, he should at least go with her. But he couldn't take Selama. Nor could he leave her. Every delay made the seas more perilous. The fever beat up and up; and then broke in another drenching sweat.

In the morning, in the lull, he put on a brave face. A sultry sky showed the monsoon weather, and Clarice maintained, over breakfast, her refusal to discuss change. By way of diversion, he read Phyllis's letter. It had been weeks delayed.

> *Dear Uncle Stan,*
>
> *I know you will have forgotten all about me. In fact when Auntie Mattie passed away you probably thought you would have got rid of us Tylers for good, and here we are turning up again like a bad penny. I'm sure I did write on the occasion of my marriage and again on the birth of our little boy, Jack,*

but unfortunately received no reply. Normally I wouldn't trouble you except Victor, my beloved husband, has lost his job, he is a shipwright at the boatyard, and is finding it hard to get another start. If there was any way you could see your way to help us through this difficult time, I can assure you we would be very grateful. I hope this letter finds you well. I always remember how kind you and Auntie Mattie were to me when you used to very kindly have me to stay with you in your country house in Suffolk.

  I remain
    Your loving niece
      Phyllis Warren (Tyler as was)

'"I remain",' Dr Pike quoted, sighing. 'She wants money, of course.'

'Who?'

'Phyllis. Her husband's lost his job.'

'Phyllis! Your letter's from Phyllis.'

'Yes.'

Her father saw the blush come to Clarice's cheeks; and I can feel it too, as I describe it.

'Is anything the matter?' he said.

'Nothing. Nothing at all.' She struggled to compose herself. 'Will you send her some? Money, I mean.'

'Not sure I've all that much left.' Dr Pike eyed her meaningfully.

'May I see?'

She took the letter, stood up, and hurried out to the veranda. The blush still prickled violently in her cheeks. Her hand was unsteady, and her knees had gone to rubber, making the short walk feel like a lurch into unsupported space. Outside, by a gap in the chick blinds, she read the letter over twice, three times, and then stared intently out at the sweep of countryside and rain forest – as if she could see all the way to England. *Victor, my beloved husband . . .*

No, I'm not Jack, the 'little boy' of Phyllis's letter. I am not yet born. I must draw up this landcape of privilege and make my portrait of the woman who should have been my mother, though her world has nothing to do with me. The past is a fable of desire, a romance, an illusion.

Why then, curled as I am, tucked away in the story, do I make these imaginative stitches, pulling Clarice Pike and my father together again? Why linger with the family connection, suturing a gash in time? And why, like my great-uncle, Dr Stan Pike, do I tackle certain monsters? Because of the hope for love, of course.

Clarice held on to the timber pole that propped the veranda roof. She tried to reinstate Robin Townely, her man of the moment – who ought to have been here by now to pick her up. But with the letter in her hand all she could think of was Vic, and London. Three years and she could still be visited by these heart-racings and shakings, these physical clichés. And still she couldn't tell whether they were genuine, or merely symptoms of her own dislocation.

On her mother's side was East London and a poverty she'd lived protected from. That was the London out of which her father had rescued her mother. That was also the London where her cousin, Phyllis, had grown up, so distressingly unrescued. But there, paradoxically, Clarice had found Vic. And what was Vic but an ordinary working man, a dockside shipwright . . .

Vic had been engaged to Phyllis; and yet instantly, shockingly, Clarice and he had been drawn to each other. They'd met for concerts, been to lectures together, stolen hours in cheap cafés. Staying at her grandmother Tyler's house, Clarice had not had long before her return to Malaya. There'd been a secret affair; then a realisation, followed by renunciation. She'd left for Southampton and her ship. He'd consented to his marriage.

Now in her mind's eye he was caught by cross-hatchings,

staring hopelessly back at her out of darkness, trapped back in that Dickensian ménage of cobwebs and candlelight that Phyllis's letter evoked for her. She pictured too, unwillingly, the marital bed, with its creaking springs, the couple panting at each other, Phyllis something triumphant, and the man who had so startled her with a meeting of minds made weak and run of the mill, ruined.

From the distance, somewhere in the plantation compound, there came the chime of gongs and a burst of drumming. She guessed there was a rehearsal for the festival to mark the end of Ramadan. Later there would be a shadow play. She turned back into the house. All the while, as she was collecting her things to meet Robin, a faint metallic music hung about her efforts. It seemed the moist air finely shook, and took on almost discernible curlicues, insinuating tendrils of sound.

AT THE COAL HOLE night-club in Betterton Street, people were ready to dance again. The band was coming back after its break, and the spotlight waited, a large empty moon half-way up the spangled backdrop. From a table beside the dance floor Victor Warren stared into the illumination. Shortly, his wife would occupy it; tonight's *chanteuse*. It was her lucky break.

Since he'd last seen Clarice, my father was not at all ruined in features. At first glance, his looks appeared quite dashing. Some negative quality, however, had certainly leaked into the rest of his appearance, and sitting with Tony Rice and Frances, the girl, he looked badly out of place. His grey flannel jacket was disreputable, his tie was skewed, and his shirt collar had too obviously been turned.

On closer inspection the face, which was thinnish with

slightly Slavic lines, revealed a brow contracted and a mouth tightened. He wore his brown hair slicked away from his face, so that his dark moustache gave him a worn and dangerous cast. It belied his earnest eyes – and his twenty-six years.

He had good reason to look grim. The feeling all along that he'd been playing for the very highest stakes seemed entirely borne out. Having done his best with Phyllis, he was sure she was trying to destroy him. In fact, it could have been the circle of his own death that glittered back at him from the stage. He, like Dr Pike, felt mightily scared. As he touched his drink to his lips he tried to convince himself he was being irrational.

The club was full. In one of Covent Garden's least promising streets, the Coal Hole was something of a find for a certain set. Or it was stumbled upon by theatre-goers after a meal at Monty's or *L'Escargot*, who told their friends. From a narrow, sandbagged door in the face of an old tobacco warehouse, a staircase led down to the cellars, where there was not only late-night alcohol but a resident dance band of four black jazzmen. If it hadn't been for the war, people said, the Coal Hole would have been set to 'take off'. In the absence, so far, of bombing or gas attacks, it was still open, still defiantly humming. For once, thank God, the idiotic situation across the Channel could be shoved firmly to the back of the mind – so long as the band proved authentically rhythmic, the singer sufficiently charming.

At the Coal Hole it wasn't a requirement to be dressed to the nines. Ordinary suits mingled with evening wear; there might be artists, addicts, a boxer or two, even an obstinate Blackshirt. There were types of unescorted girl. The Saturday-night clientele was unpredictable, and a frisson of intermixture ran in the smoke-filled air. The only real entrance qualification was a little spare cash, a commodity Vic clearly lacked. It was Tony Rice who'd brought him and Phyllis along, and it was Tony Rice, the perplexing, charmed and upwardly mobile gang boy, whose hand lay over Phyllis's career.

Yet it wasn't Tony of whom my father was afraid – it wasn't a physical fear at all. His desperation lay deeper. He was permanently wrought up, on edge.

He picked his wife out as she emerged from a side door. Her slim figure made its way towards the light. The stage was a shallow pedestal, no more than a foot high, and he watched her pause in front of it as her long dress threatened to trip her. Clutching the slink out of harm's way, she stepped up. The gown's plunge back exposed nearly the whole of her spine.

All week she'd been crippled with nerves. She despised her looks. She believed she was disfigured by a shame no amount of make-up, no glittery evening get-up could conceal. Her vocal cords, if she could force them open, would only humiliate her. All week he'd coaxed her through it, reassuring her that it was the actions of others that had left her so insecure; privately reminding himself that he'd put aside his feelings for Clarice in order to do what was right. Now he willed himself to believe that for once Phyllis could be straight with him.

When eventually she faced her audience he knew he'd been outwitted. She was completely at home, and the long wait seemed calculated. Her eyes glittered wide under plucked and pencilled brows, the cheeks were a rouged mask, the mouth a bait. For her sheer knowingness he was unprepared. She looked sly. When she let her head droop, he held his breath.

Light fell on her close-waved dark hair, the silver threads glinted in her gown, and the few bars of introduction poised on the arpeggio of a suspended chord. Chatter from the tables subsided. She lifted her eyes, childlike;

and then the voice launched itself high, virginal, and with a fashionable flutter.

> *Think of what you're losing*
> *By constantly refusing*
> *To dance with me*

From behind her a saxophone and muted trumpet picked up the phrase, and the bass threw a squib of rhythm. It was a safe number. After the success of the Branksome Revue, everyone was singing it again. The lover needed encouragement; she delivered it. With her one gloved hand on the edge of the piano, she seduced.

Then she played the man's role. Setting her head at just the coy angle, she scolded the audience with an artful smile.

> *Not this season*
> *There's a reason.*

They held up with her, and she hit the refrain:

> *I won't dance! Don't ask me;*
> *I won't dance! Don't ask me;*
> *I won't dance, madame, with you.*

The brash denial swelled out. The band swung, the bass player's free fingers vaulted the board to the springy dub-dub of the beat, and couples got up to dance. From the tables all around rose that buzz of relief which comes when the entertainment will do. Parties returned safely to their concerns: cigars were lit, and corks were popped. Aproned staff holding their trays high slid once again between casual encounters and established liaisons.

Where Vic sat a waiter hovered.

'No more, thanks.'

'I said I'll get them, Victor. We'll need three more of these, mate.' Tony indicated the cocktail glasses in front of them. 'No, make it four. Have one ready for Phylly when she comes back. Should really.'

Tony Rice was clean shaven, fleshy. He had the street looks of certain cruel young men and sported black silk lapels and neat white bow with all the sharpness Vic lacked. 'A winner, isn't she? You think so, don't you?'

'Yes.' My father glanced at his wrist-watch again: half an hour after midnight. Every passing minute ticked up feelings he couldn't cope with, costs he couldn't cover. 'She's divine,' he said. 'It's turned out a success. But I think we'd better leave as soon as she comes off. If you don't mind, Tony. Thanks so much and a bad show to break up the party, but . . .' He looked up at the waiter. 'I'd like the bill, please, actually.'

Tony cancelled him and signed the man to leave with his order.

'But our boy,' said Vic. 'Jack's on his own. We really must go.'

'Don't throw it back in my face, Vic.' There was an edge to Tony's voice, a hint of the dockside razor. He held Vic's gaze with narrowed eyes, then backed off. 'It's Phyllis's night and she deserves a break. Doesn't she, mate?'

Vic lit a cigarette, and looked over to where Phyllis was beginning her next number. Her body, such a battlefield in their marriage, seemed at ease. There, on the miniature stage, she was the idea of enchantment. There was no denying it – she was a good performer.

So he was being churlish; he was turning everything into melodrama. Tony was right, she deserved her break. Her pretty mouth, the nakedness of her neckline and arms . . . While she sang, while the music flowed, he could see her as if in a movie, briefly disentangled.

'That's more like it, Vic.'

FEMININITY FLICKERED EVERYWHERE in the smoky club.
Vic's gaze wandered. There were more attractive women
than he'd ever seen, wearing less. Out of his element, at
home neither with his own class nor the posh one, he
was wretchedly alert to them. The flash of one braceleted
wrist caught him like a blow. Voices, laughing or languid,
tempted at his ear; they underscored the chirruping of
his wife. Everywhere he looked he mustn't look, at the
eyes he mustn't meet. The place scandalised and fascinated him.

'You're a lucky bloke, Vic. You'll want to hang on to a
skirt like her. *I should like to have one, just the same as that.*'
Tony chanted softly as if all Phyllis's melody wanted was
a secret fight. '*Where'er I go they'll shout hallo where did you
get that . . . tart.*' He grinned. Vic saw his hand under the
table squeeze the thigh of the girl; he also saw the wince
that crossed her face. He was momentarily excited. 'She
deserves better, Phyllis does,' Tony said.

Vic tried to smile. 'Better than what? Better than the Coal
Hole? Or better than I can give her? That what you mean?'

'I don't know what you're playing at, Rabbit Warren,
keeping a woman like that in the manner you do.'

'Thanks.'

But Tony compelled him, turning to his female companion. 'Eh, Frankie? The boffin and the songbird. What do
you think of that?' The voice was level, the grin emotionless.

Frances opened her mouth disbelievingly at Vic. The
drinks arrived. She took hers and held it in front of her
with her little finger raised. He looked back. Thickly made
up, she might be about twenty, the same age as Clarice Pike

when they'd met, and fallen in love. . . . 'Are you, though? A boffin?' Frankie giggled.

'So I heard.' Tony's grin became a sneer.

'Evening classes,' said Vic. She even looked a little like her, like Clarice, he thought.

'Can't you just see him, duckie, with his chemistry bottles and tubes?'

'Marine engineering. I used to go up to Imperial College. On the bus. Three times a week after work. Trying to cram my physics,' Vic said again, quietly. 'It's over now. It was daft anyway.'

'Oh, *physics*, Frank. Only joking, Vic.'

Frances looked blank for a second; and then she giggled again nervously. 'I wouldn't know what that was.'

'The science of bodies,' said Vic.

'Really?' She looked him full in the eye. 'So what do you do now, then?'

'Nothing. Can't you tell?'

The girl stared one moment longer. Then she complained that Tony hadn't asked her up to dance.

At the completion of her spot Phyllis made her way through the applause. Vic stood up to greet her just as Tony and Frankie arrived back from the floor. She was breathless, on the verge of tears. 'Was it all right? Tell me honestly! I was terrible, wasn't I?'

'Knocked 'em cold,' said Tony.

'No, I was awful. I've spoilt everything. They'll never ask me back. Vic?'

He reassured her. 'It was terrific, darling. You were superb.' As he kissed the proffered cheek he heard Tony mimicking 'darling' to Frankie.

But Phyllis hardened. 'You're lying,' she said. Her ice-cold look was close up and intent.

'Honestly,' Vic said. 'Look around. They're still clapping. They loved you.' He licked his lips.

'I can't look.' Phyllis clenched her fists. 'I was so nervous.' She snatched her handbag from the table and sat down at the vacant seat, her back to the scene of her triumph. 'So bloody nervous. Is that one for me?'

'You deserve it,' said Tony. The party resumed their places. 'Doesn't she, Vic?'

'Was I really any good?' Phyllis looked from one to the other, her garish eyes again childlike over the glass, the flutter of lashes too naïve. But she allowed herself to be persuaded. 'Truly? I get positively sick. It is all right, isn't it, Vic? You don't mind?'

'You were marvellous.' Vic made himself smile. 'Completely bowled me over. I'd no idea. And the voice. I mean, I hear it at home, but . . .'

'My voice. I thought it was going to die on me. Did you hear that note in "Mexico Way"? I right muffed it, didn't I?'

'Never heard any such thing. It all sounded perfect.'

'Really, Vic?' She seemed winsome.

He smiled more genuinely, relieved, off guard. 'Perfectly perfect.'

'You hear what the engineer says. Another round, then, shall we?' Tony clicked his fingers at a waiter.

Vic tried to insist. 'Darling. I know this is boring of me . . .'

The atmosphere changed again in an instant. She was fierce. 'Vic, I told you. My sister said she'd look in on him.'

'It's incredibly late.'

'This is my night, my chance. For Christ's sake. This is my kind of place, for once. Jack'll be fast asleep. He's not a baby any more, you know.' Crossly she took out her compact and opened it. 'Oh, my God. Just look at me. Frankie, you'll come with me if I go and put things right?'

'All the same, if Tony wouldn't mind I do think we really should . . .'

Phyllis hit the table with her fist. 'No!' She shook her head, petulantly. 'No! No! No!'

'Darling, I . . .'

Tony was decisive. 'You spoil that kid. Come on. Drink up. You're a smart girl, Phylly, and if you weren't married to drearyface here . . .'

'Tony, really!' Once more Phyllis appeared the innocent. 'Whatever will you think of saying next?' Colour spread from her cheekbones and up across her forehead – the streaked powder could do nothing to contain it. Where the shaken wave of hair had worked loose from its kirby-grip, a bright little gash on her temple was visible. Her hand sprang up to touch it. Newly glazed, it reopened. A spot of blood appeared like a red pearl and fell to the table. And another. 'Christ!' It was on her fingers.

Tony cooed in mock concern. 'Now that's a nasty one, isn't it. How did you come by that, Phyllis?'

Her eyes flashed and she fumbled in her bag for a handkerchief, holding it up to the cut. 'This? Walked into a door, didn't I.' A stain spread under her varnished nails and into the cloth.

'A door, was it?'

'Yes. A door. This evening, as I was changing. Just now, in the ladies' room. Before I went on. I'll have to . . .'

Tony leant across and touched her hair. 'You'll have to be more careful, won't you, girl?'

She stood up and held out her other hand for Frances. 'Coming, Frank? Quickly!' Together they made their way off between the tables.

AT THE SIGHT of the wound he'd said nothing, done nothing. His fingers shaking, Vic lit another cigarette. The band thumped out a Latin number and the couples on the dance floor stalked each other.

Close to Phyllis there was always deceit, always pain, and he wore her chaos almost closer than his own skin; but the detail of the cut was more than anything he'd expected. Its implications stole over him like a dead faint. Tony had hit her, and she was protecting him.

The regular singer, a slight young man, was dapper in his white dinner jacket with a rose in his buttonhole; he sermonised from the stage, pinned by a searchlight:

> *Keep young and beautiful, it's your duty to be beautiful,*
> *Keep young and beautiful, if you want to be loved.*

Tony got up for the gents. 'Might as well go for a drain-off myself. Don't go away, will you.'

Vic dragged at his smoke. Despite her blushes, Phyllis wore the shiny little injury as an adornment. They were already lovers. She'd given this pimp what she always contrived to deny her husband, and Tony had taunted her with it, barefaced. They'd been carrying on here, right in front of him, knowing he was too simple to see – that even when he saw, he'd do nothing, nothing. He stubbed out his cigarette. His mouth was parched. He drank the glass in front of him too quickly. It tasted trite, bitter.

Then the others returned. The girls were quite natural, and they laughed, comparing make-up and quipping one to the other. Tony, seating himself once more, was bluff. 'There, Vic. Told you not to go away.' His eyes were clear, the sculpted lips a design on the fine skin.

A table next to them erupted with laughter. Someone was standing up on his chair, holding a champagne glass in his teeth to roars of encouragement. Phyllis turned

32

round, clapping, and then smiled in Vic's direction. 'All right, Vic?'

He smiled back. 'Fine.'

Another crackle of laughter went up. Through the din she mimed the words 'Thanks' and 'Sorry'.

Soothed, he smiled again.

Tony set the next round up, and the next. Then Vic drank wilfully. He told himself he needed to lighten up. *You're a lucky bloke, Vic. You'll want to hang on to a skirt like her*. He was confused. He wanted to dissolve the fierce nag of not knowing, never quite seeing, and to drown all the other issues, the kid, the money, the war, the awful round of his futureless days. A man at a further table held a woman's hand to his lips, nibbling the fingers; he thought of Clarice.

The club became a whirl of sensations. Noise and laughter from the tables reverberated almost visibly in the low vaults, like strips of newspaper hung out; and on the spotlit floor, bright couples wove in amongst each other. Bodies swayed, clasped, parted. A woman's naked spine was crossed by a man's hand and the crowd at the next table was trying to form itself into a conga dance. People were crying out, 'Come on, then! Are you with us?' To the frugg of the band they were a counter-chorus. Cut-glass accents aped in cockney a popular song:

> *Oh we ain't got a barrel of money,*
> *Maybe we're ragged and funny . . .*

Jack would be fine, probably.

'Vic!' Phyllis was speaking to him.

Tony was insisting on something to her. He was shouting above the swirl of noise. 'Vic here wants to make some money, Phyll. He told me.'

'You're not kidding me he does. It's only my earnings

keeping us, to tell the honest truth. If he won't do it, I have to. Don't I?'

'Eh?' Vic fought to concentrate. Frankie's young eyes were contacting his. She really did have the look of Clarice Pike, the shape of the nose, something in the line of the chin. Tony and Phyllis were linked together. There was something between them, but who was he to police her friendships? In the marriage he'd been too rigid, even a little inhuman, unfaithful at the heart, and that was why Phyllis . . . He could see now. She was right. Of course she was right. No one's life was really at stake. Truly he *should* try to be less of a bloody Nazi.

There was a twenty-pound note on the table.

IT WAS LONDON cobblestones banging under the wheels, and the car was racing east through the starlit port. Phyllis was in the front beside Tony, her mother's fox fur draped around her shoulders. The fur cast a shadow on her hair so that there was only the clouded trace of her white neck. She was resisting sleep – her head nodded and jerked as if an outside force had it in mind to break her.

Vic was slumped next to Frankie in the back. The window had been wound right down. Unlit gas lamps hung where the wind came from, then swept past. Forbidden headlights made the iron beaks of warehouse hoppers poke from speeding, eyeless cages. The night was a tall sack ripped by a car's roar, and the air driving to meet his face tasted of coal.

Still his evening replayed itself. He mustn't close his eyes. 'It's your money, Vic. Yours, mate. All you have to do is pick it up.'

He'd been wary. 'Me? Don't expect to see that kind of item in a month of Sundays.'

'More ways to skin a cat, aren't there? Come on, pick it up. Think what a difference a twenty would make. And twenty more like it.'

The tyres screeched in a left-hand corner. Frankie was forced against him. Vic's shoulder hit the right door and he was pinned under her. The car swung again. Her eyes screwed tight, she raised an arm and clung on to his neck. Then her other hand slipped across into his. He clasped at it. She made words in his ear he couldn't catch.

He'd danced with her. To the muted trumpet and the whining sax, she'd answered his arm's inclination and the nudge of his hip. When they'd sat down again Phyllis and Tony were drinking through straws from each other's glasses. Blatant and provocative, the twenty-pound note was still on the table.

Now beside them careered the black brick ends of streets, the outlines of sheds, the ironwork of a bascule bridge. A pub sign hung above the scream of another high-speed turn. Beyond Frankie's perfumed hair Vic saw the city momentarily framed, a hard silhouette that touched low cloud. He'd made a deal. The food was taken care of, the rent, and shoes for little Jack. He and Phyllis could tide themselves over, pull themselves up . . . but there was a condition attached, some codicil that he still couldn't recollect.

'Well, Vic? What *am* I worth to you, Vic? What *would* you do for me?'

Tony thrashed the engine through the gears. Tall cranes angled darker strokes on dark. A ship's hull, huge, loomed almost within touching distance.

Vic had come back from the gents, his legs loose, his brilliantined hair flopping over his eyes in strands. Through them he'd stared at the persistent banknote. There were glasses and ashtrays around it. He'd been taken up with the detail, the King's head, the faint lettering, the fine lines that looped and scrolled.

His own head reeled with the thought of it, and with the weight of the girl thrown now this way, now that by the lurching car. Frankie's fingers held on. She was managing to stroke the side of his face. So like the girl he'd fallen in love with, he could almost imagine . . . The sequence was scrambled. He'd stretched out his hand over the note, poised to give it back, or reluctant to touch it. 'Did you drop this? Tony?' The note was a test. It was Frankie's eye he'd caught, and not Phyllis's. 'I know what you mean, Tony, but you can count me out of all that.'

The engine raced hard, accelerating. 'It's yours, mate. Yours for the taking.'

The straight run was a relief, a lampless high street. Frank's eyes remained closed. Her breath was warm and damp and she was naked in his mind. No, she was slipping out of her purple evening dress and the flesh-coloured underwear. Or his hand was against the suspender hitch, where the silk of the stocking met the silkier skin of her thigh, still bearing the bruise of Tony's fingers.

Vic saw Phyllis's head loll on to the back edge of her seat. Now a long bend bumped it against the pillar and she must have felt the hurt. Her fur stole rucked up over the leather as she shifted down, curling herself out of view. Frankie moaned and hardened herself against him. He tried to speak. Literally behind his wife's back, his drunken imagination was unbuttoning a prostitute to the jazz, there on the dance floor. Or here in the car, and all the time wishing for Clarice Pike. There was a fox fur caught up on Phyllis's seat back, with its little cub mouth and eyes and sharp suggestive teeth. What *would* he do for her? 'For you, Phyllis, anything. You know that. You know that, don't you, darling. I love you . . . beyond measure.' They'd all laughed.

Vic pulled himself away. Tony braked hard, swore, and then jumped a red light. The girl's face lifted for a second, her eyes suddenly open in surprise, her lips slightly parted. On an impulse, Vic met the mouth and held the kiss. They broke off just as Tony shouted back to them, 'Enjoying yourselves, you two? Just goes to show. You can never tell with snobs, can you?' The voice had a hint of triumph. 'What do you think, Phylly?' There was no reply from Phyllis. 'Must be asleep. Tell the missus later, shall I, Vic?'

Vic recognised the occluded shop fronts of Beckton Road, Canning Town. Once more, the car accelerated fiercely. Soon there was nothing but the long stretch over the East Ham levels, the stink coming off the marshes of rot and salt and the oily wash. They were going too fast into the night and Tony had caught him red-handed – hadn't he? 'You should've gone left,' he said.

'Scenic route,' Tony called. 'Any objections?'

He'd taken the money. He remembered picking it up. The kiss, was it good or bad? Clarice would always be the other side of the world. Suddenly desperate, light-headed, Vic played up to his wife's manfriend. 'You know. We've got this little place in the country, Phyllis and I. We go there at weekends. We'd love to see you. Why don't you all come down?' He shared the laugh.

At Ripple Road he was looking into the child's room. If Phyllis's sister had called in she'd left no trace of herself. But Jack was fast asleep, as though in the child's mind there'd been no alteration, nothing of the bounce of the music and the foxy, foxtrotting on the dance floor. Frankie's kiss still stung Vic's lips. He'd made a deal.

In the chamber-pot the mess of his vomit reeked. The couple who ran the shop below had the only bathroom, half-way down the stairs. The chain cranked in the iron cistern. He cleaned up and rinsed his mouth. Back in bed there was Phyllis's body, its familiar and unfamiliar smells.

At last, the deal held its focus and he realised what he'd agreed to. It was to do a job with Tony Rice. If he loved Phyllis. His heart thumped in his chest.

'And no backing out.' Tony had sealed it, laughing.

'Yes, Vic. No backing out.' She'd hold him to it. His head ached, cracking up. In the darkness, the bright, jazz-hard lines around his wife horrified him.

AWAKE TO THE SHRILLING of birds, Jack carried his box of toys into the front room of the flat. Through half-drawn drapes the sun made a glinting, near-horizontal bar, and the child sat in the gleam of it, where the dirty brown rug stuck a plaster over the join in the floor. All along the length of the join, except for the rug, the striated, mustard-coloured lino had chipped away to show the string and glue inside it. The join was the edge of England, and when the tin bomber came Jack's mother would be all right because of the soap packet. That stood for the wooden house, lifted by low hills, which his parents always reached when they rode on the tandem. If he sat, so, on the rug, he believed he could save her.

Jack didn't like Ripple Road. There was a dog's muzzle in the coal scuttle. It was a brass creature whose gaze had cracked the leather in the two chairs. Pugs and griffons lurked behind the hat-stand; sometimes he ran at them with his wooden sword. The war was a dog in a gas mask with eyes like dinner plates. Any moment it would burst in, carrying the tin bomber on its back. Jack's mother said Ripple Road was in Barking, and from that the three-year-old imagined a perpetual canine gape ready to swallow his family.

Vic Warren stepped around my brother, or half-brother, to draw the curtains. Through dirty uneven glass, taped crosswise, the sunrise hurt his eyes. Below him, on the opposite pavement, a shirtsleeved newsagent was putting out a sign for a Sunday paper: LONDON – 200,000 CASUALTIES STILL EXPECTED.

One or two cars were parked by the post office, and a solitary Home and Colonial van stood further along. Two old men were stopped on the Vicarage Road corner to exchange greetings, and by the sandbagged shop front of Wallace's, the chemist, a black labrador sniffed and cocked its leg. The long, dry September had left all surfaces the colours of dust, and even the moist morning air was stained with tar haze.

Vic looked along the road towards the East Street traffic lights. Turn left, and, from Barking straight through the metropolis to Brentford in the West, terrace followed terrace for twenty unbroken miles. London was a working-class concentration – of window-cleaners and war cripples, clerks and typists, slaveys who lived in, skivvies who lived out, shopkeepers, journeymen. London was full, in fact, of people just like himself. Why, then, had he been singled out? His head pounded. Having slept, he wasn't sure now which ought to trouble him more, the girl or the money. The girl in the night-club had reminded him of someone he should have forgotten, and Tony had seen him kissing her. He tried to rationalise: they'd all been in high spirits, he'd drunk too much. My father was not well, but his illness was more than just a hangover. He really was cracking up.

He thought of his own parent and the little place in the country to which he'd so grandly invited Tony. It did exist. Before 1914, Percy Warren, my grandfather, worked in the same yard as Vic, at Creekmouth where they repaired the Thames barges and wooden lighters. Blunt, working craft, the staple of the river trade, they required the attentions of blunt men who knew the limits of their materials and could knock the grimy vessels back into shape.

Perce was the kind who could build a durable cabin, and did – in the countryside miles downriver, while the family watched and picnicked. That was in the one acre of England where you could buy a square inch of land – never mind that it was an Essex farmer's private racket. When most working men had scant hope of owning much at all, the tiny wooden house was something unique, a triumph, a place for holidays and sunny Georgian Sundays.

Perce had got a roof on, and glazed the windows, and would have begun decorating the inside if the Great War hadn't broken out. At Loos, he inhaled several chestfuls of gas, British, when it characteristically blew back on them. At home in East Ham he was convalescent. Vic remembered the pair of them, himself and his dad, playing together, despite the cane that lived on top of the bedroom wardrobe. Like mischievous children they avoided the mother's bitter tongue.

Most particularly he remembered all three of them at weekends, the little party going out on the train to the wooden house, where the mending rifleman pottered about with his hammer and nails. That was his true father, who loved him; and not the tetchy, shell-shocked side of the man. Vic held the good face of his dad like a precious coin kept always mounted one way. It was himself who was the 'wrong'un'. He couldn't stay the course. A marriage forced, a heart elsewhere, a perfectly good trade thrown away. Look, now, how he'd spoilt everything again.

He left the window-pane and sat for an hour, and then another, playing ludo with Jack, trying to keep his eyes open and his craziness at bay. The child insisted on the game only to sabotage it. Over Jack's breakfast leavings, Vic read him the story of the tinder-box; and at the bad end of a bad tale refused to begin again. On the Somme in 1916, Perce got a machine-gun slug that grazed the lung before passing clean through, and he came home for the second time from France. Vic was five.

A chapel bell started in one of the neighbouring streets, a monotonous clang; and Jack played up until he got slapped. His cries threatened to wake Phyllis and the Wilmots downstairs. Vic issued more threats, sick at the trap of having to back them up. During the start of the German May offensive, 1918, Perce was gassed on the skin. The shell landed right next to him on the earth parapet, tore open his uniform and splashed raw mustard compound on to it, while the fumes were sucked the other way along the trench. The contact raised a tented blister down the whole of his side – which healed in a month and spared him once again to return home alive. Vic's father, Perce, had character.

JACK UPSET HIS DRINK. There was no change of clothes. Vic sponged him off, grateful for the continuing warm weather. At half past nine, able to bear neither his son's company nor his own, he risked making Phyllis tea. Jack fidgeted round her in the bed, plucking at her nightdress. But she was laughing awake. 'I did it, Vic, didn't I.'

The room with its heavy wardrobe and bilious walls lightened suddenly and unexpectedly. 'You were marvellous.' He sat down on his side of the mattress.

'And we had a good night out on it, didn't we? Draw the curtains, Vic.'

He obeyed, still wary, afraid his guilt would show.

A prospect of hot slates and bright sky washed in as she lifted her hand to her head. 'Christ, I've got a bloody hangover.'

'Mummy!'

'Splitting.' The cut looked sore and crusted, the two laps of skin heaping on either side the neat gash.

Jack pointed: 'That's a hangover!'

A frown fleeted across her brow. She touched the place. 'Oh, that. No, it isn't. When you drink too much. Like Dad.' Her eyes were alight. She teased Vic amiably.

Relieved, he went and bustled about, heating the kettle again, finding the scissors and some lint, bringing a pudding basin of hot water from the kitchen. He settled it down beside her. With his one hand he smoothed her hair back, cradling the head on to the pillow. With the other, he hooked the warm lint out in the scissor blades and stroked it gently across the place. Her head felt small and still. There was the warm female smell of her, the damaged female skin. 'This should help.'

'That's nice.'

'You know, we ought really to get you to hospital. It ought to be stitched.'

She flared. 'I don't want someone else touching me. I don't want to think about it.' The emotion subsided. 'Anyway, they'll reckon you did it, won't they?' Her mouth softened and she smiled up at him. 'Won't show under my hair. What's a war if no one gets wounded? More important to get out to the country. Work on the cabin. That's what you want, isn't it? That's what you think. You don't want to be hanging about on my account, do you, Vic?'

'Well . . .'

'That's what you want, isn't it?'

'If you're sure. There.' He finished with the lint.

'Now we've got a bit more cash.' Her gaze followed him as he stood to go.

He paused at the door. She was genuinely compliant. Her affection confused him, and suddenly the agreement with Tony presented itself in a new light. Phyllis hadn't seen the kiss, wouldn't trouble about it if she had; it was the deal that held power with her. That alone had been the test, the chance to prove himself. What she'd really needed all along was for him to measure up, to show he cared for her. She wanted the gesture – no one would seriously hold him to it.

How grateful he was. Clarice was just infatuation. Some of the sunlight of the day filled his heart and he believed he'd broken through with his wife. There was a chance; the boy was provided for. And Tony, in the only way he knew, had been trying to help.

Soon, Phyllis was behind him on the tandem. In their shorts and shirt tops, they cut a dash in the Barking back streets. Bareheaded, healthy as Germans, they were a sculpture of modern life, threading through to the Longbridge Road with Jack in the miniature side-car they'd bought when he was a baby, holding his miniature fingers up against the breeze. Vic was taking care of his wife and child. Further out they'd be bomb safe – if it came.

Through Hornchurch and on into Upminster they steered the accustomed route. Householders were piling more sandbags, still installing Andersen shelters, digging slit trenches across prized front lawns. Under the Cranham railway bridge scuffed kerb sides gave way to verges where weed bursts frayed. He was excited, almost aroused. When he glanced down he could see her pretty feet in the toe-clips.

Soon enough, real country appeared, bright as a poster. The shorn fields stretched away, dark edged, flawless. Dotted in them here and there the last stooks were browned by the fine weather. Soon, too, solitary old oaks held ground in pastures, with gangs of cattle in their shadow. Ashes and quickbeams stood up from thorn brakes. Greenfinches from the hedgerows looped beside the bike, their beating bodies almost close enough to grab. Grasshoppers shrilled from copper tufts and dun-coloured butterflies meddled with the late white flowers.

In rhythm with the lowland, the road undulated gently, an edge of the tidal basin. Every so often a car passed. Redeemed, daring the bubble to burst, Vic breathed deeply. There was still no job for him at Everholt's, but if Phyllis was *with* him he'd find something else. His old bag of tools was strapped to the side-car. And once everything was set to rights they could uproot and do well at the little house, war or no war. He could maybe find a bit of wallpapering, distempering, odd jobs. He could sell vacuum cleaners, superior gas masks. They could live off the land, and she'd be away from the temptations of London. . . .

The heat was soon freakish; their tyres slicked a little on the tar. At Horndon, women were covering a rick in a cornfield; he heard the sound of a threshing machine in the distance – that, and a flourish of church bells driven faintly on the wind. The Englishness touched him. Then came a run-down, rather desperate stretch. No one could miss the doorless car at the back of a farm cottage, or the unusable tractor abandoned in a field further on, the harrow still attached. Barns and sheds were patched with rusting corrugated iron, doubling for pig pens, degrading into chicken runs.

They overtook a traction engine. They passed a party of hikers, tousled lads who waved, and would soon be holding rifles, being likeliest for the call-up. All along the way, telegraph wires strung out the distances. In a paddock just before the main road a dispirited cart-horse stood in the heat haze. The notion of it troubled Vic like a presentiment, and he was instantly assailed by the truth of the matter, shocked by the situation he was in. His family, all on the same bike, began the slow climb into Laindon.

HE'D TELL HER NO. He sawed new gabling for the porch, climbed up on his dad's old pair of steps, and nailed the strips carefully into place. From the roof he could see the river, wide and grey-blue in the distance. Behind him the clutter of cabins, holiday shanties, miniature follies and disused plots stretched over the roll of hills as far as the arterial road and along eastward to the village of Basildon. The locals called the settlement Slum Farm.

But Vic had always loved it. People had made dwellings out of anything, flotsam and thievings, offcuts and salvage. There were clinker-built homes, and boiler-made homes. There were railway carriages and self-assembly kits. Closest to his heart was the converted bus, six plots along the lane, where the Flatman family had lived with their ungovernable brood. Over the open top it had a crazy pitched roof with a stove-pipe sticking out, and barefaced roses groped and wrestled up the conductor's spiral staircase.

Roses grew everywhere on the encampment. They straggled over cabin porches, trailed under tiny, curtained windows or were clustered upon brick chimney stacks. They made bold and prickly hedges inside the picket stakes. Unpruned, they burst right through the tumbledowns, the failures, scratching at roofing felt and asbestos fibre. Now hip-laden in the Indian summer, they rioted.

Vic climbed down to finish the glazing he'd pinned the previous weekend. He pressed a strip of putty against the pane, shaped it deftly to the joinery with his thumb, and looked over at Phyllis. She was singing a nursery rhyme to Jack, cuddling and kissing him. He caught his breath at the slope of her shoulders, her wrists, the whiteness of her legs. In his imagination he ran his hand all along the flesh from her sandal strap to the cuff of her shorts. She was his wife. He left his work and went to put his arm around her, touching her neck with his lips whenever the boy looked away. In her ear, he whispered, 'After lunch, eh? Shall we? When he has his nap.' But Jack was hungry, and Vic stood up to lay out the picnic.

And while they were eating he plucked up his courage, a grown man, and told her that the deal was out of the question. And to his surprise she merely nodded, and frowned, and looked away. Then he imagined it was all right.

Jack licked the jam out of his last sandwich until the red sweetness was the same as his tongue. Always his mother was beautiful when they came to the wooden house. He thought of the slips of complicated words that had just flown between his parents. 'Twenty quid and my three, Vic. What about that for a night out?' He held on to the shape of them.

Still tasting his bread, he wandered away from his parents and over towards the little house. By the window where his father had been working he put his hand in the putty tin. 'The fact is, Phylly, the twenty's out of the question. You must see that. I'll have to go and see Tony and give it back.' The plump, oil-smelling stuff was warm and smooth.

Then his father caught him, picked him up, kissed him too and swung him round. His head high up next to his dad's, Jack gazed down at her, there, lying in the deck-chair. The putty lump was a feeling squeezed in his hand. She had frowned when they couldn't keep it. A crease appeared in between her eyes, just to the left of centre, and Jack remembered the cut. On the floor at Tony's place there had been red blots, as if large wet buttons had come slipping out of his mother's head and fallen to the floor. And her cream blouse dripping red.

46

Jack watched her as she lay in the deck-chair, her face clear now, her eyes fallen shut. He struggled to get down, and next thing he was climbing on her, his knee on her stomach, his head down on her soft chest, looking up under the dark wisps of curl.

'Christ, Vic. I thought you were looking after him.'

But Jack could see it, still there, a small line coming out of her hair and opening the top of her forehead with black and red. He wanted to point to it, put his finger in. Now she had her hand up to touch the wound, the ring on her finger a gleam of yellow, bright as sunshine. She had told him not to tell. He liked the gold, how one point of it shone.

Vic pulled his son off her. He said, cautiously, 'If I can just stop up that bit where the rain came in over the door. Then we'll need a couple of new panels for the sides because of that mould. I'll bike over and order them. Churchill Johnson's, that place at the station, they've got asbestos. Maybe next weekend.'

Phyllis straightened her blouse where it was tucked up. 'You're turning Tony down, then.'

'You can't seriously expect . . .'

She, too, seemed to check herself, as though she were fighting her impulses, as though she were really trying. 'Look, Vic, it's only me keeping us going, isn't it? No call for you to be looking down your nose any more at me, or my family. Or my friends. D'you think I like it or what, standing up in that club making a spectacle of myself? Those men, Victor. They do pass comments. If it wasn't for Tony . . . You do respect me, don't you?'

'I have to give it back, Phyllis. I can't get involved in all that, no matter how much we need it. . . .' He looked away.

'You say you love me, Vic.'

'I do love you.'

'*Do* you, though? You don't. You don't love me at all.'

He sighed and turned back to her. 'Look, darling. A bloke like me has to stick in the lee of the law. That's loving, isn't it? That's for you.'

'You don't want me. If you loved me you'd do what it takes. You think I've got no morals, don't you? How could I have, where I come from? Down by the docks. That's what you think. Well, love means more than lying down and taking it, Victor. It's more than, Yes boss, No boss, Thanks for the sack, boss. A man would be on my side but you never are.'

'I'd had too much to drink, for God's sake. I want . . .'

'I know exactly what you want.'

'What do I want?' he responded crossly. 'You tell me what I want. Tell me.' Then he sensed the trap he'd fallen into. 'No . . . Phyllis.'

But a line had been crossed. 'You just want to get rid of me, don't you? You want me dead.'

VIC FELT EACH colour of the world click off as the frame changed. It was always so sudden, and he always walked in. He knew every detail of what had to come next – and on, and on, until the man in him broke. Her eyes were already glazed over, hard, like an old one. Phyllis had drained out of her; she was terrible, unreachable. 'Come on. You just want me dead, don't you? You just want rid of me.'

'For pity's sake, don't start.'

'You do, though, don't you? You hate me. You do. Why don't you admit it? Go on. Admit it. Why don't you, Vic? Face facts. Well, if that's what you want . . .'

'Please . . .' Vic looked at Jack. The boy was playing ostentatiously with the tool bag, trying to save his father. 'Please, Phyllis. Not now.' Vic lowered his head into his hands. 'Look, we're having a nice day. I thought we were going to . . .' The lover's plea was feeble.

'Mummy! Stop.'

'And you can shut it,' she called. 'You and him, the two of you ganging up.'

She ran across to Jack and grabbed his arm away from the tools. The boy went limp by her side. Tears began to stream from his eyes. She shouted, 'Why are you crying at me? I'm your mother. Why are you crying? Eh? Tell me, you ungrateful little brat!'

'Stop that. He's only a child. He doesn't understand.'

'Of course he understands. He hates me. Don't you? You both do.'

Vic went to separate them. There was a byplay of hands and arms, a brief scuffle. He took Jack, quivering, and set him in a no man's land a yard or so off, triangulated between them. Neither should appear to take sides against her.

Phyllis called, 'Come here, Jack. Come to your mother.'

'Leave him be, Phyllis. Can't you see he's upset? The kid's crying, for God's sake. Can't you see? He's a child.'

'He's my child and I can do what I like with him.'

'No.'

The stare was icy in her; but Vic watched her attention as it lifted from the boy and was directed back at him. Her fists clenched and unclenched. 'If you two hate me so much, if you'd both get on so well without me, then I'll go. That's what'll make you happy, isn't it? The pair of you. You want me out of the way. Come on. You do, don't you? Face up to it, you'd both be better off without me. I'm dirt. I'm rubbish. It's a simple fact. Well, I'll do it for you. All right? It's only what you want.'

'Get inside the house, Jack. Shut the door. It's just Mummy and Daddy talking. Do as I say.'

Vic watched the boy go to the cabin, mute and sniffling. He saw the cabin door shut after his son – the hostage she kept to her demands. It was for the child's sake he held on. It was for the child's sake he'd been reduced to this. If he could break down first, she might relent; but the hurt wasn't yet great enough and nothing he could do would alter the weary routine of what was about to occur.

'I'll go then, shall I?'

'That's not what we want.'

'You do. No, listen. If I was dead you'd be free. Wouldn't you? Wouldn't you, Vic? Vic? Answer me. That's just what you want. Tell me the truth, Vic. It would solve everything if you got rid of me.'

'I don't want to have this.'

'Why don't you kill me, then? Then I'd be out of your way. That's what you think. That's what you want, isn't it?'

'Damn you!'

'What did you say?'

'Nothing, Phylly. Nothing. I didn't mean it. Truly I didn't.'

'I'm evil, aren't I? You think I'm the devil. All right I'll go, then. I will.' She made as if to gather her things. 'If that's what you want.'

'You're his mother. He needs you. We love you, Phyllis. Stay. Please stay.'

Phyllis stood, half turned away with her maroon cardigan in her hand. Vic stepped towards her and took her arm. 'I need you.'

'You don't want me. I'm filthy. That's what you think. Say it. You'd be better off without me.'

'I love you.' He wanted to smash her head. 'Phyllis. Think of the kid. Try, Phyllis. We've been through all this.' He sank down, holding his face again, turning away himself now and crouching towards the ground as if he were being beaten.

'Why don't you kill me, Vic? You know it's what you want.' She cast about as if for some implement. His bag lay in the long grass. She bent to rummage in it. He heard the scrape and edge of his tools. 'Here, then.' She had hold of a large, one-inch-wide chisel. 'Here, Vic.' She held it out to him by the blade, thrusting the yellow handle at him, its hammer-burred top fractured like the crown of a wooden dandelion. 'Take it!'

'Phyllis!' He tried ignoring her, presenting his back. But he needed to watch what she did as she jabbed words at him.

'I'll do it for you, then,' she said. 'If you're too weak. If you're not man enough, Vic, to do it yourself, I'll take it out of your hands. I will, Vic. If that's what you're after, I'll save you the bother. Save you the trouble.' She clamped both her hands on the chisel. 'Here. It's just what you've been hoping for all this time. Haven't you? Eh? Look.' Gripping the shaft of it with both hands, she poised the blade at her neck, forcing him to look.

'Phyllis!'

'It's what you want, Vic.'

'It's not what I want. Listen to me.' He dared not move. 'Let me talk to her. Let me talk to Phyllis. I know she's still there. I love her. I don't hate her.'

'You want me dead. Don't you? Then I'll do it. I'll give you what you want. I'll give you exactly what you want.'

He was on that edge for minutes. Then he broke out and grabbed a wrist. 'No! I love you, Phyllis. You know that. Sweetheart. Come on, let the thing go. Can't you? Please.' He tugged at her forearm. The chisel glinted. 'For pity's sake! Stop it!'

'Mummy!'

Vic caught a glimpse of the little face in the window he'd just glazed.

Then, once again, nothing else was alive in the garden

but the chisel and a voice, half stifled, grinding, coming remorselessly out of the fixed features.

'No. Think how much better things'll be. Think how much you want rid of me. See, I'm doing it for you. Why don't you let me? Then you'll be happy. Won't you, Vic? Won't you? You'll be happy. With me gone.' The chisel stood, pent in the inches, juddering at her throat.

All at once Vic saw himself through Jack's eyes. His one arm was around her shoulders, and he was using all the force in his other against her two hands with their woman's strength conjoined, endlessly driving the chisel towards her own throat. 'See! See! This is what you want!'

She would succeed. She was determined. This time he fully believed she would finish herself, and he felt excruciated, invaded; his soul would burst and there'd be hell to pay. He had brought her to this. At last, to his infinite relief, the pain and despair broke out of Vic's eyes. He wept in terrible, gasping sobs.

'Oh, Vic. What's the matter, love? It's all right.' It was as though she knew nothing of the steel in her hand. She ignored it, and broke her grip. The tool swung down. She might have been holding the rolled-up newspaper she'd used to chase a wasp. She wouldn't have hurt a fly.

Slowly Vic straightened and, smiling, dashed away the tears from his face. 'I thought you meant to do it that time.' His good humour was automatic, once the punishment had stopped. He wanted to soothe her, to tell her it was all right. He was strong, strong enough for both of them. Strong enough also to hide the guilty secret that in his thoughts he had held on to Clarice.

They were standing together. 'Oh, come on, Vic. Don't be so bloody daft. You know I didn't mean it.'

'I didn't know, Phyllis. I didn't.'

'Course you did.' She smiled.

Her smile was like a blessing. He was so grateful.

'Yeah.'

'Vic? When Tony comes.'

'All right, Phyllis. I'll do it. I'll do whatever he wants.'

'There,' Phyllis said.

Later, Jack watched his father sitting in the doorway to the wooden house with his long, safe legs tucked up under him. His dad was pumping the Primus until flames lapped up the sides of the kettle. In a tin box which he called his tinder-box there was a piece of thin metal, spoon pale with a wire in it which his father took and poked into the middle of the flames. The Primus roared suddenly, and hissed, and the fire turned blue so they could see holes in rows. The flame was a blue flower that never went away.

'There we go.' His father smiled at him and pumped the pump again. The metal had the same shine as the ring on her finger. Jack loved the hot smell of the Primus, the heat on his cheeks.

Much later still, when the sky was colouring up, he was clutching a piece of wood like a stick. His mother was sitting on a box drinking a cup of tea. Jack must get the wood into the cut on his mother's head. Needing both hands, he tried to bring it down from above in one clear swipe but she was too big, too high above him for it to be right. His stick was too heavy and he couldn't reach.

She smacked him hard and put him in the side-car. Then it was getting dark. Her shorts were next to him, moving. The sound was the hum, hum, of the tandem back to Ripple Road. The cars had their faint lights on. Up high were stars.

II
People and Property

CLARICE RETURNED FROM Singapore to Seremban in December. Both the monsoon and the Robin Townely affair were virtually over, and she intended to stay for Christmas. Now the sun beat down each day and the rain confined itself to half an hour every teatime. In the intense mid-afternoon, she and her father were inspecting the back garden. She wore a loose white linen dress, and her broad-brimmed straw hat was trimmed with a violet ribbon. The straw matched the raffia colour of her heeled sandals. As medicine for her feelings she held a whisky tumbler.

Glass also in hand, her father stared in silence at a large bougainvillaca plant. Then he turned and looked back at the bungalow. Clarice followed his gaze. The house appeared so old-fashioned, such a relic of the last century. The stilts pushed up and the rectangular bonnet of fringey palm thatch hung down. Sandwiched in between was her home, the only one she had. Its blue canvas awnings were pulled along most of the veranda; as far, in fact, as the servants' cottage, which was tacked on to the back with poles and more thatch. Through the one gap in the blinds was disclosed a shaded region like a winking eye next to the back steps. Clarice could see Ah Sui, her belated *amah*, moving about inside – a busy shimmer.

'I'm allowed to make up my mind,' Dr Pike said at last.

'Have you mentioned the idea to anyone else?'

57

'No.'

She gave an irritated laugh and surveyed him, as though for the first time in his own right. He had put on his old khaki bush hat, the item he tended to brood under whatever the weather. Despite his customary brown boots and gaiters, his great shorts and the loose, pocketed, sweat-stained shirt worn outside his belt, he looked anything but familiar, suddenly ineffectual.

'And this is all on my behalf?' she said.

'Yes.'

'*Why* is it? I'm grown up, aren't I? Do you think I can't take care of myself in the world?' She felt cheated. 'I've had to enough times.'

He wouldn't meet her eye, but swung his attention away now, out beyond the orchids and the young banyan tree which the turbanned gardener was busy pruning. Once again Clarice shared the prospect, past the fat-leafed succulents, the red pepper bushes and frangipanis at the fence, as far as the plantation compound, and right to the tall wild trees. Freighted with greenery, the trees reached up behind the rubber plantation towards the ridge; and would then stretch, she knew, to the next ridge, and the next, and onwards unbroken to the remote hill country. Malaya was a place of endless fruits and hardwoods, with their vines and hangers-on. She was a hanger-on herself, to the strange country that had offered her anonymity, given her a freedom she hadn't managed to claim for herself in England.

But bears and tigers and pythons dwelt in the forest, and all manner of legendary animals. Just now, near at hand, a troupe of monkeys was feeding, high up, and shooting back glances amid a continual discard of twigs, peel and droppings. The sky was streaked with fishbone cloud, growing tarnished as if baked from above. And where was truly home? Averting her eye from the stunning view, she made herself watch instead how her father shot the remainder of his whisky back into this throat. Eventually he turned to her.

'All right,' he conceded. 'It would be my last chance.'

'Your last chance at what?'

'At being a father to you.'

That made her gasp, and she sipped her own Scotch, taking it neat, as he did. Its grainy sting helped with the tears that sprang suddenly to her eyes. 'Don't be bloody silly. You've always been that.'

'Technically.'

'But why?' She dug at the lawn with the toe of her sandal like a child. 'And why England, for heaven's sake?'

'Where else is there?'

'Most of the globe, I should say. Shouldn't you, Daddy? Most of the globe would be a darned sight safer, just at the moment. Hmm?'

When she was a girl, England had just meant boarding-school, and before that a place with a train journey inside it. At one end of that railway line was the country practice in Suffolk with her mother and father. At the other was London and her cousin Phyllis. Then she'd grown up; and there had been Vic. England would force her to open up all that heartache again. In order to protect herself she was desperate to stay, and yet – dare she admit it – she also ached to see him. In her heart she was all but ready to collude with her father's wishes. The matter was beyond endurance. She half wished Robin Townely would write and take her mind off the subject of Vic Warren; for, since she'd held Phyllis's letter in her hand, she'd hardly thought of anything else.

'You've nothing to live on and most of the world's turning nasty,' Dr Pike said. 'Haven't you been reading the papers, Clarice?'

'Nothing's happened since Poland!' Exasperation filled her tone.

'Oh, nothing!'

She clicked her teeth. 'You know what I mean.'

Once, after a party at Port Dickson, a convoy of Clarice's friends had driven with her up into the villages. There she had seen her first shadow play. The performance had been done under the stars by means of a large stretched sheet. But the boozy young crowd she was with hadn't understood the formalities. The language had been poetic, a far cry from the basic chat the English had to master for their servants.

She'd been mystified by the play, its lengthy preambles, and the hesitancy about committing to the action, but had grasped there was a reason. To the accompaniment of drumbeats and the clash of cymbals, the drama had lasted late into the night, by which time most of her party had fallen asleep. Even then the story had been only half told. It was the ancient epic of the *Ramayana*: of the lovers, and the forest; of the hermitage, the war, the wickedness of the abductor; and of the great bridge across which the avenger went forth upon the sea. It occurred to her that the new war might have the same self-indulgent pace. The thought chilled her.

She stooped now to poke at a web in the flower-bed. The cords were strung thickly under the great speared arch of a leaf, and the spider came running out into the sun. It stopped. She agitated the threads again. 'I'm being a butterfly. Look. Come on, then. Can't get me, can you?' The spider raised one minutely furred leg, in suspicion. It failed to budge. 'Can't be bothered, after all.' She straightened up. 'Just like men.'

Her father's laugh was brief and preoccupied. She plucked a thought. 'Did you send Phyllis anything? Dear Phyllis and . . . Victor. And their brat. What was its name, I forget?'

'Not pregnant, are you?'

'For heaven's sake, Daddy.' He astonished her. 'Just because I mention . . . How dare you!'

'A girl without a mother. Someone has to ask. Once in a while.' He was embarrassed amidst his red mottle and doctor's manner.

'If that's what you mean by being a better father . . .'

'Sorry. I don't know how a woman would go about it. Doesn't *someone* have to? Keep tabs, I mean?'

'No, they damn well don't. And I'm not – as far as I know.'

He coughed and adjusted his hat. 'Jack. I sent him a suit of clothes.'

'All right, then.' She found herself putting her arms around her father's neck, hugging him more fiercely than she could understand. Then she broke away. 'All right, Daddy. It won't be "over by Christmas", as all the bar-room experts have been predicting. It has that in common with last time. And all right, there's an expeditionary force in France. But nothing's going on. That's why they call it "phoney", Daddy. It isn't happening.'

'It's happening to the Poles.' He shamed her. 'And something's happening to the Finns, the Jews, the poor benighted Chinese.'

'But it's not happening to me. Is it? It isn't happening to me.'

'For God's sake, Clarice!'

She bit her lip. 'It's just I don't understand you. There's always something going on in the world. Always something awful being done to someone. It's not like you to come over like this. You're not yourself. You always said, didn't you, look after the next man and the world will get better. I thought that's what you did, as a doctor. That's how I imagined you, Daddy. I admired you. I thought we were safe here. I thought you were happy. Aren't you?'

'Happy enough.' He looked sharply at her.

'Well then. Why ruin it all because of some potty idea – about *me*? What's making you like this?' She felt Singapore slipping away, Malaya itself receding. Terrified – and piercingly glad – she seized on the next unkind remark that came to mind. 'Not the Scotch, is it? You're not going the way of all white men?'

Yet he seemed in such a pinch, and she was sorry. She caught the implication of something serious going on; sensed almost his impotence. Was he in love, she wondered? Had some affair at the tennis club gone awry?

'What troubles me is that I'm probably too late. I've failed you.'

'I don't know what you're talking about. This is where we live. You're needed, Daddy. You can't leave.' She checked her emotions again, but knew he'd seen her.

'You sound just as though you were six.'

'Don't be stupid,' she said.

This time he put his arm around her. 'Look, darling. Take it on trust, will you? There's nothing for it. I've got to take the risk now. If it all goes well and everything calms down . . . You know? If there's a stand-off of some kind . . . Well, I can come back easily enough, can't I?'

'Can you? Can we?'

'Just another leave, eh?'

'If you say so.' She stood quite still. 'If you say so, Daddy.'

'*Tuan*!' Musa called to them from the veranda. Her father went to enquire. Then he came back, black bag in hand. A company employee had sent about a sick child.

'Sorry,' he said. She watched him stride up the garden and thought how he was growing old. 'Probably shan't be long,' he called over his shoulder. Then he disappeared round the side of the bungalow to get the car started.

BUT HE WAS a long time. And, yes, I do hold matters too much in abeyance, lingering here in Malaya, in paradise, because of the payment that was demanded later that evening. It was a sacrifice in return for a fair wind, so to speak, and it was Selama who chose to make it. We try to avoid coming to the pain of such things; for if Vic and Phyllis were bitterly joined in England, Dr Pike was anchored to his spot by a supreme tenderness.

It had rained and was dark before he returned, and he brought with him the Malayan nurse, Selama Yakub, whom Clarice had met several times before. She watched from the veranda as her father helped the woman out of the car and past the puddles; then she went down in the glow of the lantern to greet them.

'My assistant, Mrs Yakub,' her father said. 'Working on a case at the hospital. Of course, you know each other, don't you.'

The nurse wore a neat, white uniform, but had exchanged her headgear for a scarf. She clutched it around her face as she entered, then threw it back. 'How are you, Miss Clarice? So nice to see you again.'

'Oh fine, thanks. Nice to see you.'

'So kind of Dr Pike to invite me – after so long.' Mrs Yakub darted a piercing glance at him, then looked straight at Clarice. She seemed about to say more, but turned away instead.

Their meal of lamb curry was conventional, and the conversation strained. Selama Yakub sent the *kuki* away. She served as though she were the mistress of the house, but hardly touched her food. Clarice felt uncomfortable. The inkling of disturbance she'd felt earlier continued in the air. She hadn't known such an atmosphere for years – in fact since her mother was alive. Selama's lack of appetite did not help.

Clarice's mother had used to excuse herself from table, saying she felt a little ill; and when she thought no one could see her out beyond the veranda, Mattie had a method of making herself sick, leaving most of her meal in the back of the flower-bed – where by morning, the younger Clarice had noted with interest, all evidence of distress had been eaten by less troubled creatures.

After dinner they sat, she and her father, in the study, playing old-fashioned dance tunes on his wind-up gramophone. They were alone. Selama Yakub had claimed she wanted to dispense some of the doctor's prescriptions; but when Clarice went to use her bathroom she bumped into the nurse bringing in a tray of cups from the veranda. And someone had obviously been tidying the sitting-room.

On her return Clarice said nothing about it. With the Aladdin lamps aglow in the study, the various insects constantly getting in to crash at the flame, the air fugged and prickly with cigar smoke, she thought neither of Selama nor her mother, but of Phyllis, because of the dance tunes. She saw more vividly that leggy girl in plimsolls who, out of her element on visits to the house at the end of the railway line, would cling to the gramophone and put on certain records again and again.

She had always hated her cousin. Older than she, Phyllis claimed to know everything, to have done everything. When they'd played together Phyllis had been unremittingly spiteful. Yet Phyllis had loved the cheap songs – because a gramophone, indeed music of any kind, represented more luxury than she could imagine.

Clarice broached the subject of her father's fever again. Like his drinking, it was a touchy one. 'Has it really been troubling you?'

'Turning jaundiced, am I?'

'Why are you so difficult?'

'Clearly not wasting away.' He slapped his stomach. 'As you can see.'

'All right, Daddy. Don't take it out on me. You still enjoy work, don't you?' Ambrose and his Orchestra finished their quickstep. She got up, rewound the clockwork motor, changed the needle and set it back on the other side of the disk. A crackly tango emerged. Her father refreshed their glasses.

'I do. Except that lately . . .'

'You *are* needed, Daddy.' Something was definitely up. She wanted to pre-empt it. 'You're needed . . . to make people better.'

'How simple you make it sound.'

'I'm not naïve. I'm not.' Her fingers tapped the armrest of her chair.

He put out an awkward hand to touch them, smoothed her wrist and then drew back. 'Self-sacrifice, Clary. Yours and mine. We think if we sacrifice ourselves we can have what we want. Eh? Or have I unwittingly sacrificed my own daughter?'

'What?' She threw back her slug of whisky.

There was a knock at the door. It was Mrs Yakub. 'No need to hurry, Dr Pike. Paperwork to do,' she added with a tense smile at Clarice as if to account for her continued presence. 'Is it all right if I sit at the dining-room table? You don't mind? None of those newspaper cuttings now, I see. In your honour, no doubt, Miss Clarice. He's promised to run me to my home. My son's house. So kind, Dr Pike. You don't mind, do you? Perhaps I'd better look after this, however.' She gave another knowing grimace at Clarice and darted in to pick up the whisky bottle from beside her father's chair. Then she left, almost apologetically.

'You *are* overdoing the booze.'

He grunted. 'No more than usual. Not to excess, if that's what you mean.'

'If that's the truth then why was she so keen to take it away? And what newspaper cuttings? Did she mean all that mess I saw before?'

'Perhaps the bloody woman likes to boss people about. Perhaps she's got it in for me. I don't know. Bloody natives. Nothing feels right. Everything's out, askew.' His hand lifted suddenly, and sliced at the air, startling her. 'This war . . . Everything that's happening now seems to me so cleverly . . . planned, Clary. Down to the details. I don't know what that means but it troubles me, a scientific man. It scares me rigid. There's nothing to counter it with, no case notes, no precedent, nothing.' The gramophone needle hissed round and round in the groove at the record's end.

'I simply don't follow, Daddy. Do you go to the club? Do you speak to people? That woman, Mrs Yakub . . .' She twitched her head in the direction of the dining-room. 'Your assistant. Do you talk to her?' Under her breath, she added, 'What's she doing here? What was she up to in the sitting-room? She's been putting things away in the sideboards.'

He grunted. 'Oh, Selama likes to keep me in order. Bored, I expect. Waiting for me to drive her home. Salt of the earth, though. Damned good nurse.'

'Selama? Is she your . . . ? Daddy?' Clarice remembered another scene, of her parents by her piano. The Broadwood he'd shipped over for her had lasted only two months. From the moment of arrival its sound had become more oriental by the hour. Rust and mould had attacked it with dullness, and then excrescence. The hammers warped and the felts rotted. Whole octaves of its keyboard refused to play at all, while small lizards made homes in the soundbox. She recalled there'd been an argument.

'Good Lord, no. I'm past all that. Past all that sort of nonsense. Just good friends, I can assure you.'

'Does she often come here, then? And keep an eye on your drinking? And take a proprietary interest in your housekeeping? Do you talk to her?'

'Not much. My grasp of Malay isn't up to the subtleties of things I can't even put into English. And her grasp of English . . .'

'So there is something the matter!'

'Nothing special, I assure you. Nothing special.' But the sigh appeared only partially to discharge his feeling. She watched his lip quiver. She watched, too, as he got up and went to his desk. He took up a piece of paper and handed it to her. It was a photograph, an Associated Press cutting of the Emperor of Japan. It showed a young gentleman in a perfect Western suit and high collar posed next to Lloyd George outside a country house. And I cannot but allow my great-uncle to make his fatal speech, though the minutes were slipping away.

'Britain and Japan, Clarice. People say they're wily Orientals, inscrutable yeller fellers. People at the club explain the war in China as the Asiatic mind. They say we're safe, it'll never touch us. As though we're almost a different . . . species. As though they hardly see us, or see us as gods. Think about this, child.' He crossed the floor and turned abruptly to face her as he reached the jardinière. The potted palm on its mahogany stand fountained up next to him, and loomed over his balding head. He looked like some famous old anatomist discussing the organs.

'Two insulated, legendary pasts,' he was saying. 'Two similar knightly traditions; of kingship, honour and reticence, of the obsession with class distinctions and "the decent thing". Think, child. Isn't Japan an extraordinary mirror, as though the map of the world could be folded on to itself? The Japanese aren't like the British; no. But very like them. That small off-continental cluster's need for industrial strength ... And sea power – Nelson is as sacred in Yokohama as he is in Portsmouth. Did you know that? Think. Each of us has the same absolute conviction of racial superiority. What then? Is there truly a new order in the universe? Is there something bloodstained and Darwinian? Or have we just been mistaken about the old?'

Clarice stared at him. Now he was wry, disturbing; his delivery was enigmatic. She couldn't follow him.

He strode back to the far side of his desk, and swung round again to rest his hand on the narrow top where a lamp stood, smoking slightly from its glass. 'Japan wants the British out of the East. She hates us. The only reason British nationals were relatively safe in Shanghai was through the difficulty of murdering them. If Japan is to strike for dominance she'll need oil, rubber and tin.' He gestured at the walls of the bungalow. 'If they come ...'

She wondered if he wanted Mrs Yakub to hear. Was he trying to tell her something? 'Robin says it'll never happen.' She bit her lip. 'As for the new order. There's something in it, isn't there? I thought it had been proved scientifically. Hasn't it?'

'People become ill,' he said, 'when they're told things that aren't true. The power of words, of suggestion – it's up to us to use it ... lovingly. The more I practise, the more I believe that medicine is a kind of charm. *Influenza*! My mother – your granny – died of it. They all did. It means influence – an evil spell. Clinically, they died of magic. How primitive. It puts the doctor on the side of the angels, Clary.' He smiled, and she was relieved. 'Take my fever? Malaria means wicked air, you know. I confess to you I have such a feeling in my bones. These words, these names. You need to pay close attention. You should question what your Robin says.'

'He's not my Robin any more,' she blurted.

'Then we're in the same boat, darling.'

'I see,' she said, although she didn't.

'Except I *have* made up my mind.' Then he took a brown envelope from under the stand of a heavy brass microscope. 'I bought these. They came this morning in the post. We've simply got to get away.'

From the brown envelope he took out a slip of paper and showed it to her. It confirmed the booking of two cabins on the Dutch liner *Piet Hein* from Penang to Marseilles. The tropical night rasp seemed to force a way in through the blinds.

'You've left me no choice,' Clarice said. 'No choice at all.' Her voice was icy, but the secret yearning sprang up in triumph. 'What time do you have to drive Mrs Yakub home?'

'Oh, in a little while. Finish your drink. Put another record on, why don't you.'

She did as she was told.

But when they found Mrs Yakub in the dining-room she was already dead. She was slumped at the table, her head right against the wood. An arm dangled uselessly beside her chair, and the weight seemed to drag at her neck, stretching the skin and blurring the features lopsidedly into a gap-toothed mask. The head, at its awkward angle, had its hair partially wrapped over again, where the scarf had fallen forward. Scattered about it, there were pages torn from an opened account book. In the centre of them all, close to a fold in the fabric, lay the empty whisky bottle and the remains of the practice's digitalin supply. The keys to the drug cabinet lay in the hand that reached across the table – as if to say, by way of note, Here you are, *Tuan Doktor*. I've put everything in order.

DECEMBER. IN BARKING, in the flat, their breath was like smoke. His father sniffed at the piece of haddock on the larder shelf. Then he lit a match and touched it to the top of the old gas cooker. There was a small dull sound under the brown saucepan; but Jack was alert to his mother. He ran to watch her singing in the bedroom as she changed her clothes. She'd seen three ships come sailing in. On Christmas Day, on Christmas Day.

Then she whispered something, and the words confused him. One light bulb hung from the ceiling, and the yellow altered her skin. The bulb filled the wall with her outline.

She put on her girdle, and then a slip; only then did she shoo him away for looking. He listened outside her door. Her stockings brushed, one against the other, her dress faintly slithered. The knock on the boards was her heels as she turned herself about in front of the mirror, and when the handle rattled he stepped back against the banisters. She came out tense; he could feel the fierceness in her body. She spoke to his father in the kitchen, demanding his attention, until there was another flare-up and suddenly she was leaving again.

Down in the shop the dusty display of weighing scales was lit only from the stairs. The faces of the machines were like shadowy fish eyes. In the dark his mother kept her hand on the catch and the door was half open. Jack was cold for a long time even though he was four, now. When they all came back up, the kitchen was full of steam and the potatoes had boiled dry. His father laughed as he always did, and made a joke; but at last there was the sound of a motor bike outside in the street, and Jack remembered the words she'd used: Tony Rice was taking his father up Waltham to do the job.

Tony wore a belted mac with the collar raised. He carried his goggles in his hand as he came up the stairs.

Behind him there was another man, fat and red-faced, who was unslinging the large satchel he had over his shoulder. Jack knew his name; it was Arthur Figgis.

'Don't mind if I bring Figgsy, do you?'

Arthur Figgis winked. Jack hated him. He tried to hide. His mother held him.

'All right, Tony.'

'Like a bad penny.' Tony laughed. 'All right, sonny? You're up late. What's the score? Couldn't wait?' He laughed at his rhyme. His smooth cheek hurt Jack in a way his father's rough one didn't. 'You coming with us, Jacky boy? Eh? Coming to screw a bit of swag with your old man and his old mate?'

'Tony. Keep it shut in front of the boy.'

'What's the matter, Phylly?'

But his father spoke. 'Tony! I wasn't expecting . . . It's been so long. I thought . . .'

'Thought I'd forgotten, did you, Rabbit?'

'No, I . . . Well, yes, as a matter of fact. It can wait, can't it? I'd no idea. Tonight of all nights. Of all the bad times.'

'No time like the present. Eh, Figgsy?'

His father said, 'Tony, I . . .'

'Yes?'

Arthur Figgis said, 'Deary me.' He took his hand out of his coat. It had three heavy rings on it. Jack saw his father's face was pale. His eyes had opened wide. He'd become smaller. Tony Rice always made his father look as though he were someone else, as though Jack too should call him Vic, or Warren, or Rabbit. Tony Rice had a glitter about him, like a decoration, with his wit and sharp voice.

'Figgsy's walking home, Vic. You're coming with me.'

Jack's father was a grown man wearing his apron at the stove and holding a fish-slice. His wife's face had the faintest of smiles.

'Are you coming, or what? Eh, Rabbit. I'm talking to you.'

'Yes, Tony. I'm coming.'

'Attaboy.'

Jack saw Vic Warren put a hand in his trouser pocket and give some coins to his mother. He saw him get his raincoat from the stand and go meekly out of the house behind the other two men. When Jack ran into the front room, past the decorated tree, his shoes clumped upon the floorboards. He watched the men from the window. Vic Warren on the back of the bike was hugging Tony Rice. It was the same person doubled. The motor bike roared, and the streak appeared from the headlight, a white finger pointing the way between the lightless gas lamps on either side of Ripple Road. Vic Warren had the large bag strung over his shoulder. Gone to fetch a rabbit skin. To wrap the baby bunting in.

The bike swung and roared until he lost all sense of where they were, or how long they'd been going. In every corner the back wheel threatened to go away from under him, and all Vic could think of was that his fingers would be frostbitten and useless when he hit the ground. Then, though the road was unlit, he recognised the fringes of Epping Forest. Old crookbeams rose up on either side of them. Their bare branch tops hooked and clawed at the streaked cloud. He clung to Tony Rice's greatcoated body, sheltered his eyes from the iced and blinding wind behind the nape of Tony Rice's neck. The band of the goggles made a blank strip in Tony Rice's neat, clipped hair. The bike roared on.

They cornered sharply, leaning over together, and there were houses again, sedate black shapes, in the rushing air. Tony pointed a gauntletted hand at one of them, in a spacious row set back. It was large, detached; the bike's exhaust note rattled at its moon-glazed windows. They passed some villas, timbered and countrified. Then round in a side road, they came to a halt. Tony killed the engine. They turned the bike and left it ready, kick-start cocked.

Vic's guts churned. The side road ended in deeper darkness topped over by the shapes of trees. Tony led him into a path through the murk. Rime had formed on the iron kissing gate; it glistened. They scouted along, the two of them half crouched, feeling the leaf mould and fallen twigs through the soles of their shoes, picking their way by the flash of a torch beam. A branch creaked overhead in the trifling wind. Tony sniggered.

The way was overgrown. So long since the Coal Hole, one part of Vic had counted on Tony forgetting the deal. But another had prepared for this moment all along, dreading it, knowing with certainty that it would come to pass. It had lain between him and his wife. She'd sung at the club while he'd remained uninvited. Cash had appeared; he had no work. Though the cabin was finished he had little energy, for the child would wake in the night, twice, three times, and he would get up to calm him, or sit up with him. He and Phyllis camped out in the wastes of marriage – when she was at home. Nothing else would shift. There was only the continued ritual of her threats.

In the freezing glitter the forest hinted at its past. Twisted, silhouetted limbs took on a desperate, sardonic nature. The two men came to a fence. Five feet high, the larch strake tops wobbled underfoot. Vic landed in a vegetable patch. Among sturdy brassica stalks he stood ashamed. The tilth crunched minutely as his shoes broke the forming crust, and there rose a smell of cabbage rot. He caught the sweaty whiff of his own coat, heard his own heart. His stomach cramped him. He looked ahead and saw the black bulk of Tony ten paces further on, his breath steaming.

Vic was amazed at himself. His life was a fairy-tale.

Only the bombs, when they came, would make sense of it. Who'd stolen him and brought him here – the apprentice boy, hoicked out of his grammar-school place at fourteen because of his dad's lungs? That boy had once ridden off each morning wearing his too-manly flat cap, his jacket, waistcoat and clipped-up long trousers – as his dad had gone before him along the marsh track. Who'd picked him out – pedalling over the Roding at the Abbey Works, and then down the River Lane to the wharf to earn the family living?

As a young man he'd made cross-London voyages night after night on buses and tubes in hope of some engineering degree. He'd attended cheap concert halls, libraries, public lectures. Who had crippled his almost superhuman effort to lift himself out of the dockside backstreets?

His marriage had put a stop to it. Between lust and marriage there'd been Clarice. But he'd done the decent thing. And then Jack had been born. So why couldn't Vic Warren be left alone to make his way, bring up his family? He reminded himself that it was because of the child he was here. It was Jack who was at stake. Phyllis couldn't help herself. Nor was it the threats of violence from Tony, or Figgsy. Not really. It was what would happen to Jack, his son, if he didn't go along with her.

My father wasn't deluded. Phyllis had grown up the plaything of criminals. Now, unless Vic acted, the same fate would befall Jack. It was almost inevitable. The only chance he had of bringing Jack and even his wife out of it was to take all the guilt of the situation upon himself. The predicament was real; the trap – like all such traps – was cunning.

Therefore Tony led the way. The moon's edge slipped into a cloud, and then out again. Before them roofs, copings and chimney stacks showed up sharp against the streaked, star-pocked sky. A path cut through the garden;

it led under a trellis arch and then across the lawn. There was a shed and an outbuilding. Listening for the first shake of a chain, listening for the interrupted snort of canine breathing, they stood completely still, waiting a full minute. A snuffling sound from next door made them both start.

'Nothing. Couple of hedgehogs at it, most likely.' Tony shook his head and laughed under his breath. 'Spiky fuckers. Supposed to be asleep, aren't they?'

A cat screamed in the next garden, electrically loud. Vic jumped again. Again Tony shook his head. 'Not scared, are you? Don't you worry about a thing, mate. You've got your Uncle Tone to look after you.' They carried on. The french windows were right in front of them 'All right. Give me the doings.'

Vic had the brown paper and glue; he fished for them in the bag he'd taken over from Figgsy. The moonlight caught the fine teeth in Tony's elegant smile. He was grinning, holding the glass cutter. 'Nice, eh?' He indicated the house. 'Hope they've all hung up their stockings.'

There came the gritty score of the cutting wheel on the pane. Vic looked up at the dark building and nodded. He stood back a step, even as Tony was easing the glass. He held the two torches, ready. It was only a second or two's work to get the door open.

STRAIGHT AWAY, TO the right of him, Vic's torch beam picked out the smoked-gold frame of a painting that hung from the picture rail. Then the light sweep opened up the interior. There were several more pictures along the wall – large canvases, and some smaller. The place was lined with a distinction quite unexpected. Between and around the pictures the flickering, searchlit wallpaper

75

showed up a drab floral blue; but a great polished table was dressed with silver furnishings. It had carved upright chairs tucked beneath, and it filled much of the centre space, though there were smaller tables and a sideboard in the distance. All the surfaces were cluttered with objects, many of them glittering, cut glass, silver. There were no Christmas decorations.

Embers glowed in the grate. The torch showed the chimney breast with a poor brick fireplace, yet over the mantelshelf an astonishing high gilt mirror was mounted. Vic looked up from the eerie reflection. The ceiling had plain mouldings, but from the central rose hung a vast glass chandelier. The signs of wealth reminded him of the time when a kindly foreign professor had invited the external students to Prince's Gate for drinks. A tang of cigar smoke drifted in the air.

Chest high under the pictures ran shelves of books, so many in the torch's beam. He moved closer. The spines showed old-fashioned letter shapes which he couldn't read. Tony, gone ahead once more, was already about his own concerns.

'Come on then, brains. Finger out. No use standing here gawping. See that clock. And this bloody sideboard.'

Vic tiptoed to the far end of the room, and made himself lift the old gilded clock from its shelf. But the light from his torch was fading – the batteries must have been dud. With one hand he unhooked the long pendulum and tried to wriggle it free. The lever flicked back and forth like a live thing. He silenced it. The torch went out. He shook it back to life. A wonderful engraved bowl lay on its own tray on the sideboard. On either side of it, among the rest of the silver, stood two fine twisted candlesticks. They felt weighted by more than metal, clanking wretchedly against the clock. He imagined Tony's laugh. Ten quid, maybe. Even twenty, the lot. Something told him what he knew already – that, financially, Tony had no need of this job, or his help. A sound of ripping filled the dark beside him.

The sideboard drawers hung open, revealing cutlery in disorder. Now Tony's shape, the torch gripped under his chin, stood at a small bureau in the corner. 'Get me your light on this lot,' he whispered.

Vic shone his weakening beam on to a riffle of letters and bills. There were storage envelopes too, and a wadge of personal papers, with a passport, nipped up in a bull-dog clip. Tony shook out the envelopes and snatched at the papers. 'Not this, you bastard. Where's your bloody ill-gotten? Come on.' He flung the documents on to the floor and snickered. 'Who knows, eh?'

Vic felt a movement behind him, and smelt a trace of hair oil. His torch beam suddenly caught Tony, slipping his fingers around the edge of a long drape. The door behind it gave a moaning swish. 'Tony!' But Tony had disappeared from view, and Vic stood rooted to the soft rug by the sideboard.

Character, Perce had so often said, was about not crack-ing up. Vic's father had seen men crack up: men who couldn't move – either towards the enemy, or back. Those buggers, Perce had said, were sitting ducks. A picture by the tapestried door hanging was caught in the beam. From it a man of property in sober seventeenth-century dress stared dimly back at Vic. There was reproach in the painted eye. Beside the figure were brown water scenes with boats and houses.

He heard noises in the hall beyond, as if Tony were trying to prise something away. 'Tony!' He turned and, in the dark, inadvertently swung his own bag against the back of one of the dining chairs. The rattle was deafening. Now his torch came to rest on the large canvas above the sideboard he'd just looted. Bold smears of red might be lips, or nipples; and there were eyes, gilded, female eyes, pale, laquered skin.

It was slashed, and the hardened paint near the bottom had come off in chunks, revealing the canvas. Below the cut Vic caught a signature in the bottom corner which he couldn't read. It was as though he'd brushed up against Clarice's naked body, there in the room. He stretched to feel for the table and began backing towards the french window.

'Tony!' His nerve failed. 'Tony. I'm going back to the bike.'

'That's what you want, isn't it, Vic.' Like a tinkling whisper, out of nowhere.

He plunged after Tony into the hall where the wrenching sound had come from. A floorboard creaked above him. Across a vast chequerwork of tiles, he could just make out a front door and a large newel post at the foot of the staircase.

His torch went out and he groped for the banisters. And then holding fast on to them, he stepped sideways, several paces, still feeling for the woodwork. Above, in the stairwell, there was the faintest of gleams, the merest sense of outlines, no more.

Then a thump, and a woman's scream and footfalls overhead. Vic panicked, his arms outstretched. He heard a man's gruff voice upstairs and the sound of a door handle being turned. Something on the landing went over with a crash and there were footsteps on the stairs. Tony rushed past him in the hall and Vic turned back to follow. In the dining-room he clattered into the heavy chairs, and fell against a small table, dashing the glassware.

He was at the french windows. As he burst his wrist through a pane, a light switched on. He heard a run behind him, felt a blow to the back of his head and

he swivelled, enraged, hitting out at the pyjamaed figure, raining and pummelling blows with his strong fists
against the righteous protective arms, the plump sides, the
grunting, wet, tobacco-smelling face, feeling the glass of
spectacles against his bare knuckles, and its give.

He was escaping down the garden, his ludicrous sack
bouncing and jingling on his back. A low wall tripped him.
He crashed through stalks, was whipped by branches. He
scrambled at the fence. Next he was paralysed and the
forest was a sightless chaos. His chest was scraped and
his foot hurt. A motor bike in the distance kicked into
life: once, twice and then the roar. He inched his way
towards the trace of its sound, shuffling with his feet for
the path, feeling for tree trunks with his hands, but there
was only the unexpected ditch, the unremembered scrub,
the wicked bramble thorns. The back of his head ached
with a dull, throbbing pain and he put his knuckles in his
mouth, tasting blood.

Someone was shouting. He attempted to retrace his
steps. But he could find no fence, no house. The ground
was dropping away and frosted spines rose up and stung
his hands. He straggled back again. Then he plunged in
a different direction, and again.

He was relieved when they arrested him. His nails were
torn and his shins were barked, but the blood on his hands
showed up quite dry in the flash beams, only ten yards or
so from the back of the burgled house.

Jack wasn't dreaming when he heard the motor bike.
He was in his bed, listening, waiting. He recognised the
sound of it and knew how it stood revving in the street at
the front of the shop. Then it stopped. He got out of bed
and went into the front room. His mother and someone
else were coming up the stairs. He heard their voices.

'Where is he, then?'

'How should I know?'

Jack retreated to his bedroom and stood just beside his door.

'For heaven's sake, Tony, he is my husband!'

'What?'

'What's happened? Where is he?'

'I'm not his fucking keeper. All right. Maybe he slipped up. Maybe there was just a weensy bit of a fucking hitch.'

'A hitch?'

'Yeah.'

'What do you mean? I want to know. Where's Vic? Tell me!'

'Shut up, woman! Leave me alone, you stupid bitch. I don't know. Maybe he'll get back later. Maybe he won't. Knowing him he'll run smack in the wrong direction. And if the shite get him he'd better not open his bloody trapdoor, that's all.'

'Tony! What do you mean? What do you mean, Tony?' She was almost screaming.

'Some old Jew got fucking damaged. Rabbit was careless, that's all. All right? What's it to you, anyway?'

'Oh, Tony. What am I going to do?'

'You're going to keep quiet. That's what you're going to do, Phyllis. You're going to keep quiet for Tony, aren't you, dearest? Aren't you? Rabbit's going to keep quiet. And you're going to keep quiet. Aren't you, darling Phyllis? Poor old Bun, eh? Poor old Bunny Rabbit. Maybe he'll show up after all. And maybe not. Eh, Phyllis? Come here, then, you bloody halfwitted bitch.'

'Don't call me that.'

'I'll call you what I like.' Then Tony's voice changed. 'Come on, Phylly. You know I don't mean it. Come on, eh? There's my girl. That's what you like, isn't it? That's what you want. Eh, baby? Just like it used to be. Eh?'

Jack left the door with its rim of light. He sneaked back to his bed, touched the bristly wool of his stocking, and pulled the covers over him because he was cold, and because of the noises. He sang her song in his head to shut them out. That there was a man and his lady, on Christmas Day. It was on Christmas Day. His father would take him down to Creekmouth. Swinging their great brown sails, the three ships would come in on the tide. On one of them, the wounded lady would be standing, her arms stretched out for him.

THEIR BOAT HEADED from Penang out of the Straits of Malacca on the voyage she'd made too often before. The gesture of Selama's suicide, the pure speechless act, had drawn out from her father the story of his private life, of the dilemma of duty that had led to his buying the tickets home, and of the consequent betrayal of his lover. Clarice felt angry and let down by what had been going on behind her back; and which had come to so violent a termination.

Her own affair had drifted to its inevitable end. Robin had received his posting and with it a promotion to captain. He'd gone back to his wife, leaving Clarice only his Christmas gift of some scented notepaper. Now she saw Robin Townely just for what he was: a fairly ordinary and not particularly attractive army officer with a roving eye and stronger arms than hers. She wanted to punish both the men in her life.

But there was that triumph, too, inside her. How her heart raced every time she thought of Vic. In England her feelings would be heightened only to be mocked by the fact of his marriage. It would be a torment. Yet part of her longed to arrive. Another regretted that she would put herself through it all again.

Upon the high seas, the contradictions in her emotions

made her listless. She suffered from want of spirits, putting on a brave face. She also drank and played poker for pennies with Ted Crow and Alf McCoy, two superannuated planters trying to get home. They were both absurdly indulgent and amusing but beyond that made few demands – upon either her feelings or her conversation. On tropical evenings the three of them hung over the piano in the ship's saloon. She played popular songs: 'I've Got You Under My Skin', 'Red Sails in the Sunset', and 'Blue Moon'. They sang together, '*She went to heaven and flip-flap she flied*', and '*One man went to mow, went to mow a meadow*', and laughed, and walked about the deck under the huge stars.

More obviously distressed, Dr Pike drank to anaesthetise himself. Then he would stand on deck for hours, it seemed, watching the horizon. Clarice struggled to forgive him, with all his former talk of medicine as love and charms – and of honesty. How he'd pulled the wool over her eyes, how he'd kept up his affair behind her back. And the woman, the suicide had, yes, been very shocking; but then she'd hardly known her, Selama Yakub. Once the body had been taken away she'd cried, uncontrollably, all night in her room. She was annoyed with her, too, taking herself off like that before she even knew she might have had a stepmother.

There were U-boats in the Atlantic, which was why the *Piet Hein* ended its run at Marseilles. From there Clarice and her father made the last part of their journey across France. What should have been a fine adventure began well. She loved Marseilles the port. But the skies beyond were lacklustre. A change occurred during the rail journey up the Rhône valley; after Lyons everything grew tedious and craven cold. She saw herself and her father as two poor insects scuttling right under a web of fear and bad weather, stretched across the gloomy north from Siberia to Connemara, from Scapa Flow to the Caucasus. Her own nerve suffered, and a sense of foreboding began to preoccupy her. If Malaya had been spoiled for her, this headlong scamper over thousands of miles was pure folly.

The hotel they found in Paris had damp beds. The staff scowled, or sneered, pretending to find difficulty with her schoolroom French. Her father was even harder to manage. When there was no suitable train leaving the Gare du Nord until quite late the next morning, she had to ration his alcohol. At eleven forty-seven, an engine dawdled northwards through the Paris *banlieux* before at last getting up steam enough to tackle the countryside. By then he'd sobered up, but after Amiens and at an almost wilful snail's pace, the train turned to reconnoitre the lines of the old British trenches. She saw Albert, Bapaume, Arras, Vimy, Loos and Béthune, all under traces of snow. Trees had regrown, the broken villages had recovered; yet against an eerie little sunset framed by the train window the ordinariness of those places gave her another sharp taste of anxiety. Calais was windswept, and the Channel crossing no more than a choppy dash under the cover of night.

The final stage, from Dover to London on the morning boat train, ran them up through snow-covered hop gardens under dirty skies. The Kentish suburbs were house backs, coal dumps, or overgrown depots; and Victoria Station, heaped up with sandbags and slush, showed no interest in their arrival. Clarice noted with disbelief the air-raid shelters, the slit trenches, and the government posters about how to behave. Overcoated guns in Hyde Park looked upwards at phoney skies. Any patriotic nostalgia she'd concocted on the way evaporated. The old country was profoundly uninspiring. As for the English, how unlovely they were. After the ease and colour of the tropics, everyone looked shabby.

And would Vic look shabby too, she wondered, if by

chance she ran into him – as around every turning, almost, those first few days, she was sure she would? Would she even know him, remember his face? Perhaps she'd already passed him in the street. Urgently and involuntarily, she stopped in her tracks where she and her father were walking along the Bayswater Road, and looked behind her. Nothing – of course, nothing. But suppose he should appear; would she feel the same about him?

Her father lectured her on Disraeli's two nations. 'At least the Malayans know how to take a pride in themselves.' He held forth from Marble Arch, staggering slightly amid the traffic. 'In England there are the Privileged and the People, Property or Population. Each hates the bloody sight and sound of the other.'

'And which are we, Daddy?' she asked, steadying him. He looked her blankly in the eye, and then they crossed back to the corner of Park Lane, jinking their way by inches out of the path of a bus.

There was no relief from the cold. A bone-invading chill came in from the streets and sat down with them in their hotel, unchallenged by any of the stoves in the corners of drab rooms, the puttering gas fires or the lukewarm pipes. Ice patterns on the inside of windows persisted all day, and wherever Clarice went she took the frosty trace of her own breath. Outdoors, its shapes dissipated against the grey; inside, it mingled with the various odoriferous steams caused by boiled cabbage, by brown soup, and by the chamber-pots borne along corridors by clumping maids. Again, she wondered what on earth they'd set out upon, the two of them.

Every evening the guests in the hotel lounge tuned in to Lord Haw Haw. Londoners claimed the Germans had got what they wanted: Hitler would soon sue for peace, and be accepted by both Britain and France. It was the Bore War, they said, pleased with themselves. They were bored with the blackout and bored with rationing. Some believed the bombing threat had turned out to be an elaborate hoax. The Nazi menace would simply wither away and the kids could all come home. She latched on to the idea, and held it. She shut her mind to newspaper tales of Finnish casualties, or the continuing deportation and savagery in divided Poland. These days, apparently, it was more to enquire about the next fall of snow that Londoners surveyed the skies, than to care about Stuka dive-bombers. The winter, they said, was one of the coldest in memory. Well then, they kept on adding, it would all eventually thaw, even Hitler. About Vic, possibly so near at hand, she began to convince herself that she could feel a touch blasé. She had got through so far without seeing him; now she was perfectly in control.

The family solicitor was visited. It turned out they were Property – and therefore Privileged. By the skin of their teeth the old house in Suffolk still belonged to them. So it came about that Clarice and Dr Pike found themselves running down to the country again, this time north of the Thames through Essex and on into prettiest blanketed Suffolk. She did stare intently out of the window as the train inched through the tawdry environs of Wanstead Flats, Ilford and Seven Kings – having seen on a map how close they were to Barking, the address on Phyllis's letter. She paid particular attention as the train crossed the River Ripple. Then, past Becontree, her thoughts were a mixture of relief and overwhelming regret.

The train was ice cold, full and filthy, with soldiers sitting on their kitbags in the corridor, and trodden cigarette butts everywhere on the floors. She allowed one of the boys to engage her in conversation but disdained him a few minutes later, savouring his blushes.

After a while, as ever-thickening snowflakes began to race past the carriage, she grew excited, piqued that her window was grimy, and that smoke from the engine billowed past in such smutty reels as to blot out what might amount to a childhood recaptured. The prospect seemed to lift her father, too.

When at last the train drew up at Manningtree, she stepped out into the flickering white with amazement. The platform, the fields, the station roof were blanketed with fresh snow. She was coming to her old house; everything could be beautiful again.

AN ANCIENT MAN with a horse chaise was all the transport there was to convey daughter and father and their travelling cases the last seaward miles. She didn't mind. She clapped her hands to keep warm, and listened to the slow drawl in which the driver was remembering Dr Pike, no really, from all these years gone. His 'growen gel' Clarice smiled and offered herself to be admired. Snow-garlanded, they clopped through the village of Holbrook, after which a dip in the road and a swirl of the miniature blizzard brought them to their destination.

She dashed the snowflakes from her eyes. Pook's Hill was in the old manor-house style. Under its weight of white, the cat-slide roof seemed at once hoisted by, and sagging from, the off-centre chimney stack. At either end of the property there were gabled wings. It looked quaint as its name, touching as the scene on a card, though smaller perhaps than she remembered, with the mullioned windows of the original modest hall squeezed under the roof's vast blank perfection, and all the leads and ledges delicately iced in casements of peeling green paint. There was a simple wooden door cut in the left-hand section of wall. Snow-capped weeds had grown up on either side, while great dagger icicles hung from the eaves. Untrained stalks of a snowdrifted, leafless creeper reached away in both directions across the brickwork.

Clarice led her father inside. All at once the long journey caught up with her. The interior was only mould and damage: walls were peeled, areas of ceiling had fallen. There'd been a tenant, but nowhere had been cared for. In one of the rooms a lapse of soot had blackened everything. Her elation was dashed in a pervading smell of fungus and old rags.

A local Miss Farmer was supposed to have laid a fire and left a meal. In a dim, oak-beamed and barely furnished parlour they found a flicker in the grate; and, in the flagstoned region adjoining, a pot of unlikely stew sat on the kitchen range. Eventually, while her father prowled the bedrooms, Clarice brought herself to rummage for kindling in an outhouse. Then she perched on her high heels at the edge of the hearth, trying to revive the embers. The sticks were cold and damp and the flame did its utmost to resist.

Frustration overcame her. She stood up and stamped. Then sobs burst out, and all she could think of was Selama Yakub. Once more she cried secretly, uncontrollably; and when eventually the tears subsided, she was left drained and utterly dismal. The fire sulked. Her father's footsteps sounded somewhere overhead like the walk of a troubled ghost. Forced out of the compensations of her bright life in Singapore, whisked past any second chance of meeting Vic, she'd been thrust into an agrarian confinement so severe that the prospects of love, freedom and fulfilment were almost infinitely remote.

The phrase 'a want of spirits' had first been planted in Clarice's head by Mrs Christopher, who'd taken her under her wing in Singapore. During the voyage its elegant understatement had fitted her exactly. It reminded her of certain literary heroines she'd admired – the passionate girls held captive by circumstance or relatives, while forbidden by duty to think so.

She'd once wanted to be entirely useful: to save the world, discover radium, inspire a great composer with her playing. She'd gone on to find a man, Vic, whose flashes of warmth and intellectual openness seemed to make such things possible – had he not been trapped himself. Now her father had rushed her to the moated grange. The wooded soil of Suffolk ran away to two rivers on either side of her. Their salt and frozen mouths were only a mile or so away. An old physician and his daughter caught in the snow; it was simply too melancholic. She heard him come downstairs and go out at the back through the kitchen.

But in reality she knew she couldn't blame him. After Selama's death and the hasty inquest, her father had had half a mind to tear up the tickets. It was Clarice who'd insisted on using them, and Dr Pike had done what she told him. That was the truth of the matter, and she should come clean about it.

She pulled herself round, and was glad. The fire, too, flicked up around the sticks, the spent char deigning at last to glow. She dried her face and shouted to her father to bring in more coal.

A far-off scraping came by way of reply. Then Dr Pike appeared with the coals held out in front of him on his shovel. 'Good girl. Good girl. You make everything better.'

Her reply was a sarcastic laugh, but she was cheered. Some faded sheets of the *Daily Telegraph* made a vast newspaper skirt over the inglenook to encourage the draught, and they stood together, father and daughter, arms stretched out to hold them. The fire took, and, when the first chill was off the room, she went to the kitchen and turned her attentions to the stew.

The range, too, only needed a poke. She found bread and butter set under a cloth. There was cutlery in a drawer, dull but serviceable. Then it wasn't so long before they were able to make their meal, huddled in front of the brightening fire, their whisky bottle between them, their breath from the meal mingling with the wisps of vapour from their clothes.

'I want you to write to Phyllis.' Her father's announcement came out of nowhere. He drank off his glass.

Clarice's spoon clattered against her plate. 'I beg your pardon.'

'Phyllis. I want you to write to her.'

'But I thought you were still doing your best to keep away from the family.'

'Whenever did I ever say that, Clarice? We have a duty to family; they have a duty to us. Blood and Marriage. Aren't those the things that bind us all together? Don't you know there's a war on?'

'But you didn't make any effort to look them up, or write, or even mention them while we were in London. They were only a bus ride away, for heaven's sake.'

Seated beside the fire, my great-uncle had used up the last of his Dutch cigars, and his face looked empty under his red doming brow. His reading glasses aged him. Strapped for cash, a traitor to himself and down to his last bottle of Scotch, he'd come to a halt and was asking his daughter to co-ordinate the picking up of lost threads. There was a family, and of all its members Phyllis was the principal loose end. That couldn't be gainsaid.

Clarice's breath shortened, her head swam. 'All right. If that's what you think would be best.'

His head fell back on to the wing of the old-fashioned armchair. Though she heard him snore, she could hardly believe he was so soon asleep. It was the drink. He could issue his commands and forget for a little while that his semi-secret, semi-illicit love had sprawled Selama Yakub over the teak table in Seremban with her face screwed up. The fire leapt and crackled.

Clarice held her own glass in her lap and gazed into the hearth. Flames licked patterns around the coals, the glowing base, the blue film at the side, fluttering and reigniting itself, the fissure in one thick, black piece of rock pouring smoke upward in a stream. Outside the narrow windows the white day declined in flurries. Very well. She would write to Phyllis.

'*LADYBIRD, LADYBIRD, FLY away home, your house is on fire and your children are gone.*' The admitting officer, fully four inches taller than Vic, laid a hand on his shoulder. Then the hand dropped away and his tone changed. 'I told you. East Ham. Barking. All gone. Next.'

'D'you mean killed?' Vic gasped.

The officer punched him in the stomach. 'Don't answer me back, son. You collect your gas mask from the stores and carry it at all times. Go on. Get your bath and hair-cut, you dozy bastard, and have that stripe taken off of your lip. Where do you think you are? Fucking Hollywood? Next.'

His remand was to a converted workhouse in Middlesex. Its reception room had a barred window which looked out on to frozen fields. Vic held the bars while the pain in his gut swelled and receded.

He'd received no news for days. Stuck inside cells or handcuffed in police vans he'd heard sirens go off; sometimes he'd heard the rumble of planes. Rehearsals, they were nothing out of the ordinary, but now he strained his ears for distant explosions. In the queue he steadied himself against the registration bench. The man had lied – but if London had already been gas bombed, or fire bombed, who would smell poison or char, here to windward? The queue edged forward. He needed to be resolute. The man must have lied, and for the moment, surely, the kid was safe.

He surrendered the clothes he'd been living in since Christmas Eve. With a sliver of soap from the floor, he cleaned up in the trough. The icy water was scummed, already used by the morning's other entrants. The washroom echoed. Raw men were milling about, blue-white and misshapen in the light through frosted glass.

In the corridor beyond, at the induction process, he made his responses through teeth that kept chattering even after he was dressed in his prison clothes. The officers gave him a gas mask and took him off to a dormitory. Then there was a meal. He hardly noticed it, nor the conversations around him. He endured the first hours, the faces in strange corridors, the feeling of dumb suspension which he remembered from a lad – having taken a wrong turning, maybe, suddenly caught out on the wrong, dockside street. Figures loomed, and melted past. Voices sounded out of cells, out of entrances, out of the air. He watched his lip, his step. Locks opened in front, doors crashed shut behind him.

In his dormitory that first night he slept, or half slept, wrapped by a shapeless darkness. The dawn merely shook its alarm bell on more of the same, the next morning, the next afternoon. So the days passed. So they seemed to lose their integrity as days even. They blurred together into a first week; and then, with the constant bitter cold, into a first fortnight.

He was resolute. My father was at home with adversity and knew exactly how to cope. He knew how to rough it with his prison comrades as he'd done through the Depression years with his workmates at Everholt's. Maybe he'd dreaded a mob, but folk came and went every day; no one was long term. And if some wore a squared-up bravado, the majority still didn't know the ropes: most were men from his own background. The screws were tough local men, who did their job. No one picked on him and surprisingly, the prison routines began to calm him.

There were no German bombers. Their own planes flew overhead in skeins and gaggles. So did birds from the neighbouring gravel pits. The Thames was only a mile or so away, in these parts a tame domestic thing which self-respecting Londoners would visit only for holiday excursions to Windsor Castle; its craft flimsy pleasure boats, its watermen lock-keepers, or swan-uppers, or dredging crews. Now it threw up freezing mists. My father could get some rest in his bed; for, whatever Jack's peril, the prison held no wakeful child.

Nor was there immediate pressure on him – his case wasn't due until the middle of April. His face relaxed, gained colour. He put on the lingo of the East Ham marshes, and that way he was accepted. For his fair dealing and sharp personality he even gained a measure of status. Vic Warren was a good laugh, sometimes, a good enough bloke. Sometimes, he was able to believe as much himself, acclimatised among the damned and the doomed.

When he wasn't doubling about, or spud bashing, or washing up, he liked to walk the field, braving the cold as far as the wire and back. He took pleasure in the stubborn weeds that grew around the perimeter, their resilient greens, their blackened flower stalks, frosted seed heads. As for the Epping Forest incident, he thought nothing of it. It seemed almost as though it had never happened. The trains chuffing up to London, and down again towards the Surrey stockbroker belt, held the vacant clockwork of toys.

Then Phyllis came to visit. 'Well, we're coping,' she said. Her carefully made-up features stole eyes, turned heads. She took off her damp hat, and tried to do something with the rain-soaked ends of her hair.

'We?'

'Me and Jack. Some man in a council van wanted to evacuate us again. I told him thank you very much but we had our own arrangements. I thought you might need some cigs.' She passed a packet over. The wind outside moaned its way past the walls and into the courtyard; sleet spattered against the windows.

'I'm so glad you came.'

'Well, I have missed you.'

'I've missed you, too, Phyllis.' He heard the pitiful gratefulness in his own voice.

'Tony was really cut up.' She stroked her hair again, and looked about her in the visiting room. 'About what happened. You know. Is that stove all the heating they've got?'

'I was so stupid. Such a fool. I blew it.' He scanned her face for signs of agreement.

'Tony thought he owed it to you, you know, to see me and Jack right. He's been a real friend, Vic, helping out with the rent and such. He's given me a bit of spare cash. He said whatever he has over he'll try and see it comes my way. If he can.'

Vic shook his head. He noticed the cigarettes in his hand and stowed the packet away. 'I really am so sorry.'

'Well. It can't be helped, now, can it.'

'But there've been no attacks?'

'Attacks?' She touched her hair again, her fingers inadvertently probing the temple.

'Air raids. Bombing.'

'Oh. No. Nothing.' It was her turn to stare at him, intently, her eyes clouded in the delicate face. 'It hasn't really amounted to much, this war.'

Vic dropped his gaze and hugged his jacket around him. 'It's been on my mind a bit, that's all. I've completely spoiled everything, haven't I?'

'There's no need for that, Vic. Look, I'm sorry too. Didn't make it easy for you, did I?'

'But it's my responsibility.'

'No, Vic. Just one of those things, eh? Faults on both sides.'

'I suppose war's like prison. It's a state of mind, isn't it?' He spoke earnestly, blindly. Under his fingers, beneath its accumulation of grime, the table was brindled with the unmistakable grain of oak. He stroked the wood without thinking. 'The thing itself comes into being in its own good time. Something was waiting to happen, wasn't it?'

'Well, I don't know about that. Look, I can't stay long. Jack. . . .'

'You know I still . . . love you, don't you? You mean everything to me. You know that. Don't you?' Another squall from outside dashed on to the panes. He was ashamed of the place's smells, of ice-cold sweat and latrines, of carbolic and grey stew.

'Yes, Vic. I do.'

'It's all right, isn't it?'

'Yes. It's all right.' Phyllis looked at him squarely.

'I'll do all I can . . . to make it up to you. When this is over. Look after you.'

'I know you will, Vic.' She picked up her bag.

'Can you forgive me, then?'

'There's nothing to forgive.'

He clung to her presence. 'At Tony's job I don't know what got into me. I don't remember much about it, to tell the truth. Just panicked. Such a stupid, stupid thing, as though I almost wanted to get found out. Even on the motor bike, on the way there, I wouldn't lean enough into the corners, as though I wanted the wheel to go away from under us. As though I actually wanted to ruin it and get myself caught – or killed.'

'Well, you did, didn't you? Vic, I really have to go.'

'Yeah. You're right to be angry with me. What have you told him?'

'Who? Tony?' Her eyes flicked.

'Jack.'

'Oh. You know ... Daddy's coming soon. Vic, my train ...'

'Of course. If there's a real alert, you'll both go out to Laindon.' He tried to impress the point on her. 'Take the tandem. You promise, now. Straight away.'

'Of course we will, Vic. You know we will.'

She let him touch her hand to his lips, and then she left.

AFTER SHE'D GONE, he cursed himself again for a fool, and walked out in the slanting rain. Three perimeter trees stood black against the railway embankment. He waited for her train to pass, face dripping, collar soaked, but a warder came to round him up.

Back inside, the damp brick and whitewash, the icy tiles, the caged light bulbs and concrete floors all bore in on him. He longed to dash his head against the refectory wall, or into the iron pipes that ran beside the serving hatch. He brought himself to his dormitory and threw his body down on his bed to weep, shaking there, powerless, with his face buried against the one threadbare blanket. The men at the other end of the room, Griffith, the much tattooed ex-infantryman, and Docherty, the little one-armed bookie's runner from Hackney Wick, let him get on with it; and he cried until someone came to fetch him for work.

Over the potato peeling, he thought of his dad in the trenches, and was wretched again. The porter brought him another sackful to do, but the normally brusque head cook said no, to give the bugger a break. So Vic huddled gratefully by the kitchen door in the lee of the outside wall and lit one of Phyllis's cigarettes.

The tarmac delivery bay lay like a little school playground between the high block walls. In his head there was Clarice's voice, not Phyllis's, that time they'd talked at Phyllis's mother's house off the East India Dock Road. It was the first time they'd met, and he'd immediately wanted someone so out of his league, someone whose words had glittered so touchingly. Clarice had been the girl he hardly knew and could never have. Her essence was so desirable it shook him even now. He *had* known her. There'd been time to speak if none to waste, meeting here, talking there. It was all over in a flash. They'd found each other at the wrong hour, the wrong place.

And now he was being punished for it. He drew on the cigarette. There was no pleasure in the tobacco, and it was soon finished. He was distraught; oceans away in Malaya, she'd long since forgotten him.

It took a succession of racked and identical days, maybe even another fortnight, until Vic leant against the same wall by the same kitchen door, taking another break. There'd been a fresh fall of snow that glared white in the yard under a hard blue rectangular heaven. Smoke reeled and snaked from the glowing tip of his fag. He began to grasp where he was and what had happened to him.

He saw the mercilessness in Phyllis that he so readily forgave, and had pitied. How could he insist he loved her, and mean it, when it was precisely her own lack of pity that showed she didn't, couldn't love him?

It was a week later he told himself the story of their intimacy right from the start. He questioned her suicidal impulses. He'd imagined they were genuine. He glimpsed how a recurring private torment to which he stood pledge for his son was the defining scene of their marriage. And how well he'd marginalised it. How effectively he'd always shoved aside the part of him that had endured her, night after night poised shivering at the window in her flimsy cotton, threatening to jump, refusing to let him sleep, or escape.

Another day he realised how he'd even traded his job to protect Jack. Washing up in the kitchen, hands scalding with carbolic soap and the copper-heated water, he spun the knives out with a wipe of the dishcloth to clatter on the enamel tray. He scrubbed the crusted edge of the rectangular metal pie dish with a small piece of wire wool. The water slopped in minute spelks of rusted steel. They were almost a pleasure. He almost needn't love his wife.

The bad winter slackened its grip and once more the grounds' dull green was visible. No one visited. Phyllis sent a letter saying she'd had to take a job skivvying, and couldn't afford the train fare. His mother was unable to come because Percy's gas lung was playing up. But a sliver of Vic was at peace. Where the grass sneaked under the barbed-wire perimeter – though it ran only as far as the embankment for the Waterloo line – he stood and thought of Clarice. Then he went back to his duties, hearing the prison racket all around him, chilling his fingers in the muddy water of the chipped vitreous sink.

There'd be a reckoning for it. In his bed that same night he expected her to turn up – Phyllis. She'd appear. She'd fly in. He expected to open his eyes to find her hand there on the window frame. He expected to hear her threatening to throw herself out if he failed to submit to her banal, hours-long, Agatha Christie script, after sex or sometimes after its refusal: 'Why don't you kill me then, if you hate me so much? Why don't you get rid of me? That's what you want, isn't it? Isn't it?', the voice that wasn't her fault speaking through her, demanding Vic turn murderer, kill her, mutilate her. Always a mere word would set her off.

It was his permission that held her life and she'd do the rest herself, if he wasn't man enough. He put out a hand. She was there, next to him, under the blanket.

Eyes wide open, gasping, he sat up in the bed, fending off the past. His chest still thumping, he levered himself up on his elbows. Very slowly he was reassured. The faint starlight outlined the dormitory window and he once more took pleasure in the iron bars. What kept him in kept her out.

COME FOR THE *weekend, and bring your husband, if he can get away. It'll be lovely. And I'm quite simply desperate to see young Jack.*

They came in the spring. Clarice was exquisitely nervous. *Bring your husband* – it was flagrant, yet after three torn-up drafts she still hadn't been able to leave it out. Ever since her father's initiative beside the fire on the night of their arrival in Suffolk, she'd indulged a fantasy that she and Vic were leading parallel lives. She'd already overleapt the greatest impediment – that of distance. Now Vic would be making up the last few miles to her. It was a persistent romanticism – she knew it. But all she wanted was to be allowed to speak to him again.

From her bedroom she could just see the crest where the road from Ipswich levelled off. Clouds scudded, and a hint of rain passed the window like a moist breath. She would go down to see about the meal. But she couldn't take her eyes away. She would change her dress. But she couldn't leave the window-seat.

Finally, though, into a notch between smudges of hedge, a car rose and was immediately lost to view behind the first cottage of the street. Only then did she hear the burble of its powerful engine. She hurried downstairs adjusting her blue cotton frock as she went, fixing the grips that held her hair. She stood waiting out on the front drive. The sound of the engine came again as the car dipped into the hollow of the water-splash. She heard it accelerate, and suddenly brake. Then at last it swung in through the gap in the garden hedge. It drew to a halt, an open-top roadster, with a stylish maroon sweep in the black side panel. The gravel crackled beneath its wheels. Vic, in his coat, cap and driving goggles, was here . . . surely.

She was a jangle of anticipation. He was getting out. He was standing no more than ten yards away from her. Something was amiss. Something felt bad. Everything. Why had she written?

She'd been wrong, completely wrong. When he removed the cap and faintly stagey goggles, her spirits were thrown into confusion. It wasn't him at all. The man saluted in her direction. She felt completely bereft.

Phyllis, shedding headscarf and sunglasses, seemed unsure how to release the door catch. The man stepped round to free her, and Clarice thought she caught the name Tony, as Phyllis looked up at him. Then at last she was out of the car and the couple approached her, their faces set in greeting.

There was no question about Phyllis. Phyllis was strikingly dressed, in a long coat with a grey fur collar. It was partially unfastened, revealing the neat salmon-pink jumper beneath and the jet beads at her throat. Her face was immaculate, the hair fetchingly waved. She looked quite stunning. But the man . . . Clarice searched his face for as long as was acceptable. He returned her gaze, unwavering.

Then her fingers were in his grip. She stammered, 'I thought it was supposed to be Victor.' She forced a laugh.

The couple glanced at each other. Phyllis frowned. The husband dropped Clarice's hand and seemed non-plussed. They stood on the gravel, all three of them, awkward relations. The little boy climbed by himself out of the car, from the engine of which a hot, oily smell hung in the air, until another gust of breeze dashed it away.

It was the man who spoke decisively. 'That's right. Vic Warren.'

The lie was unashamed. It was obvious, almost flaunted, and with it disappeared a whole scheme of things that Clarice had known and built her security on.

'Pleased to meet you, Miss Pike.' He flourished his driving cap and shook hands again; an assertive, smartly dressed fellow with a pure, almost glamorous face. His voice held a trace of a London accent.

'Oh, but I think you did meet Vic before, didn't you?' Phyllis said. 'At my mother's. You probably don't remember. Why should you? Slumming it with us lot. Probably couldn't wait to get out of there and back to Malaya.' She gave a laugh. 'I was expecting, wasn't I? Before we were married.' Phyllis looked cheekily up at the man. 'Seems like ages now, doesn't it? We've all been through so many changes. And this war . . .'

'Please. Call me Clarice.' She felt her own smile, polite, automatic. The car behind them ticked as it cooled.

'Right you are,' he said. 'Clarice it is. I'll get the suitcase.'

'And my scarf and hats, please. Victor,' Phyllis called.

Clarice gazed at the car. 'My! It looks brand new.'

He was hoisting their suitcases out of the boot. He met her eye across the length of the smart leather interior. 'Riley Lynx. Picked her up last week. A problem getting hold of the gas. Still, we made it here all right.' A smile curved on his fine lip.

'And this is Jack,' Phyllis said, bobbing down to present the child. 'Say hallo to Auntie Clarice, Jack.'

The boy hung into the folds of his mother's coat, and stared up at the new person.

Clarice stared back, at the two of them, at the child's dab of a face, and his short, wind-blown hair. Then she examined once more her cousin's fine and skilfully emphasised features. She remembered the spiteful, grateful, tearful, buccaneering girl who'd bullied her in her own home behind the blind eye of her parents. She felt sorry for the kid. 'I thought Vic was . . .'

'Out of a job?' said Phyllis. 'Yes, I wrote first of all, didn't I?' She straightened up. 'We had a rocky moment.' She called over her shoulder. 'Didn't we? Darling.' Then turning back to Clarice, 'But everything's quite all right now.'

'Then who was that man I met . . . That other . . .'

'Man? What man?'

She was aware of the husband, watching her. He'd come round with the cases and set them down. She was aware of his body. It was like a threat. And Phyllis, too, was sharp, at point. Those tailored curves held an image of Clarice's own mother, together with the same scent, attar of roses. She backed down. 'Oh, well. Then I expect it was nothing,' she said.

THE CHILD WAS dressed in a brown corduroy cap and suit with leggings that buttoned all the way down the side. Clarice put out her hand to him. 'Hallo, Jack. Goodness, what a smart boy you are. I wonder what you'd like to eat. Shall we go and meet Uncle Doc?'

Her hand hung in the air like a lost limb. She was unused to children. Then, hesitantly, and somewhat to her surprise, the boy took hold of it. His small palm was warm, and there were soft, questing fingers. How disconcertingly he gazed up at her. The clasp tightened and she felt him consent. She liked the sensation.

With a glance to the parents she turned to lead them all in. 'It's so nice to see you. Why don't you come and meet Daddy.'

'Daddy?' said the child immediately. 'Where's Daddy?'

'My daddy, Jack. He's the doctor.'

Phyllis gave a strange little laugh. 'It's not such a grand house as I remember. I was almost disappointed for a minute when I saw it. I'd always thought you lived in a mansion. Not that it isn't very nice, I'm sure.'

'It's been allowed to get a bit tumbledown. We've made progress, repairs, a few sticks of furniture – but there needs a lot more doing to get it back into shape. The change isn't all in the mind's eye.'

'No. I don't suppose so. You're looking very nice, of course. I can't wait to see Stan.'

Stan! Clarice was amazed at the liberty. Just beside the door there were daffodils in newly tended beds. They rocked slightly in the April wind. 'How do you like my gardening?' she asked.

'Lovely, I'm sure.'

'We didn't actually know we still owned the buildings.' She led the way in. 'It was in Mummy's name. When she died, Daddy thought it would have gone back to . . .' She felt the embarrassment of the void she'd opened. 'I don't know, relatives.'

'Yes?'

She plunged on: 'You know, reverted somewhere. Daddy didn't much care. He thought he'd be in the East for good, you see. Since it's turned out otherwise and we own this and nothing else, there didn't seem to be much option. It's hardly worth five bob, but here's where we live, at least for the time being.' She indicated the cramped panelling in the little attempt at a lobby, and then pointed to the oak door on her right. 'Apparently, there was an old lady tenant all that time. She died and the upkeep was let go. I have to warn you, there's no running water. We have the electric, but no main drains. That's the country for you.'

Clarice ushered them into the sitting-room. 'Ethel Farmer's making lunch. She "does". I think it's nearly ready. You've arrived just in time; and here's Daddy.'

The reuniting of uncle with long-lost niece appeared to have all the natural warmth missing from her own handling of affairs. Her father hugged Phyllis to his tweeds and picked up Jack. Then he shook hands warmly with the husband. The four were animated in front of the fire while Clarice was shut out.

'I'll see about lunch,' she said, uncertainly. 'And then I'll show you to your . . .' So busy making up for lost time, they failed to hear her, and she left the room unnoticed. Suddenly the effect caught up with her, and she doubted everything about herself. *I expect it was nothing*, she'd said. As she took Phyllis's smart leather cases along the passageway and up the stairs, her eyes brimmed over. The first drops ran down her cheek and on to her dress. Then, mercifully out of earshot in the guest bedroom, she wept over the basin until the sobs hurt in her throat. She was crying again but it was nothing. What had she done or achieved? Nothing. She'd wasted her life in frivolous passages, in various passions and crazes – so they appeared to her now.

She dabbed at her face with a hand towel and looked round at the shabby furniture, the old bed. Weak English light strove in through the imperfect glass panes above the pine chest. Her father was right, he hadn't looked after her. Whatever life she'd owned had been taken away behind his back. Which was the true sham, the happy couple with their child, or the deluded girl with the ruined old man pouring what money they had left out of a black-market whisky bottle and down his throat?

Downstairs in the dining-room, as soon as she was seated, the conversation lapsed – she knew her eyes were red, her powder a tell-tale of repairs. Everyone was pointedly not looking at her. 'I'm really sorry about this beef,' she said. 'Ethel claimed she knew the ways of the range. She cooked and did for the dead Miss Lauderdale, you see.' Her voice had a desperate ring.

The husband contributed a polite chuckle. Phyllis remained as intimidating as ever. Dr Pike was insisting on finding her the reverse. Phyllis sat next to him and simpered. He engaged her in nostalgia. 'You remember the gramophone, child.'

'I believe I do.'

'Still going. We had it out in the jungle. Hardly credit it, would you? Charmed the monkeys out of the trees. Done very well for yourself, Phyllis. I'd never have dreamed that slip of a lass would turn out quite such a dazzler. Great girl, eh?'

'Oh, Stan. The things you say.'

Clarice turned her attention to the husband. 'Well, how good to see Phyllis after all these years. And to meet you too, Vic. Tell me, what line of business are you in?'

'The shipping business, actually. We ship the goods in, and then we distribute them.' The casual smile played again, a studied insincerity. They understood each other; he saw and enjoyed the fact of her tears, knew she was trying to fight back. The high stakes created an almost sexual undercurrent.

'What sort of goods?'

'All sorts, really. Anything we can get our hands on, so to speak.' He laughed. There was a fascination about him.

'We're not fussy at Figgis and Rice. Old established firm, you see.'

'Ah, quite,' broke in her father. 'So you're in the City?'

'More or less. Very handy for the port. The docks.'

She steeled herself. 'That would be the job at the . . . boatyard?'

He didn't even draw breath. 'We do have a marine construction interest. What about you, sir? Going to set up practice again? Very nice part of the world. Constable country, eh?' he grinned.

'Oh, yes. But I doubt it, Vic. I doubt it, actually. The old trouble, you know. Malaria. Physician, heal thyself.'

Phyllis told Jack to eat up his food. 'He's such a fussy eater. Do you still play the piano, Clarice? We were all expecting great things. After what we heard.'

'I'm afraid I don't.'

The pudding was more edible. Lunch closed on a reminiscence of the old East, as her father mellowed. But Clarice looked up at the low ceiling's plaster and exposed woodwork, and a deep curled presentiment of calamity stirred in her stomach. An ache the shape of the missing Victor Warren filled her heart. Where was he? What had they done with him?

SHE *WOULD* FIGHT. She was in her own kitchen, standing next to the ancient porcelain sink and looking out on to the garden hedge. Beyond it stood the trees at the edge of Appleby's farm. In her mind's eye, she could see Vic's face, quite clearly. She could almost feel his arms about her.

Recollections flooded in – of the few days they'd stolen together. Had Phyllis guessed? Among the Tyler family

Clarice had felt awkward: posh, prissy and too well dressed, as though everyone hated her but were putting her on a pedestal. Her stay had been all too brief. Eventually, she'd had to go down to Southampton to catch her ship, the *Mooltan*. At Waterloo Station she and Vic had contrived to part. She could see his eyes now, shining, yet full of desperation.

She returned to the dining-room. The two women cleared the table and then decamped with Jack to the drawing-room. The men failed to join them. Clarice excused herself once more.

Back in the kitchen she caught her father refilling the decanter, and took the bottle from him in exasperation. 'Daddy. No more. Just listen to me, please. How many times do I have to tell you, you can't expect to keep downing it at the same rate over here. There's nothing to burn it off.' She gestured at the window. The wind was tossing budded branches on the other side of the hedge. 'Whatever midday sun there might be out there won't madden a fly. In England it costs real money.'

'Thought I was being hospitable.'

'You are. Of course you are. But . . .'

'That young fellow seems to have a supply of good Havanas from somewhere.' Dr Pike took a specimen from his top jacket pocket and waved it in front of her like a trophy.

'That's the point. It's what I'm trying to speak to you about. We're out of our league. Out of our depth. They're lying. I can't believing how brazen they're being. This isn't him.'

'What?'

'I know Vic Warren. I . . . met him. Before I came out – the last time. This other . . . He's an impostor.' The word sounded puffed up.

He fixed her with his eye; and then casually pulled a spotted handkerchief, also from his top pocket, to mop the bristles on his upper lip. 'Surely not.'

'Daddy!' How could she make herself understood? 'It isn't him! Why did we have to invite them ... her? I'm frightened.'

'Turned into a very presentable young woman. What seems to be the problem?'

'Everything. I thought you'd had a letter saying Phyllis and her husband were on their uppers. Instead they arrive in a brand new Riley and he's something in the City. Daddy ... ?'

'Things change. As *we* know.'

'But it's not the right man. It's not the Vic Warren I knew. They can't be married.'

'They look very much like it to me.'

'But they're not.'

'D'you know that? For certain.'

'No. No, I don't ... Not for certain. But it isn't him!'

'I expect she just met someone else. Many a slip, my dear. Should it matter, so long as they're getting on together?' His speech was slightly slurred. She hated the loss of him, of his judgement.

'I just feel there's something terribly wrong.'

'About marriage it's never done to enquire too deeply. A private realm. To be quite frank, none of our business. Eh? Couples go through all sorts of ups and downs. Why should it matter to us what they say or what they get up to?'

'But what about me?' She was insistent.

'Can't there be some charity here?' Her father straightened up. He seemed to forget he was drunk and swayed slightly. 'Doesn't it begin at home? Phyllis was always – how can I put this – something of a refugee. Isn't it up to us to make allowances? Well, isn't it? She had an absolutely filthy time when she was a child. Did you know that? Absolutely filthy.'

'So, I expect, did Hitler. There are always some people who parade their victimhood in front of you like a banner on a pole.'

'Clarice, that's a wicked thing to say! Wicked! Once upon a time I should probably have sent you to your room.' He blinked at her as though he still might. 'As it is, all I can do is recommend a little . . . well, yes, charity. There it is. And Phyllis has never made a song and dance about all that. You can just think about it, darling. All right?' Blandly, he finished filling the decanter and began to accompany it back to the table. 'I'll bring him in to the other room, shall I?'

Clarice stood briefly once more at the kitchen window, holding on to the sink. She bit her lip. The sleeping puppy, Bentley, mewed in its basket.

In the drawing-room she sat with Phyllis on the loose-covered settee watching her father and the man in front of the fire. They stood with their backs to it in that way men did, marking their mutual territories with comments about sport and trade. The familiar, slightly lavatorial smell of cigars fugged the air. Jack was on the floor, absorbed with the clockwork train set she'd brought down from the attic. She wanted to scream. Phyllis wanted to talk to her, just loud enough for Clarice's father to hear the sweetness of her voice.

'I thought you might have been married yourself, by now. Not for want of offers, I expect,' she said.

Clarice replied, pointedly, 'We haven't all come across Mr Right, yet.' She smiled to cover the sarcasm.

Phyllis smiled back. 'Ah, you always did know how to get the attention, though. In Malaya, I can imagine . . . Don't they say those nice public-school boys out there simply worship a white woman?'

'Yes. I expect they do. Do you recommend marriage, after all?'

'Depends, doesn't it?'

'On?'

'On the man.'

'At least *you*'ve fallen on your feet.'

Phyllis glanced at her partner. 'Vic – he's a diamond. Must be to put up with a nightmare like me, eh? Coming from where I come from. That's what you think, isn't it?' She looked straight at Clarice. 'You do, don't you? Vic's a good provider. He keeps me in order. But that's the mark of a man, isn't it? What he says, goes. Makes a woman respect him. Don't you think? Not like some. Stop doing that, Jack.' Clarice knelt down to help the boy mend the track of his train.

Phyllis continued. 'He's come up the hard way, Vic. In fact we're two of a kind, really, known each other all along. Down by the river. All down in those mucky little terraces. That's what you think, don't you? But that's all we know, you see. We don't know no better – as they say. That's where you really learn what's what. And here's you coming home and finding you did own the property all along. Not so grand as we both remembered, maybe.' Her voice dropped. '*Hardly worth five bob really*. But, my, that was lucky, wasn't it? That it hadn't – what was it – "reverted" somewhere. In the family. After all. Speaking of falling on one's feet.'

Later, the sun came out. They all strolled in the garden. More daffodils were blowing in the lawn, and a random profusion of hyacinths peeped through the vegetation which Clarice hadn't yet had a chance to clear from around the edges.

'Tell us about you starting up on the stage, Phyllis,' her father said.

Clarice added, 'Yes, do. It sounds so much more exciting

than anything I've been up to. Malaya's lovely, of course, but there's so little to do, when all's said and done. Thoroughly routine if you're young, to be perfectly honest. I'm dying to hear.'

Strangely, Phyllis was reticent. 'Oh, it's nothing, really. Just to bring in a bit of extra cash. What with the kid and everything.'

'I'm sure you're being modest. Shan't we be seeing your name up in lights soon?'

'Not with this blackout we shan't.'

They all laughed.

'I keep forgetting about that. It's so unreal, isn't it? Oh, Jack. That's the well.' Clarice held the small boy so that he could peer over the brick parapet and taste the fall of dank air. The circle of water far below reflected their two heads. 'It's very mysterious, don't you think?' she said.

'You'll fall in,' said Phyllis.

Her father continued, 'But what roles have you been doing? Are you in rep?'

'It's musical shows actually. Singing and dancing. They're what I do best. The acting is just something you add on as an extra. We like to give the punters what they want. Auntie Mattie was an actress, wasn't she?'

'Yes, she was.' Charmed, pickled, Dr Pike seemed oblivious now to tragedies ancient or modern. 'An unforgiving profession, dear. Just you watch out. You will, won't you?' He slipped an arm around Phyllis's waist. 'Watch it doesn't do to you what it did to her.'

Clarice heard herself gasp. She put her hand up to the twist in her hair. Then she smoothed down the skirt of her belted cornflower-blue dress.

Little Jack brought Clarice a stick for the puppy. She looked at him intently. *And I'm quite simply desperate to see young Jack.* Now they gazed at each other, not child to adult, but almost, for an instant, person to person, and it seemed to her she read something in his small face, in his wide but guarded eyes, that understood the inexplicable disappointment in hers. Some resemblance to his father had attracted her, repelled her, frightened her.

The husband pointed to the eastern sky. 'This is where he'll come. *When* he comes.'

'I thought the Norway intervention was going to sort everything out. Once we've cut off Hitler's supply of iron he'll have to give in, won't he? I mean, whatever happens, the French army, the British navy – between the two he'll have the life squeezed out of him. Surely. And then you can go on with your trading. In the City.'

The man met her eye. 'You don't believe all that, do you? I'm telling you this is where they'll be wanting to land. When they come. All along this coast.' He smiled.

'Land? Invade? Oh, I don't suppose so. Do you? He's got his precious *Lebensraum*. Now he'll be looking for terms, won't he? Everybody says so. No one's going to try to invade *us*, for heaven's sake.' Even as he tried to intimidate her, she found herself responding to him.

'What's to stop him?'

'Surely . . .' She floundered.

'I shouldn't be surprised if he didn't come right past your doorstep.' He smiled again. Then he turned away.

'Really,' she said coldly, after him.

Phyllis was speaking. 'Of course we're tied to London, as you must understand. Or we'd probably try to move out, too. Tony's business interests . . .'

'Who is Tony?'

'Oh. Didn't I say? It's Vic's employer. Partner really. So Vic's business interests keep him close to the capital.'

'As do your own, of course.'

'Oh, yes. And that.'

In the evening, after the boy had gone to bed, they played cards.

MY BROTHER, OR half-brother, Jack. His is a voice I never heard. My brother – let me tell you.

If it didn't rain they'd go and help Boss Hayman out on the fruit farm. Hayman was the name of the neighbours. His Auntie Clarice had promised them a real taste of the outdoors. Jack had asked what the outdoors was. His great-uncle, the doctor, told him he was going with his mother and his father to the farm along the road. All night the house had creaked and ticked until morning came. Then they swept away together in the Lynx.

One field had rows of raspberry canes like a succession of hedges. Another had cherry trees in bright, white flower. A third was bare earth in turned furrows, and Jack sat in the lap of an Uncle Boss behind a tractor smaller than a motor bike. It was a mechanical snail; smoke chugged from its chimney pipe. It pulled him along on the cultivator, and he steered the front wheel, swinging the long rod as far as he could reach, this way, now that, to the furrow. All the time Jack was waiting to see his father, because of what the doctor had said; but he knew both how to wait and how to button his lip. They ploughed the brown earth by the River Stour, wide as a lake. On the water he saw one ship with tan sails, one white, but not a third.

Clarice wore shining clothes, or was there a brightness that came out of her skin? It clung to her arms, and made him want to be caught up by them, held close to her face. She stood with Tony beside the straight ridges. The brightness moved when she moved, it dwelt upon her skirt, upon the edges of her cardigan. As he jogged along on the tractor Jack could only see such light when he didn't expect to. But he liked Boss's sons, too. They wore shorts; the hair on their legs curled in dark strands. The hair moved on the wind-blown skin. Jack wanted to be as manly as them both, with their rolled-down socks and large muddy shoes. One wore glasses. He said there was a canoe but that it leaked; and in the canoe Jack thought they would sink until a kingfisher came. The canoe smelt of leaves and water lay under the seat; but though the son pointed and pointed, he couldn't see what the kingfisher was.

He turned and looked at the shore where Clarice was standing – and from far away she was reflected in the water, until the sudden ripples changed her. He knew a song his father sang when he was sawing wood: '*Hark the herald angels sing, Mrs Simpson's pinched our king.*' They must get back. On the dry land again with Clarice the birds chirruped all about: skylark, curlew, thrush, the tree creeper, the woodpecker, crows. She told him their names. She showed him, too, the first leaves coming from branches, small ears of green, unfolding, and the sticky buds. Her words matched what he could know.

Next, there was a low, boarded house in a green space, cool, in a forest. He was tired and hungry, his mother said, and they'd come away because he'd been calling out for his father. Beyond the overhanging trees Jack could still see furrows, hear the tractor's grumble, smell the pervasive farm smell; and the house was wood – but not small like the summer cabin Rabbit had made. Now Tony was the Vic. This house was old and painted dark green, as though it had grown here of its own accord, with its white decorations along the top of the roof, and a wooden spike at each end. The gable over the front door looked more like the window on Ripple Road, where they lived in the flat, than the poor hutch at Laindon. There were outside steps with a rail. They went up to knock, and his father was lost in one house after another, this one on stilts, look, underneath, where it might flood, or snakes. Uncle Doc, Uncle Boss, Vic – all men grew into a condition, and were lost.

Dark and quiet inside as the hollow tree of a story, a tall clock ticking slowly the beats, the darkness of wood, closed, still, no room, no dad. Then Jack looked everywhere in case of barking: the fire in the grate, the mantelpiece, the carved rosettes in the armchairs, the cupboards brown with china inside. The dark table legs were made into shapes, and a flat piano balanced in the air – all the wood hummed and breathed so secretly he hardly dared yawn or make his own sounds. His eyelids tried to close though he held them wide. There were thick cloths and covers, the smells of rugs, and of a real dog. He knew how always the world might turn itself away and slip into something else in a moment, and yet the patterns kept making the same shape. There were black wooden eyes in the corner near the clock, in a huge head, and Jack turned to run but his mother caught him. 'Sorry. He's always a bit difficult at first. He'll settle down.'

'It's Boss's cello. He's frightened of the cello.' The old woman knew and picked up the great face to show him what it was.

'A Cox's orange pippin.' Uncle Boss cut a piece of a large apple that was wrapped in straw. He gave it to him, like the witch his dad read about once, and it tasted of orange and smelt of straw. 'You make the most of that, boy. We shan't be seeing many oranges for a while.' Then the uncle smiled, the skin of his head moving tufts of white hair sticking up. There was a real cat there, too, in the dark house.

His mother wore a very short white skirt of Aunt Clarice's. 'Oh, I really couldn't. Are you sure? But I'm so out of practice.' Jack could see her knees. They were a small bump at the front and then white widening legs going up, and such a strange extent of skin without hair or feature, until they were hidden behind the hem, as if he were looking at her body for the first time.

The men had on old plimsolls. They'd be going to the farm again and he wanted to ride on the tractor. But they all went away without him and he thought he'd been left alone for ever with the woman, the witch aunt, her face with the small red veins, and the round lump on her lip. She smiled. His mummy and daddy would be playing tennis. He said his daddy was in Pentonville.

'Is he, dear?'

'He got three years.'

'My word. That's a long time.'

Then he was to go to sleep, there, on the leather settee. She gave him some cake because he'd had his dinner, and the sun shone in through the small window. He saw the man-jug sitting on the sill next to the china dog. His father would come soon because he was playing tennis.

In the crook of the piano his mother sang. The quiver in her voice came out of her head and was in the room. Everyone clapped. She smiled at Tony. Auntie Clarice stood up. 'Wonderful, Phyllis.' Uncle Boss sat with the cello between his legs. Jack's mother and Tony sat on the old leather settee. There were cello shapes under people's chins, and then the music came, the sounds overwhelming, full of scrolls and curls, like the cello itself, and next fierce like a saw. Clarice's arms lifted one by one from the keyboard into the air, and struck down. He wanted them to stop, but they wouldn't and the wooden room with its olden time shook and curled and filled up until it seemed there was nowhere for the music to go except inside his head and he was crying. His mother took him outside.

He looked under the house and it smelt of oil from the sons' car, a little ruby-red car with one engine cover up, the oil can on the ground, the smell of oil and mud coming up from the ground, the old dog asleep. The chain lay along the side of the stilts and was nailed up to the back of the kennel. Aunt Clarice came out too.

'You haven't forgotten my offer, have you, Phylly? Heavens, the poor slum children went, didn't they?'

'And came back, a good half of them.'

'He's very welcome, you know. I'd really like to have him.'

'It's very kind of you. I'll think about it, but I can't imagine it'll be necessary. Evacuation was just one of those silly scares, wasn't it? I don't believe in all this politics. You know me. It'll be all right on the night.'

'At the very least a holiday for him. I mean, if the noose tightens there's still a chance they'll risk the gas option. On London. If they get really rattled, don't you think?'

'Suit yourself.'

There was suddenly an ear-splitting drone. Jack thought for a moment the music was starting again and put his hands over his ears. Then three huge planes came low over the trees blanking the evening sky while they seemed to scrape at the hair on his head. He screamed and then stared as they disappeared. The grown-ups smiled at him because the aircraft were theirs, but his dad wasn't playing tennis at all and bombs would fall.

III
The Borderland

JUNE. DR PIKE followed the defeat of France with astonishment, as though it were a dream. All at once the Germans had sidestepped the Maginot Line and were through the Ardennes. While Paris seemed none the wiser, the French Ninth Army fled in rout, throwing away their rifles, joining the streams of civilians fleeing west across the fields of Champagne and Picardie.

He and Clarice saw all this at the cinema in Ipswich, the roads out of the war zones clogged with refugees, pushing carts, herding children, carrying suitcases. Strafed by Stukas and buzzed by Bf109s, lines of people were chased along a single road by the endless column of General Heinz Guderian's XIXth Armoured Corps. The *Blitzkrieg* was hypnotic. The mere sight of the thin string of panzer tanks struck terror into every heart. What was to be made of it, this extraordinary débâcle? The French Army was the largest in the world.

Its preparations had been intensive, he reflected, coldly, clearly, suddenly not drunk at all. Intensive, and yet fatally, almost wilfully flawed. Within living memory France had been attacked through the same forest – the precise spot of Guderian's crossing, Sedan, on the Meuse, was the scene of her surrender to the Prussians in 1870. Doctor Pike had learnt that at school. He had learnt, too, that the Germans were a Brothers Grimm nation of woodmen. Oak leaves and lightning were their military emblems. And yet the French had left the routes through the Ardennes undefended. The long panzer column had even been detected from the air, and allowed to advance unhindered.

In the subsequent days, at his radio, or in the news-papers, a slow-motion sequence unfolded: of the encir-clement of the armies of the north, of the exclusion of the RAF, and then of the evacuation of the British Expeditionary Force from Dunkirk. He'd seen boats go out from Ipswich docks. Not so slow after all, the sequence – for it accomplished within a matter of days what the Great War had failed to do in four years. So the two great Continental enemies, Germany and France, reformed in a line across the whole of Normandy, from the Maginot Line in the east to the Seine in the west. Outnumbered, overflown, and eventually fully engaged to the last fighting unit, France's young men gave up their lives once again to her serial assailant.

As a member of the public, very little of this last information was available to Dr Pike, for the conflict on French soil was far less reported than the rescue from the beaches. Nevertheless, by a dogged assembly of sources, he read between the lines of official broadcasts. The collision's rolling and attritional slaughter took the casualty figures for both sides into line with the Great War battles, the devastations of the seventeenth cen-tury, or the old Roman campaigns when troops unblest with gunpowder contrived to stab, poke or chew each other to death in their tens of thousands. So my great-uncle estimated; for such facts as these he had also learnt at school.

France was lost. Now the Empire he'd served, cursed, and even loved a little bit, whose myths, attitudes and mosquitoes had infected him, that arrogant, well-intentioned, shakeless guarantee of a certain way of doing things, lay exposed. Prepared all along against the bombing of her cities,

Britannia had never dreamed of invasion. It had been, in a sense, unthinkable.

All at once the mother country had proved to be nothing more than a small island made chiefly out of coal – so he joked to Clarice – on which he and his daughter had been washed up. It had a traumatised army with no guns, a mauled air force, and one or two grey boats. The world was there for the taking, and stood on the brink of the new order. Stan Pike shook himself awake. But the worst thing was that he hadn't been sleeping.

The fall of France did put a stop to his drinking – that, and a worrisome dwindling of the funds he had left over from his imperial service. He finally grasped that Selama Yakub was dead. Reality came rushing in on him, just as it rushed upon everyone else. He wanted to feel the pain. Stopping the Scotch was a way of punishing himself for her loss, because his decision to bring his daughter home now looked even more like the supreme idiocy of his life. Events had not only proved him as wrong as could be, but culpable: he'd killed one woman and placed the other in worse jeopardy.

'I'm impressed,' Clarice said. 'Though it's not one of the suggestions listed here.' She held in her hands a government leaflet – 'If the Invader Comes'. 'That other one mentions Scotland but not Scotch. Still, worth a try, perhaps. If there's time.'

'You're a cynical girl,' he replied.

'I thought I was just terrified.'

He went outside and smashed his last bottle into the dustbin. The dear fluid ran over the ash and eggshells. He saw it leak like golden urine through a rust hole at the bin's base, only to lose itself between two stones and a tuft of grass. A succession of fighters from Martlesham Heath flew overhead, angrier and more piercing than the Wattisham bombers.

Common sense argued that history would be indifferent to Dr Pike's blood alcohol levels when the *Wehrmacht* tramped over his corpse on its way up from Shotley Gate. But he recalled Selama's insistence on the religious duty to keep judgement unclouded. 'Who knows when the devil will jump out on us, Stan?' she once had said.

Now the devil *had* jumped out, and so abstinence was both a way of honouring her and her religion, and of arming himself. In fact, one way or another, Selama's spirit had been whispering over his shoulder all the time since her death, and he'd been just too soused to hear. It pleaded that one man's self-control might be as important as all the precious cannon, tanks, aircraft, and armoured cars the Army had been forced to abandon in France. It argued that the fool God saw drinking himself into oblivion at the world's moment might just turn out to be the one real fifth-columnist. Dr Pike smiled, and then choked on his emotions; but he hardened against being that fool.

THERE WERE TWO old shotguns in the boxroom of Pook's Hill, a double-barrelled twelve bore and a rusty, single four-ten. He stripped them down on the dining-room table and oiled them from a long-spouted can he found among the cobwebs in one of his sheds. There was a bottle of Johnny Walker hidden in the sideboard, at the back of the shelf. He'd known it was there all along. He brought it out and stood it next to the unscrewed locks, stocks and barrels, in order to make ready to hurl it after its companions into the dustbin. But for a while he regarded the rectangular form, since it seemed such a shame.

There came a knock at the front door. Clarice was in Ipswich where he'd sent her to buy up cartridges, and Ethel Farmer had the afternoon off. A touch guiltily, he answered the knock himself – to a gentleman in sporting tweeds from Manningtree, who gave his name as Wellbridge, and came in.

Mr Wellbridge wondered had Dr Pike considered joining the Local Defence Volunteers.

Dr Pike hadn't.

Mr Wellbridge thought the two dismantled guns were a jolly good show, and seeing the Scotch he didn't mind if he did. It had turned out fine again, though no doubt they'd have to pay for it.

They took a glass each, and at first Dr Pike warmed to the idea of becoming involved with his neighbourhood and at one with his fellow men. Having lived for so long on the fringes of society – and of the world – because of his unorthodox heart, he felt a real attraction in the prospect. The Scotch tingled on his tongue.

'After all, it could be any day now, couldn't it?' Wellbridge was saying.

'So it would seem,' said Dr Pike. 'One really ought to join. I'd had the idea the only thing we could do would be to evacuate the women and children and prepare to sell our lives as dearly as possible. Can I possibly be of any use?'

'Good Lord, yes. There's plenty of fight in the old dog yet. We'll need people to keep watch, sound the alarm.'

'But the German army, tanks and so on.'

'There'll be parachutists, first of all. They'll need rounding up.'

'Ah yes. The paratroops. I've read about them, dressed as nuns.'

Wellbridge looked quizzical, as though some old wound troubled him. Then he carried on. 'They do use disguises, yes. We'll need all our wits about us. There'll be training sessions, and drill. By the way, you're planning to hang on to those guns, are you?'

'I'd thought so.'

'It's just that we're rather short, until the rifles come through. You'd think the coast would be top priority now, wouldn't you?'

'Yes. I suppose you would.' Dr Pike laid a protective hand on his twelve-bore action.

'Please yourself,' said Wellbridge. 'But until Jerry does come there's the internal matter, of course. We'll be needed for guard duty.'

'The internal matter?'

'Traitors, doctor. Spies. The enemy within. France was undermined from the start; she never stood a chance. It's our first job to make certain the same thing doesn't happen here. Do you know, that's remarkably good Scotch. One so rarely has the opportunity, these days.'

'Have another.'

'Well, yes, why not. If you insist.'

Mr Wellbridge took his second glass. Dr Pike still sipped his first. The taste worried him. He said, 'And who exactly are these. . . ? Where shall we find them?'

'Why, the enemy aliens. Don't you read the papers? Hadn't you heard they're all being rounded up? We know exactly where they are.'

Dr Pike heaved a sigh, and pressed on with the question whose answer would confirm that he didn't, after all, wish to join the local defence force. 'Which enemy aliens would they be, exactly, Mr Wellbridge?'

Mr Wellbridge looked genuinely surprised. 'Ah, but you're only just back from the East. The Jews, of course. They're all German-speaking. You see, we've bent over backwards for years to let them all in, only to give ourselves the trouble of locking them up now. Some of them are living in luxury, you know; managed to blend completely into the community. The law. It's official. Other areas are well ahead of us. The local police have asked us to set up contingency plans – a holding centre. Not that we've actually got many of them out here.' He winked confidentially. 'Too remote. A bit too English, don't you think?'

It was always so unvarying, the tone of voice, the confidential assumption of agreement, as if some password were being slipped. Dr Pike had heard it so many times, read it, lived with it, here before, at school, at the clubs, on the ships, in the papers. But he'd only noticed it, really noticed it, after he'd taken up with Selama Yakub; and was only just beginning, at this strange last gasp with the Nazis at the gates shouting the very same password, to be profoundly, neck-pricklingly angry about it. 'Have you any idea why the Jews came over here?' he said gently. He put his glass down.

'Who knows,' said Mr Wellbridge, missing any irony. 'Maybe they were asking for it. Refujews,' he snorted. 'A good number of criminals and prostitutes, so I'm reliably informed.'

'Would we also be helping round up any former appeasers, and prominent anti-Semites? Or any of the newspaper owners, colonels, captains of industry, peers, MPs and other pillars of the community who I gather only months ago were apologists for Hitler? One or two of them might be cunningly blended in, say, as landowners, even out here. Even if, dare we say it, there were no Jews.'

'What?'

'I'm suggesting the likelier traitors.'

'Sorry, I don't get you.'

'Never mind. You'd better leave.'

'What? Look, d'you want to join, or don't you?'

'I think not. Would you mind taking this with you?' He showed both man and bottle out.

Wellbridge clutched the whisky as he stood on the gravel. His face worked between a gloat and a scowl. 'Not willing to do your bit, eh?'

'So sorry.'

'It'll get about, you know.'

'I'd an idea it might. Goodbye to you.'

Stan Pike closed the door. He wasn't surprised in the least that the appearance of Mr Wellbridge had followed directly upon his own casting aside of the demon drink. The music-hall logic helped stiffen his resolve. But Selama Yakub was lost for ever; and as he cleaned his guns he tried to keep fast to what he believed – that figures as grotesque and self-parodic as Wellbridge, or even Hitler himself, were motivated at the level of some hidden substrate by the quest for love, and the desire to be called out, named and understood. If that weren't the case then there was almost no point in resistance.

CLARICE PULLED IN her horns, like a snail. She clung to routines. As the invasion hung imminent, more likely by the week, she kept house; she concentrated on the task in hand. Everything else – the future, love, the possibility that her cousin's deception actually left her free to try to find Vic – must be put on hold.

She nursed her father, or convinced herself that she did. The loss of his drink began to work on him. It made him nervous; he had the jitters. She sat with him in the evenings, sewing, or reading, or turning the dial of the bakelite wireless through the various European stations to find music for him. Continually he'd get up to twitch the curtain, or go out prowling the garden. At last, she tried to stop him. Then he held her by the wrist and explained the situation again. He begged her forgiveness. The Nazis were everything he'd always known they were, England was at their mercy, and all he could do was shake and gibber. He was so ashamed.

The next morning she saw his preparations to fight them single-handed. With the spade in his hand, and accompanied by the ecstatic puppy, Bentley, he strode about the garden probing the earth. Then he began to dig.

'A slit trench,' he said. 'I suppose it's just that – a slit in the ground.'

'Why don't you go and join the Volunteers after all,' she suggested, her hair let loose from the comb, framing her face. 'They'd know.'

'They're the most bloody detestable collection of Fascists.'

'They can't all be, Daddy.'

'Shell-shocked old men,' he said. 'Hunting and shooting types. Yokels and village idiots. They don't know their arse from their elbow, girl. They haven't a clue what we're fighting for.'

'They might know what a slit trench was.' He exasperated her. A convoy of dull-green army lorries began to jam up in the narrow lane in front of the house. They'd been coming past every few minutes. Now one stopped by their gateway. The driver shouted and whistled. 'You could ask him,' she gestured.

'It's obviously just what it says it is,' her father said. 'A trench. You don't have to be Chief of the Imperial General Staff to know that, for God's sake.' The lorry ground on again.

'So there's no difficulty?'

'The fine detail, Clarice. Siting, drainage, slope of side. That's all I'm after.' The puppy fell into the trench, and yelped and scrabbled as he scooped it out. It proceeded to dash back and forth barking manically. 'Bentley! Here!' he shouted. 'Calm down, damn you!'

'Just join in – for God's sake. If the good men don't show up, the Wellbridges stand to win. Isn't that the whole ground of your case?'

But he wouldn't be persuaded. He sulked and sweated. She pitied his sweats, whether from going on the wagon, or reawakened malaria, or now from the sheer frustration of military engineering. By eleven o'clock the ditch he'd made under the apple trees was about two feet deep and bedded with impenetrable flint; the lorries in the lane were streaming the other way. She took him tea.

'Thanks,' he said. 'They don't give them ordinary spades, did you know? They give them entrenching tools.' He took off his Tom Mix hat, looked at his dog and fanned himself.

And she plucked a strand of hair back from her face where the warm breeze was catching it. The sun on her bare arms was precious. 'Who? The Volunteers?'

'The regular troops, girl. They issue them with entrenching tools. To be carried at all times.'

'You think one of those would do the trick, then?'

He wiped his brow; his forehead was red. 'This is real, isn't it, darling? I can't believe ... You would tell me, wouldn't you, if the whole ... If it were just an attack of the DTs?'

'As far as I know, it's real.'

'Then it's the end of everything.'

'I should think it is.'

'Christ, you're a cool one,' he said.

She wasn't. But it was after Mr Churchill's speech that she'd made a conscious decision to manage her fear – by joining in the national mood. That was the point at which she'd slammed her imagination shut. What remained was a capricious excitement. The benign epidemic, it seemed to crop up everywhere. People she didn't know stopped to talk to her in the village, or in Manningtree where she went to collect the meat ration. Everyone was buoyed up, keyed up. When the officer called around the village about the coastal zone evacuation, no one would go. It was true, she did feel such a relief to be alone and herself, not tied to allies – or even lovers – no longer mixed up with the apocalypse across the Channel, but unified with her good neighbours and resolved instead. A stand would be made. Let them come. Let the *Luftwaffe* wheel overhead in packs of bombers a hundred strong – as indeed they were alleged to be doing on the wireless and in the paper. Let them just try landing.

She made friends with a farmer's daughter called Beatrice Bligh, a strong, brown-haired, good-natured girl who taught her how to ride. And that, to her surprise, marked a turn in her morale. Bea was newly married to a young Ipswich solicitor. She poised her life uncertainly between husband and parents, town and country, apparently taking every opportunity to come up to the farm near Harkstead, much to her husband's irritation. 'He wants me to give up the horses and stay at home. You don't think I should, do you?'

'Can't see why,' Clarice replied. She was wearing borrowed jodhpurs, and one of her father's white shirts. Her brown brogue shoe swung in the stirrup. Mannish, perspiring in the afternoon's bask of cloudlessness and gnats, she guided the bay gelding, Martin, away from the gatepost just in time to prevent him crushing her knee. 'Stop it, you spiteful thing!' She could have sworn the horse sneered as she pulled his mouth. 'I do believe he actually means to do it, Bea.'

'He will. He's a rogue. Aren't you, Marty? Just be firm with him. You'll have to have your wits about you until he knows who's in charge. And don't let him stop to eat things as he goes along.'

'All very well.' Clarice wrestled with the muscled neck in front of her.

He was a rogue. Behind Bea's back and all the length of the hedge that ran the crown of Appleby's land, Martin stopped and started, ate, chewed, drooled, and threatened to bite her shin with his disgraceful brown teeth. The sun was hot; her shirt stuck to her skin. At one point flies from some decomposing kill in the hedge swarmed up around her face. They settled on her arms, her hands, and all along the horse's neck where the hair glistened with sweat below the mane. Both she and Martin flicked and shuddered, upsetting each other. She didn't know the rules. Clearly, Martin did, because each time Bea turned round he contrived to look docile and plodding. 'That's the spirit. You're doing very nicely. Just give him a slap if he plays up.'

Behind Bea's back Martin gave Clarice every impression that he cared not a fig and would do exactly as he liked. Under the elms at the edge of Bligh's farm, they eyed each other with suspicion. Nevertheless, they'd come this far, she reflected; they must have reached some grudging compromise.

The two women walked their horses down through the woods of Nether Hall and came to the banks of the Stour. The tide was out. They stood beside the mud-flats looking over the middle channel to Copperas Bay and then right along the estuary towards Harwich. Martin tossed his head incessantly, and Clarice grew incensed. 'If only he'd keep still! What is it I'm doing wrong?'

'Nothing.'

'*Your* horse isn't trying to pull your arms out.'

Bea laughed. 'I'm all right with horses. It's the men I find difficult.'

'Oh, men.'

'Geoff expects me just to be there. But I don't see why I should give up my whole life.'

'It's early days yet. I suppose there's an adjustment.'

'He wasn't at all like this when we were engaged. Sitting trot. That means you stay in the saddle. We'll get you two acquainted, shall we? Shake you out a bit.' Bea laughed. They set the horses trotting along the path beside the tide line. She shouted over her shoulder, 'I don't see that I should give up all this!'

Despite the recalcitrant animal's jogging spine and bruising sinew, for the first time Clarice felt physically connected to the little peninsula on which she'd come to live. She liked the pace she was going. Men, who needed them?

THEY WENT IN under the trees that bordered the few acres of Hayman's fruit farm, and rode right past the wooden house in the clearing, just as Boss emerged from behind it driving his miniature tractor, the trailer loaded up with sacks. It startled the horses, and they took off, one after the other, in a dash that lasted several seconds. But Clarice wasn't frightened; thrilled rather at the sudden power, ducking instinctively under a low branch that swept towards her as the path narrowed once more into the thicket, feeling her feet steadied in the stirrups, and dropping her hands down close to Martin's neck. When they pulled up, Bea turned round. 'Sorry about that. Are you all right?'

'Absolutely fine.' Breathless, she could feel her heart pounding. She'd known all along she'd come to no harm – she'd felt Martin's better nature through her hands. And though he was his former self all the walk home, dragging at passing leaves, and stumbling close to any dangerous projections, she was both tired and changed. There was, perhaps, a chance. A formation of Hurricanes went over, going back to Martlesham. They were almost close enough to touch, but the horses were as used to aircraft as the women. When she got in at Pook's Hill it was just in time for the wireless news. As always her father had his ear strained towards the set. The headlines had come and gone and he nodded the all-clear. No invasion had materialised as yet.

Then, under midsummer skies, Bea and Clarice rode almost every afternoon, defying Geoffrey, Bea's husband, and savouring the hot scents of woods and animals. When the distant sirens wailed, which they frequently did, Clarice took no notice. She grew used to the dung and rot in the buzzing ferns of the Morton plantation and the warm earthen smell off the meadow behind Harkstead church. She loved the dust from the first paths across the neighbour fields, the peppery banks along the winding lower roads, then the peculiar dappled air beneath the oaks on the long slope that led down to the river. And at the tide's various moods she snuffed up intriguing salt tangs mixed with the leathery waft of the body beneath her. She looked forward to the canters, as did Martin.

They began to rub along better after all. There was a day he forgot to try breaking her leg on the gatepost at Bligh's. That same afternoon he picked up his feet over the exposed roots through Appleby's spinney. From Shop Corner the ground on the rise lay open for a stretch where gorse still flowered. Bea nodded, and the two of them gave the horses their heads. Side by side, they raced briefly up the pasture, trampling docks and dandelions, drumming the thin turf; and Clarice was unnerved, even startled until she felt her odd confidence that Martin could look after her.

She took the moment to heart and made too much of it. If she was at one with nature she could look after everyone. She got it into her head that she and Martin created a strenuous tunnel, floored with grasses, overarched with sky – an endless chaste interim which nothing had power to smash. As long as she continued it meant no hideous development could prevent June leafing safely into July.

Then how slow was each evening, the house a watch-tower, tentatively fortified. Alone with her father, the sleeping puppy twitching in his basket, the Belgian clock on the mantelshelf, she waited. Her sense was strained, on guard for the peal of village church bells, alert for the rumble of naval gunfire off the Naze, or the diving scream of incoming bombers. She and her father lived from bulletin to bulletin, eating what Ethel Farmer had left them, or what Clarice herself prepared.

Just before dusk he'd go up to the gabled east room where the shotguns now stood loaded, propped ready beside the window frames, to take his final scan of the horizon; and she'd go up with him, throwing open the casements on the darkening view. She'd look east for flares or signals. Her sentinel thought leapt over the hedgerow pickets to inspect the chain of Martello towers strung out only a few miles away along the shore from Felixstowe, built once for this eventuality. She pictured the scatter of defenders, nursing their guns in hastily installed concrete emplacements, she conjured the mysterious wireless transmitters at Bawdsey or Little Oakley, skeletal minarets beside the fraying river mouths. So she drew a mental thicket of mines and barbed wire about her. It was as much as anyone could do.

Evening by evening, above the silhouetted elms, there was no change except the moon dropping back towards the full. It fattened, perfected, began its wane, and disappeared. In the breathless air, nothing else told the season's passage, nothing else moved or gave. There was only ever the pair of bats who hunted above the garden, wobbling in the gloam. Sometimes she heard the cries of swifts arcing high overhead. Highest of all, but only if she attuned to it, there was always the distant patrol of planes. Another dusk would grow gradually dark, and the two of them, father and daughter, would go down again to draw the blackouts.

Later, in a bedroom still full of the day's heat, the floor-boards settling, the rafters above her clicking under the tiles as they cooled, Clarice slept strangely well, her dreams linked with the dreams of her fellow-countrymen. They really would fight to the last man, woman and child. They had no memory of last month's dead, no grasp of the million and a half French prisoners of war, no under-standing at all of what a panzer division, let alone a con-centration camp, might really mean. Resolutely picturing invasion as scrums and skirmishes on the mud-flats, they closed their minds to overwhelming force. With their sharpened kitchen knives and gallant pitchforks they would never surrender.

So Clarice slumbered in this saving narcotic of mental fight, undisturbed by the Blenheim bombers dispatched overhead. She lived for riding out next day with Bea Bligh, because while she was riding there was no war at all.

OF ALL THE London jugs, Pentonville reckoned itself the spickest and most span. Evacuated briefly at the start of the war, it was thoroughly back in business. The governor was ex-Navy, the place as trim as a warship. Floors were swept and scrubbed; sinks were scrubbed and bleached; brightwork, wherever visible, was spat upon and polished, and then polished again with Brasso, issued by a bald and motherly trusty from the stores. 'Just promise me you won't try drinking the stuff, Victor, it buggers up your insides no end. The tales I could tell *you*!' He leant upon his broom. 'And anyway, what's a first-timer doing in a place like this?'

'Don't know.' Vic shrugged.

'Cock-up, if you ask me, dear.' He stretched out a hand to Vic's arm. 'Know what I'm worried about? I'm worried you won't last. Tell the truth, you're not really built for it, are you, Victor?'

Vic laughed.

'Not up here, I mean.' The storeman removed the hand and tapped his own head with it. The smells of boot black and turpentine, mothballs and disinfectant grew sharp and distinct in Vic's nostrils.

The other inmates lacked colour, or shine. They consisted largely of habitual criminals to whom a stretch was just an occupational hazard. It was a holding job, tacitly agreed to by both sides. As a rule, inmates professed to be unmoved by what they'd done.

Hemmings, Vic's cell mate, had lived a life of cons and fiddles. He'd gambled away the life savings of a score of old ladies on the dogs and horses. He'd had three wives at once. Hemmings had no regrets.

But on hearing the story of his own robbery read out in court, Vic had been struck to the core. The name of the householder, Perlmutter, felt like a millstone about his neck. Mr Perlmutter had been unable to testify in person, owing to internment regulations relating to enemy aliens. Vic's unwitting contribution to the *Reichsführer*'s racial effort came all too readily before his eyes and he hated it.

Pentonville had been purpose-built to reform sinners who would previously have been hanged or transported. The original occupants had lived in enlightened solitary. Sensory deprivation would cause their crimes to rise up before their eyes and horrify them into penitence. Their exercise was a speechless trudge in the yard, their association stifled by a full browncloth face mask, to be worn at all times except when actually in the cell or at religious observance. The pews in the chapel were sectioned off, so that each lost soul might hear only the word of God in the preacher's mouth, and never see his fellow.

That regime had long ago fallen into disuse. Vic was given another gas mask, and occasionally made to wear it; but the old Benthamite rationale, the full-blown Christianity of producing model prisoners – that vision was long gone. Lags doing time were generally law-abiding and well enough behaved, and if they weren't they got six of the cat. Hardly any of them screamed in the night.

Only the hard shell of the original design remained. There were four radiating wings, great brick blades of the old psychological turbine, jointed into the main block, itself the size of a mill. Around the whole, there ran a curtain wall. On the other side of this was Islington, right up close. The tops of buses slid by amid audible street noise, and, in the upper windows of shops, citizens dressed or dusted, enacting the fragments of their ordinary lives.

The inmates learnt not to look. When they were in the yards each concentrated on his sentence. But Vic found the outdoor exercise as soul-destroying as his labour was heartbreaking. By day until teatime he sewed mailbags, sitting on the communal benches. He did his turn – until his hands became as blistered and raw as the next man's.

A nagging infection in his index finger led to his transfer to different work. He was moved to a little shop down in D Wing where they made the cats and birches ordered by the prison service as a whole; for it was Pentonville that supplied the nation's deterrence. Clinks, cop shops, and other establishments were all equipped from the single source. Vic learnt the packing of twigs for effective scarring, and the tight knotting of ropes.

Occasionally, in the early months, the craftsmanship of making whips took his mind from despair. Sometimes it was almost soothing to handle the materials, to see, in a shaft of sunlight, ends neatly trimmed, handles turned off and sanded down. It reminded him of the boatyard. That routine and somewhat despised part of his life came often to mind, when it had been up to him to make good the damage to a swim bow, to reset the sprung timbers of a flat bilge, to judge by eye the set of a sternpost – once upon a time. He'd been a man to choose just the right piece of seasoned elm for the crook of a knee. He would rough-saw the piece across the scarred trestles and then clamp it up in the vice to be planed and shaved. There'd be an apprentice with him, looking on, learning his trade down to the smallest detail.

It was an old, unlettered tradition. Vic had once presumed to think of grander vessels; now a host of circumstances cried fool to that. He wondered what it was that had cut him off from his class. He'd sought to replace the manual world he came from with the intellectual – and with Clarice.

Vic was permitted one visit per month, and one letter. In July, his parents came. It was a shock to see them. The last time had been in court, where they'd sat next to Tony and Phyllis. There, the faces had been only partially distinct, up in the public gallery. The little group were remote signifiers of all he'd once known and held dear. Opposite him now, across the table in the prison's visiting hall, his mum and dad seemed closer up than they'd ever been. But their nearness rendered them unfamiliar. His mother's dusted skin was lined, beginning to bag under the eyes. She wore a hat he'd never seen, fastened with pins. Her brown jacket had a hole in the lapel. There was disapproval in her features – in her mouth and folded lips. Her nose jutted, reddening, from a bony ridge between her hazel eyes. Her face seemed to accuse him.

It was his father who spoke, however. 'Yes. Well. You've done it now, haven't you.'

Vic turned to him. Grey had taken his old man. The temples had greyed, the brow had fallen back, greying, the flesh, the moustache, the breath, the collarless shirt, the nondescript jacket, all told not so much of getting on a bit, but of a grey, violated lung that seemed finally to have risen up and declared itself. His father was a ghost. Only the eyes struck out at him. They were wide, pale blue, and panic-stricken.

'It's all right, Dad. I know it's a mess. But it's my mess. I'll clear it up.'

'Clear it up, will you? What about your wife? Your child? You're a grown-up. You've got responsibilities.'

'I said. I'll deal with it.'

'How will you? Eh? How do you propose to do that, in here? What's Phyllis supposed to do, I'd like to know.' He gestured with his hands.

Vic was rattled. 'Dad. Let me do the worrying, will you? I did something stupid and wrong. Now let me try to make up for it. You're angry. All right, you're furious. That's fair enough. I deserve it. And I've let everyone down. But what I can't understand is that you should be frightened.'

'Who are you calling frightened? Me? Is he looking at me?' He turned to his wife.

'No one's looking at you, Perce.' She glared at her son. 'Now listen, Vic. I don't want you making your father ill. Do you understand me? I should think you've done enough, haven't you? I should think you're proud of yourself, this time.'

'This time,' said his father, the gas voice bubbling at the back of his throat. 'It's been the same all along, hasn't it? Look where he's ended up. It's gone too far, this.' He gestured once more, around at the prison. 'Too far, I say. D'you hear me, son? Eh? You want to get some backbone in you . . . you know? Before you . . . before . . .'

Vic stared at the spectacle of his father's distress. 'Before what, Dad?'

'Before it's too damn late. That's all. That's all I've got to say to you, Victor.'

'I shouldn't think it could get much later than this, Dad.'

His mother cut in. 'I think we've had quite sufficient of smart answers.'

'Now you listen, boy. There's nothing the matter with you even now that a damn good hiding wouldn't put right. You've brought disgrace . . .' The words grated, dried. Percy was breathless and beside himself.

Vic's mother lowered her voice to a whisper. 'Look what you've done! Now look! We can't stay.' Immediately she stood up and began to lead her husband away, as he hawked and struggled for air. His father turned back, gesticulating, but his lungs overcame him.

As Vic had grown up in the sooty terraced house in East Ham, not far from the old Jews' cemetery and within smelling distance of the Beckton Levels, two great things about his father had struck him – that the man hadn't got killed on the Western Front, and that he hadn't cracked up. Back then, if his hero father had grown increasingly hard to admire, Vic had felt sorry, and a little ashamed. Now, he was saddened by the scale of his parents' outrage. It seemed he'd brought them nothing but anxiety.

Everyone in the room watched them leave. In paroxysms of coughing his father was shuffled out through the barred door between uniformed guards; and that was the last he saw of them.

Back at his workbench he regretted locking horns. He thought again of the little house out at Laindon, which, if it came to it, would still offer his wife and child a refuge from dive-bombers or phosgene; the crazy little house he'd been building like his father before him with his sweat and strong arms these last years. And Clarice? Within the scrubbed and Brassoed galleries, with their stinks and slops and bad food, he tried to hold on to her.

MY FATHER'S MADNESS was only waiting to show itself. Imagine the hermit crab caught naked on the seabed, stalk-eyed for predators. That was Vic. Madness is a soft fool on the look-out for a hard home.

A sea shell ossifies its own history. That's character. The poor little crab scuttles into its new-old container and is amazed every time at the idea of inner houses, chamber after chamber. Here's a labyrinth that winds in on itself, a tantalising, mathematical design – and that's the danger. For Vic, prison was character. Gritting his teeth, he tried so hard to make himself at home in it. And who'd begrudge the refuge – if the invader comes?

Vic's cell mate, Hemmings, spent his spare time masturbating, or telling music-hall jokes. The man fancied himself a comedian, and was going to tread the boards, when he got out. 'A lot of opportunities, moving about like that. Different towns, a lot of different suckers, women.'

Another prisoner, Sevenbanks, appeared like a poisonous *bêche-de-mer* dredged up from the river and dumped on the wharfside. Sevenbanks kept his back bent, and may have been weeping, much of the time, for whenever he did look up water oozed from his face. A former steam-crane operator, Sevenbanks spoke in short breathy statements, of drink, of tobacco, of weapons. There'd been a woman he'd pursued jealously in a stolen van. 'I fucking loved that bitch.' He hit the back of his free hand against an edge of bricks, and examined it. Blood started to seep from the cuts. He looked up. His other hand sheltered the butt-end of his cigarette. Between thumb and forefinger he fed it to his lips, sucked, and exhaled. 'Understand what I'm saying? She deserved all she got.' His pocked, murderer's face was the mask of madness and grief. Vic persisted with him – in recoil from the barrenness of Hemmings.

He was so lonely that the friendship lasted several weeks. Sevenbanks in the yard craved neat spirit. Over again in a voice choked with intensity, he spoke of the hunting knife he'd owned. How he'd fucking loved that bitch. Vic, too, waited for a visit from Phyllis that never came. But the man's mind was impenetrable; all their dialogue was confusion. It was suddenly Vic's task to keep violence from bursting out. 'See that screw over there?' Sevenbanks pointed towards the officer on duty. 'Look out for me, will you? That's the one who's trying to wind me up. I can't guarantee that fuckcr's safety.'

'Look out for you?'

'He's mine. You're mine. If you open your mouth you're fucking Smithfield, mate. I fucking loved her.'

Eventually, Vic broke away. But of all the shells he'd tried crawling into Pentonville was his hardest yet. The trusty had been right – he wasn't built for it. Soon he plunged like a burning soul in the darkness, and any link with Clarice was stretched to breaking point. He felt as though some parachute had failed to open, as though a vortex had caught him in its winds and the beauty of the entire night sky was squeezed into a retreating circle high above. Pentonville drove him in on himself, which was just what it had been designed to do. Among all that criminal congregation Vic's past alone rose up guiltily before his eyes, until he became walled off and quite blank to other people. But the more the crab huddles into its perfect form, the more perfect, and heartbreaking, the craziness.

My poor father grew quite certain that all his science had come true, and had turned against the world. Only nature's laws were being enacted – simple thermodynamics. The human body was a mere heat engine to be driven and then scrapped; a Nazi victory was guaranteed by the same equations he'd studied on his way to marine engineering. No atom could subsist; even the laws of motion had unravelled. It was inside him, this legend of disaster. He'd embraced it just as he'd embraced Phyllis, and both had seized on him, turned him robber and looter. They'd shipped him here to Pentonville, and were preparing to destroy him. He longed to pre-empt them. The flesh itself, the strength of his own body, was a prison.

Vic's spiritual collapse was a physical sensation, literally crushing. As he exercised with his fellow gaolbirds in the wedge-shaped yard, the weight of the whole building, part cathedral, part warehouse, part factory, seemed to tower over him, and he longed for it to fall. He became a prey to extreme gravity, whose force bore him downwards, ever downwards, and a voice whispered, 'Find a way, think of a way. Then you'll be free of me. It's what you want. If you won't do it, I will' – as if prison weren't sufficient payment, as if the governor, with his whips and chains, could not lay on tyrannically enough.

Though he was suicidal my father hung on. In the inmost chambers of the shell, the borderland, character turns madness into dreams. One night Vic dreamt he and Clarice walked beside a river. The scene was oppressed and monochromatic, the path overgrown. Then, in the far distance appeared a green field, unreachable, smaller than a postage stamp. Its colour was startling, its mood was joy. He was aware of her closeness, her naked breast just resting in the palm of his hand.

After that he followed his dreams in a knowing trance. He'd stalk and catch them. With the stub of a pencil in a schoolroom exercise book he scribbled his dreams down; and began to uncover the mechanics of illusion, the recurring motifs, the coy puns and tricks, the symbols and displacements by which coincidence meets design. In the midst of despair he became fascinated with despair's by-products.

Immediately, time vanished. The war didn't matter; there were always planes overhead. The attacks on the airfields – what were they to him? He held the key. His own mind grew so absorbing that he spoke only when he had to, and spurned even the dangerous Sevenbanks.

He learnt to write in the dark. An extraordinary corpus began to accumulate in his notebooks. That is how I know him. There were visions in which he flew high and effortless over the exploding cities of Europe. He saw encrusted flowers, and glittering, transcendent souls. Trees and animals told him their languages. Polish prisoners confessed their torture, spoke of suffocation and of the fires he'd started, of meals with his parents in which his own poor dad returned full of bullet holes and spoke too calmly of the trenches. There were prophetic dreams, so that Vic set down moment for moment some trivial episode which would come to pass in the yard the following day. There was his wife, in various shapes, and Clarice. Clarice alone could save him, if he could prove his worth. Savages danced. They were sacrificing animals and she was not Clarice at all, never had been, but Phyllis and all women were the same. His morale failed. For behind her was always Jack, calling out. And Vic could never reach him. No one in the prison knew or guessed what inward visitings Vic's firm-set, good-natured features concealed.

Nightmares began. The earth split and roared under his feet. He was pursued with flames by hooded figures, by secret police. Now it was him with a stick beating her and the boy to death. A body was buried; his grandmother was hanging.

Still he continued, dashing himself into the abyss. Ever further behind his own frontal bones, he was gripped by the shadow play inside his skull that made the faces of his fellow prisoners disappear. Some great revelation was on the point of bursting through. The antidote to suicide, a kind of satisfaction – of madness intermixed with one spark of grace – preoccupied him. Nothing could touch him. He lay where he belonged, beyond bombs or morality, winding his wit and intelligence into the terrible freedom of the night. Once, he dreamt of the stigmata: Christ's blood streamed from his palm. It was a triumph, of sorts.

THE SUMMER FLOWERED around Clarice. Suspended, it pollinated and burst. The streaked grass bleached to straw; empty seed heads rattled. There were giant thunderstorms, and then the corn leapt, and hedgerows rioted; but there were also mornings overcast and shorn as the hayfields, and the pinprick raids lulled folk to believe the enemy was a familiar.

Clarice heard the attack on Ipswich. The Harwich guns opened up at last. But every time she took Martin out with Bea and the mare, clouds of moths and butterflies wafted up in front of her, the ground chirred, the sky chattered and sang. She hardly dared breathe; only she must continue doing exactly what she was, not varying the least detail, keeping vigil with insouciance, lest the motion jar.

Her father's pledge held, too, despite his tremors, and July slipped away – a month, a whole month. There was even a peace offer from Berlin. No one cared, no one noticed, so rapt the mood, so fast the resolution. The charm, it seemed, was universal.

In the second week of August, Bea Bligh discovered she was pregnant. She was forbidden categorically to ride. Clarice was distraught.

'Why not? Why not? It's nothing yet. No bigger than a bug.' The tension broke and she was quick with emotion.

'He has no right. Don't you see? No right at all.' She saw herself strewn on the Pin Mill road, neatly punctured with a small red hole in the centre of her chest. She wore a white blouse and her wrap-around grey skirt. In her hand was the four-ten, its one shot discharged too late into the face of the stormtrooper. On her feet were tennis shoes.

Bea was angry with her. 'Actually, it was my doctor. He says it would be a risk. It makes a difference, don't you think?'

'Yes, of course it does. It changes everything. I was being selfish, that's all. I really am sorry, Bea.'

'You can still go out.'

'What?'

'Take Martin on your own. You'll be all right, I should think. Shouldn't you?'

Clarice was swept again, this time with gratitude. 'Are you sure?'

'Of course. Go up whenever you like. The parents won't mind. And you'll help Patrick groom. They approve of you, anyway.'

Clarice took Martin the next day, though by noon there were ominous reports on the news. The ground she knew so well with Bea Bligh felt suddenly dangerous. Supposing the horse went lame, supposing he was spooked and threw her; supposing, with Bea out of the way, he intended to lead her astray only to make a fool of her, charging off at his own whim across wheatfields, over antiglider obstacles, past the army camp, and unstoppably by highway and byway, until he came to the undefended truth: that against an invader willing to incur massive losses the British stood no chance at all. Heat had nothing to do with the sweat that broke out on her.

Martin, however, was impeccable. The ride was without incident. On her way back she glanced behind her. The southern horizon, in a glaze around the sun, was scribbled with white twists. She guessed they rose from Kent and the Thames Estuary, and was suddenly breathless, her lungs constricted. She felt the weight of her blonde hair bobbing in its net against her neck. For a second, panic held sway. Then her horse moved forward, and the prosaic fact that she could not but go forward with him was oddly inspirational – one of those moments when the commonplace appears brimful with meaning. Her fear ebbed. She was reminded of Phyllis's lie on the gravel drive in front of the Riley Lynx. A path *could* open, even into danger.

The next day there was nothing. At Knap's covert she risked a canter, collecting the horse between her hands and legs and willing herself down into the saddle. She didn't pull up until the fence with Appleby's, where she waved to the haymakers on the other side and Martin snorted to the heavy, shaggy creature that pulled the machine. She patted his neck, turned, and cantered back. Hither and thither they tired each other out. Behind her she heard the clack of the mower. A gull flew across her line of sight. Nothing else.

On 15 August, the usual paths led them down to the riverside, and Martin ambled along by the incoming tide. Overhead there were vapour trails, straight and directed seaward. At the fruit farm Clarice came across Dolly Hayman wearing a flowered overall and work gloves. She was on the point of going to help in the orchards, but offered tea. Standing beside Clarice's horse, she alluded briefly to her news. Her sons had just been called up, her husband was picking damsons. Her ridged forehead conveyed an air of abstraction.

Clarice dismounted, hooking the reins to the lopped branch of a tree, and was taken once again into the low-ceilinged room with its musical objects, its oil lamps, its excess of old-fashioned furnishings, covers and drapes. The eloquent stillness inside the wooden house moved her.

Sunlight from the tiny windows caught curious Arabian patches where dust motes drifted.

Mrs Hayman lapsed into silence while the kettle was heating, and deployed the tea things with muted ceremony, preoccupied, her grey hair scraped back in a bun, the small carbuncle poised upon her lip.

'I'm sorry,' Clarice said. 'About Ronald and Malcolm. I'm sure they'll be all right.'

'It isn't for us to complain, is it?'

Martlesham was scrambled; the engines overhead made the wooden roof ring and the teacups rattle. They talked resolutely of local matters, neither woman wanting to evoke the crisis. The piano was draped, the lid over its keyboard firmly closed. Clarice sipped her tea. She felt the mood of the room redouble, its peculiar Englishness, the grinning toby jugs and impossible china dogs. Her diamond-paned view on to the kitchen garden and the tennis court beyond looked like some intricate nursery illustration.

But Mrs Hayman remained lost in thought. Aware of intruding, Clarice felt she ought not to have come; and she'd left her horse alone where the planes might have startled him. She finished her cup and stood up awkwardly to leave.

It was then she mentioned the last time. How lucky she hadn't persuaded his parents to let Jack, the little boy, come to stay with her at Pook's Hill. Instead of rescuing him from bombs that had failed to fall, she would have taken him and placed him right in the firing line. So it seemed now.

Straight away, she could have bitten her lip with the woman's two sons destined for that same predicament, likely as not – the firing line; but Dolly Hayman looked relieved, and her face brightened at the mention of the child. She remembered how he'd cried at the cello.

'It's certainly as well he stayed in London, as it's turned out,' she said. 'Which goes to show you can never tell, can you?'

'No, indeed, Mrs Hayman.' Clarice fidgeted.

Mrs Hayman hesitated. 'That little boy told me such an unusual thing,' she said.

'Oh?'

'He was here on his own, you remember, while you and that couple played tennis. I gave him a tidbit and we stroked the cat. Then, just as I was settling him down – on the settee by the window it was, the sun coming in on his hair, bless him, quite an appealing little fellow if not for his table manners – he started fussing somewhat. You know the way they do when they're wanting a nap. I said his mummy and daddy would be coming in soon from their game.'

Dolly Hayman got up as though the story were over. She disappeared into the kitchen. Seconds passed. Then, holding a knitted tea cosy, she came back and sat down with it still in her hand, plucking at its stitches with her nail. Clarice waited.

Eventually, Mrs Hayman resumed. 'And do you know what he did next? His eyelids were getting so heavy he could hardly keep them open, poor mite.' She gazed at the glinting air in front of her. 'He nodded his head, quite deliberately, like this . . .' Mrs Hayman imitated the movement and smiled. '. . . and said the most extraordinary thing. He said, "My daddy's in Pentonville. He got three years." And the next second he was asleep.'

'Are you quite sure?'

'Certain, Clarice. It struck me at the time. And then I must have put it out of my mind because I didn't know what to make of it.'

'Was it some casual phrase, do you think? Some joke?' She had difficulty standing. She was surprised to hear her voice carrying on, apparently normal. 'Children pick up all sorts of nonsense, don't they? A thing of that kind, maybe?'

'It was with such conviction, you know. He looked me straight in the eye. And it shook me, dear.'

'Yes. I can imagine.'

'But, you see, I didn't forget it. I know you must think I'm a foolish old woman, perhaps even a cowardly one, but it stayed in my mind. You're the first person I've told.'

'Not even Boss?'

'It doesn't do to repeat things, does it, and I haven't liked to. At least not that kind of thing. As if he had any notion of what he was saying, poor child. But I think, now, that perhaps you ought to know, dear.'

'Yes. Thank you. Perhaps I should. I've never thought you were foolish. Or cowardly.' She laid a hand on her neighbour's arm.

'No mother likes to lose her sons.'

'We've no reason to jump to conclusions, have we?'

'About that other matter. I did think you ought to know.'

Martin had been unruffled by the aircraft. Riding awkwardly out of the woods and back up to Bligh's farm, Clarice glanced up. This time the sky was filled with a clear calligraphy. She could even see the planes; one, two . . . three shot down even as she pulled up her horse. It was beyond belief.

Then out of nowhere came a sound that built, as she waited, into an unearthly screaming – and she saw Stukas going down on to the Martlesham airfield; she actually saw the bombs released as the planes dived, and heard the thump, crump, thump of the explosions, the very same terror weapon here as in Guernica, Warsaw, Rotterdam. Martin's ears went back. He hopped sideways and whinnied. So close, the battle here over Ipswich and the sea off Harwich Harbour.

The war, like the first high cloud streaks of a cyclone, was sending formal notice of itself. That night neither she nor her father could contemplate sleep. They stayed up late playing cribbage and turning the radio dial around the short-wave stations. Amid hisses and crackles, she found Morse code, and voices in strange languages, but no kind of an explanation. And Vic was in Pentonville. . . ?

THE WEATHER REMAINED perfect. Battle came again the next day, and again, and again. Saturday, cold, overcast, brought only temporary respite; the following week's skies stood open again. In the South, under the sun's traverse, the edge of the Kentish air engagements painted white trails upon blue after pale ceramic blue.

Still every afternoon Clarice took the horse out, but she could bring herself to do no more than walk him on the higher ground. Like her neighbours, she was possessed with the urge to look up. Quite often, as the fight spilt away from its centre, specks of black wheeled, and silver glints corkscrewed miles above in a silent, blinding spectacle. The only accompaniments were birdcalls and the ratchet of grasshoppers, or the occasional gust stirring dry leaves. The tractor in the lane puttered to and from the harvest and Martin grew irritable.

Clarice was amazed by what she saw. Her fate was in those inscrutable white characters, that leaked and drifted with the winds while the shaven earth baked below. Always her father was waiting by the wireless when she returned, with an old dog-eared volume of Milton open on his lap by which he hoped to make sense of war in heaven. Bombs fell on suburbs. The six o'clock news relayed a daily balance sheet of Heinkels, Dorniers, Junkers and Messerschmitts, as against Hurricanes and Spitfires.

At the end of August there was low flying over Pook's Hill itself. The morning was shattered by the diving whine of two engines. All the breakfast crockery juggled to machine-gun fire, and an unexpected hail peppered the roof. She ran outdoors with her father, to see a raider being chased out to sea. Around its fuselage a smoke cocoon was billowing, through which the incongruous wings stuck out on either side. Both planes were gone while the air still pulsed with their roar. Only when she glanced down did Clarice appreciate that she'd nearly been killed – by the fall of spent cartridges and shrapnel-like debris that lay all around her. One piece was hissing and steaming in the dew.

Hitler spoke. She and her father heard it flashed one teatime. They gathered the full details at nine. The man of destiny had waited three months for Britain to stop night bombing. Such handiwork – by the English air-pirates – would be repaid one hundred fold, so help him God. The hour was coming when one of the two combatants would break. It would not be National Socialist Germany. He'd raze the English cities to the ground. 'In England, they are filled with curiosity and keep asking. "Why doesn't he come?" Be calm! *Er kommt! Er kommt!*' Clarice turned the dreadful voice off.

'Well, old thing,' her father mocked. 'That sounds like it. He means to do it. We'll soon have that swine Wellbridge ringing the church bells. *Judenrein*, they call it, don't they?' He looked quite blanched, so odd – the first time she'd seen him without the colonies in his cheeks. 'Shall I see you down to Manningtree right away and get you on that train?'

She stared at him. 'Train to where, Daddy?'

'Anywhere. Anywhere away from here.' He gripped the arms of his chair.

How rejected she felt. '"If the Invader Comes, Stay Put."'

'They've been wanting non-combatants out of here for weeks.'

She explained carefully, patronisingly. 'We only know now that it's definitely coming. We don't know where. They've been going hardest for Kent and Sussex with the air raids, haven't they? Then that's probably where they'll come ashore.'

'Inconceivable they won't hit Harwich, or Ipswich, at least with a raiding party. Let's not pretend, darling. Talk about home to roost: the blunder's mine and it looks the finish. While there's any chance of a train left running, I want to get you away to London.'

'Razing cities to the ground?'

'Talk!'

'Talk!' she echoed. 'Croydon. Wimbledon. People panicking already in Kensington shops. And Stepney, was it? Women wetting themselves at the sound of the sirens.' She struggled to come up with more telling horrors. 'You call them talk?'

'Darling! Don't you see?' He pointed at the radio. 'It's the airfields that are strategic. The rest is,' he spread his hands, 'unfortunate. No matter what *he* says to try and frighten us, London isn't the target. Paris wasn't. Londoners know it. If he's got any sense and he means to invade, he'll keep on at the airfields. It stands to reason.'

She twisted her hair. 'So this is the Pike strategy, is it?' Infuriating, his flush of logic – and after their shared vigils. 'I'm to be shipped off while you play soldiers with your old gun.'

'Don't be bloody difficult, darling. This probably won't be any place for a woman in a couple of weeks' time. Even a couple of hours. Who knows? I should have thought your going was obvious.'

'It's not what we agreed!' she cried, getting up. Her chair scraped at the floor.

'I don't remember us agreeing anything.'

'Precisely! You're not a combatant either!'

'Don't take that tone with me.' Blotches were returning to his face; his knuckles on the chair arms were white.

'Well, I'm most certainly not going. I've always had to be the one who goes, and I'm not being it again.' She stamped her foot.

'You most certainly are.' He pulled himself up to confront her.

'And leave you here, silly man, not knowing what's happening, to be shelled to bits, bombed, God knows what. The very best case would be a lot of rude soldiery tramping their boots through Pook's Hill with no one to look after it. Brewing up their whatever they call it. Bivvy.'

They both laughed suddenly. But Clarice seized the initiative. 'He needs air supremacy, does he? Has he got it? No! Anyway, where would I be supposed to stay. The Ritz?'

But her father turned towards his walnut bureau, as though the military discussion were settled. There was a letter on the open flap. 'You'll go to Phyllis's. I've written to her. Air supremacy! If he hasn't got it already he damn nearly has.' He swung round at her, suddenly blazing. 'The only thing telling us what's what is that box, Clarice!' He pointed again to the dull bakelite of the wireless. It sat innocently on the Pembroke table by the window, on its beige doily. 'We know what the bloody BBC chooses to tell! Don't you see? If he caught the French completely napping, why not us? Since matters have exceeded credibility, I've also written to your grandmother.'

'Granny Tyler. Without telling me?'

'Yes.'

'Why?'

'Why what?'

'Both! Why Phyllis and why without telling me?'

'You'll do as you're told!'

She was ready to weep with frustration. It was like an episode from her early teens, about some boyfriend, perhaps, or a late-night jaunt to a Malayan cinema. 'Over my dead body!' she yelled.

'Exactly. That, or worse.'

'Oh! For that comforting thought much thanks!'

'Clarice!'

She left, slamming the sitting-room door, stamping as loudly as she could up the stairs and into her room. It grew dark and she sat alone in the murk. Disconnected images of Vic presented themselves, but she was too wrought to assemble them. She couldn't think, she could not hold on to her mental processes. Something prevented her from placing one notion against the next. At last she undressed and cast herself into bed.

Later, she heard her father come up to his own room. He didn't knock or say good-night. She lay awake, still furious at his betrayal, and astonished that tonight of all nights – *the* night indeed, for perhaps he was right – she was tucked up in her foolish flannel nightie with the little orange and blue flowers and neither of them was in the east bedroom manning England's defences.

Disinclined to relent or make the first move, however, she lit a candle to read by. But from the assortment of favourites on her shelf she couldn't choose the one particular book with which to be defeated. It was very provoking. About midnight her temper drained away and a cramped little terror caught up with her again, rising up from her belly in waves of anguish. Her temples throbbed, she felt faint. Her father was right. The kill ratios on the wireless ... the battle might already have been lost. Hitler's boast – it could mean only one thing. What voice would come from the sea, the air, tonight?

But not all the legions of the damned would induce her to seek refuge with Phyllis. Since there was little possibility of sleep, she'd inform her cousin of the fact. She'd write to Phyllis directly.

By the flickering light at her dressing-table, with an old dip pen that blotted from the ink bottle – because her elegant Parker was nowhere to be found – she began to write, and only in the letter did she rediscover quite how much the lie Phyllis had practised against her had hurt, and quite how bitter she was towards her cousin. Good manners seasoned her diatribe of home truths with last thoughts, even appeals to reason. But *by the time you read this*, or *if this letter should ever reach you* made the scribbled testament read vexingly like a suicide note – though it lasted for three pages.

The only profit was that the fair construction of her dislike tired her out, so that finally she slumped over Robin Townely's scented notepaper and prepared to get back into bed, beyond worrying, beyond listening out for the bombardment. She scrawled a final line, *and remember me, won't you, with all affection to little Jack*. That at last gave the matter of Pentonville a chance to state its case. 'Of course. Heavens! "He got three years." I'd better go, then.' She fell asleep.

INSIDE THE CELL there were stifling ridges of sound in the darkness. Vic woke and for a moment was flummoxed. Of course it was Hemmings, snoring, three feet above him in the upper bunk. He listened intently for guns, or the drone of planes, but there was nothing beyond the breathy stertor of his cell mate. He knew where he was – the slop bucket stank in the heat. But the prickle in his eyes was not from ammonia fumes – it came from the dream that had woken him.

He yanked the side of his mattress up against himself and reached a hand down under his own weight. The school notebook with its slight nap, worn to the touch, was lodged on the wire support. He extracted his pencil from its wedge in the corner of the bed frame. Sitting up with all the practised adaptation of a blind man, he fingered for the cornered page, settled his stub against the paper, and, between his faint notches, began a line of careful but completely invisible characters.

A phrase lingered in his mind: 'the six-footed serpent'. The vision had been intoxicating, magnificent. A man was preaching from the pulpit above the left side of an aisle, the sermon a rousing affair, full of gesture and rhetorical effect. The people in the nave listened intently, craning forward in their Sunday best, worthy men, soft-haired children, the wives in coloured hats. At one point they applauded, and were on the point of bursting out in chorus; but Vic was aware of a region below the tiled floor's emblematic designs, beneath the stones and brass plates inscribed *To the memory of*. In the crypt the sinners groaned in hell. He saw them, strapped to a huge upright gear which rolled and creaked on its axle like the wheel in a wooden fair. The scene, so crabbed and medieval, was like an old woodcut; and still the preacher preached on, in his suit and gown, speaking eloquently of the modern world and the life to come. His meaningless words thumped and spattered above, like opinionated rain.

An engraving came to life. A naked man, mute, appealed directly out of torment. Eyes bulging, he stared at Vic, trying to speak. Clamped on to his back, partly concealed, and gripping the arms from behind, a hideous shape forced him to stagger. Flames started up through cracks in the dungeon floor. Some inkling crossed Vic's mind of a plate in a library book. His gas mask hung from the foot of his bed. He sniffed, wondering whether to put it on, and turned the page of his notebook to write up the next part of the dream. Beyond the preacher now, he was approaching the altar by himself. Some significant image, a womanly thing, dominated the roseate apse. Tears filled his eyes. He could only sink to his knees; at which point the dream had ended.

He stowed the book back in its hiding place beneath him. The dream was a prize specimen, a collector's item. Flies, fat bluebottles, zigzagged back and forth over the bucket. The bed wire hurt his hand. Hemmings turned over, his very real and swinish breath interrupted by the spectre of a phrase, 'Bag deem Wensdy.'

Vic fell back to sleep. A face in a cockpit was surrounded by a ring of flames. There was a man in the cell. It was Hemmings pissing into the bucket; but feathers, the white-tipped pinions of some American eagle, hung from the outstretched sleeves. He was awake again, thinking of the motor bike and the injured Jewish man. There was no other sound than his own blood pulsing and the rough breathing of his companion.

A glimmer of light came from the barred window in the top of the whitewashed wall. The scribble of birdsong touched the eaves of the silent prison – even Hemmings had snored himself out. There were no more dreams. Except one half-formed thing that was scared away by the screw hammering on the door at six fifteen. 'Hemmings! Warren! Hands off cocks! On with socks!' The weight of the prison was crushing.

IN THE MORNING, of course, everything was in its place. There'd been no assault, no bell-ringing; at breakfast, the invasion was once again conjecture. She announced her intention. 'I don't mind going to Granny Tyler for a night or two. It'll break the monotony, at any rate.'

Her father mopped his moustache on a crumpled handkerchief. 'You, my dear, can be extremely provoking. Still . . .' The sentence was left unfinished.

As it turned out she had to waste a whole day applying for a coastal region pass. Neither she nor her father had encountered that formality before. To be first turned away at Manningtree Station dismayed her, and she wondered what was she thinking of. She'd hardly seen a prison, let alone been inside one. What if the train was hit in a raid? Supposing she didn't love him after all? What if he'd committed some really loathsome crime and she still did? Surely, the boy Jack had made it up; or Dolly had muddled it.

She filled in forms and queued in Ipswich for her documentation, which took yet another day to come through. Therefore it wasn't until the 7 September, the Saturday, that Clarice drew into Liverpool Street in a train that had been several times delayed.

The mid-afternoon skies were cabled with barrage balloons. Still she felt confident that she'd left danger behind, and might, like Londoners, go about her business. The raids over London had so far seemed nominal, almost incidental – all the way it was simply the prison that had preoccupied her.

She looked at her watch. The delays had upset her plans. It was bound to be after visiting hours. She was half relieved. It was late, too, for department stores. Her best plan would be to catch a bus straight out to her grandmother in Mile End, for what real difference would a day make? On the crowded platform, she toyed with the idea of a news theatre, or a film. She thought of Vic. She thought how foolish she might appear. Emerging between the stacked sandbags of the station concourse and into Bishopsgate, she stood for a moment there on the pavement. All at once a haunting, mechanical tone rose from behind the rooftops opposite. It was the alert. It levelled out to a prolonged wail, far louder and more unsettling than the sirens she was used to hearing go off from the Ipswich quayside or from Bucklesham Wood. Some of the people around her stopped and stared upwards. Clarice looked too, taking her cue from them.

There was nothing to see. A woman said it was another false alarm, most like. A second agreed: twice in half an hour. An elderly gentleman was more circumspect, yet made no move. Nobody seemed quite to know what to do, nor how precipitate to be this time. No one carried a gas mask.

Then, leaking into the siren sound, from far off over the dirt-stained, sun-warmed buildings, came a peculiar rhythm of crumps and bangs. It was as though her thoughts and actions had acquired a strange music, some eastern accompaniment. She imagined an idle hand drumming its giant fingers. Almost immediately, a drone, felt rather than heard, rose, and continued on, as if it had always been there: a remorseless, depressing grind, swelling beside the station and throbbing into the shadows through which traffic still passed. And suddenly planes were above her, slow-moving black crosses in the hazy sky. They held a formation out of the blue to her right, one wave and still another crossing the urban gully. She stood transfixed, like the crowd beside her; and all the while the distant explosions continued, beating out the same dull, thumping tattoo.

'The docks!' The man next to her spoke, almost a whisper. At his voice, bodies moved around her, scattering. Clarice moved too; but she wasn't in the least scared. She was amazed how calm she was. One direction she might have taken was exploding; very well, she'd go elsewhere, back into the station. Perfectly composed, she walked down into the tube. And incredibly, the man behind the underground ticket window was still at his post. In fact, everything was quite normal. Travellers were passing the queue she stood in. No one was running. No one here below seemed yet to have grasped that the sword brandished so long over the city was falling. She said the first destination that came into her head.

'Pentonville, please.'

'Bona fide traveller, are you?'

'Well, yes, I suppose I am.'

'King's Cross, The Angel, or Caledonian Road?'

'What?'

'Pentonville Road or Pentonville Prison?'

'The prison,' she said.

'Caledonian Road. Fourpence.'

It was on the train that she discovered her body shaking. Still, she had no sense of danger. It was as though her link with her own sensations was anaesthetised. Clattering along in the dark tunnel, insulated from the facts, and from the other passengers, what she did feel was embarrassment. Should she mention what was going on above ground?

At King's Cross she scuttled for her connection and was horrified by the trip, trip sound of her own high-heeled shoes. She expected any moment the white tiles above her to be ripped by warheads.

Then, too soon at Caledonian Road, she forced herself to get into the lift. A stray thought plagued her: her eardrums would shatter from the blasts. She'd failed to bring earplugs or wear a cork on a string for her mouth. The blood would spoil her blouse, and her tailored jacket. In the ticket hall a crowd of people milled. Station staff herded them one way. Two wardens and a tin-hatted official marshalled them back again with shouts. She saw the sandbags of the station exit framing the outside light and made a movement towards it. A ticket inspector blew a whistle. He shouted at her. Didn't she realise there was a raid?

She was breathless; the floor seemed about to give way beneath her. 'I want the prison, please.'

The man was scornful. He swore, and told her she wanted her head looking at. But she insisted, and he let her go.

The drone was as before; the street deserted. Cars and lorries stood where they'd been abandoned by their drivers. She looked southward along the wide channel of the Caledonian Road. The bombers were clearly visible, flying upstream in tight formation. Now they broke, climbed, and wheeled away into the sun.

CLARICE STEADIED HERSELF, and walked towards them. She came upon the prison suddenly. Forbidding, set back from the main road behind a preliminary wall, it appeared rather ashamed of itself, sullen, stained. She made her way boldly down the cobbled drive inside the first barrier. She came to a great studded gate, like the entrance to a castle, with a minute postern door sealed in it. She knocked, and rang the bell. But they wouldn't let her in. And all the while the planes came overhead and the unbelievable crackle and drum continued from the other side of the city.

She walked up and down the street outside. A man wearing an armband blew his whistle at her from his bicycle; she nodded and waved. A woman yelled from an opposite window, calling her a silly cow and ordering her to get under cover. Clarice crossed and stepped into a doorway.

The raid continued. She regarded the sheer quantity of aircraft in the churned sky. She vied only with a couple of tarts for possession of the street. She walked for an hour, more, until the raid had spent itself. Back and forth, as the city came to life again, she passed the prison three times; and then wandered away into the evening on aching feet – until the bells of a church started ringing, and were taken up there, and there, and yet again there. The invasion had started.

Then the pavement was all eggshell, and she realised that her grandmother's house had been under the flight path of the attack. It dawned on her that she'd been witness to a catastrophe so great that whole fixtures and assumptions of her life had been recast. She had nowhere to go. What was dangerous and what wasn't? The sirens wailed for the all-clear while the bells still rang, the two sounds clashing with one another.

The corner of Holloway and Tufnell Park Roads held a wretched little flea-pit Odeon. They were showing a film she'd never heard of. She bought herself a ticket in order to rest a while, and found the smoky interior bizarre, the show going on, with the crackling soundtrack, the projector whirring behind her and the blue beams spreading above her head. When she came out it was quite dark, and she'd hardly any recollection of the film she'd just sat through, nor of how long she'd spent there.

Near the prison there was a labourers' café. A sign outside told the way to Highbury Fields. She ordered egg and chips, and sat sipping her tea, listening to accounts from the other customers of what had been happening. They said the docks were on fire, that the Germans had landed. They talked as though she'd always lived there. She explained her life to a couple of road menders. Another man, a brewery worker, knew the names of every ship in the P&O fleet, and the Blue Funnel Line, and could remind her of the details of those she'd sailed on herself.

She became absorbed in talking. Before she knew it, hours had gone by. Her watch must be wrong; but at her ear it ticked, the delicate little beat. Nowhere near ten o'clock, surely. Sirens warned again, and a gaggle of people crowded outside. In the blackout they were shadows beside her, looking up at the sky and trying to read it. The East glowed red, but soon enough, across the sprinkle of constellations directly above her, droning outlines tracked now from this direction; and now, as she waited, transfixed, from that. Once again she heard the irregular muffled beat of explosion after explosion.

They were bombing their earlier fires. She said as much, only to find that her companions had melted away. Then a stray fell with an immense crack not so very far from where she stood, perhaps only half a mile off. She edged along the lightless pavement. If there were shelters locally, she'd no idea where they might be. The fear returned sharp as a blade. The one certainty that loomed against the illumination of distant fires was the prison.

From the sidestreets another stray bomb echoed. So loud. At the great door she rang the bell for the second time that day – a pauper at the workhouse, a beggar at the gate; and to her surprise the postern opened and a hand beckoned her. They let her sit in the office. 'Owing to the unusual circumstances,' the porter said, and grinned. He had a pipe in his mouth. She noticed his stained teeth.

Eventually, she fell asleep in a leather chair in the dimly lit cubby-hole, hardly seeing the hand that lifted the mug of cocoa out of her slackening grip lest it spill on to the pleats of her mauve serge skirt.

'VIC, I DON'T know what to say.'

He stared across the table and knew why he'd kept her image in his heart. It wasn't her beauty, though that to his starved eyes seemed astonishing. But now that he heard it, he realised that everything had preserved itself in her voice. Her speech called his heart out.

When they'd first met, he and Clarice had been immersed, the pair of them, like birds in a duet of chatter. He could have declared anything, anything he wished. She would have received it, taken it to herself and sent it back to him. Before Clarice, he'd never truly spoken to anyone; nor, for all Phyllis's singing, truly heard anyone. Now he was tongue-tied.

'I'm sorry, Vic. Maybe I shouldn't be here. I've pushed myself on you. I thought . . .'

He forced out a sound. 'No. Please. I was sure you were thousands of miles away. Now you're crying.'

'No. You are.'

The tears spilt over. He dashed them away and looked at her. Slightly dishevelled, her blonde hair was escaping its pins; her lips were barely reddened. The natural skin of her face showed through what must have been a hasty powdering. He blinked back more tears.

She rummaged in her bag and dabbed at his face with a handkerchief. A guard's voice warned her off. The lapels of her dark green jacket were crumpled. Embarrassed again, Vic looked around him. He hadn't been in the visiting hall since his parents had come. Now it was Clarice who sat opposite him at an identical oak table. It was the same government issue, too, across which he'd faced Phyllis during his remand.

The vault buzzed with flies. It contained the echoing, awkward talk of severed intimacy. Officers stood around the perimeter, under the barred windows. They reminded Vic of his grammar school, the gowned teachers in East

Ham. He caught up with himself. He slid a glance at Clarice's gloved hand, looking for the ridge of a ring under the fabric. He wondered, ashamed, what he must look like to her, with his shaving cuts and stained clothes.

'We had to come back.'

He blinked again.

'From Malaya. I chose to come,' she said. 'I wasn't sure why.'

'When they said there was a visitor I thought it would be Phyllis, or Mum and Dad.'

'Phyllis came to us. To Daddy and me. Turning up like this out of the blue – it was something Jack said.'

'You've seen Jack? There were bombs last night. Is he all right? They've gone to the cottage, haven't they?' The words tumbled out almost angrily, and he was upset with himself, for she was the last person in the world he would wish to offend.

'I don't know. It was the spring when they came down to us. I haven't seen them since then. Vic, I hardly knew I meant to be here. I almost didn't intend . . . The bombs, you see . . . all last night. They let me stay in the porter's office. They say the docks . . . They let me shelter here.'

'You've been in the prison? In here? Overnight?'

'Don't sound so surprised. Don't say, no place for a lady. Or you'll sound like my father.' She smiled.

Vic plunged his head into his hands.

'I've said something wrong?'

He heard her voice. Slowly he raised his head, and shook it quietly from side to side. 'You smiled. I'm so sorry . . . Clarice.'

Speaking her name recaptured what had passed. He felt so poor, so acutely corrupt. He thought how he must stink of the slop bucket. He couldn't look, unable to make sense of her: the cut of her clothes, her hair, the way she sat. She was lost as she always had been.

'Vic, I did so want to see you.'

'You say you've seen Phyllis,' he repeated. 'They're alive, then.'

'Well, yes. That is . . .'

'After last night?'

'Daddy wanted me to see her. Then the bombing started and I came here. To see you instead.' There was a note of hesitation in her voice. 'Vic. I didn't know if you really existed.'

'I do exist,' he said with a sudden forced laugh. 'I'm doing three years for the stupidest thing in my life.'

'In Malaya something happened . . . Daddy lost what he had – which wasn't much. That's how it's been. There was the old house in Suffolk, you see. But when Jack mentioned his father was in here, I had to come. Phyllis and her husband . . .'

'Her husband!'

'I'm sorry.'

'Please. Tell me.'

He listened like a child. She spoke of Suffolk and the car, of Jack in the Haymans' wooden house, of Phyllis and the man playing tennis. Then of the enchantment she'd been under after the fall of France. She and her father had two guns for the invasion. The East End was on fire.

A handbell rang. The guard called from the front of the hall. She stood, picked up her gloves and handbag. Vic stood too, unable to bear losing her once more. He longed to reach out and touch her. He belonged where she didn't. 'What do you think will happen?' he said. 'About the war,' he added awkwardly, as though already presuming too much.

'If we can hold out,' she replied, 'there's the faint chance the Yanks will come in. That's what they say. A lot of influential Americans don't want to get involved. Who can blame them? But the other day Roosevelt sent fifty destroyers. I suppose it's something.' She held out her hand, but the warder called out.

'Clarice. Dearest. You've seen where I am, what I am. Will I see you again?'

'I couldn't get you out of my mind. All that time I missed you so.' She looked away.

He felt dashed. Her answer was inconclusive. He said, 'They've got to go to the cottage, the two of them. She can take the tandem on her own. Will you tell her that?'

'Phyllis? I'll try. Perhaps I shouldn't have come, after all.'

She turned, then hesitated, looking puzzled. Her mouth twitched. 'I've been sitting in the porter's office rehearsing my lines, would you believe.' Her gloved hand went up to her eye. 'I went out for some lunch – then came back.' She glanced at him and looked away again; then continued, her own voice faltering. 'You'll think me such a fool. . . . You're married, for heaven's sake. Decent girls don't do this sort of thing.' The hint of a laugh. 'It's all been so strange. The war turns peace inside out, doesn't it? Vic, I don't know what to say either.'

He watched her prepare to turn and walk out of the room. 'I fell in love with you, Clarice.'

The screw came across to chivvy her out. 'All right, miss. Come along, then.'

'I love you, Clarice,' he said again. People were looking.

The screw was taking her arm, steering her. The little crowd made up of departing wives, mothers and sweethearts swept around her.

'Then what are we going to do?' Her voice was anguished. 'What are we going to do?'

SHE PICKED HER way eastward. The smoke from at least twenty fires made a dull black haze over the dull black buildings. The filtered sunlight was unearthly. Balloons still floated, like futurist clouds. She loved him; the prison divided them, and there was no more she could do.

A section of the overground District line was running again, an act of defiance. She sat tight until the train's brakes screamed. Through the netted aperture in its window she read the sign for her station. The doors slid open. In Barking's main street a crowd blocked her path. People stood silent in rows, and beyond them wreckage was plain to see. Emergency vehicles – she'd grown used all afternoon to the clanging of their bells – were drawn up: a police car, two ambulances, a parked fire engine. Men in helmets and uniforms emerged from the shrouded centre of activity. Some wore armbands. Water dripped from the tops of their thigh boots, and there was water under her own feet. She was asking directions.

In a parade of similar properties a small shop had its display windows boarded up. Every ledge was covered with a thick layer of black dust. Above the door a sign read 'Wilmot, Trade Weights and Measures', and under a gable end with symmetrical plaster mouldings of Art Nouveau foliage, a small window, shatter-proofed with tape, showed unlined yellow curtains.

In the half-light of the shop's interior two tea chests stood amid the assortment of weighing machines and greengrocers' scales. Upstairs there was dark linoleum, and on the ugly, cluttered table a bowl of innards remained uncovered, while the ever-present flies zipped back and forth. Jack wore a grey shirt tucked into baggy grey flannel shorts; Phyllis drew on a cigarette and pointed to the banisters with her other hand. 'We went under there. They said on the wireless the church bells were a mistake. There's been no invasion. Just this . . . raid. There were hundreds of people in Woolworth's basement . . . Up the High Street. They drowned, apparently. It collapsed on them when it was hit. A burst water main, Saturday shopping. I think the neighbours . . .' She paused. Her hair had traces of fine white plaster dust.

The housecoat hung open showing the white slip underneath. A small pink rosebud was embroidered at the centre of the bust. 'Tony . . . My husband'll be here directly. In fact, I thought you were him.' The hand that flicked ash into a saucer on the table shook slightly but persistently. Clarice noted how the fingers were reddened. A large enamel basin had clothes soaking in it. And then from below there came the rattle of a door knocker. Phyllis flinched.

The whole region was ringed by fires. In the open back of the lorry Clarice sat opposite her cousin. Phyllis crouched in her best clothes – her navy suit, silk stockings, open-toed high-heeled shoes in dark taupe suede, and, perched sideways on her head, an elegant matching hat trimmed with velvet ribbon. The man – she insisted doggedly on referring to him as her husband, though she no longer called him Vic – was starting the lorry with a handle.

Jack held Clarice's arm as the airstream whipped round the cab's edges, buffeting them both. Wedged in with the tea chest and suitcases, Phyllis clung to the pretty hat with one hand. The men Tony Rice had brought with him, Figgsy and Pat, sat at the rear corners, not catching Clarice's eye, but sheltering roll-ups in their palms, and occasionally shouting to one another phrases she couldn't understand. Jack looked up at her, his eyes questioning.

She spoke to him, above the din of the lorry. 'You must have been a very brave boy when the bombs fell, Jack. It would have been quite terrible. You must have been so frightened.'

He stared back, not answering. Then his mouth opened, but he glanced away at the two men slouched in the corners of the tailboard, and closed his lips again. She cupped her hand to the child's ear. 'Yes, Jack. I did see your daddy,' she said. 'I saw him in Pentonville. And he was well, and sends you his love.'

The ride, diverting for damage, took them an hour. A stark new house lay just beyond a town's edge. It stood back from the main road in an untended compound. Weeds and fragments of concrete, wire fenced, gave on to an open field, in the middle of which sat an abandoned cement mixer. Its glowing grey-white shape amid the scrub stole attention away from the new home. It looked like a piece of minor ordnance left by an army's retreat.

As Tony, the husband, turned the key to open the front door, they were greeted by smells of new paint and unaired distemper. 'Upminster,' he announced. 'A laddie owed me.' He looked Clarice up and down and smiled as though in triumph. She hated him.

When the sirens went again, Clarice was with Phyllis and Jack next to the cement mixer in the back yard. The skies were empty. They waited, all three of them, amidst the strewn builders' rubble. Soon, out of the East, the leading planes appeared, drawing towards them above the all-too-convenient river. She caught hold of her cousin and the boy, gripping them tightly by the arms. Frantically, as if each were possessed by the same impulse, they tried to twist away. They were her own flesh and blood. She reminded herself of Vic's concern, and made them look up. 'See,' she said, suppressing the tremor in her voice. 'They're missing us. It's all right here. We really are just out of the line.' A single anti-aircraft battery opened up ineffectually a mile or so to their right.

Phyllis's arm had gone quite limp. Jack was burying his face in Clarice's skirts. She led them round the raw concrete path to the front of the house and held them up, still tightly, an arm around each. Together, they watched until the first wave of bombers, crossing the whole sky to the western horizon now, had passed on to the docks and the crowded East End houses. A drumming began. 'It's all right, Jack,' she said. 'It'll be all right.'

Jack looked back at her. 'Auntie Clarice . . .'

'You could come to me,' she said. 'You do know that, don't you? You could come to me.' She hadn't realised the husband was standing next to them, appearing as if from nowhere.

'Why would he want to do that, eh?' His fine lip curled. 'Isn't what I provide good enough for him? We stick together, our lot, don't we, Jack?' he said across her. 'Maybe we never had two ha'pennies to rub together. Sometimes we've gone hungry, I can tell you that. But we look out for one another. You understand me, don't you, Cousin Clarice?' His tone mocked her. 'We always will. The kid knows where he's well off. Don't you, Jack?'

Clarice stood her ground. She noticed his good suit, hardly creased from the lorry or the move, his smart tie, set in the crisp, perfectly starched collar. He was an attractive man. There remained always something particular about him that made her want to allow for him. She should overcome her dislike. By his own lights he did his best. Hadn't he just rescued his family – as he saw it – and her along with it?

She caught his eye and smiled. 'I just thought it was the least I could do,' she said. 'To offer to help the child.'

He said nothing in return, merely looked at her, half smiling himself. She felt disconcertingly understood.

Later, unpacking with Phyllis, a family photograph emerged from a tea chest. It was wrapped in some pages of the *News Chronicle*: the Tylers, her mother's relations. She saw her grandmother, and Phyllis's mother; and the corpulent father; the two younger sisters Moira and Beryl, and the spoilt, sullen brat of a brother, Morris; beside them all her own mother, Mattie, fey and young.

Phyllis gave her little laugh, almost as though she knew exactly where Clarice had been earlier in the day. 'Love, eh!' she said. 'Look where that gets you. Where it got me, I should say.'

'You did love him, then?' Clarice lifted her eyes and the unacknowledged fact of Vic Warren hung between the two women, undenied. For a precious moment, Phyllis seemed like a lustrous insect on the wrong leaf. Clarice studied her cousin for her true colours.

'I KNOW I can trust you.' Phyllis spoke cautiously.

Clarice made no reply.

Phyllis shifted her posture and fidgeted with her ring. 'Tony'd kill me if I . . .' She gave the little laugh again.

'I know you've only done what was for the best,' Clarice said.

'What they say. "*When a lovely flame dies*".' Phyllis breathed out cigarette smoke through her nose and then sang, shy, self-conscious:

> They said, 'Someday you'll find
> All who love are blind,
> When your heart's on fire, you must realise
> Smoke gets in your eyes.

Clarice could hear the men grumbling outside by the lorry, and the slap, slap of the boy's shoes as he ran back and forth on the concrete. Then Phyllis put her hand to her forehead. 'A fright like me needs a man who can keep her in order. All I want is a quiet life, a bit of peace. You

172

have to settle for how you are, and for how things are.'

'You knew all along?'

Phyllis made no reply. She perched on the edge of a packing case and fumbled inexpertly with a packet of Players. Her fingers still shook.

'Vic thought you might have gone to the cottage.'

Phyllis sneered sarcastically and the trance was broken. 'The cottage. Well, we do have a cottage in the country, it's true, my husband and I. Out Laindon way.' She lit up the fag. 'Bayview,' she said. 'Not that you can see the sea; or the muddy old river, even. But Upminster's a nice area, don't you think? Refined.'

Clarice sighed. The shutters had gone up.

'It's convenient for town. And everything's modern here,' Phyllis continued. She looked out of her new sitting-room window in the direction of the continuing raid. 'I don't think I could bear the country, after all. You have to be so careful these days, don't you? People around you just can't depend on. People who aren't, you know, normal.' There was no way through.

The solitary pitch-black train was a miracle – as if that one moving point on the rail could make her believe London hadn't happened. Clarice caught the connection to Manningtree nearly at midnight, and from there plunged into the dark on Ethel Farmer's unlit bicycle towards father, home, and the two small estuaries between which she'd come to live.

She was in pain. She'd blanked out a scene – Tony.

As she rode, almost gasping, her lungs oddly constricted, she thought of the bodies that had been drowned in the Woolworth's cellar. She imagined the women and children panicking down there in the sealed room as the water poured in. It was as if they alone were the answer to the question of Vic Warren's crime and she was furious with her family, furious with the whole pack of them.

Only at home did the missing image of her journey back from Phyllis's properly develop. Only then did it imprint itself, as it were, in her mind. 'Not good enough for you, aren't we? Don't talk posh enough. You fancy me all right, Miss fucking Pike. You fancy me fucking rotten.' He was giving her a lift. So indebted had she felt – not least for her safety – she hadn't felt the right to cause a scene.

At the same time she'd been intimidated by the almost lightless road ahead. As he'd rammed the shuddering, unladen lorry into narrow country corners or nearly drifted the rumbling back wheels, making the inadequate engine whine and protest, she'd hardly dared move or breathe.

He'd stopped, in the darkness, and forced her. She recalled her fingers clenched on to the lorry's window ledge, and the glint of the razor, and how he'd spoken, all the while in strangely eloquent and coldly flattering detail about what he was doing, and how she'd had it coming, along with all the other posh, stuck-up cunts like her. And she recalled how the words had formed a chain that seemed to have no meaning other than that her life and all her hopes were ended. And then he'd threatened her, vilely, but almost as though it weren't necessary – as though now he knew and was confident she'd neither do nor say anything to anybody. He'd folded the razor and dropped her at the station. 'Brentford. All right?' It was a sneering goodbye.

The word 'rape' formed itself in her mind and then melted again – exactly as the incident itself had done. The thing had happened, and then temporarily dissolved. For the intervening hours since he had put her out of the lorry's cab, the thing had not happened. Even now she could hardly believe in it, nor account for the physical state she was in.

At last the cramps in her chest let go. As her breathing deepened, each detail held so steady there could be no doubt left. She knew she'd been singled out, and was distraught. Surely, on top of everything else, it was just too much. Why her? She'd done nothing wrong. And what had become of people – her own people? Were they suddenly beasts? She'd tried to find Vic; they'd tried to bury him. She'd shown her feelings; Tony had raped her. So it was love they'd wanted to do away with. Yes, she was sure of that now, for the peculiar cruelty of her rape was that it proved genuine the one thing it so ruined. Why had he? How was love so great a threat that the whole world must jar and shudder? Again and again she tried to make sense of it. Eventually, she slept, and her dreams were dark.

When she opened her eyes in her bed at Pook's Hill the dawn was glimmering, but she couldn't imagine the day to come. It was as though she'd been sent back to school and some remorseless old textbook had been opened, whose pages would tell of nothing but the passage of armies and the slaughter of thousands. She slept again for hours, and, reawakening, felt only disgust. In the days and nights that followed, as London was progressively ripped up, she cursed her body, still stained with blood and filth, scrub as she might. For what her desire had conceived as something truly valiant, redemptive, had brought forth nothing but this bitterness.

To her father, she glossed clean over the discovery of Vic. As for the incident in the lorry, she tried to tell him but her voice wouldn't let her. She deleted the offence, behaved as though nothing had happened.

It was the drowned who wouldn't go away. She saw inside their smashed houses, their half bedrooms. She remembered one perverse sink still hanging off a wall. There were dark, peeling corners, cobwebby festoons under broken floors, shaken chimneys, summer weeds exposed through newly shattered courtyards where washing still flapped on the line. She hated England, the

England of Phyllis's family photograph, her own family. She remembered staying with them, and the sneer on the face of that tobacco-stained, beery tyrant of a father, with his waistcoat, watch-chain, and belt; and she doubted even Vic for his involvement with them all.

She couldn't get her minutes to hang together – as though some mechanism at the centre of the world had been smashed. She felt estranged from her father through no fault of his own. It was a condition she had no name for, nor could he make it better.

One thing gave her momentary hope. It was on the fifteenth, when the German daylight raiders were cut to pieces over St Paul's. She sat down to write a letter.

Dear Vic,
I must know what it was you did.

IV

A Secret America of the Heart

NIGHT AFTER NIGHT the bombing crackled and burst. Vic had virtually no view of it, and no means to shelter from it. Nor did the authorities keep their prisoners well informed. In the cells, the sounds were always mysterious. First came the sirens. Then that sinister drone of engines, sometimes so loud and overdriven it seemed the planes were brushing the roof tops. Next the ear-splitting ack-ack, and the kettledrum of hits, the distant thuds, the incongruous jingling of bells, drawn like silver combs through the matted atmosphere. The cell brimmed with noises – maddening percussion.

They told him it was mostly in the East: Limehouse, Wapping and Rotherhithe. The targets were strategic; the shelters were working well. There was no cause for exaggerated alarm on account of anyone's family, certainly not for panic.

Then Clarice's letter arrived, and in it no news of Jack. Hadn't she found Phyllis, then? What if Ripple Road had been hit, and she was just trying to protect him? He considered her request: *I must know what it was you did.* Yes, he must tell her. But the boy? Why hadn't she mentioned him? Then the detonations circled round, dancing towards him, retreating south, or west, swirling north as if a nightly thunderstorm had taken up residence above.

He stilled his nerves, tried to gather his wits, used his monthly letter to promise her an account of his crime – as soon as he could think straight. Meanwhile, he sought to describe the feelings he had for her. He made light of the danger he was in. Pentonville was still far out of the main flight path, he said. Most particularly he asked if she'd managed to find Phyllis and Jack.

Sometimes shrapnel and spent cartridges spattered past the window. He and Hemmings would stare at their own picture-framed patch of night sky. How brilliantly it flared. The reflection of searchlights flickered on the wall opposite, bright enough to scribble his notebooks by. 'Oh, that's what you fucking get up to, then?' Hemmings remarked. After that Vic dared to write openly. His journals grew fierce with reflected fact.

And by daylight, too, he noted the wry smiles, the grim camaraderie. He started talking to people. If the shocked hand could hardly stir the tea, the tongue joked bravely and struck up friendships.

She sent another letter, and they kept him waiting the regulation four weeks to receive it. November – the chance of invasion long past; only this nightly punishment remained as intense as ever. No, she said, she had not found Phyllis or Jack. Ripple Road had been empty, she said, boarded up, and she'd gone from Barking straight back to Suffolk. She repeated her request to know exactly what was the crime that had caused him to be locked away. He read a disconcerting anxiety between her lines.

All he could think of was Jack. Had Phyllis listened to his advice and ridden out to the cabin with the child? He held the letter and shook his head. Surely even Phyllis, if she'd done as he'd asked, would have sent him word that they were both safe at Laindon. Surely she would, if only because, for once, she *had* done as he'd asked.

The details didn't add up. And Clarice was insisting he tell her his crime. He guessed how it might have been once upon a time for his old man, imprisoned in the trenches and quite helpless, trying to compose a letter home while the latest rolling barrage came ever closer. Mistrustful of his wife, he wrote back again to Clarice, first giving her the address of the cabin: 'Bayview', Plot 91, Laindon, Essex. It sounded both grand and foolish – the name-plate had fallen off years ago. Somehow, he doubted she'd ever find the place, even if he dared ask her to go and look.

Then he tried to answer her request. The crime flickered in and out of his head, so hard to pin down. He wanted to hold on to her. She needed to know – yes, he could understand that. But he was afraid to encounter the details. His offence had to do with property, he said. He wrote of his concern for Jack, and tenderly, at length, of his love for her.

The Blitz continued unabated, pausing only when there was low cloud. By the time they gave him Clarice's reply it was well into December. Neither she nor her father had heard anything from Phyllis. Why did he not explain himself? She loved him but was uncertain what would become of her. Or, indeed, of the whole world. Please, Vic.

The full account of his crime lay in a cellar of his recollection like something that would explode if he touched it. It had lodged itself down there since the trial and got buried under dream and delusion. Digging it out would dig out the shame, too; yet he took prison notepaper to his cell and set himself to the task.

One freezing midnight he was trying to tell Clarice the truth. The sirens had just gone again and the Dorniers and Heinkels were right overhead. Then the whole prison seemed to jump. The cell walls, the floor, the pipework all shuddered. So also did Vic's bed frame. High up, the bulb, lit only by the raid, was left swinging wildly on its six inches of flex. He never heard the explosion, and he only remembered the whistling sound afterwards.

A house in Wheelwright Street, round the back of the prison, had been completely demolished – so they said. In the nights that followed, there were about eight other very near misses, and most of the prison windows were shattered. It should have been so simple, this plain confession of his crime, yet even now it kept slipping through his fingers, and his letter still hedged and wandered, snagged this time on whether to implicate Tony or Phyllis. When the robbery's anniversary, Christmas, came – without respite – it was the fact that his victim was a Jew. He was convinced she'd hate him.

Only during the convulsive six-hour incendiary raid of 28 December did his vision finally shift. By the odd light of those apocalyptic fires everything became clear, and he found himself able at last to set into the body of his letter what it was he'd actually done:

> *There is no excuse. I went with another man to break into someone else's house. I put some valuables in a bag and the next thing I knew we were discovered. Someone got hold of me, but I managed to escape. I ran right into the arms of the police.*

Those were the bald facts. As soon as he'd written them he wondered why it had been so hard. They showed precisely what he was, and wasn't, guilty of. He'd been justly imprisoned. He sent it off to her.

AND THEN, STRANGELY, the very next week, he was informed of his impending release. The bars of his cage melted. It was the call-up. On 10 February 1941, they were letting him go. They needed manpower.

He was dumbstruck. He found himself exchanging a flurry of hastily scribbled notes with Clarice as they attempted to make their arrangements. So promptly was Vic outside, in fact, so immediately cast upon his own devices, that he stared and blinked like a newborn. The north wind found blunt-razored skin on his cheeks. It chilled the exposed backs of his hands, and searched his close-cropped hair. Like the soldier in the song, he had no hat to put on. He looked along the street. People were going about their daily lives. He looked up. The winter sky, hung with its barrage balloons, was an intense blue quite unlike anything he'd seen from the exercise yards. So sheer was the low morning light that he stepped backwards. An angle of glass blazed at him. He strode forward. Then his knees buckled and he was nearly sick. A passer-by in uniform told him to mind where he was going. 'Sorry. Sorry, mate,' he said. The airman clicked his teeth. Vic steadied himself. 'Just got out.' He grinned.

A gust drilled at his back. It penetrated the thin rain-coat, the same one he'd worn behind Tony Rice on the motor bike. Already, he was shivering. The shoddy, wide Caledonian Road with its few cars and occasional pedestrians felt like a crevasse. To shift the weight of his prison notebooks, he slung the holdall he'd been arrested with higher on to his shoulder, and dug the other fist against the flimsy lining of his pocket. He had twenty-four hours – the time within which he was allowed by his Licence of Remission to report to the regimental depot in Leytonstone. His fingers closed around the key to Ripple Road – where his child had not been on the first night of the Blitz, so Clarice had said. The noise of two army lorries passing beside him was unbearably loud, and another gust played havoc with the skirts of his coat.

He craved a tailor-made cigarette, but couldn't go into a shop. At the pillar-box outside a labourers' café he checked below his left lapel, peering awkwardly down and pressing the fabric with his left hand. Sunlight opened the fine dun weave like a lens, and made a faint outline of the package beneath. Her letters lay against his chest, folded in his inside pocket. He had two loves, two already conflicting destinations: Clarice and Jack.

Now, he kept his head low and made the road a tunnel to get through, seeking out the patches of shadow along the left-hand side and clawing his way along. His progress was slow. By the time he'd covered the mile or so to the main intersection, he was breathing heavily. He edged away from the corner of Gray's Inn Road towards Marylebone. The traffic was again too loud, the glare from the sun; and the enormous twin stations – St Pancras, King's Cross – overbore him with their illuminated architecture. People hurried past, taking no notice.

Only then did the disconcerting fact strike him that this place was undamaged. No part of it appeared to have been the least affected by the pounding he'd heard night after night in his cell. The Victorian thoroughfare, and all the prosperous buildings opposite, stood untouched. Apart from one or two windows boarded up and some missing tiles, nothing had changed, nothing at all. It occurred to him that the whole dark complex of locks and cells in which he'd spent so long had been no more than a brainstorm. Bombs had never fallen; Clarice had never come. Some imaginative kink had slipped Pentonville in between one minute and the next, and made him lose his mind. Phyllis would be at home with Jack, like a wife in a magazine. He stood beside the St Pancras taxi rank, trembling, so disorientated he was unable to move.

A purely physical impulse carried him. It took him back across the York Way lights, where the soundless passing of trolleybuses marked Euston's transition to Pentonville Road, and pushed him towards the East End. Here and there the tramlines still lay, gleaming in the brilliant light, and Vic began at last to see signs of damage severe enough to vindicate him – houses torn out, whole roofs missing.

A bus for West Ham stopped only a few yards ahead; but

he was too shy of a crowd, and continued his slow journey on foot, past the Angel, and the Canal Basin, eventually past Shepherdess Walk. There'd been fires. Around him all the windows were shattered and a crater was fenced off in the paving. At the City Road junction with Old Street, where the route bent round, three properties had come out as if surgically, like teeth. Light gleamed on the cracked charcoal of a fallen roof timber.

Further down he saw Bunhill Fields. The terrace on his right was open like a doll's house, with every room on show in its separate furnishings, pictures and lamp brackets. He lit a roll-up. In the lee of Chiswell Street he found protection from the wind, though the air smelt of char. Inching west again towards Smithfield, he followed the tang.

Only twenty-five yards along, the frontages on the other side of the narrow road gave way to a picket fence. The scene made him gasp. Between himself and St Paul's, more than half a mile away, nothing remained except ruined stacks and the burnt-out shells of buildings. A fire-storm had reduced the heart of the capital to desolation.

He pulled at his cigarette. The black cathedral hunkered, strangely huge, seeming to escape its proportions. The great dome stood naked, the single cross silhouetted against the sun. Everywhere else an incinerated landscape stretched, a mass cremation of masonry. Walls were like blackened stumps of bone; rafters lay in heaps. The uncanny stench of burnt centuries forced its way into his nostrils; and there was the smell, too, of actual flesh, he thought, until a gust of wind swept the idea away. He finished his tobacco and threw the butt over the fence. Everything he'd heard in prison, the nightmare of the Blitz, was true. Here was the proof. He should immediately try to find his son. He put a hand to Clarice's letters in his breast pocket.

A woman clippy took his fare, a cigarette held between her lips, and in twenty minutes he was in Limehouse. The Centre and the Cut seemed intact, the rest was a shambles. The bus stopped briefly, then continued along East India Dock Road. Poplar and South Bromley had been hammered. Entire streets had been destroyed. It was a wonder that the main road was open and that people were going quietly about their business. Over Hackney Marshes a streak in the sky was thickening with the ominous yellow-grey of impending sleet.

From the muddy River Lea at Canning Town there remained the long trudge up the Barking Road. Ruin was everywhere. But he'd no time to check his own parents' house. It was only Jack he thought of as he walked through his own childhood: Plaistow, East Ham, Wallend, the next-door villages, merging into each other with their rows of densely packed and vulnerable little working-class houses. There was that strange smell again, of exploded dirt. At one point the route was roped off where a house had toppled into a flooding crater. The utility services were on hand, stanching the flows from the previous night. He saw the bodies of a family being loaded by ambulance men into a converted Green Line bus.

Ripple Road was boarded up, just as Clarice had said, but the tandem was there. He slung the holdall over his shoulder and cycled out to Laindon, pumping the perished tyres every mile. Points of snow were in the air. With fading strength, he pushed the heavy machine on as fast as he could. After Upminster the countryside was bleak, its brown shades whitening, and the exertion couldn't warm him. As he made the long slow climb up into the Langdon Hills, Spitfires from Hornchurch roared now and then between the fat snowflakes.

Either Phyllis would be at the cabin with Jack, or

Clarice would. That had been the arrangement Clarice had suggested in her most recent letter. He'd sent her precise directions and a map drawn from memory. Now, dog tired, chilled to the bone, he pressed forward. The higher ground was already carpeted; the lane curled round under the laden trees. When he reached the little wooden house, he simply let the bike fall into the snow-laced, straggling briars. There was no sign whatever of habitation. The place looked completely empty and his heart sank. His son had been stolen; his lover had baulked at his crime. He was a fool to have hoped it might be otherwise. Exhausted, he pushed open the door.

'Vic!'

THE WHITE ENAMEL bowl rocked back and forth over the blue flame with a click, click, to the water's rhythm. Clarice rinsed and warmed the flannel once more. Then she laid it to Vic's naked shoulder, drawing the cloth down, smoothing his chest and side. In washing his body, she felt she was wiping the grave dirt from him, rinsing away death and corruption. It was under her hands he'd come back to life.

His head was turned slightly away. The eyes were closed. She couldn't tell whether he was asleep, now. The breath lifted softly back and forth in his ribcage. His taut white skin with its tangle of hairs rose and fell under her touch. 'Vic, dearest.' She bent to kiss him, over his heart, and his eyes flickered open. She read the fear in them. 'It's all right, darling Vic.' With her free hand she smoothed the hair back over his forehead. 'You can sleep if you want to. You can rest now.'

Suddenly he was wide-awake. 'There isn't time,' he said. He was staring up beyond her, and trembling. She felt the ridges of agitation under her palm. He tried to sit up. 'Surely there isn't time,' he said again. 'Jack . . .'

'There is, darling. Time enough. In fact, we've got all the time in the world.'

'I've got to go back. My son.' His voice was full of urgency. And then he looked at her, and his eyes softened as he realised who she was. He smiled. 'But I want to keep hold of you. I want to make sure you're here, I'm here.'

'I am here, Vic. And you're so tired. Come on, you can rest. You haven't got to go back. You must rest.' She smoothed his brow once more and watched the eyelids droop as he fought his exhaustion. There was a pause. Then he gave a long sigh and the breathing deepened. She dried his shoulder with a corner of the shirt he'd taken off, and covered him with a blanket where he lay, on the worn mattress's thin, black-striped ticking on the floor of the little cabin.

The dusk was blue-white, underlit by the snowfall. Outside, the flakes, as they drifted past the window-panes, were already shadows on a leaden swirl. She lit a hurricane lamp – it reminded her of another life – and stood it on an orange box. Then she took her own clothes off, and crept shivering in beside Vic under the blankets. She put her arms around him, and drew herself against him. He stirred and turned over on his side. Then she pressed herself all along the length of his back, and placed her knees into the crooks of his knees.

So she rested and thought, of how she had gone down into the darkness to fetch him, and how, at the cost of her own rape, she had brought him back. And here he was wasted and frightened, with the tatters of the underworld plainly still upon him. But he was the same Vic she had fallen in love with. That love, and its determination, had brought them together, against all odds. Now even the fact of the rape, the horrible sense that Tony Rice was somehow still present inside her and that the whole world had been tainted with a grubby evil – she felt all that recede and quieten from her. It sank away. In its place came this delectable calm.

When she'd arrived at the cabin before the snowstorm to wait for him, she'd found the clustering rose briars, like tangles of barbed wire grown up around the miniature garden. She'd had to fight her way past them. Now she thought of the rose flower, even in the depths of winter. The image surfaced, a great beautiful damascus bloom, open and scented. She could even smell the Arabian perfume, and feel the heat of another exotic, alternative climate. And upon the rose in her mind's eye lay the snow of this English afternoon.

When he awoke she made love to him. There was all the while the sense of him still emerging. He was over-cautious and intemperate at the same time. She guided his awkwardness, and took him into her, pressing herself back into the thin mattress and reassuring him once more that there would be time after all.

Afterwards she let her head fall back, and the feelings streamed in her body. She remembered something of her trance, back in the weeks of the previous year – when it had seemed her mute will alone kept the invasion at bay. She wanted to hold Vic there because it was safe. If they spoke he'd become too vulnerable. And perhaps she would, too.

Vic slipped himself off her and curled up by her side. His arm remained stretched loosely over her stomach, his hand touching the base of her breast. 'Clarice, darling,' he murmured, and kissed her neck.

She edged her own arm beneath him and felt for a moment that he was her child. Then in spite of her earlier confidence, she felt time rushing in on her. He would be straight off to the army. What then? Shell fire and the front line awaited him. And his son . . . ?

In the evening, with their clothes hugged tight about them, they walked out into the snow. The night sky had cleared completely. Its winter moon hung, two days before the full, a clipped coin above the oaks. In the frozen blackout the array of stars was like brilliant dust.

'How shall we go on?' he said. He pulled her close. The voice was cautious. 'That is . . . You do want to go on?' She watched his lips. 'You've found me a wreck,' he said. 'Don't you think? It has occurred to me . . . that you might be thinking twice. Now that I'm in the flesh, as it seems.' He smiled, and then grew serious again. 'I do have to ask.'

She turned and looked out over the moonlit snow. The wind had quite dropped; the country was unimaginably still. Soon, most probably, there would be a siren going off somewhere, and the bombers would come streaming over, *en route* for London; but for a moment or two, she could imagine that all the shadowed landscape was untouchable. 'You're not a wreck to me, Vic,' she said. 'As it happens you're beautiful – in the flesh. And I want to go on. Of course I do.'

There, it was not so hard, speaking. They'd strung a few sentences and were still in love, weren't they? Nothing wretched had emerged to ruin it. Nothing about Tony Rice. . . . She felt reassured.

'We'll manage, Vic darling. They'll have to train you, the army. Then you'll get leave, won't you? They can't send you off straight away. So we can meet here. At any time. We can, Vic. What's there to stop us?'

'You're prepared to wait? However long it takes?'

'I've waited this long. And then I found you. And with the war it's the same for everyone, isn't it? We can write. We'll be just like other people.'

'And Phyllis?'

'Dearest, we don't know where Phyllis is. And in any

case what business of Phyllis's is it any more, what we do?'

'Yes,' he said. 'But I'll try everything I can to find Jack – whenever there's an opportunity. Where he is, if he's alive. If he's safe. I shan't be able to rest until I know. . . . You could help me.' He turned to her.

Her heart froze inside her. 'Yes, of course I could.' She pressed the matter away. 'We don't know how things are going to work out. But we will manage, Vic. Won't we? We'll manage. Because we love each other. We'll find a way.'

'Yes,' he said. 'We shall.'

They walked back to the cabin. She heard the glittering snow crackle beneath her shoes. And under the glittering sky she thought of the beautiful rose she had created and how it already had a worm in it.

THE MONTHS HAD flickered away like shadows and now it was high summer. They had met twice more at the cabin. He'd never even dreamt of this, back there in the prison. He lay looking up at his battledress, hung over the back of the wooden chair. Granted two days when their leaves coincided, he'd peeled her out of her shapeless WAAF uniform and the secret little house was once again a bower. This life of theirs was astonishing, and perilous. She turned, and her face brushed against his. Her eyes opened: 'Vic, darling.' Soon, they made love again. She was fierce about it, as if it were a statement.

Later, he got up and threw his unseasonable greatcoat on like a dressing-gown. He went out into the sunset, feeling the grass and stones under his bare feet. As he dropped the bucket into the well he caught the woody, dank odour in the column of cold air beneath him. He knew nothing, except that he was a soldier, and that his son was out there somewhere, spirited away.

The well was a device of his father's: rainwater came off the roof and was passed through an ingenious outdoor filter to be stored in the shallow borehole. He pulled up a bucketful and tipped it into his jug. The liquid had the colour of twilight. Returning, he stood in the minute, darkening kitchen with his greatcoat hanging open, the soft human sexual smell rising up to his nostrils from the track of his body hair.

The tandem, parked with its front wheel skewed under the one cluttered shelf, took up most of the space. Directly above its mudguard, where the shelf ended, his bag of notebooks hung on a peg. Vic turned and stood between pedal and handlebar to pour his water into the earthenware strainer on the trestle bench. Shortly, from the lip at the bottom of it, drops began to emerge though the stones, and he set his father's old tin kettle to fill. Then, squatting cramped by the door, he lit a ring of meths in the Primus and started pumping paraffin up into the jet.

Outside, against the window he'd glazed two summers before, the August sky was casually magnificent. 'Yes, all right, I'll do it,' he'd said to his wife; and that had brought him here, now, with Clarice. He glanced back through the doorway. A buttery light lay upon her neck. Her blonde hair was loosened to one side, and for a moment the gleam appeared to linger upon her nape before running off down the edge of the scruffy sheet. He put the kettle on to boil. Here, with her, the smallest actions, the most insignificant domestic routines, were charged with vehement grace.

In East Ham, when he was a child during another war, there'd been an encyclopedia with a picture of a manta ray. The creature was a sinuous black line with lobed underwater lips at its centre. The thinness had been deceptive, no more than a leading edge. Now a darkness had developed again, and lingered on his life, as it lingered upon the city. Clarice had rescued him, but still it seemed any day that the ticket of leave might expire, and the country, bankrupt, exhausted, on fragile transatlantic life support, would soon fall victim to new and more pitiless strokes. Time and tide had gone haywire. Yet this cabin subsisted, lit by the western sky and filled with their love. He looked at her once more, beautiful, too blissful. He thought of the girl in the night-club, who had so reminded him of Clarice – Frankie, the prostitute – and the sudden chaste kiss which had marked a first act of defiance.

The kettle whistled. He splashed the water on to the tea specks in the chipped brown pot. Tomorrow Clarice would have to go back to her airfield in Norfolk, and he must go back to Hayward's Heath, to a camp called Borde Hill where, ironically, his battalion had just finished building their own charmless huts amongst the trees. He would be living there thinking of her, until his unit moved again, until he snatched another day to get to London to look for Jack, until he and she next managed to steal time together.

His parents were dead, killed in the bomb that got the East Ham gasworks on Battle of Britain day. Phyllis's family – the connection Clarice shared – was bombed out, moved out, untraceable. If Phyllis herself were still alive; if Jack were . . . He was sure he was. Sometimes Vic could almost swear he heard the boy calling out to him. And it was not simply the love of a father for the loss of his closeness, his growing up, his new steps and little progresses. There was the other matter as well. More and more Vic was convinced it was Tony Rice who had the ordering of Jack's days.

Now he was pouring tea for his wife's naked cousin. Against their moments of happiness stood a seemingly endless military future, the chewed and pock-holed transits of cities, defeat in North Africa already followed by defeat; a threat on every horizon. The day would come when Vic would be sent into action. War had sent Clarice to him; it maintained them both in adultery, sin, blessedness.

He added powdered milk from his army rations and took in her cup. Her breasts lay unguarded above the bedcovers. He stared at the faint marbling of veins, the red-brown prominences of her nipples; and then, nervous, averted his gaze. She opened her eyes and looked back at him, the open coat. 'What d'you call this?' She forced his attention mockingly, indicating the cup. 'A bloody Coldstreamer?'

She'd cottoned on to his army slang. He remembered bringing Phyllis tea the morning after the Coal Hole, the open wound on her temple, the marriage pulled tight like a cord. He held out his hand for the cup. 'I'll get the pot and fill it up for you.'

'I'm not letting you go.' Then she set the teacup aside, and pulled him down close to her, stroking his head, slipping her fingers inside the greatcoat to smooth his neck and shoulder. 'It's all right, what we're doing. It's something new, you and I, don't you see?' With her free hand, she took his palm and fitted it to her breast. She seemed to sense his moods before he did. 'Be easy. Please, Vic.'

'Phyllis . . .'

'Forget Phyllis. Sometimes I think that even if we knew for definite Phyllis no longer existed you'd find a way of inventing her.' She made him sit beside her on the bed.

'Maybe.' He shifted uncomfortably, angry with himself, angry in case he couldn't be sure of her. 'It's not as though I've been at the front, or anything, is it? I haven't got so very much to complain of.'

'Are you crying?'

'No!'

'What is it, Vic? What's the matter?'

He was on the point of accusing her. She would insist on skidding away from the question of Phyllis – and, therefore, of Jack. It was as though she were concealing something, and he was suspicious of her tone. But he bit his words back, frightened of some power she had as a woman, frightened she would leave him the minute he crossed her.

They did live on a knife edge. Each of them could slip out of agreement and revert to some other state – without knowing it. That was what he'd discovered: everything could so suddenly turn about. A woman's body, that most closed field of desire, the forbidden parts, the shocking tendernesses. Sometimes they'd tear at him.

He couldn't believe she loved just him. She must have other men. Officers would be hanging round her all the time. Bile surged up in him; the whole thing was inscrutable and would make him mad again. He could never hope to satisfy her, in the real sense, in the real world. He tried to believe in their happiness, but a kind of blackness would close over him.

'You've noticed how you take the lead?' he said. 'You must have. I can't. . . . I'm all knotted up. What sort of man is that?'

'It'll be all right. Give it time, Vic. It'll be all right.'

'Time! What time have we got? A couple of days here and there. Part of me is still locked in Pentonville. Even before Phyllis . . .' He checked himself. 'I never courted you. Not properly. Look at me. You're acting as though it's all so easy.'

'You did court me. Vic, it was wonderful. We both knew. You loved me, I could tell. You courted me then.'

Now he was like a vessel on the slipway that would keep going down instead of bobbing off on its own account. How impetuously Pentonville could take hold, the great warp of the prison seemingly dragging him back. Overhead there were bombers, friend or foe – he waited to see if the guns on the Thames estuary would open up. The sky was the merest strip of egg-yolk yellow beyond the glass. 'I have no spirit, you see.' He knelt down next to her.

'Vic, darling . . .' She held his head against her chest. 'It's so hard to get you out. You think everything's against us.'

'I think something in me . . . How can you love me?'

She stroked him urgently. 'I do, Vic. You have to believe it. Yes, if she knew about us dear Phyllis would do everything possible to ruin what we've got. Yes, my father would go crazy . . . well, maybe he would. Any minute Hitler could finish with Uncle Joe and the Reds and come back with the real invasion. Tomorrow either one of us, or both, could be dead . . .'

'Clarice . . . I know.'

'Then we must be doing something very surprising, to cause all this fuss.'

He laughed with relief. 'You think it's all about us?'

She was serious. 'Don't you agree? Don't you feel that to cut through everything . . . to insist on being together . . . isn't it truly wanting to love that stirs up so much anger and hatred? I mean love that isn't all mixed up with cruelty and manipulation. Proper love. Surely something can't bear it, the thought of lovers being together. Or someone. I mean proper sexual love.'

'That might just as well be God, then. Mightn't it?'

'I shouldn't entirely think so, Vic. Should you? God wasn't quite the agency I had in mind, darling. As you well know. Though who can tell what side God's on.' She gestured impatiently at the window. 'Kiss me,' she said.

He did.

But now she was momentarily afraid. 'They won't come

after us will they, Vic? Phyllis and . . . Tony? We're safe here, aren't we?'

In the see-saw topple of emotions he was too fatherly. 'If they haven't come by now I should think they've made other arrangements, shouldn't you?'

Her fear subsided in his embrace. Some concern – he didn't know what – made him hesitate to make any further comment about Tony. Both of them were prey to sudden terrors. But now, gradually, the cabin was redrawn around them and he was himself again and her body was lovely – her neck, the vulnerable shoulders, the revelation of her bosom, the narrowing of her side as he caressed it, her skin. She smelt of black-market eau de cologne and her own fresh sweat. Both were delicious.

He looked around the bare little room with its empty fireplace. Their only furnishings were the debris of carpentry, the stepladder propped against the flimsy wall, the tools and paint pots, hurricane lamps, boatyard planks and saw-cut trestles; their only communication with the outside world was the little crystal set that only sometimes worked. Then he spoke to her of his childhood, of the brother and baby sister who'd died in the flu epidemic, of the ghosts of the Great War he thought he'd seen in the streets of East Ham.

They held on to each other. 'It'll be all right, Vic. Tell me it'll be all right.'

Later, they walked far enough for a view of the river. There was a southerly breeze from over the Kentish hop gardens on the other side – he was sure he could smell the beery tang breathing across the tide between the barbed wire and the concrete pillbox. The moon stood up on Germany, half full. He strained as if to hear the small far-off waves slapping and splashing against the concrete flood defences. 'It's so very touch and go. Everything,' he said.

Dark clouds moved between the sprinklings of bright stars. He could hardly believe she was there in his arms, and not some wraith in the night air before he woke to Hemmings and the cell and the stink of daylight. He touched her cheek.

'Vic.'

SHE WAS DETERMINED to be happy. Her life was gathered into peaks, which were with Vic; and abeyances, at the airfield in Norfolk. Now, suddenly, it was December and they had four days. The more the wind raved outside and the rain pelted slantwise at the low roof and the sounding sides, the more she conjured her secret house a nest made snug in the middle of some wild forest.

A bladed daylight broke over them in the bed. She supported herself on her elbow and smoothed Vic's chest, the wiry hairs, the shallow valley of breastbone in the breathing expanse. The cabin drummed. He was awake. The oil stove sputtered on its wick and the room filled instantly with the smoky fug she'd grown used to. Here was refuge, here lay her lover; her hand touching his heartbeat.

She let her gaze steal from the base of his throat – slowly, tantalising herself – across the chin and around the mouth, savouring his cheek, the architectural detail of his nose, only then allowing herself to link eyes. She fed on his mouth, tasting the breath and tongue, and it was as if there was no past, no war, no Tony Rice – she heard the storm outside as simple music. Her body melted, streaming to him. Afterwards she smiled up at him. 'You will love me, won't you? You will always love me, Vic?'

'I'll always love you.'

'And you'll always come back and meet me?'

'Yes.'

'And when the war's over?'

'When the war's over we'll be together.'

'Promise?'

'I promise.'

'You won't be killed?'

'I won't be killed.'

In his arms she could rest. She thought of the bunching of years and distance that had brought them together, first at disreputable Limehouse of all places; only to part them on the instant and hurl them to the opposite ends of the earth. Slowly, instinctually, along the next slope they'd reached towards one another again. Their outstretched fingers had eventually clasped here, now, and were holding firm.

Now she stroked his back, feeling him stir once more inside her and thrust softly with the embers of his passion amid the oil-stove drowse that enveloped them. Scattered, blanketed, she wanted to keep him covering her for ever. She felt they'd won. Benign rain in a squall dashed at the window-pane.

He pulled away and lolled down beside her once more, his eyes closed, his breath subsiding. It was the childlike tousle of his hair that momentarily reminded her of Jack, and then immediately, sickeningly – because for her the child was evermore blighted – of Tony Rice.

They took their breakfast in the middle of the day. She made crêpes over the Primus stove, liking to watch him eat, as though he were still a Lazarus, warming to life in her care. At her suggestion, they walked out along the lane, past the brass-band music leaking from an open window in the Flatman family's old converted bus, and on through the settlement.

There was a point quaintly named One Tree Hill, and the rain had declined into intermittent flurries. Their path was the concreted strip to one side of an unmade road. In the years the road had overgrown itself and was now a wide hedgerow between the properties. Here and there, old lords-and-ladies berries still poked up, and the last red drops of nightshade hung. There were rose-hips, too. And in the gaps, through the drenched, wind-blown scrub, they saw the homes of their neighbours, with their thorny, outhouse privies. 'The great East End land rush,' he said, as he lit his cigarette.

She laughed. 'Sounds like the wagons all lined up at the rail head.'

'Indian country east of Epping. Economic pilgrims.'

They passed a self-conscious bungalow, of a pattern she'd seen before. Its ornamental fretwork was peeling, and its chequered, patent roof showed more moss than tile. 'There, look. How grand.'

'A kit,' he said. 'Prefabricated. Still, labour full of inno-cence and reward, I guess.' He flicked his ash. 'A secret America, half an hour's journey down the line from the smoke.' He grinned and his own smoke was snatched away on the wind. 'Can you imagine? Every weekend, at the station – unloading all their bell tents and babies.' A squall of rain hit them from the side. He mimed the settlers' efforts. 'Saws, accordions, picnics, bits of timber, you name it. Up the hill they shoulder them all: rolls of picket fence, tubs of creosote. Each family dumping its necessaries on its own plot of land, nailing up cabins and shanties while their children – me for one – ran down to the marshes to watch the big ships coming in and going out. My family hoping for a new way of doing things. A bit of harmless *Lebensraum*, you might say.'

'Vic!' She laughed.

He was expansive. 'We were late in the game. By the time my old man had the five pounds to put down there were loads of others who'd already tried and failed. No water, no electricity, despite all the promises. No sewerage – nor ever likely to be. They'd come out on a dream, hadn't they?' He gestured around them; the fag end glowed. 'Onions, chickens and a pig. Freedom from bosses and religion. Freedom from the riff-raff one step below them – the unemployed stevedores and their starving kids. Pirates. Freedom from all those East End family ties and obligations: the bloody blood feuds. Pity no one told them about the local foxes. They'd never even heard of fowl pest,' he lowered his voice, '. . . nor all the mysterious fadings that pass amongst swine.'

She laughed again. He was relaxed, more himself than she'd ever known him.

'Go on,' she said. 'I want to know all about our house.'

She held on to his arm as they strode along. He told her how the vision of the settlement had been all but abandoned during the Depression. How in the heat the ground had contracted and skewed the shacks off level, so that they split apart, their asbestos linings exposed, the corrugated iron falling off the roofs. How in winter the roads became portages of sucking clay because the tarmac had never been laid.

Trapped, freezing in their freehold sheds, the emigrant cockneys had recourse neither to pub nor piano, and the natives had been less than friendly. Sometimes, miles from a doctor, without adequate provision for even the bare necessities of life, they'd seen their children sicken and die as readily as if they were still in Stepney or Whitechapel. And of the grown-ups, he supposed, none but the hardiest had endured the romance.

But now hut after rickety hut, cabin after tumbledown cabin had been reclaimed by escapees from the Blitz. In the gusts the patched-again and doubly makeshift habitations heaved and strained at their moorings, and the smoke from a score of odd, revisited smokestacks was raked sideways. Partially obscured windows spiked with candle points; lanterns and hurricane lamps glimmered before blackout.

WHEN THEY REACHED open country, Clarice and Vic followed a path along the line of the hills. The wind was scything through a copse on their left. Puddles in their way shivered, and loose branches whipped past their faces. The grass beside them rippled. At their feet resilient brown stalks pierced the rotting, lifting carpet of leaves.

Clarice squeezed the hand that held hers and wondered that it had once built barges and touched the body of her cousin. She pictured him at work in the boat sheds. She'd never seen them – beside a mud-banked tide she'd never known. It was his restless and imprisoned intelligence that from the first had attracted her. There were times when he'd try to speak to her of such matters as the Schwarzschild geometry. He said it was the folding inwards of nature. Towards the singularity, he said. She would laugh and let him talk on. The idea was impossible, he said, according to Einstein; yet there were certain equations . . . She would laugh again, finding the whole business impenetrable.

A sudden chill flurry caught her off guard and he steadied her. Their service boots slid now in the slime of a track to the village between high bending trees. When the cloud raced lower and darker and the rain began again in earnest they took shelter in the church. It was a sad little edifice, she thought, compared to the church at Holbrook, murky and smelling of mould, though neatly kept, with some vases of daffodils placed in nooks along the nave beside the pew ends. They were touches of bright yellow in the still, submarine translucency. The pelting of rain on the masonry outside sounded like the crashing of far-off waves.

She walked to the communion rail, taking in the mood, and then turned. Vic was looking at a monument let into the wall, an alabaster woman kneeling at the side of a tomb. Below it was a marble plaque. 'Look, see here,' he said. 'Here's a local family. Sons killed in the wars going right back. Local gentry. It's a family business, the manufacture of soldiers.' There was an irony in his tone. 'Like my commanding officer.'

'Like Daddy's side, you mean. Believe me, he's hardly typical. Nor am I.'

'All right then,' he said, grinning. 'I'll just have to look forward to meeting him, shall I? I'll impress him with my prospects.'

She watched him moving amiably about and her heart went out to him. The burden had been laid on her: to bring forth this love against the odds. Her father, Vic, and the redemption of her own body – she needed all these to deliver it. To deliver Jack, even. She was suddenly vehement. 'Say your promises, Vic. Say them again, in here. And I'll say mine.'

'What promises?'

'You know. Back in the cabin, in bed. I promise to love you, Vic. Say you'll always love me again, and that you won't get killed.'

'We can't.' He looked up towards the altar under the stained glass. A small ivory figure was stretched on a simple wooden cross.

'Why not?'

'Because . . . well, isn't it obvious?'

But she felt in control. 'Come on, darling. Let's do it, shall we? She took him up to the altar rail and told him how she loved him. In the defiant little ceremony they remade their improvised vows. 'Look,' she said to the crucifix. 'Do you see? We're lovers. We *are*.'

Just as they were finishing they heard the lifted door latch clack behind them, from the porch off the body of the nave. They both turned. A large, raincoated woman appeared, holding a bunch of daffodils in each hand.

She was hatted and indistinct in the half-light under the sombre vault, mysteriously enlivened by the two splashes of yellow. 'Oh, I'm sorry,' she said. 'I usually come in about this time to do the flowers. If it's not convenient . . .'

'No, of course. Carry on,' Clarice said. 'We were just passing.'

A little too quickly, embarrassed, they made their way down the nave and towards the door, smiling to the woman, and to one another, as they went by her. Clarice had her hand on the iron latch ready to leave when the soft voice called after them. 'You've heard the news, I suppose?'

'News?' Clarice said. 'What news?'

'The Yanks are in. Apparently, the Japs have bombed a big naval base in the Pacific.'

'Oh, I see. But that's marvellous. And terrible.'

Her heart was racing as they headed back along the road they'd come down. 'We should have asked her,' she said. 'Going straight out like that, as if we already knew what she meant. But isn't it wonderful; I can't believe it.' She was so excited.

'Yes, it is,' he said. 'It's wonderful news. If it's true.'

'Oh, you!' she said in exasperation.

The rain had all but left off again. On the way back he was unusually silent, as though he hadn't grasped the coincidence, as though the woman had never appeared and he resented her attempt to have their love declare itself. It was almost that he'd prefer to keep his life in boxes and hedge his bets.

He said at length, 'I've been thinking about Jack. Wondering what he looks like, now, actually. Whether I'm losing touch with . . . with his memory. It's been two years. D'you realise? Two years and no trace. I can't stop worrying about him.'

'I see.' She was immediately jealous, and there seemed nothing she could do about the spiteful mood that came over her. 'I suppose it would be too much to hope,' she sneered, 'that you might be thinking about me – about us. After what just happened. After what we've just done. And the Yanks. You know as well as I do we only ever have a few days together, don't we? I thought it might have meant something to you. Clearly, it didn't, and I was wrong.'

'Darling. What's the matter? I do care about us.' He tried to put his arm around her. 'Of course I do.'

She shook it off. The wind drove between them, as, under the tearing clouds, the sun streaked a pale line along the horizon. 'Of course you must worry about Jack,' she said, coldly. 'But coming just like that, after the church, and the news. It was the tone you used. All of a sudden I'm taken for granted.'

Seriously, she was amazed at herself, to be speaking like this, so close a moment ago, but now virtually hating him. She did hate him, the more he tried to touch her and make amends. She wanted to hit him, push him away. Her elbow caught him with force.

By the time they got back to the cabin, it was quite dark.

'You go in,' she said.

'Why?' he said. 'Where are you going?'

'I just want some space to myself, cooped up here in this rat trap. I just need time and space to myself. Can't you understand that? Life isn't all lovey-dovey, you know. I have my own life, my own work. Where I come from, people – aircrew – get killed.'

'But where are you going? Are you coming back?'

'Don't worry. I'm not my cousin. I'll go on as far as the shop, get a newspaper. And some of your fags – if they're open. You can surely manage without sex for half an hour, can't you? Or am I wrong?'

It was only on the way back in the pitch dark with the rain starting to pour down again that she began to think of what had happened. Jack and Tony Rice were chained, one to the other. When she thought of the boy, the man's crime lay there always, waiting to have its name cried out; but she couldn't speak for the shame, and so it rose up anyway and fooled her, tricked her mind. It had made her attack Vic.

She had to tell him. No matter what agony it would cost her, she must get the thing out in the open before it could do any more damage. Pausing at the door, she collected herself. Then walked in. 'Vic, dearest, I'm so sorry. Will you forgive me? I simply don't know what came over me. Well, I do, but . . .'

He was listening to the crystal set, an earpiece pressed against the side of his head. But when at last he took notice of her, his voice sounded only cold and angry in return. 'It's true,' he said. 'The Yanks are in. The Japs have bombed their fleet in the Pacific. Pearl Harbor.' And then she couldn't say it. He scared her. He just wanted to punish her for her irrationality.

Their evening was excessively formal, the meal an abomination of tinned meat and stale bread because neither would suggest a preference. Even late in the bed their rancour remained, and each huddled under the coats and blankets avoiding meticulously the touch of the other. She thought of the burning American men, the sacrificed, drowning boys, about whose death she'd been so jubilant.

In the morning he gave in and they made up. But the moment to tell him about Jack was past and she could say nothing.

JACK WAS RUNNING out of the school gates. The school sat at the crossroads of the town, right at the centre. It looked like a church, though small and made from dull red bricks. Whenever he was inside the school, there was a sick feeling in his stomach that made him yawn, and stare, and feel afraid. He couldn't get his breath. Today was a Friday, and on Friday it was Arthur Figgis who collected him at the gate for the journey up to London in the car. He'd be sick on the way.

His mother had brought him to the school. His father owned the car. His mother had lost her baby. His father worked in London, but wasn't away in the Army, or the Navy, or the RAF, like the other children's fathers. Jack was lucky, his mother said, because they had a nice house and a nice car. In the school the teachers spoke of God, and he didn't know the words of the prayers and hymns. Jack was running away down the street and past the cinema, away from the iron railings.

He was running and the town had a pall over it, yellow-ish, like jaundice, because he could never get his breath, and the days in the classroom were full of something that was too hard to bear. The workings out in his money sums, the scratchings of his pen on the grainy paper that soaked up the ink, the wooden half desk he sat at next to the fat girl with the runny nose, were incomprehensibly foreign. They were all cast over by the same yellowish light whose colour was sickness.

Now he was in full flight and the air panted hard up through the pavement and into his lungs. It was broad daylight. He ran past the shop where they sold gob-stoppers, and if he could run far enough and fast enough, his legs free and flying, almost, beneath him, he could get away from the school. When he stopped he was on the kerb of a side road, and then on again in front of a van coming fast with its horn blasting. He stopped when he was across. The air ripped in and out of his mouth.

'Where do you think you're off to, sonny?' A tall man in a long brown overcoat bent his trilby down. Jack dodged round him, and forced his way on. Level with the cinema on the other side of the main road his legs once more refused and he took stock of his situation. After the shop with the airguns and golf clubs he didn't know the route. They usually drove out by other ways, his mother and father in the big car. A sign by the municipal gardens said St Mary's Lane and he imagined he shouldn't be on it. Large full-headed poppies stood and swayed amidst the weeds.

The railway bridge ahead made a rectangle like a camera's eye, and it was as though he'd come this way before, in some other time. Walking now, because his chest was heaving his ribs, he had an intimation that if he could pass beyond that bridge a scene would unfold where his blood and body would be made good. For a second he believed there'd been another man, not his father at home at all, but some other face, some other smell, some other name than Tony Rice.

Then he managed to run on, his blazer flapping, the waistband of his worsted shorts chafing him on the slack of his braces. The cut-ended tie flew its wasp stripes into his face and streamed over his shoulder. At last there was a stitch in his guts and the distance to the bridge was too great, and the cop shop was just over the road. A couple of old women were waiting for a bus. As he stopped, panting, they stared at him. If he gave them a clue, the police would be after him in no time.

> *They'll tie you up with wire*
> *Behind a Black Maria*
> *So ring your bell*
> *And pedal like hell*
> *On your bicycle made for two.*

The playground song played over and over in his head.

When the cops took him home his mother was furious. She had the cane in her hand. 'What your father's going to say, I don't know. Why did you? Answer me. Didn't you realise the trouble you'd cause? Having that flatfoot turn up at the door. What people will think? Eh? And they'll imagine I don't look after you.' She caught him and swiped the backs of his legs three times, four, between the sock tops and the trouser ends. At each cut he screamed out and his eyes burned with tears. Then she took him upstairs and put him in his bedroom, turning the key.

'IT IS A marriage, Daddy, because we love each other. You don't understand. It's a marriage under these emergency circumstances, more than any damn parson's words can make it. And since when have you come over so bloody . . . sacramental?'

'Clarice! Do you have to swear. It's . . .'

'It's what? Unladylike? Is that so surprising now, Daddy, when I spend most of my time with boys who're going up over Germany every night? And if they swear and drink and horse about it's because the odds are tomorrow or the next day they won't be back for breakfast.'

'Darling. Let's take this matter one step at a time.' Her father sat in the surgery he'd reopened in the wing of Pook's Hill. He was silvery, and oddly impressive behind his mahogany desk. With the fingers of his right hand he squeezed and released the stethoscope tube that snaked across his blotter. The mannerism put Clarice in a frenzy of irritation.

He continued, however, in that remorselessly precise way he had sometimes of speaking to her. 'You tell me he's Phyllis's husband. But if she *is* married to the other one, the one we met, then your fellow's the impostor. You say you found him in a prison.' The pedantic tone built up. 'Some of them are very plausible, and, I've heard, even attractive to women in some way I don't pretend to understand. If, on the other hand, he's who he says he is, then he's married already. Point one.'

She bit her lip. High above the next-door fields, a lark sang; the sound streamed in through the open window. 'But Phyllis didn't want him,' she said. 'She was horrid to him, Daddy, she and that man. For God's sake, they were here. I told you something was wrong. They got him locked up.'

'So *he* says.'

'It was the boy who told me – Jack. Well, he told Dolly Hayman.'

Her father remained impassive. 'And this – Vic – has been doing time for breaking and entering.'

'So what? He was tricked into it. He's paid his debts. He's served his time.' The lark's song poured into the room.

'And now he's in the army you want my blessing.'

'I want you to meet him. He's nice, Daddy. He's a good man. You'd like him, I know you would.'

She felt she was protesting too much. She'd last been together with Vic in April when he'd got leave after a training exercise on the Isle of Wight. An electrician at her airfield had salvaged her a radio, and, excited, she'd lugged the heavy thing down to Laindon on the train. They'd danced, she and Vic, there in the cabin to American music, jitterbugging around the crates and trestles, careering into the tandem, bumping against the bag full of his notebooks.

But it hadn't all gone so swimmingly. She had to remind herself of that. They'd also rowed, badly, and at one point they'd even been on the brink of parting. And tomorrow he was coming up from Southampton; they were meeting in London. She was caught between longing and dread. For, after Pearl Harbor, that day at the church, she'd been acutely conscious of a barrier between them. Sex and her temper caused it. It seemed they had to fight before they could be intimate; and it had to go to extremes, Vic icy and withdrawn, herself raging, scornful, threatening to leave. But she couldn't help it. The rape would rule her.

Her father was treating her like a child, of course; or like a patient who'd made up a pack of lies about her symptoms and was refusing to face her true condition. Still, her father was crucial. She tried again, and her next words surprised her. 'I think you could help him.'

'Could I? Help the man who's been ruining my daughter? A criminal.'

'Oh, really! Ruining! How Victorian! This is now; and he's not a criminal.'

'He was wrongfully imprisoned, then?'

'No. But . . .'

She'd had such hopes of this discussion. She'd come home determined to bare her soul because her father was wise and cured people; but Singapore had fallen to the Japanese since she'd last seen him. 'It's the Japs, isn't it?' she said. 'It's Malaya. It's brought everything back. That's why you're being so distant. I feel it too, Daddy. I do. It's horrible. And you were right all along.'

She did feel it. Neither of them could bear what had happened to the Far East. This war had a mind of its own, and cruelty would be heaped on cruelty. No potion, charm or spell could put a stop to it, for childhood was past. Now she wished she'd never told him of her love affair. Through the window the hawthorn hedge basked deep green in the lively air, and the lark had gone so high the song was sheer vibration.

Her father looked down at his desk and then up at her once again, sharply. 'All this is leading up to some ghastly confession, I suppose? Something has happened and you're looking for a way out.'

There was a further delay before she grasped the implication. 'No! No, Daddy. It's nothing like that.' She blustered. 'For Christ's sake! We . . . We're careful.'

'I should very much hope you are. I could have wished you'd been much more so from the start.'

'I can't believe you're being like this, Daddy. I just can't understand it. I thought you'd be pleased when I fell in love.'

'With your cousin's robber husband? Or merely your accomplished deceiver.'

She left the room, but without any stamping or show of defiance.

In the afternoon she rode out with Bea Bligh, resolved not to broach the subject further. They chatted about wartime things, about Make Do and Mend with the child, Rosalind, so small. It wasn't much fun, Bea said, since Geoff had been called up. Bea relied on her parents. She envied Clarice her active life with the bomber squadron. 'Now that the Yanks are in you'd think matters would look up. But for us it just goes from bad to worse. Tobruk again! Why do we have to fight over a desert? You heard about the Hayman boys, of course?'

'Trying not to think about it, Bea. Trying my very hardest.'

'Both of them – within a week of each other. It's so awful.'

'If I thought about it, I really couldn't cope. And at the airfield. Each night some of them go down. You just have to put a brave face on it. You go numb.' She described her role, the emotions welling. 'Actually, I'm just another dogsbody – completely powerless. You can't help getting to know them. It's the same faces every time. And the same missing ones.'

Rozzie was already quite a talker, apparently. Clarice took the cue and swallowed her feelings. What remained was a sadness – if she and Vic *were* to have a child it would be a scandal rather than a blessing, so hidden away was their rationed love.

'But there is something you haven't told me, isn't there?' Bea said. They rode along the edge of a field well above Hayman's farm. The breeze rippled the tall green wheat spears while the bank beside them was alive with the chirr and chatter of insects. From high overhead in the clouds there was a lark again, and another. Clarice drew breath. She felt the comforting flex of Martin's muscles, and the thump of his powerful walk. The horse remembered her. 'No. Nothing. Nothing that I'm aware of.'

'You'll be going back to your base tomorrow, then?'

'I should really go and call in on Boss Hayman and Dolly – about the boys – but I don't think I could face it, to tell the truth. Such a funk, I know. I've got another forty-eight hours. Meeting up with a friend. A day in London. It's all a matter of who's got leave when. We seem to overlap once every few months.'

Bea set her horse into a trot. 'That would be a male friend, would it?' she shouted over her shoulder.

'Just a friend, Bea,' Clarice called after her.

'Oh, yes. Just a friend.'

Martin snorted and picked his feet up. She felt the kick of the new rhythm up through her spine.

DESPITE HER BEST intentions, though, her day with Vic in London struck a wrong note from the start. He wanted to follow a lead before going straight out to Laindon, while she wanted to find an afternoon dance, and they ended up doing neither in a succession of pubs and a British Restaurant. Then she put on a too-bright face, and went about buying an American flag, and a cheap framed picture postcard of New York to hang on their walls. When he tried to be amorous she pulled away, her chatter rising glassily, beyond her control. If the war ever ended, she said, they might even squeeze a piano into the little house with them. He said he wished they could manage a simple discussion without it all going wrong; and she flared back instantly. 'What do you mean, going wrong?'

'I mean I try to say something and you start to get upset. I can't for the life of me see why.'

'So it's always my fault.'

'Oh, for God's sake. There! That's what I'm talking about. Why is a simple, rational conversation out of the question?'

'I'm sure I don't know, Vic. Why should I? You're the scientist.'

They walked on in silence down Oxford Street.

'It's something to do with my son, isn't it?' he said. 'I feel torn in two. As if I have to look for him behind your back. You know that? You get so touchy about it.'

'Do I? Try me.'

'All right. There were a couple of hours to kill before your train this morning. I got chatting to some little lance-corporal in a bar off Leicester Square. He said a bloke called Rice was running all the trade and tarts east of Charing Cross Road. Then he got the wind up, so I told him I was an oppo. Family firm.' He snorted through his nose. 'But he clammed right up and said that was all he knew. I just wanted to throttle him.'

'I'm sorry.'

'Are you? Another lead goes begging because I can't follow it up and I'm left none the wiser.'

'I mean it. I really am sorry.'

'And there's another thing, an image I can't get out of my head – of the kid. He's caught up like an animal in some wretched net. It's awful, cobwebby, but I can see his face. He's looking at me. Everything else is dark.' He gave a grim laugh. 'Awful, yet in a way it makes me believe he's alive. If I just knew where.'

Clarice tried to speak but her voice stuck in her throat. She couldn't explain the sudden paralysis that froze her muscles. She held in her possession the missing scrap of information. It hung right on her lips, this vital jigsaw piece, of the house in Upminster where she'd been taken with Jack and Phyllis after she'd visited Vic in Pentonville. But she couldn't tell him, she couldn't. . . . Because he'd ask questions she wouldn't be able to bring herself to answer. Because it was too horrible and she'd kept silent for so long. The tears prickled in her eyes.

'I suppose the police still haven't come up with any-thing?' she said.

'A whole city full of missing persons?'

'Yes, of course.'

She would tell him; if only they could be close again. But he was always somewhere else, always thinking about something else. His heart was never really with her; he would never give her himself.

'How *is* the training going?' she said.

He looked at her in astonishment. 'You really want to know? Night combat, mine lifting, street fighting – that's what we were up to last week, Clarice. Because the tide's about to turn, isn't it? These days we do more charging than digging in. We blacken our faces. We wear leaves in our tin hats, like hunters. They're not sending us to

Burma like the other battalion – Dad's old mob. No. All bets are we're going to France.'

She was astonished in turn, at his tone. She'd been through so much for him. Her love for him was the most important thing in her life . . . A plausible rogue, her father had said, attractive to women. A criminal. She'd lost her bearings with him; her heart had gone numb and only irritation stung her. What had she seen in Vic? Just now she couldn't remember. She'd been so sure, so confident that they'd be doing something extraordinary – upon which even the outcome of the war would depend. Where were her feelings now?

He walked beside her, down Bond Street and into Mayfair, which was where neither of them wanted to go. She felt dumpy in her uniform. They didn't hold hands. He chose to carp again about their lack of proper conversation.

'Come on, Clarice. What's gone wrong?'

She drew breath; but when, outside the window of a high-class furniture shop he tried to kiss her, his hand at her breast made her flesh creep.

'Nothing's gone wrong. Just don't do that. It's the street, for God's sake.'

'No one can see.'

'Don't. That's all.'

'All right.'

She could feel him next to her, tensing as he fought to contain his anger. 'You're cross with me, aren't you?' she said.

'No.'

'Admit it, Vic.'

'I just wish we could agree on some basic principles.'

'But where's the love?'

'I do love you. I've always loved you. That church – remember?'

'You're so remote. Your voice is so cold.'

Late in the afternoon, they saw a Chicago gangster movie; and, in the early evening, they encountered their first Yanks. A party of smartly uniformed soldiers came smiling and joking out of a pub in Drury Lane. How they caught the eye, with their style and confidence. She cheered up; but then it came to thinking about the journey down into Essex. They'd spent their money too easily. They had only just had enough for the train, none for the tube. The walk was a chore. And when they did eventually get out to the little house she found for the first time she simply couldn't respond to him physically.

'It really doesn't mean I don't love you, Vic.' She was all too conscious of his disappointment. 'Because I do. I suppose it's trying to make everything just like ... to try picking up exactly where we left off. The truth is we've each lived another life in the meantime.'

'It's quite all right, darling.'

He was aroused, and frustrated. Naked, he dropped the packet of army condoms on to an upturned crate and pointedly lit a cigarette. She felt him looking at her body. It scared her. Her own frigidity scared her. From the start, she'd been the determined one. She'd coaxed him to believe in her, that she wasn't simply leading him on. It had virtually been a campaign. Bitterly, she blamed her father. Surely his words had stung her mind, and bruised her own belief.

Sitting on the mattress in her RAF bra and blackout knickers, by the weird light of the hurricane lamp, she longed for Vic to comfort her. But he kept his distance, he wouldn't just be close; and she was hurt, as if deep down he preferred his regiment to her. That rhythmic crunch of boots, that perpetually deferred gratification – he was secure in the life among men, and the more the army made a man of him the more she found his masculinity threatening. It left her out. She felt their future as lovers shrinking to a wartime talking point, like the eager London girls with black GI babies already on the way. It made her wretched.

'I'll make some cocoa, shall I?' he said, dully.

'If you like.'

While he was up, she clutched his greatcoat about her, not moving, listening to his ritual in the kitchen with the Primus. His shadow sprang and darted on the walls as his bulky male figure crossed and recrossed the door frame. And later, when they lay down to sleep, she could feel his piece of flesh poking against her skin like a reproach. She didn't like to ask him to turn away.

She woke beside him. The coats had come off the bed, and what should have been a mild night seemed to be draining all the warmth out of her. All the sorrows from the back of her mind were outside the cabin, large as wolves, and trying to get in. She wondered what someone like Vic might do to her when he found out she'd known all along about Jack? With a shock she realised she'd seen him lock the door before he got into bed. Moonlight was falling on him through the little window above their pillows – his pale, thin stranger's face. She *had* brought him back. She'd breathed love into him. But she hardly knew him. In the dark, she had no idea where the door key was.

As carefully as she could she raised herself up, pulled one of the coats around her, and slid across his sleeping body on to the bare wood floor. The moon cast only the faintest illumination, and the odd-job shapes they lived with seemed now completely unrecognisable. She felt her way to the mantelshelf and slid her fingers all along the bits and clutter she scarcely knew they had until she found the torch.

Vic was a sharp, yellow, absent face amid the strange assortment of uniform and bedclothes. He turned over, as if the light would wake him, and made a sound at the back of his throat. She didn't know what to do. In the kitchen, she tried the outside door. The lock rattled. The tandem's pedal raked her shin and she gasped with the pain. The light flashed on the bag of dreams, all that prison stuff. She fancied she heard the booming of guns from somewhere far off. As she turned, the torch swept the twin planks that served as a kitchen bench. The crusts of supper lay next to an open pot of jam.

She felt a hand on her shoulder and screamed. Then she was in his arms and he was himself again, and she pressed all the pain that was in her body against him and cried.

'There, darling. It's all right. It's all right.'

'Oh, Vic. I'm so sorry. What am I going to do? What are *we* going to do?'

JACK WAITED, SITTING on his bed, locked again in the bare room with its blackout curtains and single rag rug on the paint-spattered boards. The sky thickened outside. He thought of the purer light and the country he'd glimpsed the time before. It had been on the other side of the railway bridge. Now he grew liverish with apprehension. Next to the window, the walls stretched up, and there was a slight crack in the plaster near the ceiling, running down close to the bronze-coloured pipe. It was the continuing newness of the house he found difficult, the peculiar, insistent smell, of lime and paint and metal, which never went away.

With his gaze, he followed the pipe down again, past the small dust pits in the pink wash of distemper, and saw how it joined into the larger pipe down by the brown skirting and then went into the radiator. By the shapes of the joints, he realised for the first time how the circuit was set up to flow, how it was engineered to take the hot water about the house, to deliver it, and then to return, through the floors and along the walls downstairs, to the heavy coal boiler in the kitchen. The radiator was cold today, its bronzed cast-iron flanges dull to the touch, because they were waiting for coal. But he saw where the water would leave it, and how the pipe led away.

There were his books on the shelf, and, in their box, his toys with the tin bomber on the top. The golliwog who was losing his stuffing lay on the sheet. He put his hand to the wall above his bed. It felt perfectly flat, yet once again he could see the minute dust pits in the surface. It sucked out the heat from his fingers, from the flat of his palm, and smelt, inevitably, of lime. He couldn't get the hang of things, and the window was too high to jump from.

His mother was frightened, because any minute his father would be coming home from business. While he was allowed to the toilet, Jack could hear her on the landing, her high-heeled step trying this way, now that – indecisive upon the noisy boards. When he came out with the cistern still flushing and his own stink lingering in the air she tried to hug him. He felt the brooch she was wearing and smelt the scent on her neck. Then she took him with her into the big bedroom while she got changed, trying first one dress, then another, pulling up her skirt and fixing her stockings in the tabs, where a bruise still lay, and then, with the tops of her legs showing, sitting at the dressing-table with her hairbrushes, and bottles and powders, not talking to him while she made herself up. He looked from the skin of her thighs above the stocking tops to her face in the mirror with the lipstick poised. Her pouted mouth between the whitened cheeks was some proud razor slash she would colour in.

She stood up, blotting herself as she turned round towards him, letting her dress fall back into place. Removing the cloth she'd tied round her shoulders she began to button the gape at her front. 'I don't know what you think you're looking at.'

Involuntarily, he stepped backwards. His own shoes clomped and echoed.

'Anyone would think you'd never seen a woman before.' The small wrists pressed each bosom. Her neat, laquered fingernails fastened the last button.

Jack felt the tight lungs, the breath that would never reach down properly. The bare walls of the house still had pieces of electrical cable coming out of them, where no lights had been fixed. Everything echoed and was unfinished; and the yellow colour, that was not precisely the buttermilk distemper of her bedroom but the duller, more bilious taint that came in from outside, from the school, from the sky, and from the future, seemed to curve the world in so that the cramping of his chest was permanent. Her body stirred and frightened him; so did his own.

As she left the room to go downstairs, she allowed her fabrics to brush past him. He didn't know whether he was allowed to follow. He didn't know whether he was allowed to be present when she told his father to be cross with him. He hung about looking into her jewel box. The items were complete and secret, lying glittering there upon beds of white wadding, a necklace, a ring, the diamanté image of a bird, two pearl drops for her ears. Then he went and pressed his face into the cupboard where her clothes were hung, taking in the woollen, flesh-flavoured, mothballed smell of her. Underneath the dresses the shoes were scattered haphazardly upon some loose magazines. One heel creased a folded song sheet with a blue cover. He made out the words between the lines of the piano stave: '*I've got you under my skin.*'

Later, he smelt food and heard marches playing on the wireless. She brought him up his tea, but he was too apprehensive either to eat or to listen; and when his father arrived with Arthur Figgis, Jack peered down from the stairhead. He watched her explaining what had happened again. At first, his father appeared to lose patience. Jack heard the word 'encumbrance' and he saw his mother's slender wrist held by his father's strong grip. Next, she was both informing and interceding, and he couldn't tell whose side she was on. Voices were raised, and he caught his father's face, looking up at him in exasperation. 'All right, then,' she was saying, 'you can look after him yourself, if that's what you want. I'll go, shall I, if that's what you want? I shall if I like, and you won't stop me, Tony Rice.'

'All right, all right.'

'I'm telling you it's not my fault.'

'And I suppose it's mine, is it?'

'Make what you want of him, then. You obviously think more of him than you do of me. Don't you, Tony? You do, don't you?'

'Now then, you two lovebirds.' That was Figgsy's voice. There was laughter, for there was a job on, and what did it matter? Finally, she came up to Jack, abstracted, and told him not to worry, because this time he'd not be punished any more, and he'd still be going up for his treat. She called it that. Her eyes were far away, because she'd switched herself off from him.

The men laughed again, down by the open front door. Figgsy called up, 'Looks like you've got away with it, Jacks.'

'Come on, then,' his father said. 'Business is business. Keep you both company. Make sure you don't bloody lose him, Figgsy.'

Jack followed her back into her bedroom. He was so grateful. She was seated once more at the dressing-table, the side mirrors folded round. She was repeated, there, and there again, and he would have dashed in between and thrown himself into her arms, clung on to her and begged her to keep him, but in the doubling and trebling of her image he felt almost more beaten and overwhelmed than if he had actually been caned. 'You're going for your treat,' she said. 'You're a lucky, lucky little boy.'

Touching at her lips with the precious cotton wool, then painting, then powdering, now dabbing here, now patting the hair at her temple, she would keep looking straight ahead, and there was no use. Only when he said goodbye did she break off to kiss him on the cheek. 'Be good now, and have a nice time, won't you.'

In the back of the car he imagined her practising her songs at the piano in the parlour, in her own world of dressing up and going out, picking out the tunes with one finger, and contemplating her reflected mystery in the music on the page. He imagined her skirts pulled up again, as they had been, and the bare white expanses of skin touched by the falling notes. And the bruises, and how it was his pain that could protect her, the pain that was the business of God, they said in the school, the nails hammered through.

Then the journey through Hornchurch and on towards Romford drained all its light to the drab sunset in front. The night closed around the car in a long, tight tube, a pipe that swung and roared now this way, now that, to London.

And though he'd had nothing to eat, he had to be sick into a gutter beside some houses while the car door stood open and the engine idled. Figgsy had on his nasty face. His father threatened to slam the door on his arm if he got any mess on the leatherwork. But then they laughed again as though maybe they didn't mean it, and joked about a bad penny and a bent copper. 'The copper's bent, all right,' his father said.

The car pulled up at last. In the glow from the slitted

headlamps Jack saw the green tailgate and tarpaulin hood of a lorry. US Army.

He hadn't been to the house before. It was a large one left standing in a bombed terrace. Around it, wrecks and roofless shells showed in the faint starlight, black teeth in a bad mouth. There was a smell of old dust and the river. His father huddled him in the flap of his coat on the pavement, to keep him warm, and Jack could peer out past his buttonholes. The shadowy figures were soldiers carrying crates and packages out of the lorries. He wondered if this time they'd finally arrived at the war.

A policeman held one hand out in greeting; he carried his peaked cap in the other. 'One jump ahead, eh, Tony?'

'All right,' his father said in reply. 'Figgsy,' he gestured, and Jack felt himself move in the cloth of his father's coat. 'Oh, and the encumbrance.'

'Ah,' the policeman said, affably, looking at Jack.

'Ah, yes,' said his father. 'That's right. And the stuff's all Yank, straight off the pond. Take anything else you want, why don't you? The joint's full of it. Before it goes downriver again, or wherever.'

'Mind if I ask?'

'He ain't mine. Figgsy looks after him. He's an escaper.' Jack heard the laugh.

Inside, the house was dim. It wafted thickly of tobacco smoke. A man in uniform pushed Jack out of the way with the box he carried in. Then Mrs Lavender came who was always there before them, and Jack thought he liked her. She had lipstick that was just too big for her mouth and her eyebrows were high, pencilled lines. But her eyes were tired. Her face had small lines on her cheeks and beside her smile, and when she laughed she had a gold tooth. She held out an American chocolate bar for him. 'Don't let them see you as shouldn't.'

Then she said to Figgsy, 'Electric doesn't work but the gas does.'

'Needs teaching a lesson, that kid,' Figgsy replied. 'Cup of tea would do the trick, Sal.'

'I don't know, I'm sure. You'd better go in there, son, with Frankie.'

The girl had appeared. She was beautiful, but Jack felt sick again.

Pipe smoke in the dark front parlour was so thick it caught his throat. He was coughing. In the grate a fire burnt red. Two gas brackets were on the wall. It was the policeman who sat in a winged armchair, and a tall clock stood behind him. Jack looked round, to run, but the girl, Frankie, was stroking the velvet of the old-fashioned tablecloth. Her hand smoothed the nap. 'We're your other family, aren't we?' she said. He knew nothing, could understand nothing.

Figgsy was behind him. Mrs Lavender came in, pouring a mug of tea from a flask.

'For you, Figgsy, darling.'

'That's the ticket. All right, Frank?'

'No better for seeing you.'

'The night is young.'

'Fuck off.'

'Not in front of the child, my girl,' Mrs Lavender said.

Frankie replied, 'You're surely joking, aren't you?'

Jack watched Mrs Lavender leave.

'Old witch.'

He turned back just as Figgsy grabbed him by the collar. 'Smile for the gentleman, sonny.' Half-choked he found himself dumped in front of the hearth.

Now Jack stared into the policeman's eyes. He saw a cold dead glint with the smile that wasn't a smile, the red light from the fire making half a mask with the line of shadow from the wing chair. The smoke curled up from the man's pipe.

'None of your riff-raff,' Figgsy said. 'None of the scrawny, snot-nosed two-a-penny scum that run around here, mate. Are you, Jacks? The boss's own son.' He coughed behind his hand. 'We all have to watch our Ps and Qs, don't we?'

Jack felt the policeman's hand on his head, smoothing his hair. Outside in the hall the booted feet tramped with the sound of the crates coming in, and still coming in. He turned his head away. In the murky gaslight between the table and the policeman's fireside chair there was a box levered open. He saw the American wrappers. 'Candy, Jack,' said the pretty young woman, Frankie. She still had her hand on the table runner. 'He's got such a sweet tooth.'

His heart hurt his chest, in the upstairs room, with no light on and the curtains open. Jack fixed his eyes on the jug that stood in the water bowl. He concentrated with all his force on the jug, its black shape with the lip and handle, the full round pregnant shape where it sat in the ewer, wide, drawing a line across like a horizon. *Forgive us our trespasses.* If he could hold his mind on the shapes, the jug, the bowl, then he knew he could blank out the fact that he was not alone in the room, completely blank out the pain and the bent policeman and the breaking and entering . . .

If he could make that picture of the bridge stand in his imagination with the rectangle of bright distance in the frame of it; if he could make his mind keep on running, keep on going from where his body had given up and stopped. If he could do that, then there would come a moment when he might escape through the archway and out into the open country beyond. There was a place he'd known once, a miniature green place, and a man who'd held him in his hands, high up in the sunlight. They were making a house. He could see the sunset stretched against the sky in an intense red gold that wasn't the war, that wasn't invasion, where the streaks of cloud caught fire with a slow and kindly flame.

IT WAS A cold, damp morning. Dr Pike held his watch anxiously in the palm of his hand. He expected his daughter and her boyfriend at any moment – indeed, they might already have arrived.

He opened the surgery door. His last patient of the morning was Mrs Benedick, from Bolt's Grove. At the sight of him she stood up and came forward; but as she did so, Clarice entered the waiting-room from the hallway. Dr Pike caught a glimpse of the soldier with her and smiled involuntarily. Mrs Benedick smiled back, and he felt awkwardly exposed between the two.

Blushing, though he had no reason to, he nodded to his daughter, ushered his patient in, and closed his door. Mrs Benedick, in her threadbare but exquisitely tailored brown suit, hovered. A pretty little hat perched sideways on her head; she was an elegant, well-preserved woman who'd taken obvious pains. Her gloves and shoes were stylish, banded with fawn suede. Yet with a gesture that verged on the ungallant, Dr Pike indicated the upright chair and turned away to extract her file from his cabinet.

Seated once more at his desk, he attempted to collect his thoughts. He had no fever this morning. He was certainly more himself, these days. Since he'd entered practice again, the months had begun to hurry by. Mrs Benedick was a problematically menopausal woman – so he'd always thought. He was sure he had no fever.

She waited demurely in front of him. Something about her always unsettled him. She was the widow of the local landowner's agent. In his mind, he'd almost made a point of being unkind to her. He'd invested her, for example, with political prejudices he'd no evidence she actually held, simply on account of her deceased husband's profession. For some reason it suited him, this failure to see her as a woman in her own right. He'd found himself sketchy with her, reluctant to offer her his due attention. As a result she continued to present herself.

He peered above his half-moon spectacles at the composed, rather delicate little figure. She was putting her own spectacle case into her bag. An apprehension prickled the hairs on the back of his neck. Mrs Benedick was in her early fifties. Her features were good; rather than detracting, the faint lines in her complexion added distinction – a handsome woman, even. She was known to live modestly; her son ran what was left of the business.

For a moment he couldn't take his eyes off her. Then, when she lifted her own gaze, he felt again caught out, and turned away, patting his waistcoat and pretending to reassure himself about his watch. He made himself skim her notes. Clarice had written to say she was coming over on a day's pass. Her last letter had sounded buoyant enough, but she masked her difficulties; there was an undertone. He'd be relieved, at last, to see the young man and have the chance of forming his own opinion. Last time he'd been too hard on her.

When he looked up again his eyes met those of his patient, and once more veered apart from them. But Mrs Benedick's expression was warm, and trusting. Instantly he regretted the unprofessional comments he'd made only the previous week, at a reunion dinner in London for the benefit of a couple of long-lost fellow students. Glancing back at the lady now, he wondered what he could have been thinking of to have misread her so. She appeared almost stately, and he'd been churlish.

'Good morning, Mrs Benedick. What seems to be the trouble today?'

Mrs Benedick looked down at her gloved hands. The suede was very fine; one of the seams had come unstitched. 'I'm not entirely sure, doctor. I still don't believe everything's quite as it should be.' She went over her symptoms for him. They were vague, shifting discomforts. Her voice was cultured, liquid. She'd hurt her knee on last winter's ice and after so long it still gave her pain.

He was moved. 'It's a sad fact that as we get on, Mrs Benedick, our bodies take longer to heal.'

'But if one could discipline one's thoughts, Dr Pike, surely that would help. I find I sleep so badly, what with everything: the world, the news. Even the successes. Perhaps because of the successes. This over Rommel, say . . . Certain distressing items, they will insist . . .'

She'd hit it exactly. Certain distressing items: no more than his own thoughts. They turned constantly to Seremban, under Japanese occupation. But the woman herself . . . Only last week he'd baulked at a full examination, having convinced himself she was perfectly healthy. She was not neurasthenic. Nor did she complain of the precise discomforts of the natural process. Instead of flushes and mood swings she produced a disorganised malaise, and, as a rule, he gave such patients short shrift. Yet once again today he saw her in a different light. 'I'm sorry to hear that.'

She smiled. The ready play of her mouth was touching, and honest.

His daughter was waiting. But with Mrs Benedick he'd been too hasty too often. 'I think I ought to have a proper look at you, then, don't you?' he said. 'And we'll see if we can do something about that knee.'

He set the screen around the couch and waited at the window until he heard the springs creak. Then he hung his stethoscope round his neck, stuck the heavy man-ometer box in his coat pocket and opened the screen's end panel. She lay in her underclothes upon the couch beneath the unglazed reproduction of Flatford Mill. Her slip was pulled up and her hands were laced loosely together under her bosom. He hovered like a lover – the word went off in his head like a gun. That damned intuitive gift of his, it ran so contrary to science. The sight of her bare neck and shoulders made him blush, right to his unstarched collar. Her thighs, even with their slight sag of flesh, perhaps even because of it, were quite beautiful.

Lethargy; diffuse pain; headaches; lesion in right knee owing to fall, failure to mend. He tried to remain clini-cal, and failed profoundly. For, once he'd touched her, nothing could block the true diagnosis that had evaded him all along. Indeed, one slight, involuntary movement of Mrs Benedick's leg taught him in a flash what he should have seen months ago. Unfortunately, there was nothing medical about it. She – her head just turned away and the line of the underside of her jaw made visible – was attracted to him. Ten times worse, it was quite on the cards that he – judging by certain unmistakable sensations occurring parasympathetically with the contact – felt exactly the same.

He folded her slip back down in haste. He checked her breathing. All he could hear was his own heartbeat. He took her blood pressure but his hand tingled from her pulse and he broke off with the mercury unread and the band dangling from her arm. He went to wash. 'I can find nothing specifically wrong, Mrs Benedick.' His voice quavered, formulaic. 'But I'll try you on a different tonic, if you like. We'll see if that suits you better. And we could have some blood tests done, if things don't clear up. Of their own accord, I mean.' His throat was dry. 'The aches and pains . . . Well, we must all come to expect that sort of thing, I'm afraid.'

'Very well,' she said. 'Thank you, doctor.' Her own sound was sweetness. From where he stood by the ewer and basin, he heard her get up. He heard her hands smoothing her linen. She didn't reposition the screen. In the corner of his eye he caught her adjusting her lace hem. She stepped into her skirt, fastened it, and then pointed her toes into the worn brown high-heeled shoes. As she bent down to tie the laces he saw the bodice of her slip fall just a fraction away from her breasts. And when she stood up the soft, grey-streaked hair rolled upon the nape of her neck.

He moved to his desk to write up her notes. She emerged from the other side of the screen, buttoning her blouse and pulling on the fitted suit jacket with its moth holes in the lapel. There was nothing knowing or coquettish about her. She thanked him again, and he was desperate she should go at once, desolated that she would. He'd send the prescription. She thanked him once more, decorously. In leaving she gave no sign that she thought tuppence about him. Yet he knew he was right, and when he'd recovered himself, he was tempted to laugh out loud.

Dr Pike hadn't remained entirely impotent; it was more that he'd grown used to regarding himself as something of a hopeless case in that department. Now it seemed his long penance had ended. But even as he emerged from it, so the old difficulties loomed, as fresh and unresolved as if he were somehow picking up exactly where he'd left off, with Mattie, with Selama. Here stood the same moral dilemma, of forbidden territory. Mrs Benedick was his patient, and therefore sacrosanct. For that he was tempted to groan out loud. To complete the recurring picture there impended, of course, the matter of his daughter.

THAT AFTERNOON, THE black specks of American Flying Fortresses were visible, climbing in jagged formations up the November clouds and out over the North Sea. It was their raiding hour. And from the lane at the edge of the field came the inevitable growl and camouflaged canvas roof of an army lorry.

They were walking in the top meadow, Clarice, Vic and himself, wrapped up against the damp, still air. There was a hint of mist gathering. Bentley, the dog, visited them every so often before tearing off after some scent or flicker. Ethel Farmer had followed a rationing recipe in which grated carrot and powdered egg featured prominently. Now they were all uneasy with each other, trying to make light.

Yet Vic cut a reasonable enough figure in his khaki: the tanned, rather distinguished-looking face, the clipped brown hair. He was tall and strong. There was nothing about him as a man that would make one uneasy. Indeed, to his surprise, Dr Pike was disposed to like Vic very much, and as the day had worn on something of a father–son bond seemed primed and ready to spring up between them. But there was the matter he couldn't fathom, something Clarice wasn't telling him. It was too unconvincing that she simply craved his permission.

He hesitated. Clarice and Vic stopped beside him, expectantly. He felt cornered by circumstances, being asked to override a better judgement. He needed to think. 'I suppose if we've come to a natural break in the proceedings,' he said to Vic, half joking, 'I should ask you what your prospects are.'

'I'm afraid that's a difficult one, sir.' There was that trace of a London accent, just like the other one.

'Yes, I'm afraid it is.' Dr Pike sighed. They walked on

together. Vic threw another stick and Bentley plunged after it. The dog disappeared in a streaked green sea which frothed spent cow-parsley heads. Every few seconds a shower of shaken moisture showed his position. Then he returned, panting and empty mouthed. The parted grass revealed damp celandines, and another remnant of the Queen Anne's lace. 'Fetch,' Vic said. 'You're supposed to fetch!'

'He's completely barmy,' said Dr Pike. 'They're not bred for intellect, setters.'

Vic searched for something else to throw. The dog bounded up, and then crouched excitedly beside him. Clarice walked on a few paces ahead while Dr Pike brooded. His mind turned for the hundredth time to Mrs Benedick, and he wondered in which direction Bolt's Grove lay from where they stood. With a certain reluctance, he brought his attention back. Clarice looked peaked, certainly no advertisement for love's young dream. Her happiness lay in his hands; or in Vic's.

He ran over the facts, hoping for fresh insight. Blindly, blunderingly, but eventually, he'd got her out of the way of the Japanese. Crazily, he and she had managed the threat of invasion together. She'd survived being bombed. Now the war, at least against the Germans, showed signs of ameli-oration. She'd got off scot-free, hadn't she? Then where was the problem? Why wasn't Vic making her happy?

He tried to allow for any jealousy or frustration of his own. Diligently, he sought to put aside his liking for Vic as a man. Vic had striven, he knew, had built his barges and showed brains enough to want to better himself. Did that make him right for Clarice? Dr Pike detected a hint of suppressed violence – there was a holding back, a tension. But then the man was a soldier, and it was wartime; towards Clarice his movements showed nothing but care and affection.

Dr Pike knew he missed the nub of the matter. Some trouble was sapping Clarice from within. That was the problem and for all Vic's good nature he doubted the young man had much clue how to deal with it. Then again, could he really be trusted? He still wasn't sure – he felt he had too little to go on. He took out his watch and put it back in its pocket.

Rooks cawed from high up in the elms by Top Barn, and the sharp sound came like a saw down the long air of the meadow. Bentley barked. Vic Warren had already let down one woman in the family. He had been in prison for a serious crime. The whole subsequent situation was so full of legal tangles and familial awkwardnesses, it was irregular even for wartime. Dr Pike found himself coming to his position. Honestly – in all heartfelt honesty – he couldn't see the way through for her. And if that were the case, it was up to him to say so, wasn't it, as kindly as possible? To begin, at least, to air the matter?

He took the plunge. 'Everything I've been told, every-thing that's been said . . . Believe me, I have thought long and hard about it. Look, it's difficult for me to do this, but if you're looking for my blessing, I can't honestly say . . .'

'We're not.' Clarice turned round and glared at him. Everyone stood still.

'I see.'

'We're looking for your acceptance.'

He was aware of the sudden silence all about him. It took a moment for the distant country sounds to filter back: Appleby's tractor, woodpigeons, the receding army lorry, the rooks. He spread his hands. 'Acceptance of what, exactly?' The dog, Bentley, launched himself off after a fieldfare. 'I'm not quite sure of my duty here. From what you've told me, Vic isn't in a position to ask for your hand in marriage. But my role as your father in that area seems to have been pre-empted by events. As far as I've been given to understand, he's already married to Phyllis. Phyllis, on the other hand, who seems to be maintaining radio silence, showed up here with a different husband – also called Vic. And a goddamned child!'

He saw the pain that crossed Vic's face and was instantly sorry.

'Daddy. I thought you'd promised not to bring all that up. Vic and I have already pieced together exactly what must have happened that weekend. It all makes sense.'

'It may make sense, but where does it lead?' He stood his ground.

She lost her temper. 'What about love, Daddy? What about love?'

'According to the papers, we're all going to have a new start – apparently. When the war's over. What about you two? What will you be and what will you live on?'

'We'll manage. We'll sort something out. People do. Daddy, I can't believe you're making problems where none exist. Why are you being so difficult? You're all I've got.' She was staring at him, but she was already withdrawn and her gaze was stony.

He looked away. 'Why indeed? I'm sure I've no idea. Maybe it's just because I'm an old spoilsport.'

'It's not as though *you*'ve got much of a moral leg to stand on,' she said. 'All things considered.'

'Ah,' was all he replied, because the thrust was even more telling than she knew – in the light of Mrs Benedick.

'Well, is it?'

'Probably not, darling.' They walked on in silence, following the field's edge. 'And we've no idea what's become of the boy?' he said.

'Vic's trying to find him. He loves him. I . . .'

The church steeple came into view. 'Yes . . . ?' he said.

'I loved him too.'

When the three of them reached the gate into the lane,

he said, 'It's getting quite late for the trains. You're both welcome to stay over. Shall I ask Ethel to make Vic up a bed?'

'No need to worry Ethel. We'll be quite all right in my room. Thanks.'

Late into the evening, he sat up in his surgery listening for the night bombers. The picture – Flatford Mill – above the couch where a half-clad Mrs Benedick had so recently reclined, flickered with the lamplight. And beside the lamp stood an empty quinine bottle. Since the Japanese army had turned the Far East into a torture chamber and German submarines had made a charnel house of the high seas there was no quinine to be had. Not for love nor money.

He reflected on the long thin Panzer column of General Guderian, back in 1940. Its segments were fine soldiers, winding their way through the supposedly impenetrable forest of the Ardennes, racial ambassadors of the most advanced scientific nation in the world. He thought of the Japanese army – delegates of the most exquisite culture – *Lymphangitis* in the Malayan jungle, psychotic tourists threading the forest paths on bicycles, raping and killing in rubber gym shoes. He had on his desk a single cutting from an American magazine. It was, he felt *the* single cutting, for there had been no news elsewhere that he'd been able to discover. A well-placed German industrialist had smuggled intelligence out though Geneva. It concerned extermination by gas.

He'd *believed* in bloody myths. He'd bloody swallowed them. He'd believed there was peace and that war was parasitic on it. Now peace was the worm and Britain's dream nothing but a sentimental growth. 'What about love?' Clarice had cried out. Either way he'd alienated her. And Mary Benedick, a cruel tag snipped out of a prayer-book, Mary Benedick must be condemned to her diffuse symptoms because she had the power to strike him out of the register, his life and his living. Feeling bruised, he drew in his horns. Vic and Clarice must continue in their piecemeal love, fine soldiers in a kaleidoscope. Any new start would be long delayed, he knew, and the war would grind them apart. He took up his thermometer to check himself for fever. Sure enough his temperature was 101 degrees, and climbing.

V
The Tempter

MY BROTHER HAD fallen among thieves. Thieves were everywhere. All over the world they were having a field-day, making hay while the law couldn't touch them. In occupied Europe, thieves were stripping whole populations down to their hair and teeth.

Dr Pike's fragment of information had turned out correct – within days of him finding it, the story of the Final Solution had broken in the newspapers. Somewhere in Poland people really were disappearing into a vortex. On 17 December 1942, the entire House of Commons had stood in silence with heads bowed over a death toll already estimated at a million.

The tale was at once too true and too shocking; the furore it caused ended as soon as it began. When no new facts emerged a silence fell, and the subject was no longer reported. To the English, in the first weary months of another war year, the technicalities of melting the last shred of value out of a human being remained a mystery. Most still preferred not to believe in them.

Jack was already seven, and God saw whatever he did. The barn was dim and the straw stacked up in fraying steps. The stalks were sharp. On his shins they left scratch marks that were thin and red. On his arms, too. The shape of them, curving away into wisps at the end, reminded him of wind-blown vapour trails left in the sky by American bombers. His actions had become overlaid with guilt; some great responsibility lay on his shoulders.

Still the war would not truly show itself. Sometimes it was a thing of air, of theirs and ours. Through dud slats in the wooden walls farmyard smells came in with the chickens. Jack watched them, the muttering clockwork hens, pecking at trodden stalks beside the two farm machines. Colin, the other boy, jumped down to scatter the creatures, chasing one bantam over a pile of sheaves. Then he sat on the seat of the horse-hoe and pretended to be firing a machine-gun. Sometimes, the war was a toy drama of tanks and sand in comic books, a game of win or lose. Sometimes it was the sound of guns and of buildings rocking – a woman's hand sticking out from a pile of bricks.

Now, even inside the barn the air was discoloured, and somehow rotten, like snot, or phlegm. No excitements. Jack thought what a joyless drudgery it was at the little red school. These days he envied the younger ones, the tots who played so carelessly in the smaller playground. He was a miscreation who couldn't get his breath.

The straw prickled and itched against the skin where his clothing was disarranged. He was certainly not like his classmates. He watched Colin, now darting after this chicken, now chasing that. Colin ought not to chase the hens. The farmer might come. They must go.

Jack pulled on his balaclava. Grabbing his coat, he scrambled down from the stack of straw. He called to Colin and they took straw kindling and dry sticks, buttoning them inside their jackets before slipping out of the great creaking barn door and into the farmyard. There were puddles with ice on them, and wisps of corn were frozen into the ruts. More chickens strutted around a tractor; in his stall the cart-horse stamped. Jack regretted the jaded outbuildings, the mud, the dung clamp, and the pile of jag-iced hardcore beside the open gate. Picking his way across muck and worn concrete, there was no relief.

He remembered a puttering tractor in a place beside an estuary. Far away, one ship had tan sails, one white. Aunt Clarice had taught him the names of birds, of the leaves and buds, and the emergent flowers. And beyond the railway arch, a lost land, forever fleeting.

Then he understood something. It came like a buzz in his head, mixed up with the buzz of cars and lorries from the Southend arterial road. He and Colin were at the end of the long lane that led up from the farm, and the thing that had so perplexed him, the yellowness, the persistent tainting of the town he'd come to live in – that *was the war*. Why hadn't he realised? All along it had been right under his nose, the word grown-ups used so casually. He'd taken to heart what they took for granted. Now, as he and Colin walked back along the cold track towards his house, he didn't know if he knew too much, or too little. He was set apart. What about the words Clarice had whispered in his ear, that day on the lorry?

I see my poor brother, through the gap in the years. The child thrown back on himself is never-endingly thoughtful, and maybe there'd be no philosophising at all but for unhappy children. Who'd have to fathom the world but those for whom it makes no sense? Who'd invent systems but those subject to strangeness and disruption? Jack had lost his youth in the move from Ripple Road. Now he was filled with sin – they said so at the school.

HE TRUDGED WITH Colin back up the steep rise. The morning's frost still lay in pockets behind the hedge. There were spider's webs with drops of water clinging to them. They were strung between the thorn branches and headless stalks beside the path. Jack took out one of his sticks to slash them through, clamping the rest more tightly with his arm against his body. His house came into view.

Behind the back fence, a scrub-lined gully ran through the waste ground. There, out of sight of windows, the two boys lit their fire. Flames ate into the pieces of old magazines, *Picture Post* and *Reveille*, and the newspapers a deserter had left smeared from wiping his backside. White rime lay upon the single empty beer bottle. A sardine can had the lid wound back on the metal key. When the bottle smashed on the sharp pointed stone, the pieces flew like shrapnel.

Suddenly, at the crest of the gully's wall, two other boys were standing, watching them. He hadn't heard them sneak up. Their pullovers and trousers had the stained grey colour of poor kids' clothes and their legs were marked over with mud smears. One had a glue of snivel hanging from his nostril. They came down and started talking.

Jack was glad when the fight started, trying to wrestle the kid's legs out from under him. But he still couldn't reckon the seriousness. How would it end? There were shards of glass on the floor. He identified a blade-shaped sliver lying next to the sharp stone. He might be able to stretch and pick it up.

He could glean nothing from the look in the kid's eye. When he got him down, he jammed his mucky head against the stone until he cried out. The other one was kneeling on Colin's arms, ready to punch his face.

'Let him go or your mate gets it.'

Jack let his victim up.

The boy was shocked. 'Grind my head, would you?'

The newcomers swapped positions and started punching. Jack put his arms up to protect himself. He let the other boy's fists land on him, soaking up the thumps until, beside his shoulder, he heard Colin start to cry. His first assailant broke off to kick out their fire.

'Come on, Rodge,' he said. 'His dad's Rice. That kid's Tony Rice's son.'

'Oh, yeah?'

'He is, Rodge. Come on, that's enough.'

Rodge kicked Jack in the leg, swore, and put his boot on what was left of the embers. 'Lucky for you then, mate. Or you'd have got smashed.' Then the two scrambled back up the bank the way they'd come, agile as monkeys. At the top Rodge turned and looked down.

'Cunts!' he called, loud enough for the sound to carry to Jack's house, and for his mother to hear. 'Fucking cunts, you are!' They laughed and ran off.

Jack wanted to run after them, and burn the backs of their necks with one of the stick ends from the trashed fire. But he would not. And once more he'd failed. Because the other children at the school made light of the war, and wanted a fight, and would have made friends afterwards and known where they stood; while he had to make do with Colin.

In his house, the new baby, Melia, was crying upstairs. A man in uniform was still putting up wallpaper in the front room and the tang of his cigarette smoke hung in the newly carpeted hallway. Past the clutter of stacked furniture, Jack made his way to the kitchen. As he did so, he thought of the man with the light behind him who was making a house. More and more the picture came to him these days, of how he had been held up in those arms.

IN THE RECREATION ground the witch's hat was draped in April snow. At an angle off the black central pole, it made the long white lines of a wigwam. Freak snow lay an inch thick on the roundabout. It was already melting on the slide and had fallen into a heap at the chute bottom.

Blue straggly hyacinths, dripping, pressed up out of the unexpected covering. The sky was grey and heavy; and from all around came the faint noises of the thaw, the patter of the drips. He could sense the give of collapsing crystals. Further off, a white mist shrouded the trees by the fence and it screened the flint church walls.

Jack cleared the snow from a swing. As he touched his feet to the wet ground the cold soaked to his skin through the seat of his trousers. He took from his pockets the three German cartridge cases and the piece of twisted shrapnel. The hymn they'd sung at the school kept cropping up in his head. The song forced him to see its pictures. A far green hill was stuck through with daffodils, their fraught colour and soft, earthen perfume. Pennies of blood dripped on to them. He could not bear it. Harmonies out of the ill-tuned piano in the school hall made him feel sorry.

The headmaster had exhorted the children to take up the cross. How brave the other children seemed. In the playground they marched and shouted, unabashed by the duty that was laid on them: to die. They would gladly go to the sacrifice. But he, Jack, was frightened.

He made himself stay put on the swing, trying to gauge his discomfort. His fingers were numb. His legs were chapped from where the trouser hems rubbed his thighs. None of these counted. In church they gave the children something. There was some secret, perhaps, that took away the pain. That was how they got courage enough to fight. That was what he'd missed out on, coming from London.

He wondered, as always, what was inside the building of the church, behind the big door where the comfortable folk went in; what faces the saints wore. Women were married. Something was done to a woman in church that made a child grow inside her belly, every so often. To have it cut out how resolute must she be, once she'd come from the arched doorway.

That night he was dreaming. There was a thump, thump. When he opened his eyes he could hear nothing. He waited. His radiator hissed in the dark. He put out his hand to feel its scalding metal. Then there were muffled shouts from beyond his door, and another hit. Something broke.

He put his head beneath the pillow and pulled its ends about his ears, but it was useless to filter out the sounds. His mother's persistent pleas or complaints were like the line of a song, savage but indistinct. Punctuated by his father's outbursts, they forced their way into his head. Eventually, he sat up and threw back the covers. The winter night was mild, and the air in his blacked-out bedroom had become oppressive. A black wind was soughing outside. He stepped from the bed, feeling his way towards the door, his toes sinking with each footfall into the pile of the new rug. Then he reached the bare boards and found the handle. It opened soundlessly. Crouched on the landing next to his parents' door he could hear the precise words.

'You're a liar. You've always been a liar, you bloody bitch.'

'All right, then. Hit me again, then. You know you want to. Kill me. Go on.'

And then he heard the blows land, and his mother's whimper. There was a moment of complete silence, before the sound of the sobs began, a terrible drawn-out weeping that seemed to swell and then maintain itself as though it might never stop.

There were other noises, too, as of slight ineffectual movements. He sensed his father's exasperation. 'Shut it! D'you hear me! Just fucking shut it, all right! Shut it, for Christ's sake. Do you want some more?'

There was a change. He heard his mother groan. And then his father's voice came, deeper, softer. 'Come on, you silly bitch. I'm not going to hurt you. Come on, will you. Come on, Phylly, for fuck's sake. That's enough now. That's enough. Did you think I was going to do you in? Eh? Silly cunt. You know me. Don't you. Eh? You know me.'

He heard his mother's faint laugh, gritted and far away, sounding almost as though Jack were still in his own bedroom. Then she spoke. 'Yes, but I wasn't fibbing, Tony. All right? I wasn't. He could be yours. Why couldn't he?'

'Could he hell.'

'I'm telling you.'

'You're telling me, are you. Why now? Why now, Phyllis? Why tell me now?'

'I'm telling you, all right. You could have worked it out as well as me, couldn't you? Eh? You could. If you'd have been bothered.'

JACK WAITED. THEN he sensed that his parents' door was about to open. As quietly as he could he hurried back along the stairhead to his room, teasing the catch shut behind him, and slipped himself into bed. A moment later, sure enough, he felt the draft as his own door swished wide, and recognised, through lidded eyes, the glare of the landing light. He heard one step, two, of hard bare feet.

A presence was bending over him. He knew his father's eyes were peering intently at him. He endured the scrutiny of his face, almost X-raying the bone. What was he trying to know? He lay as still as he could, counterfeiting sleep. At last there was the scuff and pad again of the bare feet on the boards, and the door closed once more.

In the morning, he searched his mother's face for marks while she cooked him breakfast; but she was heavily made up and wore a turban round her newly washed hair, she said, that fitted like a charlady's closely to her temples. Nor did she move far, or fast. He saw, out of the dining-room window, the birds that came to the strips of bacon rind she'd hung up, sparrows and blue tits, and a bullfinch. And there were yellowhammers that perched, inquisitive, upon the wire fence next to them.

He studied her again when she couldn't avoid leaning close to him across the table to pick up the milk jug. Her turban seemed to slip slightly to one side, and before she could put the striped china jug down again to set it right there was revealed the bruised end of a split in her skin, just in the hair above her ear. All kinds of impressions flooded him – though he scarcely had an idea of what they were, or what they might portend.

On the bus to school, he'd forgotten his fare money. The conductress stood him on the footplate at the back, telling him not to worry, an arm resting on his shoulder where the satchel strap went across. He rode, standing, nearer and nearer to the school, past the big houses set back in gardens behind their fences, and on into the town beside the first shops. The satchel bobbed at his back as the bus hit a bump in the road beside the tube station. He remembered the other wound in her head and the man in the garden who had lifted him up – like a father.

He sat in his desk near the window. In a jamjar on the sill there was a stem of pussy willow. He made it sharp and clear, and the sky beyond it through the pane was like a sheet of paper, a background of blue-white. When he looked at the cloud streaks high and fine above the elm tree in the corner of the schoolyard, it was the dusted buds that were doubled, turned to nothing more than dabs of grey on two blurred stalks. He made the effect go back and forth, back and forth.

He remembered Ripple Road, the cut in her forehead, her voice: *what's a war if no one gets wounded?* He heard the sound of her voice. Yes, he'd seen her hurt exactly like that before. Not just the ordinary bruises but a bright, clear cut, he remembered, with the drops of blood coming out like buttons, then falling to the floor. At Tony's place years ago: bright red pennies. Gone to buy a rabbit skin.

His yellow-striped school tie lay against his grey shirt-front. How queer he felt. The house, that new brick house slammed down, so it appeared, beside a peculiar arrangement of creases, gashes, and steep fallings away upon a piece of waste ground; today he could almost taste the pall over it and the school and the bus ride between them.

He sat next to a boy called Timmy Mott. At the double desk, they'd each copied the map of Sinai, and the Red Sea. Underneath it he was writing in ink the words from the blackboard: *The enemy said, I will pursue, I will overtake, I will divide the spoil; my lust shall be satisfied upon them; I will draw my sword, my hand shall* . . . His pen had blotted on the word '*spoil*' and Mrs Penruddock was annoyed. She pulled the hair on the top of his head before moving on to the desk in front. The clouds had rearranged themselves. Jack watched the wisps in the window's frame detach, and their ends curl upward and round. Then he caught the exact moment at which they moved across the bar in the window into the next pane. So, too, did the movement of the clock hands become visible if he fixed his gaze. The passage of the minute hand between the marks made him feel as though he were floating.

In the distance there was the sound of anti-aircraft guns. All the heads in the class lifted, and then returned to their work. 'Dagenham,' Timmy Mott whispered. Now a whole spear of fuller, thicker cloud appeared, and the wisps were nowhere to be seen. There'd been a succession of miracles. Jack knew their names: Pearl Harbor, El Alamein. There'd been a special assembly and thanks to God. Now there was no movement, only waiting. They were waiting for the Yanks to roll up the Pacific. He did not understand. They were waiting for more Yanks to arrive with more tanks and more jeeps.

He began to write again: . . . *destroy them. Thou did'st blow with thy wind, the sea covered them: they sank as lead in the mighty waters.*

He could be yours, his mother had said. The words hung in Jack's mind. A face other than Tony's, another man's: with his hammer and nails, he was making a little wooden house. It was in the country beyond the railway bridge. Jack could picture the roses. Their heady smell drifted momentarily upon his recollection. The grass was dry and sharp bladed, straw coloured in the warm sun. It was a strange, higgledy-piggledy town, perhaps in a story, or not a town at all. A bus was a house and had its own chimney-pipe sticking out of it. His mother lay in a garden, asleep, the bright little cut like a jewel at the edge of her hair. His father . . .

'You, boy. Jack Warren. Get on with your work. Don't you know there's a war on?'

AS THE UNTIMELY snow melted next morning, its fog rolled northward from the estuary over the coastlands where the Essex marsh merged with the Suffolk shore. Fog began to blanket that whole system of flatted rivers and inlets by which the outflux of the Thames, across a shallow sea, mirrored that of the Rhine.

By mid-morning, it was so dense that Dr Pike, newly arrived, could hardly see the gates of Woodbridge Airbase. He stood in his trilby, scarf and sports jacket, holding the handlebar grips of Ethel Farmer's bicycle. Quite how he'd managed the ten miles from Pook's Hill he wasn't quite sure. Since Martlesham, the landscape had been reduced to guesswork. Now before and behind him the road was only a nuance of metalled grey, its line lost amid the dripping shapes of tall fir trees.

The sound of a lorry made him turn. Its engine was whining in a low gear. He moved hurriedly out of the way as it swung in at the guard post and stopped. A barrier lifted. Two brief red tail-lights were drawn by the truck into the mist, until they, too, vanished.

He peered after them. There was precious little to see of his daughter's world, nor did the mist make so much difference. The air force, with its ever-increasing network of runways, was in the habit of fencing itself off. They had their own lingo, their own ways, these heroes and their warrior maidens. He hardly knew her.

He felt his fingers patting at his watch through the fob of his waistcoat. Pulling the scuffed hunter out, he opened it and squinted down at the face. His half-moon spectacles were in a different pocket. He fished for them. Clarice had said eleven. It was twenty past. He'd misread her note. He had the day wrong. There were two airbases. Something had happened to her.

Eventually, however, a WAAF emerged from beside the sentry-box. He recognised her outline immediately, the distinctive sway of her body, the carriage of her head. Capped and skirted, she, too, was wheeling a bicycle. Trails of frozen breath appeared from her mouth. Only when she was almost close enough to touch was there any colour in her cheeks or tone to her uniform. He embraced her. And before his spectacles themselves misted up he saw tiny droplets of water on her eyebrows, on her eyelashes, and beaded on the strands of hair that strayed from under her cap brim.

'Daddy. I'm so glad you could come.'

The two bicycle frames had locked horns. They pulled them apart. 'It's so good to see you, darling.'

She needed to explain. 'A crew of ours had to put down here. I came yesterday with the transport, to pick them up. It's an emergency field. If they're limping and losing height on the way back from the Ruhr, this is one of the nearest points. Home, you see.' She looked up at him. 'They've even got a fog system.'

'Have they?'

'Yes. Flares and all that. I've had to come here quite a few times actually, since . . . since we last spoke. It's part of my job. But I've never taken the chance before. To get in touch, I mean. I just wanted to see you. I know you're cross with me.'

'Cross with you?'

'Yes.'

'Of course I'm not.'

She insisted. 'You are, Daddy. You don't like Vic. And you think I'm . . . loose. Don't you? You think I'm irresponsible. A tart.'

'I can assure you, my dear. Nothing has been further from my mind.'

'Then why . . . ? Oh, but don't let's start. Don't let's. If we talk we'll spoil things. I wanted to see you. Sometimes I feel . . . low; and you're the one who can make it better.'

He smiled. 'I do my best.' The bicycles were unwieldy again. He faced around. 'If you don't want to talk, darling, then we shan't. What about trying to find our way back to the town? There'll probably be a teashop or something.'

She pointed in the other direction. 'A few minutes and you come to the shore. I'd really like to see the sea.'

'Aren't beaches supposed to be out of bounds?'

'Who cares?'

At Shingle Street they left the bikes between two cottages and trudged across the wide pebble strand. There was no horizon, only fogged military defences: tangles of rusted wire amid tufts of sea cabbage, and a weather-beaten post warning of mines. The sea marge sloped, and at its foot waves arrived hurriedly from nowhere, lapping and swirling into a diminutive lagoon. There was a short spit loaded with pieces of armoured wreckage, beached as though some failed invasion had occurred which no one dared mention. Stan Pike thought he could make out the black and white of an iron cross.

'Well,' she said. 'What have you been up to?'

'Oh, the usual,' he grinned. 'But what about you? Oh, Lord. You're a corporal.'

She touched her sleeve and grinned back. 'Proud of me? I went on a course in Wales. I get to be a duty clerk.'

'At which station now?'

'Attlebridge. It's up near Norwich. All very rustic.'

'And what do you do?'

'Everything. Typing. Admin. Making sure A happens and B doesn't. Getting C delivered. Driving Squadron Leader D here, there and everywhere, and fending off his advances. And every night the boys go up and bomb something.'

'You're kept busy.'

'I enjoy it. How about you?'

'I practise, though it rarely makes perfect.'

'Very funny, Daddy. And still no . . . ?'

Her question hung in the air. He wondered whether she meant the progress of his malaria, or even if she'd managed to tune in to his feelings for Mrs Benedick. 'No what?'

'No backslidings. The bottle.'

'Oh, that. God, no. A glass now and then. Nothing immoderate, I assure you. Poor Selama . . .'

'You still think of her.'

'Of course. And she of me, so it feels sometimes.' His voice tailed off.

Clarice turned to the left. They began to trudge once more along the shingle, following the line of the breakers.

A stir of wind caught the back of Stan's hair and lifted the brim of his hat; and another. The mist began to move, tearing and forming clumps.

'No more bloody paper cuttings everywhere, though,' Clarice said.

'On the contrary. I keep an eye on things, and have my scraps laid out on my desk. Ethel relentlessly tidies them. I relentlessly weight them down with my more embarrassing gynaecological instruments. In the hope of scaring her off.'

'Does it?'

'Heavens, no. She has a stronger stomach than mine. Rural life, you see. What *has* been bothering me recently, though, has been a shortage of material.'

'Isn't there enough bad news for you?'

'I mean specifically about one thing.'

'Ah. The atrocity stories. I'd rather you spared me the details, if you wouldn't mind.'

He put his arm around her. 'Yes. I quite understand.'

'Do you, though?' She spoke angrily. Then she turned in mid-stride and hugged him so that they both nearly fell down the pebble bank.

He found himself staggering wildly amid a grind of stones. 'Hey, look out!'

She laughed at him. 'Sorry. Sorry about that. It's just that I do love you, Daddy. And I get cross with you – because I always think you're cross with me.'

'Well, I'm not. I've told you I'm not.' He scrambled to rescue his hat from down near the water's edge. 'I just want what's best for you, that's all.'

She linked arms when he returned. 'And that's what we said we weren't going to discuss. My, my. How difficult it all is, not to talk of things.'

'My point exactly – that it's fishy. The lack of information. After so much last December. The ghettoes.

The routes taken by the trains. It's bloody fishy, darling.'

'Please! I have to be getting back, soon. And look, the
mist's clearing.'

The mist ripped apart even as they watched. It was
heaping back upon the pine woods inshore, and suddenly
there was a view right through to Orford Ness. They
looked, and then turned to walk back. Within minutes it
was a spring day. Against a bright blue sky, Bawdsey radar
masts were visible, and the Martello towers.

Along the road, glistening water-meadows lay beside
the streams. They crossed small, flat bridges. He couldn't
refrain from asking her, 'How are things with Vic?'

'Vic's fine,' she said. 'And so am I. Look! There are the
flares, still burning on the runway.'

She pointed across the distance. Far off there was the
wire boundary fence of the base, and through it, evenly
spaced, a row of minute, delicate fires could be seen
kindling in the furze. Stan Pike sighed to himself. He
was unable to make things better for his daughter at all.
She would set flames, as it were, around herself, and there
was no approaching her.

ONLY NOW, FOR some reason, did Jack's mother begin to
remark in the evenings that it would be for the best if he
were to be evacuated, 'like all the other children'. She said
the Germans had started bombing schools.

There had been no really serious raids since the one in
January, when the very first snows had lain all about. On
that frozen night, the gaggles of bombers had once more
been audible overhead. Jack had watched from his window
the play of searchlights, and the streaked colours of ack-ack
going up into the darkness. A German bomber had been

caught, the topmost point of a pyramid of white rays. He'd seen the brilliant shells exploding round it, like starbursts, while he was supposed to be asleep. There'd been nothing like it since.

No, there were always noises in the air, but hardly ever the menace of bombs any more. And another thing. He'd never seen Tony Rice, his father, put out before. The man he was used to, and scared of, the man who had that sardonic way with him, and that decisive opinion about everything, the man who would spend several days of each week absent 'on business', so his mother said, had always been inclined to wear at home a certain smile. The mouth in the smooth face was very clearly shaped, and there'd been many a tense supper time when Jack would look out of the corner of his eye at it, while the man ate. He would try to read the mouth's movements – until Tony, his father, turned and stared ironically back at him.

Now the smile seemed to have grown tighter and thinner. Jack had the idea that Tony Rice no longer operated in quite so cavalier a manner, believed a mite less securely that the war's crippling yellow breath could never bloody touch *him*. A vague knowledge fluttered at Jack like some insect against a pane of glass, that Tony was finding his presence too troubling to cope with.

Now, in the mild April evenings, there was one further question. The mother of a little girl along the road came complaining about him. Something had been done, or said. The matter was confused; some scenes of Jack's life were broken and mixed up. The girl had told her mother. His own mother had been in a rage. And she was frightened. He'd been punished and sent to his room where he'd recited the Lord's Prayer over and over again, to make the thoughts leave his head. He'd tried pulling the dressing-gown cord tight around his neck.

No more had been said, but the incident gave Jack the

impression that the moody discipline which bound his family so tightly and insulated it so effectively, no longer had quite the force to contain him.

Then his mother let it drop that it wasn't some common-or-garden government scheme that he would be sent to, but actually a school – a boarding school. He was being offered an opportunity, a chance to get education. It would make a man of him, and nothing was wrong nor ever had been.

A certain Tuesday, when he got in from the bus, there were cardboard cartons and boxes, wrapped and tied, that had just been delivered. Stacked one on top of the other in the hall they looked exactly like American PX supplies. He stopped in his tracks, horrified to see London matters blatantly on display at his home. His mother came from the front room with the baby on her hip. She beckoned to him. 'Aren't you going to open them, then?' She laid Melia in her pram.

He did as he was told. He started to fumble the knot out of a string, expecting any moment that he and his mother would be joined by Frankie, or Mrs Lavender, the woman with pencilled eyebrows. Mrs Lavender's ragged laughter would herald some terrible consequence. His fingers began to shake. He listened for the tramping of soldiers' boots on the concrete path outside. Break your mother's heart to know the half of what you get up to, Figgsy had said. I'd have to rip yours out, wouldn't I, you shitty little tramp.

But the cardboard contained not candy, nor Camel cigarettes, nor watches, nylons, revolvers, nor the packets with the curious names – Benzedrine, Penicillin, Morphine, Cocaine – nor any other blazon of an underworld where walls had ears and careless talk would cost you dearly. He took out instead a perfect school cap, ring striped in silver and blue and stuffed with tissue paper. Where the tissue fell away, a badge fell with it, waiting to be sewn in. The sweat cooled on his brow, and the faint subsided. His mother smiled.

She pulled out the rest of the contents and held up the blazer. It was made from the same colours and had the same badge. There were silver buttons. 'Try it, Jack. Why don't you. It's for you.'

He put it on. She put the hat on his head. 'There. My! Aren't you the smart one? Come on, let's look at you.' She took him up to her bedroom. He saw himself in her dressing-table mirror, the top half of a strange new creature in the stiff, slightly-too-big clothes. Standing behind him, touching him, she was holding the badge over the peak of his cap. 'Well,' she said. 'What do we think of that?' The clutter of her brushes, lotions and lipsticks appeared twice in front of him, and again in the side mirrors. The flavours of her perfumes drifted. He looked around, feeling the pressure of her body against his new collar. One of her lace-edged slips was thrown over the back of the chair; a pair of nylons lay strewn on the floor.

'Don't you just look the part? Little Lord Fauntleroy!' Excited, she took him downstairs again, her arm about his shoulder. In one package there were towels and sheets, pyjamas, a new dressing-gown. In another a pair of cricket boots, white plimsolls, black shoes. Yet another held the stack of grey shirts, the grey corduroy trousers, the thick grey socks.

She was in a kind of transport, unpacking the lavish, best-quality items, as if there were no rationing nor had ever been, nothing make do nor threadbare in the world. A typed list had the items ticked off. 'They call the socks stockings, Jack. What do you think of that? You won't want to speak to the likes of us any more, once you go to a toff school. Not with your Latin and French. It'll be Physics next, I'll be bound.' Then she mimicked a high-faluting tone. 'Every Sunday the boys attend matins at the cathedral. Won't want to know your own mother, will you?'

Jack couldn't think how to answer.

Her voice changed. 'But then you never wanted me anyway, did you? Couldn't wait to get out of the door, half the time. You hate me, don't you? Well, you'll be pleased now. You've got out of here, eh? Joining the posh side of the family.' She laughed mockingly. 'You'll be better off without me, won't you, holding you back?'

She began to stuff the clothes back anyhow inside their wrappings. 'That's what you think, don't you? Like your dear Auntie Clarice.' A roll of name-tapes fell on to the floorboards and came slightly undone: J Warren, J Warren, J Warren. Then she turned her back on both him and the task and went fiercely upstairs in her high-heeled shoes. He watched the seams of her nylons running up under the hem of her fine American skirt, her shapely calves moving under the pressed fabric with that tantalising near-nakedness.

Halfway up, she turned, her hand on the banister. 'The bloody ground she treads on. Still worship it, don't you? You don't give a tinker's for me. Nothing I've done for you has ever been good enough. That's what you think, isn't it? And now all this.' She gestured about inclusively. 'The things I've had to do. You take it all in your stride, don't you? Oh, yes. You're just a dirty-minded, ungrateful little boy. If I had my way, I'd take the bloody hide off you. Just you think yourself lucky, that's all.' She faced about again and continued angrily up the stairs.

Across the road from the front gate, there was a high, untidy hedge, and beyond it a field where the drills of new corn bristled, so that the sunlit clay had a shimmer of green running all the way down its slope. At the corner of the field a beech tree rose up tall. He climbed into the crook of a branch, and looked out towards London from under a fringe of young, almost transparent leaves. Two fighter planes were circling over Hornchurch. Beyond the golf course, he could see glinting railway lines, and the red caterpillar of the tube train crawling under the sun towards Dagenham.

She was jealous of him. He ought to have been punished. Instead, a parcel had arrived, and it was for him. Then surely his Aunt Clarice had been as good as her word. He remembered her soft fair hair pinned up, and the sound of her voice. She'd tried to persuade his mother to let him come to her. Instead, they'd settled on this boarding-school education. He recalled the faint perfume of flowers that came from her clothes, the sweet sound of her voice. She was almost present.

A POOL OF sick had formed outside the station canteen. The doorway to the bar looked in on to a dark wood counter cluttered with half-filled bottles and soda syphons. The man inside stroked his white moustaches. Jack's mother wiped the splashes off his shoes with her handkerchief. It was a Saturday afternoon. The hot sun had filled the air with so much moisture and pollen that it tasted sweet, peppery, near liquid. The clouds hinted at thunder. He had heard nothing from Clarice.

Jack watched the shop fronts, with their poor displays and empty shelves, flick across the taxi window like the scenes in a film. People were going about their business. There was a market square. The car edged its way between shouts and jostle. Then came the sharp smell of cattle. Jack saw them being driven, lowing, into iron pens by men in brown coats. The driver swung to avoid a greengrocer's horse and cart with 'Finest in Chelmsford' painted upon it.

There were more shops, canopied windows in three-storey brick house fronts.

The next moment they were among side roads, and after that in broader streets flanked by villas. He shifted himself on the leather seat, and his new trousers squeaked. The taxi-driver's cigarette smoke drifted back in thick strands; he put up his hand to touch one of them.

His father began speaking to the driver about the taxi's year and model. Then he made a joke about the nabob in the back seat. They'd all better mind their manners, he said. From now on, they'd have to do their business without leaving a smell. Jack looked to see what the nabob was. All at once unlikely hedges had closed in on both sides. It was a narrow lane with a pair of old-fashioned country cottages at the bottom. A gateway had a gravel drive under tall, gloomy trees which, for a second, quite blotted out the sky. Then ahead, so that the branches framed its grey façade, there was an imposing villa of the type they'd passed only a few minutes earlier. On the tight little gravel drive two or three large cars waited before them at the entrance, a central portico with stone pillars. One of the cars was painted khaki with a regimental badge on it.

Jack squinted through the plate glass from under his peaked cap. The smell of sick still hung about, because his mother had the handkerchief in her handbag. Now he fingered the embroidered blazer badge. The jacket seemed made of bright blue cardboard, and his bare knees stuck out in front of him as though from some corduroy furnishing. If he bent forward and looked down, his black toecaps shone back at him. His shoes pinched his feet, laced too tightly over the thick, ribbed stockings.

The taxi came to a stop. The driver got out, opened the doors and fetched the case from the boot. Jack walked forward on the gravel and mounted the steps. He shook the hand of a tall, grey-haired lady with a lined face and plucked eyebrows. Her skin was dry and curiously cold. She cast an eye over his parents and then took him in. Almost, he had no conception of being inside his body.

Now he stood beside an iron-framed bed and three boys were gathered round him. One of them was studying his wrist. The boy asked him if his American watch were his own, and then told Jack to take it off.

'Why?'

'Because you're going to get bashed up.' The boy who spoke thumped the bed with his fist. Jack should say goodbye to his mother now, another said, in case she didn't recognise him after what he was going to get.

A white-coated young woman, like a nurse, appeared at the door of the dormitory. 'All right, Warren. Your parents are just off now. You can pop down to see them go. Just leave your things on your bed, for a minute.' She disappeared back beyond the open door.

'Well,' the first boy said. 'What are you waiting for? Hadn't you better go and do what Matron said? Just mind you don't sneak, that's all. Know what sneaks get? I tell you: sneak, and it'll be all the worse for you. Understand?'

Warren went to the door and stepped out into a narrow, polished corridor. It was quite dark and only comfortably wide enough for one person. Seven years old, he clomped firmly down upon the boards in his new shoes, not sneaking, and descended the great, carpeted stairway, to where his parents were standing in the front hall, next to the grey-haired lady. His mother was toying with one of the buttons on her fur coat. His father, in his cravat and dog-tooth suit, holding his trilby hat in his hand, was making a joke about not forgetting Jack's holdall. He called it a johnny bag, and sneered.

The lady turned apologetically to another couple by the door. She was sure parents would understand the difficulties for schools in maintaining a full complement of boys during the present unfortunate circumstances. She coughed and hurried on. And also of masters. Geography was with the Marines; while Scripture – the young Revd McGilligan, who'd been showing such promise, had been sent as a padre to Iceland of all places. And her own son was in training somewhere in Southern England, which was all a mother was permitted to know. Then she looked round again. 'Ah, yes. Young Warren. Well, Mr and Mrs Rice. You can rest assured he's in safe hands.'

Jack shook hands with them; and then his family was gone.

THE PARQUET FLOOR smelt of polish and sour milk and the inside of shoes. The hallway was lined with name boards and mounted shields. Boys spilt from behind solid oak doors, talking breezily and laughing. Jack blinked hard and swallowed. The boys swirled away in a crowd and disappeared.

An older lad, dressed in a pullover and long trousers, was left reading a notice. The grey-haired lady asked him to take Warren back up. 'He's in Plantagenet, I think. Aren't you, Warren? There was talk of putting some of them in Hanover, but I don't think we had enough beds in there. Matron will know.'

As he climbed the thick staircarpet, in his thick corduroy, Jack remembered the word, hangover, his mother smiling: *When you drink too much. Like Dad.*

'New, are you?' said the boy.

'Yes.' Jack's holdall with his towel and pyjamas and washing kit grazed against his leg.

'It's not too bad here. Once you get used to it.'

On the great galleried landing boys milled in through

the open doorways, and rows of beds with cabin trunks beside them were briefly visible in the light from huge distant windows. He passed a washroom on his right with two enormous enamel baths and a row of sinks and was delivered back to his bed.

'Well,' said the boy who'd threatened him. 'Did you sneak? I bet you did, didn't you? I bet he sneaked.' He looked round at the others.

'I didn't,' Jack said. 'I didn't sneak at all.'

'You better not have. What's your name?'

'Warren.'

'I'm Temple. What form are you in?'

Jack stared at him. He could make no sense of the question. He wondered whether he was allowed to defend himself.

'Bet he's in Gordon,' said one of the others. 'Bet he doesn't know anything.'

'Bet he's an evacuee.'

'Bet he's a Jew.'

'Come on, where do you live?'

'Bet he's an oick. Talks a bit like one.'

'What outfit's your father in?'

A tall boy of about twelve strolled towards a bed in the corner by the fireplace, and threw himself languidly upon it. 'So this is the billet I've drawn this term. God, what a hole. Temple, you can unpack my trunk. Neatly, mind. The rest of you can get your own things sorted out. And no noise.' He pulled a magazine from his blazer pocket. 'I've got an *Illustrated London News* I want to read, to see how my brother's getting on. He's kicking Fritz out of Africa, for your information. Anyone who disturbs me gets the regulation three.'

How extraordinary a world he'd been transported to. Jack thought of *The Tinder-box*, and of the voice that used to read it to him. When you drink too much. Like Dad. And how he'd liked that story, especially the part where the soldier came with his money to live in the town, and was a gentleman. Now that his parents had gone, he could even imagine that Clarice would come in to explain, that she would walk in like the princess, wearing her pretty green jacket and mauve serge skirt to tell him that the war was over.

Much later that evening he was standing in the washroom, not sneaking, holding his new towel, wearing his new pyjamas, new slippers, and new, regulation dressinggown, while his fellows were at the sinks, washing and larking about in the mysterious twilight. In the huge sash windows the last of the daylight made silhouettes of the trees. There was a cry from outside.

At once the boys left what they were doing and the windows were run up. Half-naked bodies craned out into the darkness. Two boys broke away suddenly, their faces intent, excited, as they ran past Warren out of the room. A prefect appeared, grey-corduroyed. 'It's a bug called Wiseman. They caught him beside the spinney. His face was all bloody, but he escaped.'

'He's a plucky little fighter, actually, but he's taken an awful pounding.'

'He tripped over a root by the lawn and smashed his mouth, before they could do it for him.'

Warren stared at the high washroom walls. They stretched up and beyond, steam-grey and scarred with pipework. From a long wire in the ceiling, a single unlit light bulb dangled over the rows of outdated wash-basins.

'What sort of name is that? Wise man? Not so sensible now, is he?'

'He's a Jew boy. Or a spy. He's a German. They come over here and change their names.'

'Refujew!'

The windows were slung up like guillotines, and his fellows were leaning out.

266

'There he goes! They're all after him again.'

He heard the din of running feet. He kept wiping his mouth.

'He's down. They've got him. He's done for.' At last another prefect came in, with long trousers and a badge. 'It's all over. Now, any other new bugs, get along to your beds. It'll be your turn tomorrow.'

But tomorrow his Aunt Clarice would be coming for him, and there would be another man with her, the man from the garden.

IT WAS SUNDAY already. They were at the top of a high street, passing along beside the larger shops and the coaching inns with their heraldic signs and arched gateways, their quaint latticed windows without shatter tape. The sun sparkled off the grit on the road. Rutherford's hand in his was firm and civil. Every so often the other boy broke off his grip to scratch his ear. 'Damned itch. Can you see anything in there?'

Warren looked. 'No.'

'Tell you what. I'll ask Matron to have a look at it when we get back.'

'I should,' said Warren. He would have laughed, but he was worried about what might happen next. Still Clarice had not got word to him.

The whole column was turning left into an alleyway between two old houses. The stones underfoot were ancient cobbles, and the walls, with their miniature, leaded windows, rose up patched and stained on either side. The few noises of the street fell away behind them, and a sense of stillness prevailed.

And then all at once there were flagstones underfoot, and railings around a bright green space with gravestones, like an island out of time. The great church stood in the centre of it.

Warren half halted, and was pulled forward again. He found his gaze taken up the height of the sunlit tower, up higher still to the tip of the thin green spire with its glinting weathercock. The air all about it was the clearest blue. The procession of boys that was called a crocodile was moving towards the church.

There were mothers, black-hatted old ladies, children in short coats, a father in uniform. Ahead, at the end of a brief approach, the notes of an organ leaked from behind a black door. Now Warren wanted to run away, but the shuffling progress of the crocodile took him forward.

Shadowed wood met huge shadowed stone. He was seated near the front, on the right, where the school had the first rows. All about him a filtered light was like the dust of dried roses. Boys were on their knees, pressing their faces against the wooden shelves in front of them. He sat, still, preparing himself. He looked for something to fasten his attention to.

Ahead, past the soaring stone columns, past the wood-work – more of it, darkened and banked, hooded and carved into some frenzy of ornament – there was a cloth-covered table, gold-worked, with a cross and candles. And above it blazed a coloured window with a man on the cross. The nails were perfectly visible, driven through his hands and feet.

Behind them there was some movement and they all rose to their feet. The music swelled and filled the space, and he looked up past the line of tattered flags, hanging like an arrangement of cobwebs, to where, high up in the roof, carved roses and painted cherubs' heads stared back down at him. A spy, a sinner, he would be exposed. If he could only pass through the ordeal of these next minutes, or hours. He saw the procession of robed men and boys

268

crossing the stones, stepping up under the arch towards the cross. In another window he saw a crucified snake.

The crowd stood and spoke or dropped to its knees, or stood again and sang. He tried to join in, struggled to keep up, mumbling along, mouthing the tunes. There was a story of the Israelites from the Bible, just as at the little red school, but deeper, and longer, and more magnificent. The choir sang. A letter was read out. Still there were no deeds, and no one spotted him. It was nothing but words; but such words that struck fear into him, and thrilled him, too.

For when a frocked man climbed into a wooden turret, Jack heard: '*I sent to know your faith, lest by some means the tempter have tempted you, and our labour be in vain.*' And then, for a second, he seemed to look directly at Jack: '*When the Comforter is come, whom I will send unto you from the Father, even the Spirit of truth, which proceedeth from the Father, he shall testify of me. And ye also shall bear witness, because ye have been with me from the beginning. These things have I spoken unto you, that ye should not be offended. They shall put you out of the synagogues: yea the time cometh, that whosoever killeth you will think that he doeth God service. And these things will they do unto you, because they have not known the Father, nor me. But these things have I told you, that, when the time shall come, ye may remember that I told you of them.*'

And as the priest spoke and spoke, and the great vault filled with his words, Jack held on to the hint about the father sending a comforter, and about remembering – until the prayers were said for the King, for the empire, for the soldiers in Burma, the sailors holding the seas, and the bomber crews over Germany; until, in the lapse of time and more time, the hymn was sung and the priests and choir withdrew and nothing was left in the air except the organ, its peals and runs

269

making the same shapes and colours as the stained glass.

That night, in his iron bed, he tried to return to the cathedral in his imagination, summoning again those moments when the singing voices blended and changed themselves, rising up into the immense overarching space. He tried to bring Clarice there with him, and the indistinct figure whom he had once known, the father from the rose garden. Then tears came unstoppably, because he didn't know where he was.

A CAR HORN honked furiously, and when Vic emerged from the cabin still holding his paintbrush he saw Clarice jumping out of a USAAF car. She hauled her bundles out after her, then posed with him against the front woodwork. The obliging Kodak owner departed in a blare of trumpeting and Vic led Clarice indoors. She'd been transferred to Lincolnshire; she had one day and one night.

After they'd made love she wanted to see everything in detail. The inside window frames were picked out in a stolen camouflage green, while the neat plank table was entirely white. Expanses of decently stained floor had two fibre PT mats for rugs. On the walls, he'd fastened up her pieces of fanciful Americana, the crossed flags, a picture of a B-17 Flying Fortress, a view of the plains of Colorado with some Rocky Mountains in the distance, and her New York. An odd assortment of chairs had appeared, courtesy of a sergeant in Vic's battalion who'd delivered them in a truck, no questions asked. Now they were neatly arranged, all painted the same shade of camouflage buff.

'Oh, Vic. It's marvellous!' She kissed him.

Their old air force radio stood on an ammunition box

behind him. He backed their embrace slightly towards the wall, and with his free hand switched it on. Soon, as it warmed up, notes of American dance music jostled their way out from the little speaker.

'Vic! You're an angel!'

They swayed together softly. He steered her around the new furniture, distrustful of her exclamations, and of the man who'd brought her.

She broke away, and proceeded to take out from her bags samples of an astonishing, brash chintz. She held them up to the window. 'A dead navigator's mother gave them to me,' she said. 'We'll be such pioneers of taste.'

He laughed awkwardly and tried to embrace her again, but it seemed to him there was already an implication in the air, as though just a few moments ago he'd made her submit against her will. He wanted to argue it out with her but bit his tongue. Instead, for the next two hours while she was busy cutting and pinning her curtains over the blackouts, he took up his paintbrush again.

Every now and then, he paused for a cigarette and turned to look at her. He thought how blissful she was, and of the first summer, and how he was losing her. He watched her slight arms holding the fabric up, her fingers deft at the pins – how beautiful was the fine blonde hair that lay loose upon her shoulders, caught in the streak of sunlight through the window.

Before she'd finished, he had to go over and stand behind her, kissing her neck, touching her breasts with his fingertips. She flinched, yet angled her head back to kiss him. But when he tried to go further, smoothing his hand over her skirt, nudging her towards the old, makeshift bed again, she tensed and squirmed free.

'Vic, darling,' she said. 'The room is absolutely transformed.' There was a bright, unreal note to her voice. The new paint smells seemed to stick in his nostrils.

Down by the Thames where they strolled, she told him the gossip of her squadron. The night bombing offensive was to continue, of course. He told her of his unit's proposed six-week move to Wales for a joint operation with the Black Watch. She said it would make a change for him. The mended tandem lay on the straggling salt-meadow grass behind them. Sounds of war drifted across the wide river, the unremarkable booming of anti-aircraft fire, and he slipped an arm about her waist. The local kids played at the water's edge, barefoot with their fishing nets in the cow-trodden estuary mud.

They walked to where talkative wavelets lapped into a tiny bay. At the end of a roll of barbed wire a piece of iron was hammered into the water's edge. Beside it, one or two of last year's reeds stood tall, and their spiked featherheads fringed the view of the oil refinery. He was angry, frustrated. Always their time together was like this, like treading on eggshells.

She seemed to read his thoughts. 'What is it, Vic? I'd rather you told me?'

He felt immediately cornered. 'It's about us, as usual.'

'All right.' She was defensive. 'Talk, then. I wish you would, sometimes. I wish you did show your feelings more, Vic.'

'About how we are, where we're going.'

She made no reply, but turned her face away.

He plunged on. 'I mean, the more free of that prison I feel, the more I desire you . . .'

She'd become quite silent. Now she stopped walking. They turned rather awkwardly to face one another. The sun was westering. It struck long bars of fleeting gold in the river surface. Out in midstream a grey torpedo boat was plying towards the sea.

'It seems to me we were perfectly happy only a moment

ago,' she said. 'And then you want to make some kind of an accusation.'

'I don't expect it as a right. I just wish we could talk about it. That's all. You go cold.'

'Oh yes, I'm frigid, aren't I?'

'That's not what I mean, darling. You know it's not. Don't you see? It almost has nothing to do with sex.'

'Almost.' She spoke scornfully.

'Why! Why is it always so difficult? We're trapped. We've got nowhere in all this time. Everything is still exactly as it's always been. That airman who dropped you off . . .'

'Don't start, Vic. Of course not. He's just a chum, for God's sake.'

'Your God,' he said glumly. 'What's He bloody playing at, I wonder?'

She slapped him suddenly, fiercely on the cheek. 'What do we know of God, either of us?'

He was astonished. 'Why did you do that?' The sting of the blow throbbed up around the corner of his eye.

'I came down for you, Vic. To see you. And all you want to do is spoil it. Why can't you just tell me you love me? I just need reassurance, that's all.'

'Why can't you tell *me*? Why can't you reassure *me*?' It was becoming that same weary struggle over who would back down first. She was as obstructive as Phyllis.

They pedalled back along the main road, and up the hill to the cottage, in silence. When they arrived, he stalked off to the waste ground to stand and smoke. She didn't love him. He wanted to burn the house down. Wasn't this crude, rickety, and absurdly tricked-out shack plainly an image of himself. He looked at the outline of it, against the late afternoon – a joke. She could take her pick of any number of glamorous American officers, men who risked their lives. What could she see in him?

Later, when he returned to the cabin, he saw her huddled up in front of the empty grate. There were tear stains on her face. And yet they still held apart from one another, offering only functional snippets of speech, about the tea, the washing-up, what they might eat. Then he collapsed and she was in his arms. 'Oh, Vic,' she said. 'I do love you. I do.'

'And I love you, darling.'

He lay in the dark, kissing her mouth. Her body was soft beside him. When she slept he heard guns again, far away. He got up, tiptoeing naked across the bare floorboards to his newly painted window, and twitched the dressing of floral chintz aside. Beyond Upminster, a roving crown of searchlights, from Dagenham, Romford and Barking, threw the nearby branches into silhouette. Between the beams, incredible colours, neon reds and fluorescent greens, flared suddenly. Golden strings of tracer bullets arced into the sky. His son was either under it somewhere . . . or maybe he *was* dead, after all. He felt powerless, missing him: his face, his voice, the way he perched his cheeky head sideways when he misbehaved, the way he clambered up and down the stairs one at a time at the flat. The three-year-old was years gone. Vic was losing hope.

A SMELL LIKE smouldering fibre hung in the air and mingled with the oily whiff from the West India Docks. She clung to his arm before the burnt-out wreckage of the house in which they'd first met, her aunt's in Morant Street – Phyllis's mother's. The sky was a mottled haze through which only driblets of sun filtered down.

Curiously angled crane tips speared the line of the missing rooftops, and half a ship's funnel projected from behind a blackened chimney-stack.

In a café on the Commercial Road they looked at each other over the stained red-and-white tablecloth. Their mugs of tea steamed in the space between them. He could see she was wound up. He knew the way he tapped his match at the ashtray threatened to drive her to distraction. Through the window he could see the communist slogan daubed on the shell of a building opposite: 'SECOND FRONT NOW'. The summer had gone.

At last he got round to lighting his cigarette.

She sought to comfort him. 'It's natural, Vic.'

'But you don't want to help,' he said. 'That Tony Rice . . .'

He could almost see her heart stop. All along there'd been something, something she held back. How tired he was of the struggle with her. 'What is it? Tell me. Why won't you tell me?'

He watched her mouth move, as though she tried desperately to frame some formula of explanation. She could not. Even now as she stirred her tea, staring into the muddy liquid in its stark white enamel, he saw that she would deny him.

'No,' she said. 'It's nothing. Nothing at all. Why do you keep on at me?'

Vic looked at her intently. He saw how defiantly she met his eye.

'The Blitz is long over,' she said. 'You can't just go on worrying like this. You're here with me. What about us, Vic? Don't *I* matter to you?'

'Of course you matter to me. You're everything, darling.'

They drank their tea in silence. A car passed in the road outside.

Back in Laindon, she said she needed to feel his arms around her. If he so much as touched her more intimately, she flinched away. He caught sight of his face in her mirror; he looked strained and withdrawn. He blamed her.

'Why do you make me feel this way?' he said.

'I'm not making you feel any way.'

And he knew she was right. But he watched her withdrawing in turn, and it made him furious. Then the anger would fill him up, despite all his efforts, just waiting to be discharged against her. And there she was, angry too, her defences on a hair trigger, as she sat opposite him at their white table. The slightest thing would set it off.

He made an effort to be light, whistling as he cleared the table, but his best intentions were subtly ironised, and she sensed it.

'Do you have to do that?'

'Do what?'

'You know very well. You know it irritates me.'

'Doing what?'

'Your bloody whistling, of course.'

'Was I?'

'You just do it to annoy me.'

'Do I?'

'Christ!'

Then he was hurt and gloomy, and his mood seemed to exasperate her. They bore the soured atmosphere between them all evening and went to bed in silence.

AND IN THE morning he lay beside her as the dawn broke, alert to birds shuffling and chattering in the cold wooden eaves, and to the sudden whirrings of their wings. He remembered a dozen such mornings and the passing away of hours, days, months of the love that had brought her to him. How vile, the way it could be switched out; to be replaced with a dull resentment.

He watched the delicacy of her eyelashes, flickering every now and then with her dream. The fair hair, loose-permed these days, straggled waywardly. As her skin gave slightly towards the pillow, her right cheekbone was the more softly defined, and the faintest down of hairs lay upon it.

Somewhere he still loved her. He wanted to stroke her hair, and whisper in her ear, as she always had to him, to convince her that it would be all right again, it really would. If only he could believe it himself.

Her eyes opened and for a moment he looked straight into the blue waking irises. When he spoke, however, and put out a hand to her, he found her resisting. She blamed the approach of her period and briskly announced her intention to get straight up and make them a breakfast. As she dressed, he watched her coldly, supporting his weight on one elbow. He saw her tuck a towel about her as if for the first time she felt embarrassed. The cloth made a soft disturbing line across her naked back. The dark hairs on his own forearm saddened him.

She brought the meagre bread and marge, and placed it in front of him.

'It's not easy, Vic. What we're doing.'

'If you say so.' He heard his voice come out hard and controlled. He saw it made her wince.

'Listen.' She was making herself ignore him. 'There's a fine line between us. Don't you see? It's not class, Vic, it's just a line. Below the line you stand to spiral downwards, for ever. Above it, love has a chance, if we choose.'

He made no reply. He got out of the bed and rummaged in his trousers for his tin of makings. Then at length, after he'd rolled his cigarette, he spoke. 'And intimacy?'

'Damn you! I knew that was going to be it.'

He knew she felt wretched; yet she insisted and he couldn't stop himself. She took off her clothes and submitted herself to be embraced. He thought she'd almost prefer him to be violent. The cottage seemed drear and remote, and he sensed she wanted nothing so much as to get away from it. He knew she forced herself to kiss, clenched her teeth against the pain as he came into her. When it was over, he simply felt puzzled.

In the afternoon they took the tandem out. They stopped on the crest of the ridge and looked across to the west. 'Down there's Upminster,' he said. 'That's the way Phyllis and I used to come up every weekend, to get the cottage finished. Through Upminster, past the red school and through the railway bridge. Shall we ride down there and have a look round? A cup of tea? It wouldn't take long. Anyway, we've got time.'

'No.' Her voice was shaky. 'I'd rather not. Do you mind?'

'No. I don't mind. Just thought it might be something to do. Take us out of ourselves. There'd probably be somewhere to get a cup of tea.'

'No, Vic. I've said I don't want to. Is that all right?'

'I've said yes. Of course it's perfectly all right.'

Late the next night, when they were parting at the little local station, they clung to each other in the blue, shrouded light.

'I do love you, Clarice.'

'I love you too, Vic.' She seemed suddenly happy. 'Perhaps he's been safe after all. Jack, I mean. All this time.' She touched his cheek.

'What?' he said.

'Perhaps it's only your old bag of dreams, you know. It's been putting a jinx on us.'

'It's just a lot of old nonsense. Next time, if it makes you any happier, you can chuck the lot away.'

'I'm so sorry, darling. It's me, isn't it? I'll find a way, I promise. I'll write and explain. Everything is so difficult.'

BUT SHE COULD not explain and they could not see each other.

On Monday 18 October 1943, not without a certain pride of achievement, Mrs Benedick handed Dr Pike a single snippet. It had been cut from the *Sunday People*. She'd found it left behind at a Spitfire fund-raising sale in the church hall at Stutton.

HITLER MURDERED 3 MILLION JEWS IN EUROPE – so ran the small headline to a minute article. It was tucked away at the bottom of a front page packed with other war news. The information was indelibly there, right in front of his eyes. But because of the way it was presented, so isolated and apparently insignificant, he was almost unable to pay attention to it, or to make it fit with anything else he held to be normal or natural. He would have liked to discuss the matter with Clarice. He would have liked even more to discuss it with Mrs Benedick. But she'd brought it in almost apologetically, as a result of a conversation they'd had weeks previously, and had run away again almost as soon as she'd arrived.

Dr Pike took the cutting to his desk. It was a prize. He had a map of pre-war Poland, traced from an atlas by means of a piece of greaseproof paper. On it he'd marked the names of certain towns that had cropped up earlier that year in similar, very brief reports in more respectable journals, and had plotted the directions of the trains so far referred to. It wasn't a hard thing to do, in fact disarmingly easy; yet most of the time it felt as though he sat in a vacuum, the only person anywhere trying to find a name for the monstrosity that emerged once two and two were put together. Nobody spoke about it. Nobody mentioned it – ever.

The conclusions were chilling. Sobibor, Chelmno, Belzec, Majdanek, Oswiecim. There was no news of the resettlement transports, in fact no information at all. 'All trace of the cattle waggons was lost after Crakow.' 'Beyond Warsaw no information was available.' And yet the trains still ran, and were now apparently setting out from Hungary, far to the south-east. The pull of the Polish region seemed intense, its end profound obscurity. He wondered what laws operated there. He felt challenged to the core.

Clarice, shackled to the daily grind of RAF vengeance upon Germany, grew inured to loss and suffering. Her father stifled his heart and collected his news cuttings. Vic trained at Bournemouth, then at Durham, then at Fimber in the Yorkshire Wolds for a 'realistic exercise', then Durham again, and then seaside Clacton, of all places, in Essex. Then Scotland. Now the invasion of France was a talked-of thing, and he was practised at crawling, bayonet fixed, under live fire.

Then she was transferred back from Lincolnshire to Norfolk. Leave had been cancelled, but he was to meet her on his way down from the Highlands at her airfield, a newly concreted and reopened one. His combined operations had left him with a broken rib, and all the way from Inveraray, his battalion had crossed the mountains in a convoy of painfully bone-shaking lorries.

After that, the Army had brought him back down from Glasgow to London by overnight train; and almost immediately, he'd set out again from Liverpool Street to make the journey up to Norwich to meet her. He was exhausted. As to Clarice, he didn't know what to expect. He'd been with his mates. Now he was on his own, and he guessed this stolen visit to her was their one last chance. The beat of the wheels on the rail joints lulled him. He closed his eyes and let his head fall softly against the headrest next to the window.

When he looked up again, the flat reaches of Cambridgeshire stretched away beside the train. He made himself a cigarette. It was always either training, travelling – or not travelling, because of the coal strike – or sitting around, and any one of these could quickly turn into the others. After three years in the mimicry of combat he longed for battle, for the release of it. Then there was the old suicidal feeling again, that it didn't matter, that nothing was worth staying around for. And he knew it was a dangerous state for a soldier to get into, this verge of frenzy. He knew, but he flirted with it, because he could see no solution to his life, and this feeling of abandon seemed to whisper a promise to take him through the crisis when it came.

It would come soon enough, he knew. At any time within the next few weeks or so. Wherever a man turned these days there were Americans gathering for the invasion. Wherever one looked in southern England there were movements of troops, movements of tanks, movements of heavy lorries. Here in East Anglia you could hardly get between two wayside stations without evidence of concrete construction, or petrol delivery, or of the machines that required these two, the heavy bombers. The island was filling up; the towns, the countryside, the air above the humdrum little country of his experience was filling up with American production. And caught up in it there was Clarice; and there was not Jack. The smoke rose up from the lighted tip of his fag.

He unbuttoned his top pocket and took out the latest of her letters to him. He read her sentences over once again, hearing her voice. The tone was just that shade too hale, too matter-of-fact.

From Norwich he hitched, although he had plenty of back pay in his pocket book. But it was late afternoon by the time he arrived at the gate of her airfield. She'd managed to arrange him entry and a bunk for the night. The airman on the barrier made a phone call, and he overheard himself referred to as 'some bloody brown job'. Nevertheless the permission was confirmed and he wandered in to try to find who he should report to.

Oulton was to be a shared base. Two B-17 Flying Fortresses had already arrived and stood on the newly tarred concrete outside a half-completed hangar. As he walked beneath their wing tips, he was impressed by the size of the planes, and imagined himself cooped up in one of those swivelling perspex bubbles. In the distance, parked in echelon along the side of the vast concrete strip, were the Lancasters of the RAF.

Then Clarice found him. She had another woman with her. 'Vic, this is Yvain. Yvain Beaumont. She works with me.' They were constrained from embracing, here on military ground. In the presence of the third party, they smiled awkwardly into one another's eyes.

The girl, Yvain, stretched out her hand. 'How do you do.' She was an angular, rather striking, but serious-faced young woman with a cultured accent. Hints of her black curls clustered at her ears, and her uniform looked too big on her. A gust of wind tugged at her heavy blue skirt.

They found a section of the mess where they might be able to sit for a while, all three of them, without offending discipline. There Vic was given food from the canteen and a cup of tea. A party of American officers was standing nearby, snatches of their talk drifting across the room. Their dashing USAAF uniforms lent them a poise and style he could only wonder at.

'Oh, them!' Clarice said, noticing his interest. 'I'm sure they're very sweet boys, once you get to know them; but so full of themselves. Vic, darling? Is there something the matter?'

His rib was hurting him. 'It's nothing much,' he said. 'When the landing craft hit the beach, so-called, I was thrown against some metal sticking-out thing with all my kit on my back.'

'You poor chap,' Yvain said. 'Have you had it seen to?'

'Oh, yes,' he said. 'The medical orderly lent me the jar of regimental liniment with a mark on the side and strict instructions not to take more than my share.'

But any lightheartedness was temporary, and the conversation proceeded in rather stilted fashion along predictable lines. The girls told him the details of their routine, and he revealed as much as he was allowed to of his recent escapades. He wondered whether it was the station that had insisted on Yvain being present while he was on site, or whether it was some ruse of Clarice's to cover the awkwardness between them.

'Yvain is an ardent communist,' Clarice said.

'I see,' he replied.

IT WAS EVENING before they could be alone together. Clarice borrowed him a lady's bicycle and they rode down to the village pub. There was a large contingent of aircrew there, apparently celebrating the arrival of the B-17s.

'Come on, Vic, don't be a spoilsport. I'll introduce you.'

And soon he was part of a gang, all drinking and joking noisily, and talking shop. Later, there was the inevitable singsong.

Buzzed by the jeeps of the returning revellers, they rode back in the dark. 'Can't we stop a minute?' he called.

'Why?' She braked and turned round, her feet planted into the darkness either side of her pedals. Moonlight touched the shape of her stockinged calves below the hem of her skirt, lit faintly the chrome of her handlebars, and revealed no more than the surface of her cheek framed silver by her loosened hair.

'I thought we could . . .' His voice died away.

'Thought we could what?'

'Well. You know. Take a little time to ourselves.'

He saw her lower the machine into the verge, and then come towards him. She put her arms around his neck. But the kiss was perfunctory. He could neither taste her, nor feel her tongue. He broke off and pressed her head to his shoulder. 'Clarice, darling. I'm missing you so much.' He gazed emptily at the forms of trees beyond the hedge, the pepper-pot of a windmill sticking up as if at the end of the road, and the sharp black box of the airfield control tower with its wind-sock on the skyline.

He stroked the back of her neck and she softened slightly, and huddled herself closer against him. 'I'm sorry, Vic. I am trying, really I am.'

'Are you?'

'Honestly. It's just . . . difficult.'

'How? Why? Why is it so difficult?'

'I don't know.' She lifted her face to him again, covering his cheek with her small kisses. 'Your poor ribs.' She caressed his chest. 'You poor, poor boy.'

He ran his hand down her back, feeling for her waist under the thick tunic, and on to the swell of her hip. 'I love you, Clarice. I've always loved you.'

'And I love you too, Vic. I swear it.'

He nuzzled her ear with his mouth. They stood clasped together. Almost he could hear her heartbeat. Then, stupidly, he slipped his hand further, feeling for the back of her thigh, and then round to the front. He found, through the fabric, the slight bump of her suspender. It made her laugh. Then he ran the back of his hand suddenly up across her belly and away again.

She started away from him. 'No!'

He let go of her. They stood together, their breaths smoking slightly in the falling cold. He was conscious of the big Norfolk sky over them, the tiny, sharpened points of the stars, the air itself about to crystallise and crack around them.

He said, 'I don't understand how it could be so easy and straightforward at the start – "Oh Vic" this; and "darling" that, when I was such a shambles myself; but now I'm on the eve of going into action it's somehow impossible. I simply don't understand. Did you only want me when I was a cripple? Was it something like that?'

She went silently to pick up her bike and rode off ahead of him.

He called, 'I don't get it! Understand?'

Inside the perimeter, they passed beside the asphalt plant. It loomed over him, its complicated hoppers and tubes like the mistaken corner of a factory, risen suddenly blacker out of the black ground. It smelt of frosted tar. She said nothing until they reached the huts. Then it was merely, 'I'll show you to your bunk.'

He lay sick with remorse, and with his own tiredness. Precisely what would he be fighting for, when it came to D-Day and the invasion?

With an unholy noise the Lancasters, plane after plane, took off over the hut, shaking the tin roof and rattling the window frames. The concentration of troops in the

South of England was already beginning, and he would be going soon enough.

In the morning, at the gate, he made one more effort. 'There's something I never told you,' he said. 'When I was getting out of that house, at the robbery, I lost my temper. I tried to blind the old man. I tried to smash his glasses into his eyes. I've been ashamed of it, hardly even admitted it to myself, certainly not to you. I'm telling you now, so that you know what I'm like. I thought maybe it was something you could tell about me. I thought you could see through me to the nastiness inside, and that was why . . .' He shook his head. 'I thought if I owned up to it, it might clear the air. Of course it's a risk, and the risk is that it'll confirm your worst suspicions. There, it's done now, and I feel better for getting it off my chest, even if it means you hate me for it. Do you see what I'm trying to say? I thought perhaps some falsehood between us was what was causing the problem.'

Her face was blanched. 'Yes,' she said, 'I see.' She looked away and cleared her throat. 'I see,' she said again, abstractedly. She turned back to him. 'But you're still you, Vic. You're no different.' She dropped her gaze, biting her lip. 'I'm glad you told me. I am, really.'

'I love you, Clarice.'

'I love you, too, Vic.' She looked away.

'Truly? In spite of what I've just told you?'

She laid her hand on his arm and met his eye again. 'We will make it, darling. We will.'

He didn't believe her.

THE VERY NEXT evening he passed Phyllis on the steps at Waterloo Station. She wore a hat that slanted down over her face, and a half veil, but she was unmistakable, her walk, the way she'd pulled at her coat as she negotiated the steps in her high heels, in fact everything about her. He was sure of it and called after her. She had almost gone down under the railway bridge, and turned back once, before hurrying on into the twilight, the heels clicking audibly on the pavement. He shouldered his kitbag and ran after her, the broken rib grinding painfully with his breaths. But he was fit from his training and caught up with her by the bomb craters. 'Hallo, Phyllis.'

'Vic!' She pretended surprise. 'Long time no see.'

He gasped, 'Where is he? The boy? Is he all right? Where have you been?'

'You mean Jack? He's well enough.'

'He's alive! You're both alive!'

'Why shouldn't we be?'

'In the Blitz. I thought, when I didn't hear from you . . .'

'You thought we'd caught a packet. We nearly did, as it happens, that first night. Then we got out.'

'But not the cottage.'

'No. As it happens. We were offered somewhere else.' She turned away.

'Yes . . . ?'

'That's all.' She stepped back slightly and looked down the line of her elegant skirt. Casually she wagged the toe of her shoe back and forth on its heel, as though to inspect it for a scuff. Then she looked up at him, straight in the eye. 'My cousin Clarice helped us move out of the flat. Kind of her, don't you think?'

'The flat . . . ? You mean Ripple Road?'

'Can't think of any other flats we lived in. Can you?'

'But . . . You mean Clarice was there with you. And Jack?'

'Yes, she was. Oh, of course,' she eyed him meaning-fully. 'I'd forgotten you two once knew each other, didn't you. Quite well, wasn't it? In fact . . . let me see if I can remember. . . .' Phyllis frowned and put her finger up to her chin. 'Yes. If I'm not very much mistaken, she'd just come from visiting you. Well, then, and how have you been, Vic? I've missed you something terrible. Vic? Have you missed me? Well, have you?'

Standing there with her chin slightly raised towards him she seemed once again to be daring him to strike her. He felt his fists clench involuntarily, yet he was amazed at how calm he was otherwise. Only his lower lip trembled. He twisted away. The old black bricks of the bridge were damp; dark weeds grew in the mortar. In the twilight vapour that was coming off the river, the structure that arched over their meeting seemed almost visibly to corrode.

'Where is he, then?'

'We had to evacuate him.'

'We?'

'Times have been hard, Vic. What with this war and everything. I shouldn't need to tell you that.'

'All right. Where to?'

'Vic, dearest.' She looked at her watch. 'I'm singing tonight. At the Coal Hole, would you believe. Quite a coincidence really, isn't it? It's only just reopened.' She looked at her watch. 'But just now I do really have to dash. Meeting someone. Why don't you come and find me there? After the show we can catch up, can't we? On everything.' How much of what she'd told him was true? 'How about it, Vic, love? For old time's sake. No hard feelings, eh?'

She knew where Jack was. 'Yes. Of course. Why not?' He had to find out. 'All right, then. I will.'

Phyllis was hurrying off along the cobbles. Only then did his emotion catch him like a blow in the chest. It welled at the back of his eyes like acid. But he had to know.

Why should I be surprised, then, that he kept his rendezvous, and that he ended up spending the drunken night with her?

VI
The Comforter

NOW, IN THE boats at Southampton, I am with him in spirit. He's ready, about to launch out into the Channel. That night in May, when he learned Clarice had known all along, was the night I was conceived, and now on the eve of battle the only profit he has of it is Jack's address. He has written to him at boarding-school. In his breast pocket he has a letter from Clarice, desperately explaining, so late in the day, the fact of the rape. She asks for his understanding. She asks forgiveness.

Forty-eight hours his company had been confined to their open-topped vessel, with breaks only for trips up on to the wharf for meals at the mobile canteens. Vic was intensely familiar with the inside of the little ship, its painted metal and latrine-like smells. It was more like a flimsy kind of lighter than a barge.

A hundred and eighty men were its principal cargo, divided between four holds. He said to his pal, Norton, that if he'd been back at Everholt's yard he could have welded the thing together in an afternoon. It had a tower structure over the engines at the back and a pair of drop ramps at the front. The installation of both was for one purpose only: the negotiation of the far beach.

Vic looked down at the items he held in his hands. They were the latest issue: bags for vomit, and pills for seasickness. He was impressed by the army's attention to detail. It showed a certain loving kindness. Nevertheless, it was obvious enough that one well-aimed bomb could finish him and his mates – together with their officers, who'd come forward from their cabins to sit with them. Or one shell would be enough to empty them all out into the briny. And even if they did get across . . . ?

He stowed the pills and sick bag in one of his innumerable fastenings and looked around him. His fellows, squashed in *en masse*, wearing their tin hats and Mae Wests, took up every square inch of floor space. A few were standing, smoking or drinking tea. Most were seated, resting against their equipment, gambling, talking, writing letters.

Rifles and entrenching tools bristled amidst the throng. At the far end of the hold the rations were packed; beside them, bizarrely, were the bicycles. Here, moored up in the midst of a fleet of similar craft at Southampton Docks, Vic felt he had more or less arrived at the end of the line.

Yet it came as a relief when the engines started. Everyone left what they were doing and stood up to get a view. He craned to see their crew unlash the tangle of strappings to the next boat. They cast off and joined the queue, of similar transports and similar soldiers; one by one they left the security of the docks.

Gradually, Vic felt the American-built vessel pick up the dip and rise of open water; the men braced themselves against their kitbags. He noted that the great assembly they'd passed on their way in – of much larger vessels at anchor, camouflaged troop-ships with their tugs and attendants – was no longer there.

'Only back to Lymington, most like. Eh, Vic? It's all off, isn't it?' Matthieson smiled sarcastically. He held on to the hull. 'Those soft sailor bastards. All gone home. Didn't like the look of the weather after all.'

But it was clear within the next five minutes that they were heading down the Solent towards the Channel in force, and that the event they had spent the last three years preparing for was finally under way. Vic peered above the steel bulwark at the black, feathered water. Going to be a sea and a half out there, he thought.

Norton twisted to get a glance back at the receding shore. Then he turned to Vic. 'How long to get clear of the Isle of Wight, then?' He cocked his head to one side, as if to savour the home waters. 'You're the fucking water rat round here.'

'Hour, maybe.' Vic said. 'Depends on the swell. Depends on what this thing'll do.' He lit a cigarette. The cumbersome landing craft broke into heavier water. It chucked and danced into the broadening estuary.

The men sat down again, squatted in spaces, renewed card-games. Some read. Some said prayers. A sergeant-major seated a couple of yards away was already looking ill, his face green in the overcast evening. And Vic, sharpened, purposeful, could feel the anxiety sluice back and forth along some bilge in his own stomach.

For more than a week since the receipt of Clarice's letter his thoughts had been in turmoil. He'd found himself enraged for hours; his anger for her concealment of Jack blinded him to her predicament. The affair had always been a cruel sham; she was exactly like Phyllis. Love was delusion, since all women were false. At other times, his own importunate demands on her disgusted him, now that he knew the score. The torment was his own blind insensitivity. He thought of the sweetness of revenge: for what Tony Rice had done to her, for his son, and for his own terrible feelings. The Army and the moment were providing the supreme opportunity. In the release of violence he'd feel clean.

IT WAS TRUE. HE was ready, a loaded gun, a trained killer. Other soldiers – decent men doing a job – stowed lucky coins, rabbits' feet, family photographs in their pockets. Vic had his hatred curled about his heart.

During the last two weeks, while the last briefings had gone down and the live rounds were issued, he'd learnt to rely on this feeling growing inside him. It would see him through. It had kept him warm, hot. Suddenly, in mid-Channel, it deserted him. Seasickness? He'd never been seasick in his life. The body took over, and an unnerving faintness swept him. He could barely move, let alone fight.

He found himself acutely preoccupied with the enemy. The young German who would take his life was having his evening meal in a concrete bunker, maybe, or chatting to a girl in some wind-whipped seaside bar. Or there was some Russian conscript – troops they'd been told about – with nothing much to hope for, but nothing to lose either. Vic's thoughts raced ahead, leaping over the sea, collapsing too precipitately the hours and miles. It was the worst thing, this breakdown of *character*, so soon. It took him by surprise.

He stood up again, next to Matthieson, to smoke.

'Done your letters, then?' said Matthieson.

'One to my son,' Vic said. His nerves subsided a little. 'Couldn't think what to put to anyone else. When it came to it.'

'Know what you mean.' Matthieson shifted his boots on the steel floor with a grating sound. He looked up at the clouds. 'Sitting ducks, us. If the fuckers catch on.'

But there was no attack, even though a glimmer of twilight lingered until late, and the boat plunged on exposed, riding the heavy swell. Vic reckoned the odds. There was little chance of success. The conditions were disastrous. It would be another Dieppe, on a massive scale. Another Somme. Three times his father had been wounded; three times Percy recovered. Ironically named Victor, this son of his was in a blue funk before getting anywhere near the combat zone. Always with the image of his father before him, Vic cringed at the poor show. His wasn't even an assault unit, but second wave. His fighting was supposed to be inland, not on the beach.

The unseasonable wind whipped the tops off waves and spattered the hull behind Vic's head with a premonition of machine-gun fire. At midnight, when their young officer, Lieutenant Fairfax, informed them they were in mid-Channel, he judged the seas were a good four or five feet high. They had been shipping spray for hours. The unkind craft would kick up and then smash down. Men were being repeatedly sick over their clothes; the sound was awful. On a few spare inches of wet deck, between Norton, Matthieson and a pair of stubborn boots he thought might be Fairbrother's, he tried unsuccessfully to sleep.

At one o'clock, he sat up and looked across the heaving steel darkness. His comrades were shapes, black upon black. Some lay stretched out. Some groaned in their *mal de mer*. Others were in groups, still gambling, or talking quietly amongst themselves. They were already ghosts, the sea destabilised them, back and forth, their cigarette tips glowing, sudden red points in the catching wind. Over Vic's head a corporal held a box like a tray of ices at the cinema.

'Kidney soup? Cocoa?'

Vic fumbled with his self-heating can. He set his tins unopened beside him and lay back against his rucksack. If he closed his eyes he felt nauseous, almost as though he were drunk. He thought of the Coal Hole – he deserved everything he got. Back in Tony Rice's car, that first time – 'We've got this little place in the country. Why don't you all come down?' – how ridiculous he'd been.

Then he'd lain next to Phyllis in the bed, his head full of jazz and the tart and the contract. The boat shook and tumbled, its screws racing. He fell asleep – letting go at last.

While he lay in the slop of stomach acids and sea water, the fleet began to position itself. The Americans were to the right, the Canadians to the left. Sea corridors had been swept of mines, the depths had been cleared of U-boats, and the air overhead had been quite extinguished of its last bandits and angels. Now, the big warships turned broadside to the shore. Everything was thrown into the balance.

HE WAS WOKEN by gunfire. The sound was like nothing he'd heard before, deeper and more penetrating, but still far off. Something metallic behind his head was vibrating, almost ringing, and then the floor bucked up and fell. It was still dark. He groped for his rifle, and sat up.

'All right, mate?' It was Norton.

'Christ.'

'Not long now.'

His bowels churned. He would have run, if he could, for the bucket. Anything, he thought, as he returned, staggering, would be better than this. A glimmer of grey light was leaking in the east. A shadowy officer was coming down one of the ladders, Major Whitton. He held a mug of liquid. 'All right, you men?' he said. 'Nice day for it.' He was fatherly. With him stood Lieutenant Fairfax, biting his lip, fingering the pistol in its case on his belt.

Vic shut his mind to the cold in his wet clothes. He stayed standing and made a cigarette, bracing himself, fumbling for the lighter and materials with his trembling hands. When he next looked up he was amazed. The cold summer's day had inked in a Channel strewn with the silhouettes of ships. On their own port quarter, almost close enough to touch, the black bulk of a tank lander was riding out its own rhythm. Men on board were inflating a great grey shape, a barrage balloon. And as Vic watched and swept his gaze across the seascape, similar toy balloons began to mushroom and then float up, to hover eerily above the funnels and superstructures that shaped the horizon.

There was a roar overhead. Lightnings in echelon were above them, and then a wave of Spitfires. The distant guns boomed and thudded. A streamer of rockets went up from somewhere far to the right, then another, and another.

He thought of the Hampshires and Dorsets well on ahead, ready to go in. Even now they were preparing to drop into their miniature landing craft, sardines packing into their tins, primed to come to salty life and run up that beach. He envied them, going in, getting it over – heroes. Upon them, most probably, would depend whether he saw the day's end.

He cast his mind back to the sweltering tent at Beaulieu, where he'd done his best to memorise the sand model of the approaches to Arromanches. He imagined his father queueing in the supply trenches, inching along under the shattering bombardment while the first men went over the top. And then there were all the generations of his family, crowding in and leading down to this moment. Had they any conception of what they were passing on? Thames folk, scrabbling for a bit of a life on the mud of the Essex marshes. Making a bit, taking a bit, trying to look respectable – the women struggling with the washing, cooking, the kids and the laying out; the men poling lighters on the river, odd-jobbing, serving every so often for king and country. He saw them coming home, parading. He saw the brilliance of a thousand uniforms. He conjured them now, with their breastplates and flashing swords after Waterloo, say. The cavalry horses had tossed their heads, and shaken their bridles. Their hooves had struck sparks out of the stones. Would he, Vic Warren, acquit himself well in the brown squalor of modern warfare? In the wind and waves it was almost possible to hear the dead generations – the adulation, the shouts of command, the tramp of feet in perfect unison. There, the jingle of harnesses, and the rattle of the field guns as they passed by on their carriages. And there were the captured cannon, the cartloads of spears and spoils and trophies. The men were coming home; once more, everything was in place.

Then Perce, coughing his lungs up ever after. And now this. Vic looked up from his kidney soup. Four hours to wait. The naval barrage intensified. The little ship shuddered, still driving on. England was draining away from him. What ties did he have? What concern did he have for that ridiculous little place – with its dwarfish factory workers and mawkish sentimental songs – that had stumbled on the world and tried to give it good government? If he survived, what should he have to look forward to? Not love. Not Clarice, now. What then? Forty more years of drudgery punctuated by spare weeks at the Brighton seaside and tawdry penny entertainments. His gut burnt with the longing for revenge. 'Why don't you kill me then? That's what you want, isn't it? Eh, Vic? Then you'd be happy, wouldn't you? Then you'd be free.'

He fingered his rifle and prepared himself to die.

WHEN THE RAMP went down there was no gunfire to encounter. Two and a half hours adrift of schedule, the whole flotilla of the second contingent was adrift, too, of its position. Under mortar and artillery bombardment from Le Hamel, they had nudged helplessly against the wind and the high tide. The glistening remains of a British ship, American canisters, petrol tanks, unidentifiable pieces of camouflaged equipment held up by tricks of buoyancy – the morning's debris from Gold and even Omaha – had begun to float past them. Vic could see shelled seaside villas and burning tanks, the mined spikes, entanglements and confusion of the esplanade. Major Whitton, damning the maps for the loss of a mile, ordered the landing. Uncertain of any success or failures that might have gone on before him, Vic jumped into deep water close under the timbered sea wall of the wrong beach.

His boots touched the shingled bottom and his Mae West bobbed up in front of him. His pack threatened to drown him. Then a wave flung him forward on to his face. Men crowded past, but he was determined and staggered after Norton. The Major had found a way up the wall. Water sluiced out of Vic's clothes. He forced his way through the shallows, hearing nothing, feeling nothing, expecting the seabed to explode at any minute.

On the higher level, instead of raking machine-gun fire, there was disconcerting good order. The thin remaining strip between the beach and the road was more like the entrance to a municipal event than a corner of a battlefield. Vic's major was chatting unconcernedly with a traffic officer. Companies of dripping men were moving on ahead along a wide strip of coconut matting. The matting was reddish brown, like the PT rugs he'd put down in the little cabin. It ran off across pitted clay where the mines had been cleared by a flail tank. All about were the signs of a competent occupation. Matthieson caught up with him, together with Lieutenant Fairfax.

'Jesus!'

'Get going, you two. Movement is of the essence,' said the major. 'I'll be along directly.'

'Jesus Christ!'

Vic glanced to his right. Along the high tide there were companies of men starting to trek inshore from the landing craft. They were concentrating on to other strips of matting, which looked, in the distance, like black snakes between the milling vehicles, the miniature flags, and the officers who waved – far-off car-park attendants. And there were little mobs of different soldiers, standing stationary, unarmed. Dare he imagine they were prisoners? His heart exulted as he marched. He was glad at the sight of them. Beyond, still further off, some intermittent detonation continued. Out of the corner of his eye, Vic caught the plumes of water still leaping up. A tank was engaged, two of them, three. He pressed on along the corridor, holding his rifle, the brine squelching in his boots. His legs felt rubbery, as though he had no knee joints. He looked down, surprised to see them intact. There was blood – yes, a graze on the knuckle of his first finger. He sucked it. The keen wind smelt of smoke.

At a village called Meuvaines the whole brigade was assembled. Still to the right there was the sound of fighting. Rations were taken quickly, rifles stripped and cleaned, tea brewed. French children, clattering on the flagstones in their wooden shoes, came asking for food – treating the battle zone around their houses as the most ordinary thing in the world. About a quarter of a mile away, tank turrets were visible behind a hedge. Every so often, cannons were fired. Map in hand, Major Whitton came up beside Vic's company together with a captain of the Second Gloucesters. 'Getting the hang of this bloody place,' he said. 'Someone's going to sort out that Le Hamel battery. But it's not us, apparently.' Bren-gun carriers appeared in the road. Strapped on to them were the precious bicycles. Vic laughed out loud.

His uniform was dry when they set out again. On the left of a broad front his battalion was advancing across country towards Bayeux – the first day's objective. They had passed through the left wing of the assault troops, the Green Howards. While his own company had been still wallowing at sea these soldiers had taken casualties enough. The tide had covered them.

But Vic could hardly recall the morning. Nor had the faces of the advance troops touched him. A happiness filled him. His body was doing what it had been trained for, and his thoughts were in abeyance. All along the basin of a small river stretched a profusion of meadow flowers: kingcups, cow parsleys, vetches, clovers. Clusters of ox-eye daisies straggled down from the banks among the nettles. Close to the water there were yellow flag irises, and at a field's edge, poppies blinked in the green corn crop. Beside a fresh bomb crater, tall trees arched, their tops rustling and bending in the wind.

Then they were marching in a lane. On either side, hedgerows towered up out of steep earthen walls, and, under great curds of elderflower, the road twisted amidst a maze of paddocks. They crossed a field between gates. Suddenly there were shots out of the trees that rose up on top of the far boundary. Men dropped to the ground all round him. He found himself pressed flat to the damp, sweet-smelling grasses, with dock leaves and shepherd's purse, his heart hammering, his rifle levelled towards the grey-green rampart in front of him.

Somehow, then, the landscape contained an exchange of fire. He was awestruck – only yards to his left, cows were grazing. Next, on a command, he was running forward across the pasture, his pack jolting and straining. Norton was five yards away. They threw themselves down again. A shot cracked from the hedge. Vic and a dozen others returned fire.

The enemy here put up no determined resistance. The greater part of the defenders had fallen back, or found themselves outflanked. He didn't see the bodies afterwards, only a knot of prisoners, looking dejected – or was it relieved? So high was his mood he found it hard to believe he might have done anyone harm. They pressed on, more cautious now.

From the hamlet of Ryes in the late afternoon there was a road to St Sulpice. The land was not entirely land, the sky not quite sky. Birds sang that he couldn't precisely identify, and now he trod like a sleepwalker, hardly feeling his feet starting to blister from the salt water that had got into his boots. How long had they been going? He looked at his watch. It recorded twelve thirty-three, the exact moment he'd jumped off the ramp under the sea wall. His shoulders ached from the pack.

IT WAS EVENING by the time they occupied St Sulpice. There'd been contact with the defenders of Bayeux. On the battalion's right the South Wales Borderers were engaged and there would be a head-on attack before the end of the day. Vic tried to ready himself, picture himself going forward somewhere beyond this village.

There was a flurry of organisation. Officers passed in front of them to confer. He looked across at Norton who leant against the wall of a house. 'Your matches dried out yet?'

'Parky's got some. Eh, Parky. Give Vic a light, will you?'

No one spoke of the fire-fight that had occurred, nor of

the attack that was imminent. Men swore, checked their equipment. The cries of swifts above the little church mingled with the intimate gunfire from the next sector. Then an artillery shell passed close as a breath overhead, suggesting a flak gun in the town was shooting wildly into the evening. It exploded somewhere in the distance. There came a rumour of casualties from the sniper fire. Two patrols were sent forward while the battalion waited.

When the patrols returned they told of a manned anti-tank ditch that lay ahead, and a decision hung almost palpably in the air for twenty minutes. Then the attack was called off. Vic looked up at the grey clouds scudding under the west. He felt first disappointment, next inordinate relief. While they dug in, he mused as to why it should have been that way round. How unreal the place felt, only a hundred miles or so from England. How different everything was.

He was not detailed for night patrol, so he slept fitfully to the sound of intermittent rifle fire, frightened, alert for the dawn, dreaming back to the sea passage. In the morning there were tanks alongside the position. The Sherwood Rangers had driven up from the coast to support the attack. An order was given, and the movement forward under grey streamers of cloud and into the outskirts of the town was stealthy, full of intent.

Bayeux was deserted. They made their entry warily, cautiously, amongst the parks and old houses that were dawn-lit across the bridges of the Aure. There was no hand-to-hand fighting, no rush and raid amidst the screams of civilians. It seemed the enemy had withdrawn in the night.

And when they had stolen into the medieval town, their boots loud on the cobbles, their whispered, incredulous voices echoing on the silent walls, then, as if some secret signal had been given, shutters were suddenly flung open. Shouts and laughter rang out instead of gunfire, and women were waving from windows. Vic found himself a liberator; he came into his name. Tricolours appeared from balconies and the streets were full of children. They sang the song of the lark, *Alouette*.

He stood in the town square, sipping calvados and nodding to the girl who'd brought it. She threw her arms around his neck and then hung back, smiling. He smiled at her in turn. How unearthly. So they nodded to one another, and spoke without understanding. And he felt himself caught up with the celebration under the cathedral that was quite different from anything he'd known in England. Tinged with brandy and Catholicism, it assumed some direct acquaintance with heaven and hell. A family rushed out of a house to shake his hand. They were introducing themselves, the chattering woman and her father in his loose black jacket, and a little boy in baggy grey shorts. He thought instantly of Jack. They brought bread and cheese and more calvados.

So the town swirled and cheered as the tanks came rumbling through. Someone had found a group of Germans. They brought them along the Rue Larcher in front of the cathedral, poor bewildered lads in their uniforms, one with a beaten mask of a face. The South Wales Borderers were guarding them. He wondered what the crowd would have done to the boys if they'd been left to it, if these good folk had all decided to turn nasty – as they had every right to. And he remembered suddenly the carnivalesque, shell-shocked world he'd grown up in. He'd seen grotesques. In East Ham, the amputees – even the dead – were everywhere, slain youths and men who refused to go away. He'd seen them, or imagined he did: ruined tailors and gasping lathe operators, and pierced chemical workers, and shoemakers without heads. Yet the little cream-painted structure far away amid grass and trees, the cottage with its slatted sides and corrugated roof, stood always at the back of his mind.

When evening came bringing rain, they dug in and made camp in a public garden. Major Whitton had a book instead of a map. Vic overheard him. 'Bayeux,' he said, looking up as though from the pages of a guidebook. 'So lofty in its noble coronet of rusty lace. Ever care for Proust, Fairfax?'

'Not that I was frightfully aware of, sir,' said Lieutenant Fairfax, saluting.

A FIELD STRETCHED away to the south under skies still overcast in the late afternoon. Green corn waved in the gusting breeze, spattered here and there with the bright heads of poppies. For the hundredth time Vic scanned the low hedgerow at the field's far boundary, its base obscured both by the half-grown stand of wheat and by the slight downward contour of the terrain. There had been rain for most of the previous night, and again at midday. A mouldy waft rose up from his clothes. He finished his bread and tinned meat, and checked his rifle, clicking the bolt back and forth.

'Put the bloody thing down, Warren. I expect it'll work.' Second Lieutenant Fairfax turned his head irritably. His fresh face under his helmet looked painfully young and vulnerable, the eyes pale blue and the lashes invisible.

'Yes, sir.'

'And you, Norton.'

Norton snapped to attention, his tin mug held, slopping, against his trouser seam.

'No, no. At ease, man. Stand easy. Drink your damn tea.' He looked pleadingly for a moment, as though he would have given anything to be able to break through the formalities of command and apologise for his nerves. 'Never mind. Carry on.'

'Very good, sir.'

A jeep revved in the lane behind them, then swerved in at the gate. Major Whitton leapt out of the passenger seat, holding a solid-looking field compass in his left hand and his map case in his right. Vic watched as he spread the map out on the jeep's bonnet and then called his captains and junior officers around. Then Lieutenant Fairfax came back to relay the details. The battalion in entirety was to advance on a selected bearing at eighteen hundred hours and take an orchard about a mile away down the slope. The lieutenant indicated the direction across the cornfield. Enemy troops with tanks had been seen there. They'd been identified as belonging to a Panzer training unit.

'Hardly a pushover, I'd say. Would you?' Lieutenant Fairfax set his lips. 'This is to be the battalion's first full-scale attack. But, in fact, it's pretty much a textbook situation. About the only bit of open country for miles.' He looked the platoon up and down, his jaw thrust forward meaningfully. 'More or less what we've all been trained for.' He snorted through his nose.

Then, with his nervous little smile, he outlined the distances of the attack, and wished his platoon luck. 'At the moment we're well ahead of the Yanks on our right. Some of them had a pretty bad show on the beaches, by all accounts, but they're right back in contention just over there.' He pointed to the west. 'And more or less level pegging. We have linkage with all Canadian and British troops to our left. But they've run into big resistance at Caen.' A schoolboy grin appeared on his lips and he laughed again nervously. Vic noticed how he held on to the strap of his webbing, where the knuckles were white. 'Well. All right? Today is our chance to show them all what we're made of. I know I can say with absolute confidence that none of you men will let me, or the regiment, down.'

A moment of silence followed. Vic noticed the chatter of the sparrows in the brake next to him suddenly grow louder. But it was only a moment, for in the next minute their own field guns in the *bocage* behind them opened up. Shells whined overhead; faint drifts of smoke seeped from beyond the drop of the terrain. He watched them until the command came from the sergeants all along the line to form up.

It *was* what he'd been trained for. Precisely at six, they started forward. Nearly a thousand yards wide, the advance proceeded on a two-company front in perfect formation. Lieutenant Fairfax strode purposefully through the corn, his revolver drawn. To Vic's left was Norton, partially obscuring the major and his map. To his right Williams, the Dunkirk veteran. Behind him, he could feel the presence of Matthieson and Fairbrother, and occasionally hear their movements.

In an odd, arrhythmic music the shells from the twenty-five pounders sliced the air above, almost close enough to touch. The effect was hypnotic: it was like a training exercise, yet nothing like, a sense of *déjà vu* which had no relation to any former experience. His heart raced, his fingers were slippery on the wooden stock of his gun. Under his boots the corn stalks cricked and dragged against his legs like the shallows of some soft persistent tide.

They came to the hedge. Compared to the obstacles of the early afternoon, it was no more than a flimsy marker between one crop and the next. But even the recent past and its landscape were already a blur. Bayeux was forgotten. Was it only a few hours ago there'd been a monastery, and a farmhouse? Had more prisoners been taken? The whole of Vic's former life had fallen away. Before the invasion, there had been some drama of love, some wrestling with sensibilities. The woman was lost. Only this gradually declining slope with its swaying corn and whirring, punctuated air had ever existed.

Steady pace; he made himself count the steps. One hundred yards filled nearly two minutes. He disciplined his fear. Two hundred yards and through the next low line of thorn, still to its own sounds, still with its own deliberate momentum, the advance continued. Then it was some necessary repetition, some meaningful machinery of nature, surely, this deliberate walk towards the enemy. It was a condition of manhood, and had to be gone through. They broke the next boundary.

Now there was a far horizon, a dark blue-green shading off, purple against the grey sky. But as they proceeded across the new field, sown waist high with some inconvenient vegetable Vic didn't recognise, there arose on a sight-line of the middle distance a fringe of paler green rising as though out of a fold. He fixed his eyes on it. As he walked, it thickened and gained definition, and then he could see clearly that it was the topmost boughs of pruned orchard apple trees.

It occurred to him that the barrage from their own guns had stopped. But the pace kept up, coordinated, deliberate. Vic held his position; the major in front and to the left, glancing down at his compass; the lieutenant, striding forward stiff-legged, with his boyish, rather self-conscious gait; Norton, with his long, loping walk. Vic felt the common sense in his own legs that wanted to stop him in his tracks and turn him around. He overruled it. But he knew that now each further step down the gradual slope could only offer up ever more candidly the strung-out lines of men. It *was* a textbook situation, and he knew the name of it. It was a killing ground.

NOW THE TREES were the green tops of lollipops, teasing and innocent. Now they'd acquired the suggestion of their sticks below. Still the line continued forward, eight hundred yards from the wood, seven hundred, six. He felt light-headed, almost already dead. He was not walking but floating. A lark burst up in front of him, hovering suddenly with a distressed, heart-rending call. Vic started, and then nearly cried out himself for the delicious, ludicrous song that poured down out of it. Another, and he was convinced the whole business had gone quite into madness. *Je te plumerai.* In his imagination he could already hear the rattle of machine-gun fire, feel the hot bullets in his chest. He entered the next field. It was a crop of cabbages, and the orchard was fully in view.

Then at last the command came and he dropped gratefully to the ground. The gun barrel smashed one globing plant from its fat stalk. A minute stream of trapped water trickled on to his hand from the fat blue leaf of another. Norton was getting up in front of him. Vic raced after him and they both crashed down into the wet brassicas. Then up once more. And down again. New shells from their own guns whined above them for the final softener. Fragments fountained amongst the fruit trees. One smashed and toppled. Smoke boiled under the low clouds and was then blown sideways. The breath tore in and out of Vic's lungs.

The new rhythm took hold. He had a sensation of the land all around him on the move in this strange irregular ripple of khaki battledress, like a visible earthquake that crept forward harmlessly, carefully, under a blanket of sprouting soil. Now their own barrage had fallen silent. Yet there had been no returned fire, no indication of an enemy at all.

An impulse, almost irresistible in its folly, to stand up and walk just as they'd been doing at the start, began to take hold of him. He should stroll, even. There was no opposition. How could there be? How odd the major looked when he threw himself down only to scramble up again. There was nothing between the tree-trunks. Vic stood up and ran forward. The base of the wood turned orange.

He was pressed into the earth. The grit was in his mouth, on his tongue. Clods were falling on him. He felt them thump into his back like punches. His head was under something. Above him the air tore and snarled. He tried to force himself flatter. Then the ground only feet away kicked up in deafening fire and he felt himself blown back and twisted round by the blast.

A large figure was running past him, Platoon Sergeant Bell. Vic followed an instruction he didn't know he'd heard and reached for his bayonet. As he was trying to fix it to the front of his rifle, he saw the sergeant lifted and thrown backwards as though by colossal impact. The body hung for a moment with its own weapon spinning slowly in the air, the strap passing only a few inches from the outstretched hand. It collapsed down heavily on to its pack, even seeming to bounce slightly amid a shower of stones and pieces of earth.

Vic was up once more and dashing on. As he neared the sergeant there was another flash from the wood and a patter of small-arms fire. He swerved. The ground in front of him offered a gaping hole and he jumped into it. Ahead of him in amongst the trees he saw the swivelling turret of a tank. The flash came again and the body of the tank shuddered.

He stole a glance to his left. The shot had torn away a great part of the field, but the line was still moving forward. Further along it was broken in places. And, close at hand, though there was smoke drifting in great wreaths out of other new pits in the field, he thought he could make out Norton.

The wood flashed and flashed again; it crackled as though it were on fire. He ran forward. Three hundred yards remained. The earth crashed and heaved. He ran forward. He could see figures under the apple trees, little puffs of white smoke beside them. Then there was another tank. The blast from a cannon round exploding to his right threw him sideways. He picked himself up and ran forward.

At one hundred yards there were shouts. He dropped down. The dozen rounds of rapid fire went off, the heavy wooden stock of his rifle bruising back into his shoulder, the stark black spike of his foresight ranging now here, now there, upon confused and dark green shapes amidst the smoke-filled trees. He could see the tanks as they reversed. The turrets swung and flashed again. But he heard nothing. He was briefly immune to noise.

Then they were all charging, all at once, along the whole front, borne forward by a shout that seemed to have welled up from deep inside him. The shout had filled him up and was sweeping him along. One shape beside him crumpled. Another stumbled. He ran through smoke and flying debris, intent only on getting in under the branches to stab and hack at whatever blind retreating figures dodged between the orderly, knobbled tree-trunks.

Under a canopy of leaves he stopped, exhausted, leaning on his gun. There were figures all about him, but no sign of Norton. Nor of the veteran, Williams. The major was calling for a defensive box formation to be organised.

The two companies who'd been bringing up the rear were already starting to stream through into the more forward positions. He saw Matthieson. 'All right?'

'Yeah. You?'

'Yeah. Don't know about the others, though.'

Lieutenant Fairfax appeared. He began to check off numbers. Norton was indeed missing. And Fairbrother. A lance-corporal from another platoon arrived with Williams. He was groaning from a stomach wound. Vic fought back nausea at the sight of it. Then he was detailed to a defensive post.

It seemed almost immediately that the popping sound of mortar shells began, exploding up ahead in the forward positions, right in the centre of the wood, and there were more cries and shouts. Vic couldn't get the hang of what ought to be done. Men behind him were digging slit trenches. He crouched at his post, his gun on the crook of a branch, ready aimed. Five yards in front of him, in the long grass, lay the body of a German boy. Its eyes stared over Vic's head.

There was small-arms fire. The mortar stopped. Now a touch of evening was in the air. The wood had begun to darken, the breeze to die down. But like a summer storm reluctant to pass, the engagement was still active. Flashes and sounds continued to come out of the gloom ahead. There were rifle shots, and every now and then bursts from a machine pistol, disagreeably close like an unpleasant insect. Vic waited. The platoon waited, gathered on the edge of the orchard. No armoured support appeared to have arrived.

It was at about nine o'clock that the counter-attack started. All at once the mortar fire was renewed and concentrated. In the intervals between hits on the forward line, Vic could hear the insistent creak and grind of tanks. Suddenly the enemy cannon were blasting, it felt

314

at point-blank range. The detonations were shatteringly loud, and the wood seemed perpetually erupting in fire and flame. Trees splintered. Branches fell, burning. All at once the air was contaminated with the sweet, sickly smell of high explosives.

Vic saw movement before him. He prepared to fire. There was a command from Lieutenant Fairfax, and he realised just as he heard it that their own forward company was in retreat towards them. Men were visible not twenty yards in front of him. A fireball engulfed them as he watched. He saw a pair of tanks reverse and turn together amid the apple trees, and then race off towards the left and out of sight.

And from the left flank, he heard the din of half a dozen other engagements. The two tanks were working back on a new line, and shelling point blank. Once more, great swathes were cut out of the cover, and in between the terrifying reports, rifle bullets zipped and stung as they knocked splinters out of broken stumps.

Yet by some miracle of resistance with their own mortars and anti-tank Piats the battalion was not entirely overrun. And when eventually night fell, the tanks actually retreated, and the troops they supported appeared to have melted away. But the darkness was charged with danger, and filled with the intermittent groans from the wounded in front. In an earthern trench Vic waited once again, holding his hot rifle.

At about midnight he heard the major's voice. He was cursing a useless radio under his breath. One fresh shellburst that lit up the landscape like a flash bulb signalled a renewed counter-attack. Another came in, and another. Ahead there was a tremendous volley of shots and the chaos of hand-to-hand fighting.

It was then that Vic experienced what he thought must have been a hallucination – an enormous millipede or glow-worm, walking for an instant amid the far-off groves. He put a hand up to his face. He saw it coming nearer, a strange monstrous thing, like a dragon's tongue. And to the right, a second one appeared, much nearer, its roar terrible now, backed by the chug of an engine.

'Fucking hell,' said a voice. 'They're using bloody flame-throwers.' It was the last thing Vic remembered.

HE RAN AWAY because he thought he'd killed one of the other boys. It was a Sunday, after breakfast, and they were getting ready for kit inspection. In the dormitory, Rutherford was helping him with his tartan travelling rug. His shorts, sets of flannel shirts, pullovers, underwear, socks, lay precisely arranged on the bed cover. The iron-framed bed was lit through the sash window, and all his corduroy ridges were grey and gold in a sunstream. Far off, there were bending poplars under scudding clouds. It was the middle of summer.

The Comforter was in its envelope, hidden under the mattress. Signed, *Your Loving Father, Victor Warren*, it was a letter that didn't make sense. Since Aubrey had come everything had changed in any case; and now there were flying bombs. And right in Warren's nose the dust from the tartan rug had a prickling, maddening smell: new wool, old wood, someone else's mother. He and Rutherford found the folds.

Then Aubrey started. It was always the same. He came over from his own bed and dodged between the two of them, yanked the coverlet where it never quite tucked in properly. The piles of kit were mucked up. Aubrey thrust his round face with its brat sneer at Warren. Go on, Warren. Get me back. Punish me. You know you want to.

Aubrey, the six-year-old nose-picker, his finger garlanded. Wipe it on your pillow, shall I? Aubrey the troubled one who knew how to take the room hostage, like an infected splinter. On your bed now, shall I? They should put kids like him somewhere else. They should lock them up.

If it weren't for him, Warren might have been happy at the school. There were rules; he'd felt safe. Now his fingers itched for a cane, or a horsewhip. Tavy, their prefect, had been called downstairs. But there was no discipline in the dorm, because Tavy was weak; unlike Briggs, whose slippers were leather and could really hurt.

'Shut up, Aubrey. Bloody cut it out.' Warren took the folded rug from Rutherford, placed it, and began straightening the mess.

'Swear*ing*!'

'Just ignore him.' Rutherford turned to his own bed. 'Pity we're not in Tudor. The people in there know how to behave.'

But Aubrey put on that cocksure face of his with its grin, a mocking, leering affair of the lips and fat little cheeks – a nursery-rhyme face. Outside, beyond the lawns, the neighbours' houses stood in their green tufting. A pattern of roofs and chimney-stacks marked the road down to the city. Jack's father had scoffed at the name, city, that time when his parents had visited. 'Not much more than a big country town.' They *were* his parents, weren't they? Jack called the letter the Comforter, because in a way it was. The Bible was true. The letter had a regimental stamp on, but it seemed too late, and was too made up, somehow, like a cruel kind of joke; he couldn't really believe in it. The father said he was on the point of going abroad. The tip of the sharp cathedral spire could just be seen from the school. Soon the distant bells would ring for matins.

'Warren wants to get me but he's too wet. Wet Warren wees his willy. He does. Don't you, Warren? He wets his bed.'

'Damn well don't.'

'Ooh!'

None of the other boys noticed quite how far things had come, how bad the Aubrey business was. Pacey and Mortimer complained and jeered, but it seemed not to bother them so much. Nor Bintcliffe, hiding his silk-worms under his bed frame in their cardboard box. Aubrey should have been stamped on at birth, crunched like a snail on concrete. Should have been smashed, hammered, fried alive.

Aubrey was standing on his own bed, the one next to the door, trampolining slightly, prancing on his kit. He didn't care if he got the cane. 'Better tidy up quick smart, Warren. Listen. Isn't that Matron coming? No, it's the Widow already. Clickey-click high heels. Don't want to get into trouble now, do we, Warren? Big goody-goody, aren't you? Yes sir, no sir, my big toe, sir. What about you, Bintcliffe? You've got worms, Bintcliffe. He's got silkworms coming out of his bum. Shall I tell the Widow, Bintcliffe. About your bum?'

AUBREY HAD COME in the winter. He'd had it too easy, was too young, too recent to know how things were done at the school – behaved still as though there were Mummy and Daddy, and you could push the limits. Warren had warned him. He could get killed. All sorts of ways. One day there'd be another hunt.

But instead Aubrey mimicked him, mincing and pulling up his skirts. 'Warren thinks he's so clever. Yes, Mrs Fairfax, I do say my prayers. See him kneeling beside his bed at night. Yes, Ma Fairfax. He prays to see Ginny all bare. At the keyhole, he saw her hair. They couldn't get him away. Hairfax, barefax. Ginny barefax, Warren.'

The other boys laughed.

'Shut it, though, Aubrey, she might be in her bedroom.' And Bintcliffe eyed Warren as he polished a toecap with his pyjama sleeve. Ginny's door, with its keyhole, was just across the passage.

Smythe Minor came back in, the wild one with sunken eyes and hospital breath. His parents were in India. Once he had punched Miss Leeson in the bosom, and got caned for it, of course. He wore an untidy glory. 'They're doing Tudor now. That gives us about five minutes.' Sloping to his bed he parked his towel beside his washbag. 'I'm about finished. Where's Tavy?'

'Duty, I think.' Rutherford took out his handkerchief, looked at it, and put it back in his pocket.

'He would be. That means we have to do his kit. I hate Tavy. I hate the lot of 'em.'

Warren was worried. For inspection Mrs Fairfax always came, Ma Fairfax in her high-heeled shoes. They would click down the polished floorboards of the passage outside. Then she would appear in the door frame. She was like a steel spring in her perfect clothes. Her face was severely, perfectly painted, her eyebrows plucked, her grey hair permed. And wherever she went in the dormitory, poking at clothes, examining beds, checking, questioning, Matron slipped in her wake, wearing a white nurse's dress – slipped silently on rubber shoes, white too. They would find the Comforter. They would find something out. His father had called his holdall a johnny bag. The Widow had given him a look.

'There's a big fart on its way. Could be a Cunarder.' Aubrey smirked round for approval. 'Oh, no. It's Warren. Pooh, Warren.' He fanned his hand in front of his face.

One of the quiet boys spoke, Mortimer. 'That's enough, Aubrey. Get down and sort your kit or we'll all be responsible.'

'Responsible. Ooh, big words, Mortimer. Responsible. What did you say your father was? A country solicitor? In Bishop's Stortford? A silly-sitter. A shilly-shitter.'

'Yes, and he'll sue you.'

'I'm scared. How many Germans has he killed?'

'More than yours.'

'Hasn't.'

'Has. He's in the Commandos. He's gone over in the invasion.'

'Where will he sue me, then? In my bottom?' Aubrey crouched on his bed. As he did so the promised fart ripped out.

'For God's sake.'

Aubrey sniggered and broadcast his air. He made paddling movements with the backs of his small hands. 'Will your farter put me in farters' prison?'

Warren caught the whiff. 'You're disgusting. Why don't you ever do what you're told? Just tidy your things, you little . . .'

'Little what, Warren?' Grinning, Aubrey straightened up again and pointed a finger towards his nostril. 'Shall I see what I've got in here?' He searched the finger inside his nose and came out with a trace of slime. It dangled from the delicate, childish tip. He held Warren's eye.

'Don't you bloody dare!'

Smythe Minor hustled back past Aubrey's bed and peered out of the door. 'They'll be here any minute. Cut it out.' Then he went to the triangular sink in Warren's corner and began sprucing it with the wooden brush. 'The Widow's got it in for me. I hate her. I bloody well hate her.'

Aubrey's kit and bedclothes were crumpled under his

feet. 'Mine's killed more than Warren's, any rate. What does Warren's father do? Eh, Warren? What does old man Warren get up to?' He bounced again, slightly. 'We all know what Warren's father does, don't we?' There was a significant pause. The other boys looked up.

If the room were not right, they'd be given lines, made to learn a poem, forced to copy out some Holy Bible in the prep study. They would miss games next week. They might even miss swimming. It was not that, though.

He had lived his double life. But had been equal to it, except for Aubrey. Aubrey would invent an insulting career for his father. Any minute. The boys would laugh in spite of themselves – for most were decent enough. He must do nothing, only endure. One day Clarice would send a letter. Now Mrs Fairfax was coming. The name at the end of the Comforter was Victor Warren. If he could believe in it, it would explain why he, too, was called Warren, while his father's name was Rice. Mrs Fairfax would find out. She would know. What might she find out?

'Warren's father . . .'

Warren clenched his eyes tight shut. He felt the blood behind them. He could not think.

'We know what Warren's father does. Yes, Warren.' Aubrey held his laughter in. His eyes bulged, comically. They were all in the palm of his hand. 'Warren's old man does oo-ah, oo-ah with Ma Warren up the bum. Oo-ah. Oo-ah.'

Rutherford gasped. 'Christ!' It was catastrophic. Warren knew. They all knew. The line was crossed by miles. His mother! Tony Rice was in love with her.

For Warren there was an absolute release. He was standing now on Aubrey's bed, the little boy's round, unbearable face right under his jaw, the eyes wide and frightened, but almost satisfied, the kid's fringe of straight, nut-coloured hair smelling of Warren's old school in

321

Upminster, of crayons and nature study. The two were wrestling. Then Aubrey's face made an arc through the air as he toppled.

Warren didn't hear the sound of the head hitting the cast-iron radiator. He only saw the blood. At first it was a beautiful red mist in front of his eyes. He wanted to get right in close and taste it. Then he was down from the bed too, somehow, making to finish the job with his fists. But he felt himself gripped all at once, held back by the others. He was thankful for it. He'd seen the mess his father had made of Figgsy. At that moment heels sounded in the corridor. Mrs Fairfax walked in. Aubrey's body lay across her path, his head crooked up against the flange of the radiator. Red drenched the side of his face and his collar.

SEVERAL MINUTES MUST have passed. From where he sat in the Widow's big drawing-room, Warren heard someone in the head's study. Matron, it might be. She was winding the handle on the school telephone.

Once the ambulance had gone, he would be beaten. And if Aubrey were dead he would be hanged. Warren perched on the unaccustomed chintz. He sat quite still and there were no tears, no emotions. Rubber shoes squeaked outside, but no one came in. He had always known the room from piano lessons, from long evenings when most of the boys had gone home for the holidays. Sometimes Mrs Fairfax herself had admitted him, kindly, absently, before rejoining on the distant carpet a vicar, a doctor, perhaps a magistrate, holding a delicate china teacup with his back to the fire. On the piano keys Warren's fingers had faltered. The walls were a deep, religious eggshell blue. Oil paintings in gilt frames hung from the white picture rail. And there were Japanese prints of swordsmen, and bamboo.

He was on his honour not to escape. But his head was filled with confused thoughts. He, Jack, was Warren. His father's name was Rice. Until the Comforter arrived, it was a difference he'd always known about but never understood. One more queer thing – no one had ever questioned him on it.

He thought of what hell would really look like, and of the filthy image of his parents that Aubrey had summoned up. He thought of *The Pilgrim's Progress* which they had read in class, and Ginny Fairfax, the Widow's daughter, and this elegant room, the trim lawns outside it, the Latin-Algebra-Scripture-Games. He was shocked with himself.

And then he found himself walking across the room to one of the pairs of french windows. His legs seemed to move of their own accord. The brass handle turned easily. Why should the Widow have had them locked, after all? She knew he could never dream of running away.

He shut the latch behind. There was no one on the lawn between the steps and the shrubbery. Before long he was right in the far corner of the grounds, close to the swimming-pool, concealed among laurels, camouflaged amidst rhododendron blooms. The pool was clearly visible through the branches, a circle of concrete in which the water lay dark green in some parts, in others a sky-bright mirror, ruffled now and then by the wind. Leaves lay on the top, bobbing occasionally, or skidding sideways.

He recalled the pool's strange taste, like a trapped river, woody, leafy. It was just water from a pipe, which ran for a week at the start of summer. Each day the boys would look to see how far it had crept up the stained concrete walls. As it did fill, slowly and teasingly, so it turned yellow-green and became eventually quite opaque. He was filled with regret, for his friends the other schoolboys.

A green ambulance was in the lane, ringing and screeching its tyres, racing along the fence behind him. Then it turned into the school drive. Warren skirted along the inside of the fence, and, taking advantage of the commotion, slipped out of the school gates in the other direction. He ran as fast as he could.

THE COLCHESTER EXPRESS hammered a streak right under Warren's escape, where the school lane crossed the railway track. Grey sulphur billows broke over the parapet. While the carriages raced and drummed beneath him, he threw his tie over. The swirl caught and snagged it on a carriage-top vent, where it streamed out like a pennant just as the train swept it under the bridge. Turning, he saw the trapped smoke roil up the cutting slope on the opposite side.

Then, just for one moment, he let himself look back to the schoolhouse, the top of which he could see through the trees. He made out Ginny's window, so close to the scene of the killing. They'd be searching the building, scouring the grounds. He hadn't long to get away. The Widow would get the police. All the masters would be summoned up to hunt him in earnest, just as the boys had hunted the Jew, Wiseman, on his first night. He imagined Cathcart and Cicero with sticks rampaging after him in their hopeless trousers.

But at Ginny's window he saw a figure. He ducked behind the brickwork and then peered cautiously back. Surely Ginny Fairfax was waving from her bedroom, standing up in her best dress. He was mistaken. There was nothing but the movement of her curtain in a gust of the breeze.

A man cycling behind him said, 'Aye aye?' but Warren hardly turned his head. He stared again at the schoolhouse framed by chestnut trees and their blown leaves, and then turned and ran as quickly as he was able. A knot of village kids came out from behind the shop. They had dirty faces, unbrushed hair, scruffy clothes. He burst through the middle of them.

'Sorry!'

'Oy, oy! Watch out!'

They were caught too unawares to give chase, and he was well away before they began even to jeer, spotting his uniform grey and the clean backs of his knees. It wasn't until he passed a baker's horse and cart loaded up with sacks, towards the roundabout and the village end, that he paused to draw breath.

Across the dual carriageway stood the thin village church, hemmed in by trees, with the vicarage behind it. But Jack made automatically for the sports field. Sharp left, it was about half a mile further on at the foot of the hill. The boys trekked there every afternoon for rugby or cricket. He coasted down easily, while a car or two swished past on his right. There was a lorry as well. The first few sports of rain began to fall.

A ditch ran beside the road, full of willows and scrub, and once all the boys had seen a man and a woman right inside the bushes, lying down. The rickety five-barred gate stood always open. Here, the sports field, a soft, green sea, the rain suddenly leaping and bouncing up out of its surface, stretched in the low between road and railway embankment. At the far corner like a small white ark stood the cricket pavilion.

The little shed was dim inside, almost murky, divided by a partition into Home, and Away. Warren went to the right, Away. He liked the special smell coming up off the dry wood. An umpire's coat hung on a peg. Hundreds of cricket studs had jagged the floor into fibres. The slatted walls smelt of resin and plimsolls and silence. Last summer he had scored three runs against Braintree, in his pads and whites and batting gloves, and the fellows had clapped when he came in.

A bench seat ran all round the inside of the changing-room. He pressed his nose against the dusty window to look back up at the school on the rise, half pretending he was in another wooden hut, a flimsy shelter inside a rose garden – he could just see the back of the schoolhouse next to it, the roofs and dormitory windows, where the boys still lived. Circling above it were rooks, dark specks coming his way. They grew larger and then veered off, disappearing, leading his eye over the high bank to his right.

There was a route across the railway tracks because one wet day in their gaberdine raincoats the boys had taken it. Someone had put a penny on the line. A further turning led eventually to a wild thicket, and he was sure he could find that route again – now that he'd lost everything: the winter evenings sitting on the study window ledge with the old wireless, the games in the yard, the big boys making model aeroplanes in the upper-form workshop with its smells of dope and the miniature petrol engines buzzing and spitting as they ran, the midnight feasts. He looked down at his fingers. They needed attention. Matron was due any day to come round and cut the boys' nails, sitting on each bed in turn, holding his hand in hers.

The boys he'd known were brave, and briefly he'd been numbered among them. It was all over, he knew it. And now his only chance was to make his way east to search for his aunt, and for that other figure, the man he'd once known, who'd held him up in the light. But he'd left the Comforter behind.

326

IT WAS A simple enough task. It was one of her duties. All she had to do was type a letter. She'd done it often enough before.

The heavy machine sat on her desk in front of the metal window. Its bank of keys showed the alphabet white on black. Somebody had marked indelibly across its bodywork 'WAR DEPARTMENT, PROPERTY OF 100 GROUP, RAF'. She had only to play it – just as she might a piano. And yet she could not get started. It made her almost beside herself with a kind of pent-up fury. The squadron crest at the top of her sheet of paper mocked her from the triangular eye of the platen carriage.

Her hut window at Oulton looked directly over part of the base where the Americans of the 803rd parked their Flying Fortresses. They were the B-17s and B-24s scheduled to assemble over the North Sea for the hitherto unimaginable thousand-bomber raids. The first in the line of huge planes was so close she could virtually see the rivets that held it together. It cocked its perspex nose up against the wide Norfolk sky, its machine-guns poking the June air from under the bombsight panel. A naked, poster-painted woman sprawled next to her name: *Donna Louise*. From just behind the nose-compartment windows, the teeth in *Donna Louise*'s bright blonde head flashed a million-dollar smile back at Clarice.

Clarice punched her fingers down as hard as she could on to the keys. The big khaki typewriter rattled and ratcheted. When the chime rang at the end of her line she collared the return lever so harshly that the carriage almost crashed through its stops. It was a routine letter to a boy's mother and she had the format by heart. The station commander's records were clear and uncomplicated; there should be no further difficulties.

It was not until she was about to type the word 'instantaneously' that she hesitated again. Her fingers hovered. The word formed and reformed itself in her mind. Just for the moment, she couldn't for the life of her recall how to spell it. There was an 'e' instead of an 'i'. But she wasn't quite sure where. 'Killed instantaneously'.

It would come to her. She had only to wait a second while her thoughts cleared. The solution was certain to pop into her head. After all, she'd written the word countless times before without a hitch – 'instantaneously'. It was part of a formula, necessary, professional. Of course, she *knew* how to spell it. It was just for the moment that . . . It was just at the minute she was unable . . . She was just now having trouble focusing . . .

There was a sensation on her cheeks. When she put up her hand she found she was crying. It made her furious. So many tears in a war – why should she have to cry them? It made her simply incandescent with rage that she was sitting at her desk with her face streaming, unable to finish a straightforward, simple, stupid, bloody letter.

Later, on the train down to London, she still couldn't for the life of her see why they'd placed her on compassionate leave. What incensed her most was her own failure. A letter, the simplest of things. Not to be able to do one's work – it was deeply humiliating. The stupid train would keep stopping for no reason; she should really go straight back to Oulton. At the base she was useful, she was needed. Apart from the letter, there were countless things she had to attend to which just wouldn't get done if she weren't there. The letter was nothing. There were the operations schedules, and duty rosters and a hundred and one administrative issues that only she knew how to deal with properly. She was the one who'd set up the systems, after all. If Marjory Peters or even Yvain tried to take over, they wouldn't know how to read the service charts. For heaven's sake, they'd order the wrong parts for the wrong planes. One little thing could ground the whole squadron. She'd have to telephone as soon as she got in to Liverpool Street.

It had all started – the bouts of uncontrollable crying – after she'd written the letter to Vic, describing what had happened to her. From Vic she'd heard nothing in return. Did he still care for her? Could he ever forgive her? Was he alive, or dead? She'd needed, briefly, to lean on Yvain. But she would have pulled herself together. Why hadn't they at least given her the chance?

Now her files would get hopelessly muddled, and she'd have to spend weeks when she came back sorting everything out. Why couldn't Wing Commander Hedges get it through his thick military head that there'd truly been no need to send her away? She was *needed*. Didn't they realise there was a war on?

Outside Liverpool Street Station, exactly where she'd heard the first raid of the Blitz, the CP had fly-postered a wall: 'Comrades ... This Imperialist War ... Strike Now! Support the Miners! Action on Right to Strike NOW!' Just there, by a spook coincidence, she heard her first flying bomb. She recognised at once the curious puttering engine note: it was just like its own rumours. And, just as had happened before, everyone in Bishopsgate stopped what they were doing – and seemed not to want to be the first to take cover. The pilotless machine passed overhead under the hazy clouds. Officially it didn't exist. Thirty seconds later its engine cut out and the sound of its explosion made the paving-stone judder under Clarice's feet.

She walked down to Fenchurch Street. On the train for Laindon, through the heart of the East End, she caught glimpses of the Thames through the missing parts of Shadwell. The river was busy again, now that the seas had been made safe. American ships in various colours lay along the battered wharfsides. Dockers were at work. Another distant explosion rattled the glass in the carriage door. And then her eye was caught by a row of old dismasted sailing barges, hooked up between two buoys against the opposite bank, straining at the current. How it hurt to think of Vic. Really, she had no business coming down here. Behind the barges, against the ruined wharves and dark chimneys of the Surrey shore, a tier of lighters, huge sullen things, were strung one to another, floating quarries, three abreast. And then the train veered northward behind warehouses, shutting the river out, and on past the potholed side-streets and bombsites of Stepney and Limehouse. In back yards, headscarved women hung out washing on bits of string, attended by their frightful staring children. Beside Burdett Road, a demolition crane and bulldozer were at work where a roofless slum terrace abutted the railway embankment. And there, right next to the tracks, a girl stood with a baby in a piece of blanket. The girl stared up at the train as it passed. Three other children waited next to a broken wall behind her. All were filthy, without shoes.

She hated them. Bluestockings like Yvain expected everyone to think nobly of such class victims. They're comrades, Clarice. I've always envied you, Clarice. You really know working people, Clarice. She shook with disgust. She was glad the slums had been blown to pieces. And now she welcomed the flying bombs. Because vermin like Tony Rice stood a chance of being exterminated. She wanted it wiped out, the filthy mark that had been left inside her.

The train crossed the mud flats of the River Lea and ran on between the gasworks and the Abbey Mills sewage beds. She hated Phyllis. She hated Vic because he so obviously now hated her for getting raped. Especially she hated herself, who'd tried to save him from the cesspit he'd plunged himself into, but had succeeded merely in allowing herself to be contaminated. Most of all she hated Jack – because if she hadn't had to go and find him and his viper of a mother in the first place, then the harm would never have been done. Everything she'd ever attempted had turned to ashes and disgrace.

SOME FANTASY OCCUPIED her that Vic might be at the cabin, after all – that all the time he might have been waiting for her. Walking up the hill from the station, as she had so many times in the past, she became almost convinced that as soon as she opened the door she would see him, there, in his uniform, his cigarette stuck in the corner of his mouth, making some improvement, his figure in a gesture she could already picture, or loose-limbed in his singlet with his tunic top thrown over one of the chairs, at work with his saw, or his hammer and nails. When she entered, he would look up, and smile. Everything would be put right.

The same tangled briars greeted her, their coils across the path, their flowers blatant in the sultry afternoon. She turned her key and pushed open the door. There was no one there.

Even so, her stomach fluttered with a curious anxiety. She had to make sure. Couldn't he still be in the little kitchen, having known she was coming? Might she not even now still find him, before he quite expected her, still setting the jug under his filter and pumping the Primus stove, all in preparation to make her some tea? She crossed the floor he'd painted, and passed the pictures he'd put up, and the camouflage colours where they clashed with the curtains. She would not cry.

The kitchen was occupied only by the tandem which stood in its usual position under his bag of dreams. She leant across the bike and lifted the bag from its peg. She took it back into the living-room and sat down with it on the mattress.

Shafts of brilliant sunlight laid fiery squares across the brown PT mats and dull floorboards. She sat staring across at the pictures of America he'd put up for her. The GIs had all gone over to Normandy. And so had Vic. And now she hated even the big painted USAAF bombers at the airbase. She picked out a notebook from his bag, and began to read the scribbled lines, as though that might bring him back again. Then she tore out the page and began ripping it carefully into shreds.

She didn't hear the door shift on its hinges. Only when she felt the sun suddenly hot on her neck did she turn round towards the light. In the blinding entrance a figure stood.

'Vic?' She screwed up her eyes. 'Is that you? Vic?' The figure wasn't Vic at all – how could it be? No – it was a woman. It was Phyllis.

The cousins stared at each other. Clarice rose to her feet and the scraps of paper fell from her skirt.

Phyllis took a step inside. 'What ... ?' she said. She carried a handbag in the crook of her arm and was wearing one of her hats, but she was steely, and threatening. Her eyes were narrowed, her shoulders, in the padded black suit, squared. 'What do you think you're doing here?' She looked quickly around, her eye taking everything in. 'What's been going on?'

Clarice took a step back. 'I'm on compassionate leave. I just came by to ...'

Phyllis reached behind her and pushed the door shut.

'Just came by! Someone's been living here. Someone's actually been bloody living here. It's you, isn't it?'

'No. I haven't actually.'

'You've been here in this bloody little dump. Or something's been going on. Behind my back.' She strode over and fingered the chintz curtain, glanced at one of the pictures. The sunlight laid a bright bar beside her. Dust glinted. 'Oh, I see. I get it. It's him, isn't it?' She gave a gritted little laugh. 'Not for me, though. It's for you. He's done it for you.'

Clarice spoke up. 'Why have you come? Are you on your own?' She gripped the edge of the table, and darted a glance through the window.

'What, frightened I've got Tony with me, are you? Frightened I've come mob-handed? Over this? You must be joking, dear. I can fight my own battles, thank you very much.'

'Yes, I am frightened of him, actually. I've got every right to be. After what he did to me.'

Phyllis's eyes widened for a moment. 'After what he did to *you*?'

'Yes. After what he did to me.'

Phyllis looked genuinely taken aback. Then she snorted. 'You.' She put her bag down on a chair and came forward, defiant, her slant hat wobbling slightly on her perm. 'You can sling your hook, dear. This is my property.'

Clarice made herself stand fast. She held the table hard and returned the stare. She could smell Phyllis's scent drifting in the air between them. 'Your property? Why is it yours?'

'What is a man's is his wife's. It belongs to me and my husband. That's why.'

'Your husband,' said Clarice. 'That would be the charming Mr Rice, would it?'

'You know very well who I mean. It's mine and Vic's.

It's mine, and you can bloody get out.' Phyllis advanced on her high heels. 'Because I'm entitled, aren't I? I'm bloody entitled, I should think.' She thrust her face close. Clarice felt the force of her. Phyllis could always put her in the wrong.

'I haven't been . . .'

But Phyllis changed. She turned on her heel. Now she was familiar, almost. She touched the oil stove, she rested a finger on the top of the radio where it stood on its painted crate. Vic's notebooks lay spilt from his bag across the mattress. 'I came out here to get a bit of peace,' she said. 'That's all I want. That's all I ever wanted. A bit of peace and a quiet life. I came out here because things were finally getting on top of me. You know? I can handle most of it, Clarice. I have handled it, haven't I, most of the time? But my dear husband *as was* was always going on at me that if there was *real* danger I should take the kid and come out here.' She breathed out through her nose, half smiling, half contemptuous, confiding. 'Well, now it seems the kid's gone missing and the boys in blue are out looking for him. And my husband *as is* is not best pleased. To say the least. You get the idea? So I've just come myself. Because it's not my fault and I've had enough.' Phyllis looked tired, even abstracted for a moment. 'These buzz bombs or whatever they are. I just can't be doing with them, somehow. Don't you agree?'

'Missing? Then you haven't got him? Jack's gone missing?'

But Phyllis ignored her. She was indignant again. Once more her face altered, and her eyes clouded. 'But what do I bloody find, here in my property – yes, in the little place I've had in the back of my mind all along in case things got really bad? I mean desperate. I don't find woodworm and rot. Not spiders and cobwebs, and a dirty little corner for me to hide in where no one will think to look.' She tossed

334

her head. 'No. I find my blue-eyed cousin, and the place all patched and tarted out like a barracks boudoir.'

She advanced again, and then paused. Clarice put her hand to the wall behind her. Her body wanted to flatten itself against it. She tried to stop her right knee from quivering. Her cousin took another step towards her. 'And I put two and two together, Clarice – as I might, Clarice, because I'm not a fool – and I put what I do know, with what I don't know, and I realise that all along I've not had anything – anything – but it's been taken off me. Do you see that? And I've met some people in my time, Clarice, but out of all of them – yes, out of the lot of them – the person that's had the most off of me, when I really come to think of it . . . And this is the most surprising thing in the world, isn't it, my dear little innocent cousin . . . when you really come to add it all up – that even before I half started or had the beginning of a chance, there was someone there before me. And that someone was you, wasn't it, Clarice?'

Despite herself Clarice felt ashamed. So powerful was the offence in Phyllis's tone that she could have believed her. Even the sound of a train passing far off caught her ear accusingly. She'd had no business to poke her nose in. *She* was the tramp, the tart who went about wrecking families, stealing women's husbands.

'Yes, it was you,' Phyllis went on. 'Who could believe that? You know, it wouldn't have surprised me, deep down – now that I come to think of it – it wouldn't have surprised me one bit if you hadn't have got Jack here with you, already. Before I even showed up.'

The mention of the child freed Clarice from her spell. 'He isn't here. Why should I have him?'

'Because you always wanted him! Because he was mine!'

'Because I showed a child a little bit of kindness!' The rage that had been burning inside her all day suddenly flared. 'You're his mother!' she cried. 'Vic told me what it was like. You never lifted a finger for Jack. If you had, he'd be running to you, wouldn't he! But you're a selfish, spiteful woman, Phyllis, just as you were a selfish, spiteful girl. I tried to like you. I tried to make allowances. I didn't want to take anything from you.'

'You took my husband!'

'And you wanted him? Really wanted him?'

'He was mine, and you took him!'

'He wasn't yours. You can't own people, to torment them and get them shut up. Your sort of person only wants someone to hurt. You're a bloodsucker, Phyllis. A liar and a bloodsucking whore.'

There was a can-opener on the table. Phyllis's eyes flicked sideways at it. Her laquered nails stretched towards its handle. She picked it up and looked at it. Then she looked straight at Clarice. The can-opener's little black knife blade poked ominously out of her pretty fist. Her fingers clenched and unclenched on the grip of it. Then she came forward. Clarice had no idea what the woman was capable of. She screwed up her eyes. Her hands came up involuntarily to shield them. As she backed away, the bright sunlight from the window fell across her knuckles.

Phyllis came on nearer. Clarice was acutely conscious of the tiny, black, crescent-shaped blade. She felt her cheek already laid open, or her mouth slashed across.

Then all at once Phyllis reversed the instrument in her hand. 'Why don't you kill me, if you hate me so much?'

'What?'

'That's what you want, isn't it? You want me dead. Go on, then. Why don't you do it? Here. Take it.' She thrust the handle at Clarice.

'Don't be stupid. I don't want to kill you.'

'You do. You think I'm rubbish. You hate me. If I was dead you'd be free of me. You would, wouldn't you? And then you could have your precious Vic, couldn't you? And your beloved Jack? You could make sure his dirty slut of a mother never comes near him, couldn't you? Then he'd be all right, wouldn't he? Then he'd be safe. Go on, then. If that's what you want, you can do it, then, can't you?' Now she was holding up the cutting edge between her thumb and forefinger. 'Take it, then.'

Clarice swallowed hard. She couldn't believe what she was hearing.

'All right,' Phyllis said. 'If you haven't got the nerve to do it, I will. I'll do it for you, shall I? Then you'll be pleased. That's what you want, isn't it?'

Phyllis had the blade at her throat. Her two hands were clamped around the grip, and her head was tilted to the side. In the glare that streamed through the window, Clarice could almost see right through the pearl-white skin to the artery. A little peak of tissue was already prised up on the blade's tip.

Something finally snapped inside her. She drew her right arm swiftly across her body. Before she knew it the back of her hand had hit Phyllis's cheek with all the force she could muster. The face jolted. The tin-opener clattered on to the floorboards. Clarice darted down to secure it.

She straightened up to see her cousin staggering slightly. There was a minute spot of red on the collar of Phyllis's blouse, and the perch hat was clinging ludicrously by its pins to the hair at one side of her head. Phyllis put her hands up to it. From under the tangle she glared furiously.

'You'd better sit down.' Clarice pulled one of Vic's painted chairs out from under the painted table. Sulkily, Phyllis lowered herself on to it and tucked her fine shoes at an angle underneath her. Clarice remained standing. Mistress of the situation, now, she swallowed her outrage at it. 'Here, take my handkerchief. I'd offer you tea, except it's something of a palaver. You'd better tell me about Jack, hadn't you?'

'What's it to you?'

'A child is missing. How did it happen? When did it happen? Where exactly did he go missing from?'

'From the boarding-school. A couple of days ago. We got this telegram.'

'Boarding-school? What boarding-school?'

'He got to be . . . a cause of friction.' Phyllis looked up from under her ruined hair. 'That's how someone like you would want to put it, isn't it? He started to . . . Well, we've got little Melia to think of, and everything.'

'Melia?'

'The little girl. We put him in this school. A good school, mind. Tony wanted . . . Tony couldn't . . . But that's all a long story. All very complicated. I . . . You wouldn't get it. You wouldn't get the fucking half of it, dear.' Phyllis put her hand up to her reddening cheek. The fingertips strayed over the powdered skin, caressing it faintly.

'So what's happened to Jack? Why has he. . . ?'

'Oh, he smacked open some kid's head. A scrap in the *dorm*, so it seems. Runs in the fucking family. His fucking father's son. What's a war, eh, if no one gets wounded?' Phyllis laughed, bitterly. 'But he bunked off somewhere. And then there was a flap. And the school had to call in the fucking police, didn't they? And that . . . well, perhaps you can imagine. Or perhaps you can't. Let's say Tony won't be easy to live with when he gets back.'

'When he gets back?'

'He's out with some of the blokes looking for the boy. Pick him up before the coppers do.'

'I see,' Clarice said.

Phyllis continued. 'I just needed to get away.' She nursed her face. She was so plausible, now. 'And do you know, it did cross my mind that my son might have found his way here. He might have done, mightn't he? It's where we used to come, after all. Why not, Clarice? Eh? Why not? And all along, myself, I haven't had the luxury of getting away, you know. Not so very often, you see.' She forced the breath out again through her nose. 'Because my husband *as is*,' she sighed, 'because my husband likes to know exactly where I am. At all times. And that I'm doing exactly what he wants me to do, and what he tells me to do. You see?' Phyllis paused and dropped her gaze. 'Where I come from it's what we call bettering ourselves. Well, you have to try. Don't you?'

'You should go,' said Clarice.

'Where?'

'Don't look at me. You've made your bed, Phyllis. Hadn't you better lie in it?'

'He'll kill me.'

'A couple of minutes ago you were asking me to.'

Phyllis stood up. 'I'm two weeks late, you know.'

'So what?'

'It's Vic's.'

Clarice screamed, 'Get out! Just get out, will you!'

'All right, I'm going. That's what you want, isn't it? I'm doing what you want.'

She watched Phyllis pick up her handbag and go meekly enough, out through the doorway. She saw her step down on to the path. Shaking with anger, she went to the door frame and stood there looking after the ridiculous, dangerous, carefully dressed woman who picked her way on her heels past the thorns. Some strange sense of kindred stirred for an instant in her breast. She called, 'Phyllis!'

Her cousin gave no sign she'd heard. But at the gateway

to the lane, she turned and looked round. 'What do you want?'

'You could come to my father's with me. If you . . .'

'I know where I belong, dear.' Phyllis jerked her head towards London. 'But don't you worry. I expect a buzz bomb will get me. Us.' She laid a hand to her belly. 'You'll be happy then, won't you? You will, won't you? All right, I'll go then.' She turned her back again and disappeared behind the hedgerow.

Clarice shut the door after her. She didn't know whether she'd witnessed Phyllis's true self or her true insanity. She didn't really care. Yet again, she'd been terrified, cornered, forced to take part. Her cousin had succeeded, once again, in rattling her to the core with her vicious drama of poverty and need, her tendentious victimhood, and had left her feeling trashed. She might have wished she hadn't hit her – but then she had asked for it.

Still shaking, she dropped down beside the bag of dreams and picked out a few of the notebooks at random. They were almost indecipherable. They were nothing, nothing at all, and she could make no sense of anything that had happened to her. Whatever glamour the world might once have possessed for her had all fallen away. She'd no heart left, no feelings. Words had almost lost their meanings.

It was like the ending to the shadow play, she recalled. She'd gone behind the screen – a mere tablecloth stretched up in the jungle clearing – and what had she found? After the clashing of cymbals and beating of drums, nothing but a toothless old man sitting beside his pressure lamp with the sweat rolling down his face, with his leather cut-outs, his sticks and instruments, his different swazzles and pipes for mimicking the gods.

She stood up. Mechanically, she smoothed the curtains, straightened the mats, placed the chairs beside the table.

In about half an hour's time, once the reaction had set in, she'd probably have to put up with another crying fit. She stooped to pick up her kitbag, ready to leave. Then a detail she'd forgotten struck her. The shadow man had given her one of the cut-out, jointed puppets to look at. On the side away from the lamp, the leather was fully painted, the features and dress intricately picked out in extraordinary, detailed colours – colours that would never be seen by the audience. He had only smiled and shaken his head, shrugging his shoulders.

VII
Remedy

A COUNTRY PATH ran along the whaleback of land towards Erwarton and Shotley. For the last two years Dr Pike had refrained from taking it, because it led past Mary Benedick's house at Bolt's Grove.

Now he set out from Pook's Hill and turned deliberately eastward by the gate to Appleby's top meadow. The walk would take perhaps forty-five minutes. He squared his shoulders. All around him the midsummer air was twitched at and tugged by the activities of birds. A single oak hung over the hedgerow. Bright feathered streaks darted up from the bushes, until the fat, serrated leaves above him gossiped and whirred.

His route took him under the eaves of Appleby's barn. He stopped to bend down and touch sorrel and herb Robert. The fragile plants, growing by the foot of the wall, delighted him. A few rabbits bolted from the nibbled clearing opposite, their scuts bobbing up. A yard dog barked. Dr Pike walked on, skirting the mud that lay between the farm wall and a nettle bed. He was going courting at last.

He'd been strictly ethical. There had come a point, more than a year before, when he'd declared there was nothing more he could do for Mrs Benedick. He'd referred her to Dr Molson at Shotley Gate. Once he'd said his piece a poignant silence had fallen between them, by which he'd guessed that she too was quite aware of her emotions.

Nevertheless, he'd done his duty. Dutifully, too, the lady

had borne her complaints away. He'd thrown himself into the care of the ordinary patients who were left on his panel; and he'd tried to meditate generously upon the coming of the welfare state.

The path ran through a wood. Chequered light fell upon the strewn floor, and his shoes cracked dead twigs. Ferns rustled. He'd worked hard; there'd been consolation in that. He had patients enough who were suffering from enforced separation, whose present loneliness or sexual frustration was none of their own choosing. He'd been the better able to sympathise with the lovelorn.

For how the woman at Bolt's Grove had captivated him, with her soft eyes and puzzled, delicate ways. There'd been no denying his feelings for her. They'd hurt him. He'd wanted Mary Benedick in his life: speaking, touching, intimate, and had been required to set her aside.

Still under the trees, the path joined up with a cart track. He was relieved not to have brought Bentley along – it would hardly do to arrive flustered and bespattered. Nervous about his appearance, he stopped to stroke down what was left of his hair. He adjusted his collar and licked his lips. For a moment the sensation on his tongue of the luxuriance of his old-fashioned moustache embarrassed him, and he wished he'd shaved it off. Then he remembered her smile. Fighters from Martlesham droned invisibly overhead. A solitary stag beetle clattered its wings brusquely across his path like some small pilotless weapon.

Without her there had been compensations. He'd made friends. The goatish Wellbridge had left the vicinity. Dr Pike was even on wrangling terms with the vicar, Colin Passmore, and Nora, his wife; and had become quite used to taking a harmless glass of black-market Scotch with them. The feeling of being at one with his society, rather than at odds with it, was intriguing. He'd made the effort to savour in wartime what years of peace had never brought.

And he'd kept his old eye upon hidden events. For months his greaseproof-paper map of Poland had sat on the window ledge of his surgery. Then had come President Roosevelt's declaration. Intelligence now confirmed both the systematic Nazi extermination policy and the limitless Japanese war crimes.

He hadn't been in the least surprised. What did surprise him was his body's reaction. Hearing the incredible made official, he'd been physically sick. How should one respond? History itself was changed, metaphysics had invaded the everyday. Even now, as he made his way seaward, the sheer scale of the wickedness let loose gave him pause. Did he – did anyone in such times – have the right even to think about the embraces of a woman?

He thought about her all the time. He wanted her. He wanted to be with her. It was as simple as that. On occasions when he must meet her socially, implication darted between their eyes, he was sure of it. It was blindingly obvious. He smiled, now, on the dry track across a patch of heath. Bees hummed. Small clouds of gnats smoked above the standing puddles. He'd been scared of trying again; that was all.

Once he'd made up his mind, though, he'd sent her a note directly, asking permission to call. She had replied at once. Now he walked between the tall flowering grasses, and saw with gladness the hordes of meadow brown butterflies attending the thistle heads. Clovers were both white and pink among the stems. Trefoils made bright points of yellow beside the path. The air buzzed and hummed again; it smelt of cattle, and of salt. He climbed a stile. In the next field he felt all the agitation in his stomach of a glassful of neat adrenalin.

By another big oak, he came to the ridge that gave a

clear lookout over the Stour estuary. The river lay in its mud-flats before Harwich on the far bank. Two open boats, oared like naval insects, were scuffing their way towards Shotley Gate against the incoming tide – new recruits at the infamous old shore school. He was inclined to linger. He felt his journey across a mere two or three miles of the peninsula had been transected not just by reverie and desire, but somehow by the trace of every event that had followed from the suicide of Selama Yakub.

Could he be mistaken about Mary? Clarice had arrived home, cracking up, just at the instant he'd decided to pursue his own love. The coincidence was an omen, wasn't it? He brushed the thought aside.

And his worn brown brogues, polished up today as best he could, and protruding from the turn-ups of the only good pair of tweed trousers he had left, seemed to insist upon his appointment. They strode him on towards Bolt's Grove; and, as he went, he prodded the dry ground with his ivory-handled stick.

JACK SAW BOATS were moored up under the church. He went down to the waterside. There were masts and a bend of water opening out. Beyond that, as far as to the horizon, reed beds grew up from rafts of floating grass and from strands of mud. He played wishful games with his knowledge: that this was Ipswich already and that by some miracle he'd managed to walk as far as the sea. The gold-lettered sign on the board outside the church said 'Maldon'.

He was cold from the rain that had soaked him under a tree. He was very hungry. As he walked back past the church and up the slope into the town, he tried to make it appear to anyone who looked that his grey shirt and corduroy shorts were nothing out of the ordinary in that part of the world. There were knots of inquisitive children hanging about in the main street. He knew he must steal food before the shops shut.

That deed was done right at the edge of town, and just as he was on the point of giving up. There was a metal bridge. Some yards before that, an isolated wooden building stood next to a pair of petrol pumps. It called itself a general store, but there was nothing on display in the dingy window except a large black cat and a sponge cake. The one was asleep on the other.

A notice on the door said 'Closed'. Jack tried the handle. The door opened, and a bell on a spring jangled. He darted in. As the cake came out from under the cat's head, its claws caught his hand and drew blood. And that was the only price of his meal. He was out of the door and clean away. He didn't look back until he'd crossed the bridge.

There was a place called Goldhanger. Under a broken haystack, he ate the last piece of his prize. It tasted of carrots and artificial egg. The sky had cleared and there were stars just beginning to appear. His father was not Tony Rice. His father was called Vic Warren. That was why he, Jack, was also called Warren. Once, at Christmas time, his father had gone out and not come back.

Aunt Clarice had said he could come to her – at Ipswich. He'd remembered the name because it was so odd. If he could get to Ipswich the people there would know where to find her. And she would know where his real father was. He watched the stars come out, one by one. He was sure she held the key. Soon the bombers would be going up.

In the morning he stood by the roadside until an American lorry gave him a lift. The driver said he was lost, too, and trying to find the route to Heckford Bridge. What sort of a name was that? So why didn't Jack come along and they could both get lost together. This was a lame-brained country where the roads wound like cart-tracks and led to goddamn nowhere. The driver had upside-down stripes on his shirtsleeve. He had enough pieces of airplane on board, he guessed, to think about trying to get up his own raid on Berlin. Unfortunately, though, if the regular flyboys didn't get the parts by midday, he'd get his ass quite badly bitten. Did Jack like cold frankfurters? Jack did.

The lorry lumbered on across the flat salt land. Near a spinney beside a farm gate, a single signpost pointed to Tolleshunt D'Arcy, Great Wigborough, Layer-de-la-Haye and Colchester. 'Oh, for Christ's sake!' the driver said.

I HAVE WRITTEN myself into it. My pilgrim brother, Jack, runs between earth and sky; and, for all the unlikeliness of my own start in life, this is a tale of redemption.

Jack is for ever divided from me. I never had his nerve, nor his opportunity; you've seen enough of my mother to get the picture. I was Vic's child raised in Tony Rice's world and my early life was what Jack escaped. But something unites us, my brother and me. My story picks its way between snapshots and I shape myself inside it. As the family that should have been mine assembles under my hands, I make a portrait of the father who doesn't know me, because I've no other way to reach him.

I should add that my great-uncle Pike is not deluded, or feverish, setting forth on his latest encounter. There's an urgency about the matter of our conclusions, and of my commitment to them. What is to follow is the only possible outcome, and should be taken notice of.

LEFT TO HER own devices much of the time at Pook's Hill, Clarice could think of no one but Jack. Whether she occupied herself in housewifely fashion, with dusting, hoovering, or polishing, or attending to her father's backlog of darning; or whether she set herself punitive war work, such as sorting the salvage, it was Jack's small face that haunted her. The police were out hunting for him. It had even been on the announcements after the midday news that there was a boy missing from an Essex boarding-school. Colchester was handling it, since a child answering his description had been sighted in that vicinity.

The irony that among so many unrecorded and un-remarked losses the magic words 'boarding-school' could still secure Jack a mention on the wireless was not lost on Clarice. But if the authorities were exercised about a little gentleman going missing, so too, she knew, were the associates of Tony Rice. She remained very worried.

She didn't think of Vic, alive or dead. Vic and she were finished. Since her meeting with Phyllis, she'd evaluated the whole affair. They'd never stood a chance. Look at the assumptions he'd had to live with. He hadn't been able to accept her; and she was even quite matter-of-fact about it.

From the start their coming together had been built upon impossibilities. Too much had lain between them for love to overcome, even if, as she acknowledged ruefully to herself while putting Dr Pike's filing system to rights, it had drawn her across thousands of miles and tugged him through the bars of his prison.

She tidied her father's desk. She put the stethoscope ready in his black bag. She sterilised the thermometers. A patient had left a specimen of urine in a jamjar. An amorphous piece of tissue lay in a dish. Used dressings had been thrown into the waste-paper basket. She set the place in order. All it needed was a woman's touch. Maybe if there hadn't been a war she and Vic might have been all right. But in the world that surrounded them now, where only the brutish seemed to survive, truly there'd never been any real hope. If Vic were alive and had wanted to respond to her letter, he would have done so by now. She'd heard nothing. He either held her in contempt for her long deceit; or he was dead. She'd switched herself off from him. He had slept with Phyllis.

What focused her tears as she sought to carry out her self-appointed tasks – and she wept nearly all the time and over almost everything she touched, so that there were always splashes on her father's notes, and over Ethel Farmer's recipes, and on the ironing, and on Bentley's coat when she bent down to pat him – was the child she hadn't seen since the Upminster episode. And that day of the visit, standing on the gravel in front of the house, in front of the stolen Riley Lynx, the boy had placed his hand in hers. He'd wanted to trust her, and she remembered her surprise.

They'd said Colchester on the news, but in her state it took another six hours of brusque housekeeping and ineffectual anxiety for her to cotton on to what she should be doing about it. She should be looking for him, of course. Now it was too late in the day to start. She cursed herself for her muddle-headedness.

AT ARDLEIGH HEATH he'd slept in a barn. Over a wall in a twist of scarlet flowers he found runner beans to eat. They were half formed, sweet. He looked through the rack of beanpoles at Colchester on the hill.

Outside a village sweetshop, he asked a woman the way to Ipswich. She gave him a pained look and stepped away. There was a greengrocer with his horse and cart. Jack sat up on the front as they went along. Then the man pointed out the direction, and winked, and adjusted his flat cap. He took out his cigarettes. 'Want one?' he said. Jack declined. He took his road. His legs were tired. He even drank from a cattle trough.

CLARICE THOUGHT SHE could take the train to Colchester. She'd woken early and planned a course of action. She could ride to Manningtree, put Ethel's bike in the guard's van and then use it to comb the countryside. A rather loosely conceived plan, it relied on nothing but chance; but she couldn't think of a better one. She stood in the parlour in her WAAF jumper and slacks checking the railway timetable and waiting for her father to come down from shaving. He seemed much more preoccupied with his *toilette* these days than she would ever have expected, and still hadn't appeared when she happened to glance out of the window. She was surprised to see a slim, somewhat birdlike woman in middle age approaching up the gravel drive. She went to the door.

At first Clarice thought the woman was selling something – she had a copy of the *Eastern Daily Press* with her. Then she held her hand out. 'You must be Clarice. I'm so pleased to meet you. I'm Mary Benedick.'

'Oh, yes?' Clarice shook the delicate, gloved fingers.

'I've heard such a lot about you.' She smiled, brightly.

'Really? I'm afraid I . . .'

'It is early, I know. But I wondered whether the

doctor was up yet.' The woman peered past Clarice's shoulder.

'I'm afraid surgery doesn't start for another couple of hours. Of course, if it's an emergency . . .'

Her father appeared, hastily pulling his jacket on over his waistcoat. 'Mrs Benedick! Ah . . . Mary. Do come in. You two haven't met. My daughter Clarice. Clarice, this is Mrs Benedick.' He looked embarrassed, and at the same time rather pleased with himself. Clarice was mystified.

In the parlour, Mrs Benedick held the newspaper out to them. It was folded so that only half of the front page was showing. 'I thought you might be interested in this, Dr Pike. Have you seen it? Oh, please don't tell me you've seen it already. You'll think me . . .'

She was pointing to an item about a Lowestoft woman who had escaped the fall of Singapore back in 1942 and had finally made it home, bringing first-hand accounts of the hurried withdrawals from Malacca and Seremban. Dr Pike took the paper and fished in his top pocket for his spectacles. Clarice looked briefly at the headline and was about to ask what was going on. Then a picture at the corner of the fold, partially obscured by Mrs Benedick's hand, caught her eye. 'Excuse me a moment,' she said. She pulled the paper rudely out of her father's grasp and stared at it. 'That's him!' she cried out. 'That's Jack.'

Sure enough, there was a brief article under the picture, and a tally of sightings and conjectures. Sandwiched between a fire in Stowmarket and a decision by Norwich City Council, the story had caught somebody's imagination. From Chelmsford the runaway scholar had struck north-east and was clearly making for the coast, stealing as he went. After Colchester it was thought likely he might try to reach Harwich or Ipswich, perhaps in the hope of stowing away on a coaster.

Clarice made hurried excuses and virtually ran out of

the house. Bentley ran after her. At Bligh's she saddled up Martin. The horse sniffed the morning air and whinnied; the dog looked at her expectantly, and then tagged after her as she rode down the track and headed west along the Stutton road.

Her mind worked quickly, now that she knew what she was doing. The boy must be travelling under cover, hiding, sleeping rough. So far he'd avoided capture. If he were simply blundering across country she'd no hope at all of finding him. But the newspaper article had suggested a clear line of intention: Harwich or Ipswich. Her hunch was that the boy was trying to reach her. It was a long shot and she had no real basis for it but she decided to back it, because it was her only chance of getting to him before Tony or the police did. She looked round for the dog. Bentley had given up and gone home. She rode on towards Cattawade. At Blantham, she turned up north towards Ipswich and the Orwell.

A TRACTOR PULLED the hay cart across the river Stour. Jack crouched down on top of the heap, in case the tractor driver, coming to the bridge, should turn round and spot him. The stream lay at low tide between the mud-flats. He spied out from his vantage point to where the water opened up – almost as wide as the sea. The sea couldn't be far away. Something about the place was familiar; there was a feel to the wooded slopes, a certain taste in the air.

But almost immediately after reaching the other bank he found himself parked in a farmyard, where the dogs barked incessantly and the farmer and his wife bustled about, and the land-girl mucked out the pigs, and the farmer's children played endless war games. Hiding on top of it all, he was forced hour after hour to lose the best part of his day. His stomach churning, he could only keep his head down and wait, amid the sweet damp hay.

It was late afternoon when he got the all-clear. He clambered down. There was a woman with a handcart in the lane. 'Excuse me, please. I was wondering if you know where a lady lives. Her name's Clarice. She's my aunt. And the doctor. At Pook's Hill, I think. I was wondering . . .'

'Oh, you mean Dr Pike. That's just along at Holbrook, there.' The woman pointed the way with a knobbly finger. 'That's a good walk from here, though, boy; and you don't look so grand. Hey! Wait a minute, though. Aren't you that kid . . .'

Jack had legged it out of her clutches and got clean away before she could shout or raise the alarm. He put the corner of a cottage between him and the old witch and slipped over a five-barred gate to make sure. But he knew they'd be on to him and he hadn't much time.

SHE FOUND NOTHING. Martin was starting to play up. By teatime she'd touched the outskirts of the county town, and, with numerous detours, had made the circle right round to Wherstead. The horse plodded dully up the hill; it was clear he'd had enough.

She was exhausted herself as she walked back home from Bligh's farm. It was a wasted effort. Yet in the night she woke up twice, imagining she heard Jack's voice. She sat bolt upright, but there was nothing except the sounds of the house as the woodwork cooled. She went to the window and peered into the moonlit dark. Then a vixen yelled from somewhere deep in the lane. She put it down to that.

In the morning she was out again by nine, taking the same route as on the previous day, scanning the fields and the hedgerows for any sign at all.

JACK THOUGHT HE would die of hunger. All night he'd lain under a hedge and he'd been too cold to sleep. Then it had rained. A village was called Cattawade, and his feet hurt so much from blisters that he had to keep stopping and taking off his shoes. He'd tried padding dock leaves over the blood. Now he limped along inside a cornfield with a scarecrow in it. The green ears tasted only of grass; he spat them out. Rooks cawed from the high elms.

He felt faint. It was strange how the trees at the far end of the field seemed to shiver. Planes roared overhead. He believed they were looking for him, and he thought there might be bombing. In that case he should move out of the open. Under the elms, though, there was a gate into the road, and as far as he could tell it went the right way.

Clarice discovered him on her way back from the bridge at Manningtree. He was tucked up asleep by the side of the drainage ditch just outside Upper Street. At first sight she thought a bundle of clothes had been left in the verge. When she dismounted, and parted the grass, she found herself looking into his sleeping face. His cheeks were filthy and smeared, his hair stuck through with pieces of straw. Yet there was no doubt it was Jack – she recognised him at once.

As she lifted his head, his eyes opened. He looked at her intently. 'Jack,' she said. His mouth formed a word but he was unable to articulate it. 'Jack. It's me, Aunt Clarice. I've found you.' He seemed still to be fighting sleep. She pulled his hand around her neck. How chilled were the backs of his fingers. 'Jack! Jack! Listen to me!' This time, he made no response at all.

Using all her strength she stood him up. His damp grey clothes stank. As she leant him against the horse's side he began to shake, and only incoherent sounds came out of his mouth. She was so desperate for him to be all right she wanted to slap him. The horse turned its head round to watch.

Jack opened his lips once more but still no voice emerged. 'You have to be all right,' she said. 'Please, Jack! Please!'

He stirred his arms feebly. She draped them over the saddle and lifted his foot until she could just about force it into the stirrup. Then she pushed and manoeuvred him up on to the horse's back, held him, and scrambled up herself. She set him astride Martin's withers in front of her. Despite wrapping her jacket around him and embracing him for all she was worth, she couldn't put a stop to his shivering.

IN THE RAINY half-light of dawn the old steamer bit down at the Channel swell, and then as it came up again dashed the streaks of froth from its blunted snout. Twenty minutes out from France the water was grey-black; the breeze was just catching the crests and beginning to ruffle them over. The last of the gulls had flown back to the smashed-up Mulberry Harbour.

Vic wedged himself against a bulkhead and stared across the waves. The corporal next to him took out his tobacco tin. 'Want one?'

'Thanks.'

The corporal measured out the shredded leaf into a paper, nipped it tightly against the wind and passed it across. Careful for his broken arm, Vic steadied his wrists on the ship's rail. With practised fingers both men rolled and lit up in the lee of their own bodies. Vic looked down inside the folds of his sling. A stub of apple wood had gone in and split the bone. The wound was still oozing into its dressing. The sun came up under the rim of the clouds, and a fire path stretched away towards Germany.

When he thought of Clarice, his ruined skin ached all down the side of his head where the filaments of the flame-thrower had brushed it. And there was an odd cooked ring around his scalp from the heat of the steel helmet. But the bullet wound that had passed straight through his chest hurt only if he inhaled too deeply on his cigarette – at least until the painkilling jabs wore off.

And Jack, dumped in some school or other – he wondered whether his letter had got through. The camouflaged steamer ducked its head into another wave. A blazing line had been drawn across his life. Behind it he was some other man. Now he saw clearly how much Clarice had suffered, and actually how brave she'd been. He couldn't imagine living without her. The boat wallowed. He sucked at his cigarette. The pain seared up from the hole in his ribcage.

CLARICE WOKE SUDDENLY in the chair beside Jack's bed. She'd sat with him all night. Birds chattering in the eaves outside his window were at full pitch; but what had awakened her was the soft knock at the door she now heard repeated. She got up to let her father in.

He looked at her enquiringly. She nodded. Together they approached the sleeping child. A night-light on a saucer still flickered on the bedside table. She laid the back of her hand across his brow. The skin was hot but not burning. The child sighed in his dream and murmured, and she turned her hand over and smoothed his hair with her palm. Then she looked again at her father. 'First he could hardly speak. Then suddenly he was talking about a man,' she whispered. 'Before he went to sleep he kept talking about the man.'

'Was it troubling him? Was it someone he was frightened of?'

'I think he meant Vic, Daddy. He sounds so odd, so stilted. He said the man at the house, at the little house. He seemed to think I'd cotton on. It was Vic; I know it was.'

'It would make sense of a lot of things,' Dr Pike said. 'Things that I can't begin to apologise for.'

'Oh, Daddy.' She put her arms around his neck. Then she drew back a little. 'We can't keep him here, though, can we? What if the police come again; and what if they don't believe you this time? Or some of Tony's bully-boys.'

Her father walked to the window and peered out. 'I don't know which would be safer,' he said. 'Here, or your cabin.'

'Surely the cabin,' she said.

'What about Phyllis? That's where you ran into her, wasn't it? Supposing this Rice fellow has someone posted there.'

'They all know Jack's somewhere round here, don't they? The cabin is the best bet. I'm willing to take the chance.'

'Very well, then. Mary's son has a car. He could run you both down to the station as soon as it's fully light. If there are still no trains, he can take you on. I'll see him right about it.'

'What's that?'

'Take one of the guns.'

She laughed. 'You're not serious.'

'Quite serious. Promise me you will.'

'All right, Daddy. I will if you insist. If it makes you feel any better.'

'A good deal better, dear. As it happens.'

Jack stirred and opened his eyes. He looked at Clarice. He had the same expression she remembered from four years earlier. She bent down and kissed his cheek. 'I'm so glad you're all right,' she said.

She laid her hand on his brow again. 'You must rest a bit more, Jack. Then I'll make you something to eat. And then we'll have to go, I'm afraid.' She sat down on the bed. 'Because there are people who want to find you.' The child bit his lip. She took his hand, and continued. 'You were talking yesterday about a little house, Jack. I think I know where you mean. Do you think you'd like to go there? To see if it's the same one?'

The boy rubbed his eyes and stretched. 'I should say so,' he said in his odd-sounding schoolboy tones. 'I rather think I should. If it's no trouble, that is.'

SET DOWN IN London, Vic wondered where a man should go who'd been shot up. The Army had neglected to instruct him. He crossed the river by the footbridge and hung about in Trafalgar Square. Pigeons and women eyed him suspiciously; no fountains played. The city looked more battered and filthy than he could have imagined; and, every now and then, some distant explosion marked the fall of another flying bomb. The slabs beneath his feet still held the sea rhythm of the Channel.

At the top of the concourse, he saw one or two others in the same condition as himself – uniformed men with burns and bandages, sitting quietly on the steps, waiting for the pictureless picture gallery to open. He shifted his kitbag on to his good shoulder. He should get himself out to Laindon. From there he could sort out a plan of campaign. It was the closest thing to a home that he had, full of memories both of Clarice and of Jack. He should make his way to Fenchurch Street, then, without more delay.

There were no trains. Coal deliveries had failed owing to the strike. All movements on that line were cancelled until further notice. When would that be? The ticket man pursed his lips and sucked in his breath. 'Now you're asking me. Could be tonight. Could be tomorrow. Could be next week, mate, for all they tell me. Don't you know there's a war on?'

The swing bridge in the road across the dock entrance was open. In front of him tugs were pulling out a rusty grey-hulled liberty ship through the lock and into the stream. The ship was fat and ugly, close up, easing itself between the concrete piers. One of the tugs manoeuvred near where Vic stood, then took up the strain again, slewing sideways under Tower Bridge as if to get a better grip on the water.

Vic stared, a little enviously, at the men in the wheel-house. One stoking, one at the helm, they both wore the river get-up of collarless shirt, waistcoat, and moleskin trousers. The tide swung the stern close. Wavelets on the brown river slopped up against the swags of thick filthy rope that hung from the gunnels. The stoker put down his shovel, turned, and came aft. As he lifted his cap, he ran his hand back over his grey hair, tugging at his sweat cloth in a mannerism that struck Vic as familiar. He knew the man. He'd worked at the boatyard with him. It was Alfie Coats.

He called, 'Hey, Alf!'

The man stared back. 'It's not Vic Warren, is it? Christ, it fucking is.'

The tug went into reverse and belched clouds of sable smoke.

'Just wait till we get this old Yankee bitch out of her kennel and then we'll have a natter. And what sort of a bloody mess have you been making of yourself?'

Vic and Alfie Coats left the Earl Howard and walked down towards Shadwell. Soon the warehouses loomed above them on either side, closing out the light, and the narrow cobbled street was busy with vehicles trying to force a route through. The High Street was crossed with aerial catwalks between the upper floors. Vic's injuries throbbed. He swigged another dose from the syrup the medical officer had given him, and tried to keep up.

In little engine houses glued high up to the walls, men controlled the ropes from top gibbets. The bulging sacks swung as dead weights lifted off open drop-doors. The loaders hung out after them, cigarettes stuck in their mouths, guiding the fall with serious, smoke-wreathed faces. A lad was rolling barrels where the raids had knocked out a fifty-yard gap. Suddenly exposed, a parade of crane jibs reared up on the far bank. Vic and his mate walked on past Shadwell New Basin.

'Just a bit further,' Alfie said.

Vic grimaced.

Alf laughed and tugged his white moustache. 'You poor bugger. Off of the old Free Trade.'

They turned down an alley off Stepney Broad Street and came out where a small pier jutted from the Free Trade Wharf. About twenty lifeless stack barges were lashed together in an oblong block formation.

'It's the one on the end,' Alf said. 'All the rest are bloody laid up. Kenny Wright's the geezer's name. He takes odds and ends down to Southend. Seems to muddle along.' He laid his finger to the side of his nose. 'If you know what I mean.'

Vic nodded and smiled. 'Thanks a lot, mate.' He shook Alf's hand.

'Think nothing of it. Reckon you've done your bit, son.'

THE BROWN SAIL bellied and flapped; the sprit swung wide off the mast. Kenny Wright switched the leeboards on the winch and picked up his cigarette. Rounding the point on Blackwall Reach, the old barge began her sedate heel under Vic's hand. He knew the vessel. At the yard, they'd refitted her.

'That's the tricky bit over,' Kenny said. 'From here on it's plain sailing.' He laughed. 'Think you can manage that, soldier boy?'

'I'll give it a go,' Vic said. He smiled again to himself, at the impossible romance of his situation. The wood creaked, the water began to swish away under the *Irene*'s stern. The cargo was salvaged, sulphur-coloured bricks, but under the tarpaulin, there were dozens of boxes of American luxury goods. The Artillery were flying their flag beneath a barrage balloon on Woolwich Common, and Vic lined up the boat's head on it. Greenwich gasworks slipped past. Soon the old familiar stink began to come from off the marshes.

Kenny lounged in the bow. An equally lazy breeze drifted the barge down with the tide. They passed Woolwich power station. As the broadening river slid between wetlands, a late sun made bright drifts of the eastern cloud. He must contact her; he must show her that he understood. He would write to her at Oulton, and tell her he was at the cabin. At least he knew where Jack was. He could reassure her about that. Concerning the other matter, Phyllis, well, he'd just have to make a clean breast of it, and hope for the best.

364

What wind there was dropped off as they passed Everholt's yard at Creekmouth. They drifted on in midstream towards Grays. A minesweeper came up, and part of a convoy: three great, rusty, beaten-looking ships in line astern. Vic took more of his painkiller and turned round to gaze after them. He saw a sunset baulked by the anvil shapes of thunderclouds.

'No sweat,' said Kenny. 'We'll find ourselves a nice little mud-flat. Don't worry, mate. You'll be there by tomorrow.'

STAN PIKE LAY awake in the four-poster bed at Pook's Hill. Outside, the July storm clattered on his roof and the air he breathed seemed alive with minute droplets, as though the rain had learnt to bounce through the terracotta tiles and horsehair plaster ceiling above him.

As soon as there was a lull, an odd flurry of wind trembled for a second or two in the chimney, and a dormer casement rattled. The overwhelming conviction struck him that Selama was in the room.

Then the downpour re-established itself, leaving only a faint, unmistakably English smell of wood soot that crept towards him from the fireplace; and when he tried to recreate in his nostrils the human sweat, and coconut, the cloves, pepper and peat, by which he might have remembered Selama and her country, he couldn't do it.

The woman next to him stirred in her sleep, turned over and sighed. Her flavours were her own: of salt, of the fringing shore, and of the sea that twice a day came flooding up past the sloping lawns of her garden. In the absolute dark, the only other evidence of her presence was her breathing. Each exhalation caught slightly in her throat, like the echo of a snore.

Under the covers he put out a hand to her. Mary Benedick's haunches were naked where her nightdress had ridden up. Her skin felt soft and full. Her flesh covered membranous walls and liquid systems – a lover's anatomy. Here on the hip, connective structures anchored them at no very great depth to the prominence of her femur, and deeper within to the engagement of that bone with her pelvis.

He recalled how scrupulously, tremulously, medically, he'd once been accustomed to reading her colours, palpating her discrete minor debilities. Now he stroked her side under her nightdress, running his hand upon the indentations of her ribs and then down across the sternum, just grazing with the back of his fingers the undersides of her breasts. His touch woke her.

Only a little later, while she whispered amorous reproaches into his ear, and he, careful of her slight frame, rolled his panting weight away, did he become aware of the rain again.

THE BOY HELD her hand as they turned into the lane. She felt the quickening in his step as they came in sight of the Flatman's bus with its comical stove-pipe sticking through the roof. She wished she could ask him straight out, 'Well, then, what do you think, Jack?' and then catch, as though she were a camera, all the emotions that were crossing his small face. Water from the storm lay in large puddles here and there across the path, and the loaded gun felt heavy and awkward tucked under her arm. But through the hand that held his she could sense Jack's quivering excitement.

They unfastened the gate. The child stood stock still amid the wet briars. For a moment she felt disappointed in the cabin – she'd let the boy down. The gabling over the porch was flaked, a window-sill was hanging off. Various weatherboards were riven and twisted, and the roof distinctly sagged at the corner. They were details she'd hardly noticed when, only a week ago in her furious state, she'd had her battle with his mother; and how small and insignificant the frame of her affair with his father looked now.

Jack twisted his hand out of hers and ran towards the front door. 'Look!' he cried. 'Auntie Clarice! The wooden house. The house through the bridge!'

'Careful!' she shouted. She hurried after him. Cautiously, together, with the barrel of the gun poking forward, they pushed open the door, and as the inside came into view, she heard Jack give a gasp. He ran to the middle of the room, stared at the mattress, ran to the window with its flowery curtains, touched the wall, touched the table, and the chairs, knelt down and touched the floorboards. He turned back towards her, his eyes wide, his mouth open. 'It's really here,' he said.

'Your father made it,' she said. She could have bitten her tongue.

He frowned and shook his head. 'No. He can't have done. My father's name's Rice. That's us. I shouldn't really be here at all. If he finds out ... I ... I had a letter, you see. At the school. It was ... It's probably just something I made up.'

He smiled in embarrassment, such a sweet smile, but so out of place, far too old for him. And how strangely grown up were his mannerisms. She put the gun down on the table and sloughed off the sack of groceries from her shoulder. A flying bomb was somewhere high overhead.

'Some of the boys, you know, they do tell stories. It's living away from home, I expect. This letter ... I called it the Comforter.' He smiled again, nervously. 'From a Victor Warren. He said he was . . .'

She was desperate to hug him to herself and explain that everything was fine; everything would be all right.

'But then I went and killed somebody.' He said it so matter-of-factly. Now there were drops in his eyes, welling at his lower lids. She had to watch him struggling with his too-formal words. 'There. Now I've told you. You've been so kind, Aunt Clarice, but . . . I'm afraid . . . I'm afraid I'm actually a bad lot. I shouldn't like you to get into trouble.' He lowered his gaze. 'Actually, you'd jolly well better turn me in, after all. That's what you want, isn't it?'

It was too much. She simply ran and grabbed him in her arms. He clung to her as though he could never let go and she let him sob against her breast. 'You poor boy.' She smoothed his hair. 'You poor, poor boy. It's all over, Jack. Nobody got killed, nobody has to get turned in. You and me, here. We'll be safe, Jack. We will. We'll be safe.'

THE WIND HAD gone round southerly and was coming fresh off the North Downs and the Kentish Weald. *Irene* leant into the morning tide and picked up speed. Waves splashed under the stubby boat's black chines, and the heavy length of beech wood that made up the tiller kicked slightly under Vic's good hand. Then Kenny Wright slackened the port sheets, and she was running northward up the Tilbury bend between the twin forts of Coalhouse and Shornmead.

When he looked across at each of them, now this side, now that, Vic could see the heavy cannon sticking out from their concrete emplacements. Just for a moment all his injuries gave a collective twinge as he imagined the little contraband-carrying barge caught in some whistling crossfire.

They drove close to the marshlands and quarries at Cliffe, sailing straight for a full half hour. As the reach under Pitsea and then the oil refinery came in sight, he fancied he could pinpoint the handmade house up on the opposite hill, even when the whole rise was still no more than a green blur in the distance. Nearer and nearer they came. The brown sail tugged and the timbers creaked with all the little noises of an old boat. He was at home with wood, and how it could be shaped and jointed to keep out the water, or the wind.

Kenny took the helm to go about and bring the nose up to the jetty. Then he drifted *Irene*'s side just close enough in, still moving, with the heavy sail flapping its block and tackle back and forth, and the tiny mizzen shivering. Vic grabbed his kit and jumped ashore. 'Thanks a lot. I owe you one, mate.'

'All right.'

Vic watched the barge catch the wind again and circle about. Then he waved and turned, and set off from the flood defences along the road up towards the hill.

IF THE THING Jack hardly dared imagine turned out to be true, then what of the war, and his mother? And most of all what of Tony Rice? When he caught up with him, Tony Rice would kill him. Tony Rice would have his guts out of him. He could not stay.

Clarice was in the tiny kitchen, making him sandwiches. He could see her fair hair, her arms, the line of her skirt. He waited until her back was turned, and then ran out of the door.

At the end of the lane, he paused. He looked one way.

A dispatch rider was coaxing his motor bike along the concrete strip between the hedgerows. Jack turned and looked the other way down the hill. He was too late. A man in uniform was coming towards him.

He ran back. He shouted in terror, 'Auntie Clarice! Auntie Clarice! Get the gun! They're coming!' Then he slammed the door shut.

She came out of the kitchen holding a breadknife.

'They're coming this way!'

His aunt took hold of the double-barrelled shotgun. She told him to open the door. Trembling, he opened it the merest crack. He watched her kneel and point the gun out through the gap. And then all at once he saw her face change. She gave a cry, let the gun drop down, and pulled Jack out from behind the door. 'Jack,' she said. 'Jack. Look!'

When he looked out he saw a soldier with his arm in a sling coming towards them. And as he stared at the man's face it was as though he walked exactly into the memory he always had at the back of his mind. There was a spray of light behind the man's shoulder. His arm crooked and punched, crooked and punched. He remembered him sawing. On either side of the cut in the wood, dust the same shade as his mother's face powder jumped itself into heaps. There were summer birds singing. On his cheeks were buds of water, which rolled into the hairs of his moustache. One large drop rolled down the side of his chin. The man straightened, and wiped his face with a rolled-up sleeve. The saw glittered in his hand. He was out of breath, and when he bent down again to pick Jack up the smell was his father's waistcoat, and brilliantine, and the inside of wood.

Acknowledgements

My particular thanks are due to Sam Boyce, Bill Hamilton and Nicholas Pearson for help, more help, tolerance, brilliant judgement and terrific support. In addition I should like to acknowledge my indebtedness to Patricia Browning, Mary Chamberlain, Joan and Philip Cooley, Michael Emmett, Leo Hollis, Jack and Pearl Holloway, Jonathan Kaplan, Peter Lamb, Sylvia Legge, Caroline Saville and Susan Utting.

Special thanks are also due to the London Corporation for records of bomb damage, and to the staff of Barking Reference Library, the local studies staff of Chelmsford Library, the staff of the Essex Regiment Museum, and the Met. Office.

In describing the military actions in this novel, I have had to tread the line between reconstruction and invention. On the one hand it is the duty of the novelist not to seek to alter the details of history; on the other, I had no intention of writing 'faction'. Above all a novel should not seek to trespass on the experience and suffering of real soldiers – and those of their families – while the events in question remain in living memory. For these reasons Vic's regiment is never specified; it remains an imaginary one.

Vic's military career is *based* on true events, however, for the sake of authenticity. His movements shadow those of the 2nd Battalion of the Essex Regiment, as recorded in T. A. Martin's book, *The Essex Regiment 1929–1950*. The battle of Verrières Wood ('Essex Wood') took place on 11 June 1944. Whether my evocation of such an engagement rings true or not, I should like it to stand as a tribute to the astonishing courage of the men involved in the real thing.

The battalion held the wood with 'severe casualties' until the morning, and were then pulled back. There were many individual acts of bravery. The battalion chaplain, the Reverend F. Thomas, 'remained with the forward platoons throughout the night, shielding the bodies of the wounded with his own and entirely disregarding his own safety, gallantry for which he was given an immediate award of the Military Cross'. Major M. W. Hulme is also recorded as particularly distinguishing himself. The many unrecorded deeds of bravery by ordinary soldiers can only be imagined.

The battalion continued to fight its way through France, Holland and Germany.

The very severe civilian casualties mentioned as occurring in Barking on Saturday 7 September 1940 are a matter of record. I should like to extend my deepest sympathy to the relatives of all those killed, and to the injured and their families.

Note: the 'plotland' settlements at Laindon, Vange and Pitsea are well documented. They were bulldozed under compulsory purchase order after the war, and the new town of Basildon was built over them.

374